QUEEN OF THE UNION

QUEEN OF THE UNION

JR ZINK

Copyright © 2022 JR Zink
All rights reserved.
Cover design by PixelStudio
Cover Photo: Middleton, Strobridge & Co., Lithographer, and Alfred Edward Mathews. The 21st Reg't Wisconsin Vol., crossing the pontoon bridge, at Cincinnati, Saturday, Sept. 13,/ sketched by A.E. Mathews, 31st Reg't. O.V. Sept. 30. Photograph. Retrieved from the Library of Congress, <www.loc.gov/item/2008675450/>
ISBN (paperback): 979-8-9863053-2-5
ISBN (ebook): 979-8-9863053-3-2

CHAPTER 1

Central Kentucky 1846

"Excuse me, Master Johnson, have you seen my mammy?" The twelve-year-old boy stood in the library doorway tentatively. "Today is Tuesday. I have Master Aaron's clothes for her to wash."

The middle-aged man, dressed in dark pants, shirt, and waistcoat, looked up from his papers. "Come in, John."

"Yes, sir." John approached the desk, holding a basket of clothes.

"Put that down. Close the door and take a seat."

"Yes, sir." The boy moved slowly to the wooden chair that faced the desk and sat on the edge of the seat. He gripped the front of the chair between his legs and looked at the floor.

"She's gone," said William Johnson.

"Where'd she go?" asked John without looking up.

"She's not coming back. Mrs. Johnson sold your mammy to a plantation in Mississippi. We needed the money, so she had to go down river."

"Who's going to do the laundry then and look after Mrs. Johnson?"

"Your sister Martha will move into the big house and take on her duties," said William.

"Why Mammy and not one of the field hands?"

"I'm sorry, John. It wasn't my decision. Mrs. Johnson and your mammy didn't get along, so this is best for peace in the house."

"She didn't say goodbye."

Distressed, William rubbed his fingertips against his forehead. "She wanted to, but there wasn't time when they came for her. It will be all right. Your sister and your brother are still here for you."

"Are you going to sell any more of us if you need more money?" asked John.

"You're a good boy and a hard worker."

"What if Master Aaron decides we don't get along anymore? What if you don't need me while he's away at school in Cincinnati?"

"I won't let her sell you, John."

"What about Martha and Harry? Are they going to be sold?"

"Don't you worry yourself. We need you all to keep Given House running smoothly. We'd be lost without all your help. You hear me?"

"Yes, sir."

William looked at the boy, started to speak, then made a choking sound as he took a long breath. "That's all. Get on with your chores now."

"Yes, sir." He picked up the laundry basket and started for the door.

"John."

John stopped and turned to William. "Yes, sir?"

"She loved you. She'll be fine, and you'll be fine. You're strong." William nodded his head.

John blinked away tears. "Yes, sir."

#

Lydia Johnson sat under the covers, propped up with pillows in the large bed. Her twelve-year-old son lay on top of the bedclothes on his back next to her. She stroked his hair gently.

"You are growing up to be so handsome. Those Yankee boys at school won't hold a candle to you. You come from a great family, one touched by the grace of God. Your great-granddaddy was one of the great men who settled Mississippi. He built one of the largest plantations from nothing, with over one hundred slaves working it, raising the finest cotton in America. When he died, your granddaddy took over the plantation. He's the one who bought this land and built this house as a place for us to spend the summers. I came here as a young girl and was one of the most sought-after belles of Kentucky. All the handsome men wanted to dance with me at our parties."

"That's where you and father met, right?" said Aaron, enjoying hearing the story of his parents' young love again.

"Yes. Your father did business with your grandad, and he came to one of our parties during a visit to Given House."

"Why did you marry father instead of one of the Southern gentlemen?" asked Aaron.

"Your father was handsome and very savvy in business. He worked for the insurance company in Cincinnati. Granddaddy thought it would be an advantageous match to bring his business into the family."

"So that's when you moved from Mississippi to Kentucky?" said Aaron.

"Yes. Granddaddy gave us Given House as a wedding present. Granddaddy gave Uncle Lyle the other half of his land here in Kentucky. That's when Uncle Lyle built his house down the road. Your daddy kept his house in Cincinnati, so he had a place to stay when he was there on business."

"Mother? What's going to happen to Given House when you…" Aaron fell silent

"When I'm gone?" She touched his cheek.

"Yes."

"All of my property will become your father's and one day yours. Your father will own Given House. He and Uncle Lyle will share ownership of the slaves."

"It makes me sad to think about you dying," said Aaron.

"Me too, my darling. I wanted to see you rise to be master of your own estate. Be in charge of running a farm and a house and marry a beautiful belle. You're already a wonderful horseman. One day you'll host sporting events and hunting weekends. It breaks my heart knowing I won't see you become a man." She caressed his arm.

"John's mammy won't get to see him become a man either."

"Dear, darkies don't get attached to their families as we do. She's probably already over leaving her children. She'll forget them in no time. They're not like us."

"But John is very sad about losing his mammy," said Aaron.

"Well, he'll soon forget too. Why are you worried about him? He's your valet and nothing more."

"Today, when we were playing, he was different. He didn't talk much."

"Well, he's not like you. Darkies' brains aren't as developed, and they don't have the capacity for feelings or thinking as we do. You can tell that by looking at them."

"John was pretty quick to learn during our lessons," said Aaron.

"He was probably just mimicking you. Your father insisted he be schooled for a few years so you'd have someone to study with. He was a fine playmate for you as a boy, but you need to put him in his place now that you're becoming a man. His education is over. You're off to college. He'll never be more than a houseboy. You see the difference, don't you?"

"Yes, but he's feeling sad."

"Never let your emotions interfere with your actions as master over your slaves. It's undignified. Besides, some of them can be sly and try to take advantage of a soft heart. You're too strong a man for that."

"Yes, ma'am."

"Have confidence in yourself, Aaron. You have a strong bloodline. There's a pecking order in life, with families like ours at the top. You must lead; that's your destiny. Others of lesser lineage will naturally take places in society below you. You'll meet them at school and in your commerce dealings. There's you, there's men from less prominent families that aren't equipped to lead, there's immigrants, and there's darkies. It's the ladder of society. That makes perfect sense, doesn't it?"

"Yes, ma'am."

"Now give me a kiss, and go enjoy your ride."

#

After the Johnson family had all retired, John, his sister Martha, and Miss Clara, the head house servant, sat in their room in the basement of the big house. As domestic servants, they lived in the basement room instead of the cabin, so they would be nearby to assist the family. The room contained two beds, a wooden chair, a chest of drawers, and a chamber pot. Miss Clara pulled the chair close to where John and Martha sat on the bed.

"Why, Miss Clara? Why did Mrs. Johnson sell our mammy down the river?" asked John. "She's the devil herself. What did Mama do to deserve that?"

"Hush, child," said Miss Clara. "Someone hear you talking bad about the Missus, and you'll be right behind her. You don't want to go down river. Working those cotton plantations is a hard life, and the drivers beat you if you don't work hard enough."

Martha started crying. "Mammy. Oh, they're going to beat Mammy."

"She'll be all right, now. Come here," said Miss Clara, extending her arms. Martha went to her and sobbed into Miss

Clara's embrace. She rocked with the girl in her arms. "Shh. Shh. We're going to be all right, the three of us. Look at you now, moving up to work in the big house."

"I don't want to work for that witch. She sold Mammy," said Martha.

"What I say to your brother?" said Miss Clara. "You can't be talking those sort of words about the Missus. You can think 'em, but you don't say 'em. You keep those words to yourself."

"I don't want to work in the house and live with these white people. I want to go back to the cabin," said Martha.

"You don't have a choice. You got to do what the Master and Missus say. And they say your job now is to look after Mrs. Johnson."

"I don't know how to look after the Missus."

"I'll show you what to do. You're a smart girl. None of this work is so hard that any of us couldn't do it. Hardest part is learning to use a stitch, but I'll show you."

"Miss Clara, where do you think Mammy is now?" asked John. "Master Johnson said she's in Mississippi. Why did they send her so far away?"

Miss Clara said, "Mrs. Johnson didn't want your mammy 'round cause she didn't want her tempting Master Johnson no more. She likely gone to her daddy's plantation in Mississippi."

"What do you mean tempting Master Johnson?" asked John.

"Master Johnson had a liking for your mammy. I think that's why he sold Ray, her husband. Every now and then over the years, Master Johnson spent time alone with your mammy. After Mrs. Johnson came down with the fever, he started back up with your mammy, and Mrs. Johnson found out about it. I heard her screaming at him, and Master Johnson promised to stop seeing your mammy. He said he was sorry, and he sounded like he meant it. The Missus told him to get rid of her. He tried to talk her out of it, but she ordered him like she was the master, not him."

"If Mr. Johnson liked Mammy, why'd he agree to it?" said John.

"Mmm-mmm. Boy, here's how it works. If a white man has a white woman, she is the queen. His Black woman is someone he can be with and may even love, but white people don't like Blacks and whites to mix in that way. If white men do it, they got to be sneaky about it. The white queen don't want nobody knowing her man with a Black woman. Besides, Mrs. Johnson's family own us. When she married William, he became the master, but Mrs. Johnson runs this house. You see it. She's in charge until she dies."

"When the fever takes Mrs. Johnson, could they sell us all?" asked John.

"Then I don't know what happens. We all either go to Master Johnson or her brother, Master Lyle. Nobody told me what's gonna happen. We have to wait and see," said Miss Clara.

"No, they can't sell any more of us. All I got left is my brother and my sister," said John.

Martha started shaking her head and crying again.

"John, you settle yourself. You don't know what's going to happen. Don't you be getting your sissy all upset over something you don't know."

"I won't let it happen," said John.

"You can't stop that from happening any more than you can stop the wind from blowing."

"Mr. Johnson likes me," said John. "I'll talk to him. I'll promise him that we'll work harder. He has to keep us together."

Martha hung her arms tightly around her brother's neck. "My mammy, Mammy," she cried. "John, don't let them take anyone else away."

"I won't, Martha. You, Harry, and me will stay together. And I'm going to find Mammy. Somehow, someday, I'm going to find her and bring her back to us."

"Really?" said Martha.

"If it's the last thing I do. I promise," said John.

Miss Clara shook her head. "Foolishness. She's gone. You both need to get all your crying out tonight. Tomorrow morning, we got work to do. Martha, you wake up and put a smile on your face, and you do what you're told. Mrs. Johnson don't have many days left on this earth, and you make them the best you can. That's your best chance of staying in the big house where the living is easier."

"She's right, Martha," said John.

"All right. I'll do it."

"We'll get you a bath with hot water," said Miss Clara. "We can't have you waiting on Mrs. Johnson dirty like a field worker. I'll fix one of the dresses to fit you, and we'll find you some shoes. House servants wear shoes. One more thing. Watch out for Master Johnson. You be nice to him, but not too nice. If you let him have his way with you, you might end up down the river just like your mammy."

"How I know he having his way?" asked Martha.

"Don't let him touch you, and don't be alone with him."

"What I do if he does?"

"You holler loud as you can for somebody. Now, time to sleep. The sun will be up early tomorrow. Martha, you sleep in that bed with John." Miss Clara blew out the lamp.

"I'll find her, Martha. I promise. I'll find her, and we'll all be together again. I will," whispered John.

John and Martha clung to each other in the dark.

CHAPTER 2

Cincinnati 1859 – Thirteen years later

Max Mueller stood almost six feet, with blond hair and sharp facial features. The clerk took his hat, led him down the hall of the second-floor law offices, and knocked on the door.

"Come in."

Max opened the door into a sunshine-filled room with a large wooden table and windows overlooking Court Street. Four men stood as he entered.

"Good morning, Max," said Aaron Johnson. "Thank you for coming." He extended his hand and shook.

Max and Aaron spent five years together at Saint Xavier College, where Aaron had bullied Max, deriding him for his German heritage. They crossed paths again later in life at a campaign event, where Aaron disparaged Max's character and contributed to his loss in his first city councilman race.

Aaron had invited Max to this meeting the week prior, indicating a legal matter requiring Max's attendance. Max was intrigued and agreed to the meeting but approached it skeptically.

Max exchanged handshakes with each of the other men as Aaron introduced them. "This is my senior partner, Thomas Wilson. Duane Dawson, from the firm of Dawson & Riley in Lexington, Kentucky; and my uncle, Lyle Reed. Please, have a seat."

Max sat down with the others and waited for one of them to say something.

Dawson, the Lexington lawyer, broke the silence, "Mr. Mueller, we've asked you here today because you have been named as a beneficiary in the last will and testament of the late Mr. William Johnson of Georgetown, Kentucky and Cincinnati, Ohio. His will is being executed by the courts in Lexington by my firm. Due to the Ohio residency of you and Aaron Johnson as beneficiaries, we have retained Aaron's partner, Mr. Wilson, to assist with the interstate complexities."

Aaron's uncle, Lyle Reed, scowled and sat back in his chair, folding his arms across his chest. Dawson nodded at him and held up a hand, attempting to settle apparent discomfort on Uncle Lyle's part.

Max said, "I apologize. I am not familiar with William Johnson. Who is he, and why am I named in his will?"

Aaron spoke, "William Johnson was my father."

"I don't understand. Why would your father include me in his will?"

"Well, Max, he was also your father," said Aaron.

"What? No, that can't be. My father was…" Max stopped, thinking for a moment, "Are you certain?" His face paled as he processed the implications of the revelation.

"Yes," said Dawson. "William spelled it out in his will, which I helped him draw up several years ago. As he explained to me, William spent much of his time at his house in Cincinnati, apart from his wife, attending his insurance business. In 1835, his wife Lydia was pregnant with Aaron. William found himself attracted to your mother, Katharina, who was in his employ as a domestic servant at his Cincinnati house. He acted upon his attraction and had relations with Katharina. When she informed him of her pregnancy, he discharged her and paid her a sum of money for her silence about their relationship."

"He was the man who raped my mother," Max said mostly to himself. "That's where she got the money to buy the saloon."

Dawson said, "He didn't divulge the exact nature of their relations to me. He didn't portray it that way, but he did say he felt remorse for causing her the trouble. He also felt regret for not knowing his son. He was aware of you and your circumstances. William said he felt he owed you the same in death as he did his other son, Aaron, even though he couldn't acknowledge you during his life."

"He was a soft coward," said Lyle. "No way a bastard Dutch boy deserves half of my sister's property."

Dawson said, "Lyle, we've been through this. William's will is valid and legal and will be executed according to its instructions. I know you don't like it, but let's proceed."

Lyle shook his head, "It's not right. William screwing everything in sight and messing with our family's legacy." He looked at Aaron, "Your daddy was a shame to our family. Your mother, Lydia, was sorry she ever married him, and she's turning over in her grave now at the disgrace he's cast upon the Reed family name. Look at the both of you," he said, eyeing Aaron and Max, "Northern businessmen with no sense of honor, just like your father."

Max turned to Aaron, a new realization dawning, "So, we're brothers?"

"We both have the same father," said Aaron flatly.

"My word. Who would have thought?" said Max.

"Can we move on to the specifics of the bequeath then?" said Dawson. "Max, here's a copy of the will, but I'll summarize for you."

"When did he die?" asked Max stoically.

"He passed the third of September. The doctor said his heart gave out on him. He died in his sleep." Dawson continued, "William had substantial property of his own entering his marriage to Lydia, including his home here in Cincinnati and financial investments. He also had a life insurance policy in which you and Aaron are named beneficiaries. When he married Lydia, he became the owner of Given House and the farmland, outbuildings, and material on the property. All of this will be divided equally between Aaron and Max. We'll need to discuss whether you two want to own the title jointly, one wants to buy the other out, or you want to sell some or all of it and divide the proceeds. As to the matter of the slaves. Lyle and William jointly owned them; thus, they need to be divided, half to Lyle and half to Aaron and Max."

"Slaves?" asked Max. "How many?"

Dawson said, "There are twelve of them. Six support the operations at Given House and the rest at Lyle's plantation, but they move back and forth depending on the season. There was a special bequeath in William's will for one of the Negroes, John Johnson. William manumits John and bequeaths him $1,000 from Aaron and Max's proceeds. He executed the proper documents to grant him his freedom upon his death."

"I'm suing to prevent that one," said Lyle. "We jointly own those Negroes. He had no right to free John."

"Why did he only free the one?" asked Max.

The men were silent.

"Why not free them all?" said Max.

"Geez, a Negro lover just like his daddy," scoffed Lyle. "Do you know what they're worth? More than the land he left you. If we free all of them, who will plow the fields, milk the cows, and keep up the house? My God."

"Calm down, Lyle," said Dawson.

"He might as well know," said Aaron.

Max turned to Aaron.

"William was John's father too," said Aaron.

"Christ," muttered Max.

"Amen," said Lyle. "Your daddy wasn't very discriminating when it came to the women he bed—Dutch, Negroes. If we look hard, we'll probably find a Mick too. I'm not standing for it."

Dawson interjected, "Lyle, we've been over this. You can fight this, but it will be easiest if you let the boy go. I'm sure you gentlemen can come to a fair arrangement. If you keep John on, he'll be trouble amongst the other slaves."

Lyle said, "You're probably right. That one has always been uppity. He reads and writes and talks shit among the others, putting ideas about the federal government ending slavery in their heads. Just makes them more ornery and harder to control."

"Is there anything else?" asked Max.

"Those are the most important terms. You and Aaron have some decisions to make before I address the titling of the property and financials. I suggest you set up meetings to work through it, and then we can all get back together to lay out the settlement. Any questions?" said Dawson.

"When is John going to be told? I'd like to meet him," said Max.

"What for?" asked Lyle.

"I think I should meet him."

"Why don't you arrange a trip to Given House?" suggested Dawson.

Aaron said, "Max, why don't you and your wife spend a weekend with Mary and me at Given House? It will be good if you know the property before we decide its fate."

"That's very gracious of you, Aaron. That makes sense. I'll discuss it with Annie."

"We done here? I need to get back home. I have a farm to run," said Lyle.

"I think so," said Dawson.

The men stood. Lyle shook Max's hand coldly. Aaron and Max stood in the corner and shook hands.

Aaron said, "Max, I'm sure this is a lot to take in. I know it was for me."

"Yes, I'm stunned. I have three brothers but have always had a sense of disconnectedness with them. Now I have you too. And we share a father that I never knew. I hope you can tell me about him so I can fill in that part of me that's been missing." Max looked at Aaron, searching for recognition of his missing family. He only saw a slight physical resemblance.

Aaron said, "Let me know when you can meet at Given House or here in town."

"I will. Goodbye."

#

On his walk back to the shop, Max detoured to Saint Xavier Church. He quietly entered the main doors and knelt in a pew near the altar. Max was raised Catholic, attended boarding school at Saint Xavier College, and went to mass in the church weekly. He also used the Jesuit Examen of Consciousness nightly as a meditation to guide him spiritually. Saint Xavier had felt more like home to him than his family's residence over the Eichen Garten saloon. He found solace in the church when he was struggling with things. Max thought about the morning's revelations and the turn of events that spanned his lifetime. He couldn't change any of it, and he couldn't judge or blame his mother, father, stepfather, or anyone else. They were all trying to get through life, one day at a time. He pondered if things had been different. His life could have been easier if he had been born in Aaron's place. He wouldn't have had to fight for his place in society as the son of German immigrants. He and Aaron had both gone to the same school and received the same education, but everything was a little easier for Aaron because of the circumstances of his birth. What if they had been switched?

He told himself to stop thinking about what might have been. It didn't matter. He now had to decide what to do with these new developments. How much could he reveal to his family? His siblings didn't even know that he wasn't their full brother. Did his mother know anything about William's life once he paid her off? How would she react to this news? What would they all think about John? These revelations could mar his reputation and jeopardize his business. He vowed that nothing would get in the way of his quest to rise above his birth and become a respected civic leader.

He prayed for guidance.

CHAPTER 3

Dressed in a tailored suit and hat, worn to make him appear older than his twenty-four years, Max led his wife, Annie, sister, Marie, and three-year-old daughter, Lizzie, up Vine Street. It was a sunny Sunday, unusually warm for late October.

Max turned to find the three women lagging. In their Sunday dresses, Annie and Marie held Lizzie's hands. "Here, Lizzie, let Papa carry you." He scooped her up and put her on his broad shoulders. She laughed with delight and clapped her hands. They crossed the canal bridge into the Over-the-Rhine neighborhood where Max, Marie, and four siblings had been raised. It was less German than it had been when they were young, and the wave of German immigrants was settling after the 1848 unrest, but it still had the qualities of a "little Germany" in the middle of America. The working-class neighborhood was dominated by two- and three-story buildings with street-level shops, topped with housing on the upper floors.

A heavily bearded man sporting a soft cap and long pipe sticking out of the side of his mouth greeted them in German. "Good morning, Max, Marie. How are you? How is your mother?"

They returned the greeting in German, and then Max continued in English. "She is well. We're headed to the Eichen Garten to see her now. How is Mrs. Klein?"

"She's well, thank you. And who is this little princess?"

"This is my daughter Lizzie, and my wife, Annie."

Annie said, "It is a pleasure to meet you."

"Mr. Klein used to run the bakery up the street from us," said Max. "I would visit his store to buy the bread and pretzels Mother served in the saloon. Mrs. Klein would give me a roll or bun. I have fond memories of the wonderful smells."

Mr. Klein laughed, "You would bring the growlers of beer around in the afternoon to serve our bakers at the end of their workday. You could barely carry them on the stick across your shoulders. We looked forward to seeing you as much as you enjoyed coming to the bakery. We're proud of you, Max, and your work on city council. It is good to have a voice of reason, a man raised with German morals, and a man of the Church helping guide our city."

"Thank you; I am happy to serve," said Max.

"Please pass my regards to your mother for me." He tipped his hat and continued down the street.

Once the man was out of earshot, Max said to Annie, "It never ceases to amaze me—the way I'm welcomed as one of their own, even though I haven't lived in Over-the-Rhine since I left for boarding school when I was eleven."

"Why wouldn't they?" said his sister Marie. "Papa and Mother lived above the saloon since you were born. Families have been gathering at the Eichen Garten on Sundays for years. The community is proud of you and what you've done to help Cincinnatians accept Germans."

"The reason I've been successful is because I don't act German. My education at Saint Xavier taught me how to act like an American. I haven't been successful because of my German upbringing, but rather in spite of it."

"Max, why do you downplay your heritage? It pained Papa before he died, and it pains Mother to see you do it now. You're German and always will be."

"I wish people would stop categorizing me as a German. We're all Americans," said Max.

Max had always wanted to be treated like the Anglos who considered themselves American natives. Cincinnati had periods of staunch anti-immigrant and anti-Catholic sentiments, and he was on the wrong side of both.

They approached the Eichen Garten on Vine Street. Max had memories of Sundays spent in the beer garden behind the saloon. Growing up, he felt embarrassed to be the son of immigrants whose parents spoke German and clung to aspects of their homeland. His stepfather's coldness toward him further pushed him to find his way out, which was to attend the Jesuit college downtown. One of the wealthiest men in Cincinnati, Nicholas Longworth, had paid for his schooling, which was his ticket to the world outside of Over-the-Rhine. He was still seeking his version of the American dream—to make it as a businessman and leader in Cincinnati.

Max took Lizzie down from his shoulders and opened the wooden door. He could still smell remnants of the fire that destroyed the pub's interior and caused the tragic death of his stepfather and his younger sister, Elli, four years earlier. The pub had been restored, but the lingering odor evoked the memory of the burned remains that he had to identify for the undertaker. They walked past the long wooden bar to the back door, greeting familiar patrons along the way. Max nodded to the bartender, a young man from the neighborhood, as they made their way through the crowded room.

They walked into the sunshine on the back patio, shaded by a large oak tree that was the pub's namesake; *Eichen Garten* is "Oak Garden" in German. Dozens of families sat on benches around large wooden tables. A table filled with food stood against the building, and an accordion player played music near the back fence.

They approached their usual table, and their family greeted them with cheers and smiles. Max leaned down to kiss his mother, Katharina, and she touched his cheek and gave him a blessing in German. Lizzie climbed into her oma's lap, where Katharina had a pile of wooden blocks and rings ready for her to play. Marie appeared with her nineteen-year-old sister Helene, holding six mugs of lager beer. The family raised the mugs with the traditional German toast of "Prost!"

Max hugged Helene. "How goes business?"

"Robust. Crowds have been large, and we have good hired help, so Mother and I supervise now," said Helene. "They do most of the work. It is much more manageable."

"You seem to have everything under control now. I'm proud of you," said Max.

Max admired Annie sitting at the table. At twenty-three, she still had dewy skin with a few freckles and light red hair pulled back into a bun. Annie comfortably joined her in-laws' conversation. She had almost refused to marry Max, fearing that marriage would shackle her to domestic life, void of the freedom to pursue her passions. After conversing with her father's cousin, Elizabeth Cady Stanton, a national women's movement leader, she convinced herself that she and Max could have a non-traditional marriage like Elizabeth's, where they were equals. Annie had all but abandoned her mother and family, as they never understood her forward nature and tried to prevent her from marrying Max, a man below her position in society.

Max's brother Peter, who had recently graduated from Ohio University and begun working as a reporter for the *Cincinnati Daily Commercial* newspaper, recounted Abraham Lincoln's speech in Cincinnati the prior week. "It was as if he was addressing the people across the Ohio River in Kentucky, and we Ohioans were secondary."

Annie, who had attended Lincoln's address with Max, said, "I think that was part of it. He hoped he might turn a few of those slaveholders toward him, but he knows neither he nor Stephen Douglas, the Democrat presidential candidate, can count on slaveholders' votes. He wanted to ensure that we, the voters in Ohio, knew he was the better alternative."

Max said, "But Lincoln's a Republican. Many of the former Know-Nothing party have joined the Republican party. The Know-Nothings pushed an anti-Catholic, anti-immigrant platform and worked to keep the native-born Americans in control of the government. That's not democracy!"

Annie replied, "That's not what Lincoln stands for. You objected to the Know-Nothing party's tactics in the local Cincinnati elections, but you need to set that aside. Who we elect as president will likely determine the future of this country—whether we stay a united country and allow slavery here. Most of the other civilized countries in the world no longer permit it. Stephen Douglas helped put popular sovereignty in place, allowing slavery to continue to grow in new territories. That goes against God and the original Founding Fathers' plan that slavery would be resolved twenty years after the Constitution was ratified. We can't let Douglas be elected."

Max said, "If Lincoln is elected, the South will secede, and our country will be ruined. We can't force the issue right now."

"Why not?" Annie was raising her voice now. "It's gone on too long. The Negro has been systematically exploited, and individual's lives have been ruined in the name of profit and money."

"Annie, I agree slavery is morally wrong," said Max. "I've held my nose when I deal with slave owners in business, but we can't just pull the rug out from under the whole Southern economy. It will have ripple effects in the North. My business will be negatively impacted. A big part of my business is developing new steam engine mills for the cotton mills in Georgia."

"You're going to let your profits get in the way of doing the right thing? Your Jesuit teachers would be ashamed," said Annie.

"It's not just that. What will happen to all the Negroes if they're suddenly free? How will they take care of themselves and their families? Where will they live? Many will come north, across the river to Ohio and beyond. I'm afraid of the reaction if we suddenly ask Cincinnatians to live among the Negroes. They hate the Germans and the Catholics enough. Imagine it."

Peter jumped in, "President Lincoln made it very clear he's not a pure abolitionist. He reiterated several times in his speech that he has no intention of setting the slaves free and wouldn't have the power to do so. The Constitution gives the states the right to regulate that. He will, however, fight to prevent the further spread of slavery."

Max raised his voice, "And that leaves us stuck where we are now. The South feels like the North is holding them hostage—their way of life and economy, and they have no way to protect it."

Annie said, "Lincoln declared slavery morally, socially, and politically wrong. Douglas hasn't said that. How can you support the man?"

Max said, "In politics, sometimes it's the lesser of two evils. We don't want a war to break this country apart."

His sister Helene asked, "Would the South go as far as waging war over this?"

"Yes," said Max. "This is their livelihood. They feed their families and have millions of dollars invested in their plantations and the labor to work them. This threatens generations of a way of life. There's no simple solution to get out of it. Even the moderate Southerners who don't own slaves fear the impact of the end of slavery. They see it as a necessary evil with no good alternative."

Oskar, Max's youngest brother, studying at Saint Xavier College, said, "If there's a war against the South, we will crush them. They don't have the factories to build guns or even supply an army. I go to school with Southern gentlemen who crow about their fighting abilities. They may know how to ride a horse and look good at it, but most are a bit soft."

Their mother, Katharina, interjected, "Enough talk about slavery and war. I'm tired of the arguments. Peter, I read your newspaper article. It was a balanced perspective. You published Lincoln's entire speech, so we could read it and decide for ourselves. I'm proud of your reporting. It's Sunday. Let's enjoy ourselves."

"Yes, Mother," said Max. He leaned over, kissed Annie, and whispered, "I look forward to continuing our debate."

At the far end of the table, Peter said to the group, "I didn't write the article; I took notes and edited the reporter's copy. Does Mother know that?"

Helene said, "Let her think you wrote it, Peter. It makes her happy."

Katharina caught the attention of the accordion player and motioned him over to the table. "How about we have Joseph play us some music? I want to see you young people dance."

Joseph played a traditional German folk song on his accordion, and both young and old joined the dance.

#

Annie left the office on the second floor of Miller Industries mid-afternoon and shopped at the Fifth Street market on her way home. She entered their two-story home on Eighth Street, hung her coat in the front hall, and carried her burlap bag of groceries into the kitchen. "Hi, Marie."

"Hi, Annie. Say hi, Mama," Marie said to Lizzie in her baby talk voice.

Annie lifted Lizzie and gave her a long hug. "How's Miss Lizzie today?"

"Mama. You're wet," said Lizzie.

"Yes, it's raining outside. Mama is wet from the rain," said Annie.

"I found everything on your list, except they had no carrots, so I bought sweet potatoes to mash for Lizzie's vegetable."

"Thank you. I'll start cooking dinner. You take Lizzie now?" said Marie.

"You're a godsend, Marie. I appreciate you. You know that."

"I'm happy to be here, and I love taking care of Lizzie. I couldn't make what you pay me working for someone else as a domestic, and I feel blessed to be among family."

"Max said he has a meeting, so he will be home at eight," said Annie.

"I'll fix Lizzie's dinner at her normal time, then have things ready for you, Max, and Oskar at eight. I am seeing Hugo tonight," said Marie.

#

When Max arrived home, Annie was reading a newspaper in the kitchen. She stood, and they kissed and embraced.

"How was my angel today?" asked Max.

"Getting more active by the day," said Annie. "I don't know how Marie can stay with her all day, clean the house, cook, and everything else. I read Lizzie a story, fed her dinner, and she went right to sleep. I think Marie wore her out with their errands today. How was the rest of your day at the shop?"

"Good, they finished one of the cotton mill machines. We'll test it for a few weeks and make adjustments. I hope to ship it to Georgia by the end of November. Can you start looking for a train route to ship it?"

"I'll start working on it tomorrow," said Annie.

"Where are Marie and Oskar?" Max asked.

"Oskar is studying late at school. Marie is with Hugo."

"Hugo and Marie have been spending so much time together. He's almost ten years older than her. Should I be worried about their relationship?" said Max.

"Let her be happy. She enjoys being with him. He's such a gentleman."

"All men are polite when they meet the family of their beau. Remember how nice I was to your mother and stepfather, even though they thought I was a low life from the wrong side of the canal? When we were alone, you saw the real me," said Max.

"You were a gentleman…mostly."

"And I'm the exception. They have more opportunity to be alone than we did."

"You sound like a father. Imagine what you'll be like when men start calling on Lizzie."

"She's only three. Please don't rush it."

"You are a protective and doting father. That's a good thing. That's how my father was with me. I know what you missed. I'm grateful Lizzie has you for a father."

CHAPTER 4

Annie and Max took a ferry across the river from Cincinnati to Covington, walked to the Kentucky Central Railroad station, and boarded a train bound for Lexington, Kentucky. They sat close, holding hands, conversing quietly.

Annie asked, "How are you feeling about this visit?"

"I'm not sure what to expect," said Max. "Aaron has been cordial to me in our encounters since the meeting in his law office, but I'm still having trouble letting my guard down with him. He was such a bully to me in school—he terrorized me. Do you think people change?"

"I do," said Annie. "Our perspectives as children are influenced by our families and others close to us. When we experience the world ourselves, we learn things aren't always as our parents told us. I've learned that Catholics aren't heathens, Germans aren't sloths, and men are primarily concerned with protecting their superior position in the world."

He pulled his hand from hers. "We're not all pigs!"

"My point is, Aaron, like you, has experienced much since you were in school together. He's also had significant revelations about his family in the last few months. I imagine he's trying to adjust to those, just like you are."

"I suppose you're right," said Max.

"Do you have any interest in owning Given House? As an investment or a place to get away from the city?" said Annie.

"I haven't seen it yet, and I've never been to a plantation, but my inclination is no. I know nothing about running a farm and don't desire to own one. I think our new house up on the hill will be respite enough. We'll have fresh air, a garden where Lizzie can run around, and trees for her to climb."

Annie leaned her head on his shoulder and retook his hand, "The house will be lovely. What about the Johnson family slaves?"

"Well, I couldn't sleep at night owning them. But the plantation can't run without them. They're kind of a package deal. Maybe Aaron wants to keep the plantation and the hands," said Max.

Annie said, "We have an opportunity in front of us. Make a small impact on the South's peculiar institution. Do more than talk about abolishing slavery in this country."

"You mean free them?" said Max.

"It's the moral thing to do," said Annie.

"It would be costly. The market value of each is $500 to $1,000 or more."

"We talk about them like horses or materials we buy for the shop. They're people," said Annie.

"I know, but it's the economic reality. That's part of the reason Southerners are so against abolition. They have too much capital invested in the labor of slaves. Immediate emancipation of all the slaves would bankrupt many rich and powerful men in the South."

"Aren't you going to inherit a substantial sum from your father's estate?" said Annie. "Can't we use that money to free them? That's money we don't have today anyway. It's tainted money, earned by years of labor from those men and women."

"Not all of it. A portion of the estate proceeds comes from William's insurance business and life insurance policy. I could use the inheritance to help expand Miller Industries and grow our sales in the west. But I've been thinking the same thing—the money from Given House is blood money.

What can I do with the money for good? My mentor, Nicholas Longworth, donated money to the American Colonization Society. The group's solution to slavery is to buy land in Liberia in Africa. They plan to pay slave owners for their slaves and their passage back to Africa. They will be free in their own country among people equal to them, and the United States won't have to worry about where they live or supporting them. It seems like the best all-around solution for everyone."

"Max, listen to yourself."

"What?"

"How would your German-American friends feel if Americans decided to send them back to their country after several generations? You really think that's right?"

"It's different. The Negroes aren't suited to live amongst the whites as equals. They're an inferior race," said Max.

"They're not suited because they've been treated like animals, not people. I met educated Black men when I lived in New York City. They have equal capacity as others if given a chance. Besides—I've read there are an estimated three and a half million slaves in the country. That's a lot of shiploads. It's not practical!"

"Well, I don't know what to do with them. It will be chaos if they're all freed."

"I'm not talking about all of them right now," said Annie. "I'm talking about the ones who live on the plantation you'll soon own with Aaron. You have to decide what the right thing for them is."

"I don't know. Uncle Lyle's going to be a problem. Aaron and I jointly own the slaves with him. You're not going to like him."

"He sounds horrid. What about John?"

"What about him?" said Max.

"Where's he going to go when he's free?"

"I don't know. I hadn't considered it. I think that's up to him. William left him a substantial sum of money."

"He'll need more than money," said Annie. "A Black man has limited options. Limited places to live. Limited employment opportunities, especially in the South. He also risks being re-enslaved if he stays in the South. It happens. Freedmen have been captured, dragged back, and trapped again on plantations."

"How do you know so much about this? What are you reading?" said Max.

"My friend, Katie Coffin. and her husband Levi are Quakers and advocates for the Negro. I meet with them and a group of ladies from the Anti-Slavery Sewing Society."

"You—belong to a sewing society?" Max laughed, "What's your role? Head rabble-rouser?"

Annie said indignantly, "I don't sew, but I contribute in other ways."

Max raised his eyebrows. "You don't bake biscuits for the ladies, so what then?"

"Let's call it scheduling and organizing."

He shook his head. "You're good at that. I don't think I want to know the details."

Annie said, "We're talking about John. I think he should go north. Come to Cincinnati or go further north. We could let him stay with us until he gets on his feet."

"You would have a Black man in our house? With Lizzie?" said Max.

"Why not?"

"I can give you multiple reasons. First and foremost, it wouldn't be safe. What if he did something to her?"

"Such as?" she said.

"I don't know; what if he did something to you? Forced himself on you? I've heard Black men have a very aggressive nature with white women."

"Have you observed this yourself?" said Annie.

"No."

"Have you ever become acquainted with a Black man? Beyond niceties or allowing them to open a door for you?

"No."

"Several Black men and women attended the salons I went to in New York. I even met Frederick Douglass once—he is a proper gentleman. Not all Black men want to ravage white women. This man is your half-brother. You have an opportunity to help him. You should consider it."

"Annie, I don't know. What would the voters in Cincinnati say if one of their city councilmen had a Black man living in his home?"

"They should say—what a charitable man that Max Mueller is; helping a man born into even less fortunate circumstances than himself, a poor lad from Over-the-Rhine. But I understand. I know most won't say that. Will you think about it?"

"Let me meet him first," said Max.

A man in the row in front of them stood, turned and leaned over his seat back, "Excuse me, but I couldn't help overhearing your conversation about the Negroes. I know their ways, as I own a dozen of 'em. You Northerners are quite naive about what it would be like to have them living amongst yourselves. I can attest to their foul stench, ill manners, ravaging carnal appetites and dense intellect. Trust me; you don't want to bring that on your neighbors. People like yourselves and that John Brown—inciting the slaves to revolt and presuming them to be our equals will lead to the substantial demise of American civilization."

"I beg your pardon, sir, but my husband and I were having a private conversation," said Annie.

Max jumped in. "Thank you for sharing your experiences with us. However, as a gentleman, I'm sure you can respect our desire to be left to ourselves. We do appreciate it."

The man eyed Annie and Max disapprovingly, nodded and retook his seat.

Annie whispered, "See what we're up against?"

"Let's keep our voices down. You never know who is riding these trains," said Max.

They watched the rolling hills of central Kentucky go by. The trees had lost their leaves, leaving a gray landscape.

"I've never been this far south," said Annie. "I imagine it's pretty in the summertime. It reminds me of rural New York, near Aunt Lizzie's house. So much unsettled land and farms. Look at the horses." She pointed to a group of horses grazing in an open field. "Are they wild?"

"I don't think so. This part of Kentucky has horse farms. They raise them for horse racing," said Max.

"They look so happy with so much room to run around. So free. Freer than the slaves at Given House," said Annie.

Max nodded in agreement. He watched the landscape rush by for several minutes, then drifted asleep.

Annie nudged. "Max, wake up. We're at the Paris station."

He stretched and looked out the window at the small platform and building. As the train stopped, they gathered their things and moved to the end of the car. The attendant helped Max carry their trunk onto the platform. After a few passengers got off, several climbed on as the train whistle blew.

A young Black man dressed in ragged work clothes approached them. "Mr. Mueller?"

"Yes, I'm Max Mueller."

"I'm Harry. I'll drive you and your Missus to Given House."

Max reached out to shake the man's hand. Harry shook limply, glanced at Max in the face, crossed himself, then looked down at the ground.

"This your trunk?" Harry asked.

"Yes, can you assist me, please?" said Max.

"I'll carry it, sir. You tend to your Missus." Harry hoisted the trunk and waddled ahead, carrying the heavy wide load. "This way." He led them to a carriage and secured the trunk to the back. Max helped Annie step up before climbing in himself.

Harry climbed up front and took the reins.

"How long a ride is it?" Max asked through the open window.

"Not too long, sir."

Max whispered to Annie, "What does that mean?"

"He doesn't have a watch. Don't worry about it," said Annie.

Max said, "I have to use a privy."

"You should have done that at the station. You can ask him to stop once we get away from town."

"Why doesn't he run away?" said Max.

"What do you mean?"

"They trust him to drive a buggy by himself into town? Aren't they afraid he won't come back? I'd head for the hills."

"I don't know. It is strange. Is he a freedman, maybe?" said Annie.

"I don't think there are many free Negroes in central Kentucky."

Max had Harry stop so he could step into some bushes. He climbed back into the carriage. "Thank you. How much farther is it?"

"Just a ways down this road, and then we almost there," said Harry.

Max looked at Annie and muttered, "He's no sense of time or distance, but he seems to know the way."

"Look at that house. It's beautiful," said Annie, pointing to a large plantation house with rows of hedges surrounding the front lawn.

"It looks like a courthouse with those pillars. It's huge," said Max.

They rode for miles passing more grand homes, smaller farmhouses and a horse farm with acres of fenced fields. After about two hours, Harry turned the carriage up a lane. When they reached a fork, he veered right and drove into a clearing where the main house stood.

Given House was a two-story brick building with four white fluted Corinthian columns across the front porch.

"It's pretty," said Annie.

"Yes, it is."

Harry helped them down from the carriage and led them up the porch stairs. He opened the large front door. A man in matching dark pants and jacket and a white shirt met them in a long hallway decorated with rich carpets and papered walls. "Mr. and Mrs. Mueller, I'm John. Welcome to Given House." John studied Max, then bowed slightly. "Please come in." He led them into a large parlor with a brick fireplace and elegant, upholstered furniture. "Please make yourself comfortable. I'll let Master Aaron and Missus Johnson know you arrived. May I take your overcoats?"

"Max, welcome." The tall, blond, muscular Aaron strode into the room and greeted them. "You must be Annie." He took her hand lightly. Annie noticed his blue eyes, the same as Max's.

"I'm Aaron."

"It's nice to meet you, Aaron."

A tall, slender woman with curls of blonde hair stepped from behind Aaron and smiled. "This is my wife, Mary." The women dipped toward each other and exchanged greetings. Max stepped forward and took her hand.

"How was your journey?" asked Mary.

"The train ride was beautiful, but the last two hours in the carriage were a little cold and rough," said Max.

Mary said, "You must be tired. We came in yesterday and have had a chance to recover, although Aaron's been working nonstop since he got here. Why don't you get settled in your room? We'll have dinner at seven, so that gives you a few hours to relax while I help Martha in the kitchen."

"We'll introduce you to the house later, but let me show you to your room," said Aaron. He led them up a curved staircase with polished mahogany railing to the second floor, containing four bedrooms. "John has lit the fire in your fireplace, and there's plenty of wood if you need it. Please let John or me know if you need anything." Aaron lowered his voice. "We haven't said anything to the staff yet about you, John's situation or the estate. No sense in upsetting them unnecessarily. I think you and I should sit down with John tomorrow after we've agreed on our plan, Max."

"Of course. Thank you for your hospitality, Aaron," said Max.

"My pleasure. It's your house too, for now." Aaron left and closed the door.

"My word," said Max. "This is some house."

"It's fantastic," agreed Annie.

"He grew up here. No wonder he looked down his nose at me," said Max. "It's a palace. He's being so gracious. I think it's odd that he hasn't said anything to the staff. Aren't they wondering what's going to happen since William passed?"

"He called them staff, but they're slaves. When I lived in New York City, we had staff, but they were paid and could leave any time they wanted. They went home at night."

"Relax, Annie."

"I'm uncomfortable being party to a weekend in a house where our hosts are holding people captive and forcing them to wait on me. I'm working to advance women's position in the world, but women's place seems elevated in comparison. I'm embarrassed. I don't know if I can do this." She started tearing up. "I can't imagine."

Max went to her and hugged her. "We just have to get through the weekend. We came here to understand what I am inheriting so we can make the right decisions. This is part of it."

Annie nodded her head.

"There's a basin. You want to wash up? I'll pour some water from the kettle for you." Annie washed while Max began to unpack their things from the trunk. He said, "That bed looks comfortable. Should we rest before dinner?"

"Napping is a luxury we might as well take advantage of without Lizzie. I may need the strength to get through dinner," said Annie.

CHAPTER 5

The two couples sat in the middle of a polished mahogany table with seats for a dozen diners. The table was set with painted china, silver, and a vase of flowers in the center. Candles from a cut-glass chandelier lit the room. Martha and John served roast chicken, succotash, boiled eggs, potatoes, and bread. They sat silently as the two servants made their way around the table.

Mary broke the silence, "Well, Martha and I did our best with what's left of the summer vegetables. Martha baked the bread and made an apple pie for dessert."

"It all looks delicious. Thank you, Martha and Mary," said Max.

"Yes, thank you," said Annie.

Aaron lifted his wine glass, "A toast? To our guests."

Max responded. "To our hosts and to families."

They began to sip. Annie added, "To equal opportunities for all."

They resumed their sips.

"Very nice, Aaron," said Max, eyeing the wine through the crystal glass.

"You can thank my father. He left a full wine cellar."

"May he rest in peace," said Mary.

"John and Martha, please leave us with our dinners. We'll let you know should we need anything," instructed Aaron.

John bowed slightly, and Martha said, "Yes, sir."

"We really should get to know each other. How did you two meet?" asked Aaron.

Max began, "We met on a steamship. I was traveling back from Pittsburgh after visiting some suppliers. At the time, I was working for the Niles ironworks. Annie was traveling with her mother, brothers, and sister, moving from New York to Cincinnati. I discovered her on the lower deck, studying the steam engine and paddlewheel mechanics. We had a brief conversation and went our separate ways. Several weeks later, I happened to be installing the iron railings at Annie's stepfather's home on Chestnut Street when she appeared at the door and came back into my life. I was smitten from the start."

"You're not from Cincinnati, Annie?" said Aaron.

"No, I grew up in New York City, on Fifth Avenue. My father was a banker but died from cholera when I was a teenager. My mother remarried Mr. Stephen Neltner, an attorney in Cincinnati, and that's when we moved."

"I've met Mr. Neltner. He has a solid reputation with the attorneys in town," said Aaron.

"I'm somewhat estranged from Stephen and my family," said Annie. "They disapproved of our marriage. I write to my brother, who is an army officer, but I don't see the rest."

"I'm sorry," said Mary. "That must have been very difficult for you."

"It was. It was more than my marrying Max. My mother never understood me or supported my efforts as an independent woman. Sometimes I miss them, but Max's family has taken me in. They're wonderful."

"Yes, if I remember, you were a vocal advocate for the women's movement. Something about sharing your views with the girls in the school where you were teaching?" said Aaron.

Annie's tone sharpened, "Yes, you brought that up at a city council election speech Max made the first time he ran. He lost."

"What's this?" asked Mary, turning to Aaron.

Aaron said, "I should apologize for that, Max. It wasn't personal. It was politics. I'm sorry I did that."

Max nodded, acknowledging the apology.

"Do you have children at home?" asked Mary.

"We have one daughter, Lizzie, who is three. Unfortunately, her birth was complicated, and I can't have more children. Max's sister Marie lives with us and helps care for her. I work as the accountant at Miller Industries with Max. I took on the role when he bought out the Niles brothers."

"How progressive of you," said Mary. "Don't you miss her while you're at work?"

"I see her plenty; my schedule is flexible. My nature is such that I am bored easily, so I need the challenge of a profession in addition to child-rearing. It's a juggling act at times, but I truly feel blessed to have the opportunity to do both. How about you, Mary? Do you have children?"

"Yes, we have three children. Two boys and a girl, ages five, four, and one."

"Three—that's a handful. Are they here?"

"No, this is a holiday for me. They are staying with my sister this weekend. She and her husband live near us in Clifton. I'm enjoying the peace and quiet. Where do you and Max live?"

"We are in a house on Eighth Street right now, but we're building a house in Mount Auburn," said Annie.

"There are some lovely views from there. How is the construction progressing, Max?" asked Aaron.

"It hasn't started yet. We are still finalizing the drawings."

Annie said, "How did the two of you meet?"

Aaron said, "We met at a party. Our fathers met through business dealings, and our families have known each other for years. More wine?" He poured wine for them.

Mary said, "Let me see about dessert."

John and Martha cleared the table and served the pie. It was dark outside, and some of the candles had burned out.

"Max, shall we have a drink?" said Aaron.

"I'd love to."

They all stood up. "Annie, I'm going to help Martha in the kitchen. Would you like to join me?" said Mary.

"Yes, I can do that. You men go have your drink," said Annie.

Max winked at her.

Aaron led Max into the library. Bookcases filled two walls, and a third had floor-to-ceiling windows and a fireplace. He called out, "John, can you light a fire in here for us, please?"

"Yes, sir," he called from somewhere in the house. A few minutes later, John quietly arranged the wood and lit the fire. "Anything else, Master Aaron?"

"No, thank you, John."

He left and closed the door behind him.

"Bourbon whiskey?" asked Aaron.

"Yes, thank you," said Max.

Aaron poured from a decanter into two short glasses. They each took a chair in front of the fireplace. They raised their glasses, "Cheers."

"It's excellent," said Max.

"Yes, there are some fine distillers here in Bluegrass country. They make their whiskey with mostly corn—as opposed to Irish or Scotch whisky, made from malted barley or other grains; the corn makes it sweeter. Then they age it in oak barrels," said Aaron.

"I'm usually a beer man, but I could get used to this," said Max.

"How is your business doing? Tell me about buying out the Niles brothers."

"About five years ago, I bought the machine tool and ironworks portions of their business and created Miller Industries. Since we took over, I've focused on creating specialty steam engine equipment for manufacturers. We've tripled in size and profits as more factories look for ways to manufacture using machines. Proprietors are looking for ways to create ready-made products at lower costs, as opposed to hiring artisans to create custom goods. We've seen it in shoes, furniture, and even clothing. I think the trend is just beginning. It's the future."

"You were always bloody smart," said Aaron.

"What about you? What kind of law do you practice?"

"Primarily insurance claims and fraud. My father introduced me to men in the insurance industry, and I've argued some of their cases. I find those most interesting. You'd be surprised what men try to claim from their insurance companies. I had a case where a man set fire to his failing business, hoping to receive an insurance payout, rather than accepting the consequences of his mismanagement.

"I plan to start my own firm soon. I want to build a specialty practice around insurance. I'm establishing the personal relationships I'll need to do that now. Father's passing is a mixed blessing. The capital from his estate should help me open my firm sooner, but a revelation about John or you would be an inconvenience I don't need. I ask for your discretion. You'll each get what you're due after we settle the estate, but the knowledge of your relationships could be detrimental to my reputation."

Max said nothing. He thought it was ironic that Aaron, the boy who had derided him for his German heritage, now had a family background that he was ashamed of and wanted to conceal.

They talked and drank into the late evening. John knocked on the door and entered. "Anything else this evening, Master Aaron?"

"No, thank you, John. We won't require anything else of you tonight. Goodnight."

John said goodnight and left them.

"What do you think about all this, Max—your newfound father and a substantial inheritance?"

"The inheritance is an unexpected blessing. I'm not sure what I think about the man, our father. He wreaked some havoc in his life, didn't he? I am curious about him. Tell me what he was like."

Aaron sighed and thought before answering. "I don't think I ever truly knew him. He was complicated… He treated me kindly… He loved women." He laughed. "He wasn't a good match for my mother. She didn't respect him. They were from different worlds. She was a Southern belle, a part of a prominent family, and he wasn't comfortable with it. He valued commerce and enjoyed the thrill of living in the city. She wanted to have parties and socialize with the families in her circle. I don't think he liked spending time here. I felt it when I was young. He spent as much time at his city house as he could. He was the one who sent me to Saint Xavier in Cincinnati. I don't know if it was another excuse for him to be away or if he wanted to take me out of this environment. They fought about where I would spend my summers. She always won. After she passed away, he only came here when he had to. He turned over the day-to-day running of the house to John. Uncle Lyle oversaw the farming and the slaves."

"Did you have any idea about John?" asked Max.

"When I was young, I didn't. We were playmates and schoolmates, but he was also my valet. I didn't see my father treat John any differently than the other Negroes. He was good to all of them. He let Lyle discipline them as he didn't have it in him to dole out the punishments required. As I got older and came home, I noticed that he had put a lot of trust in John. John maintained the house and helped William track expenses. He even trusted John with a small amount of cash. I thought it was reckless. I found it strange, but it never crossed my mind that he might be John's father."

"Do you think John had any idea?"

"I don't know," said Aaron. "John has a pretty hard shell. He doesn't let on what he's thinking."

"How do you feel about John being your brother?" said Max.

"He's not my brother."

"You share a father."

"That doesn't make us brothers."

Aaron poured bourbon into both their glasses.

"What about me?" said Max.

"We share a father also, so technically, we're half-brothers, but I don't see us as family."

"Am I just one step above John to you?"

"No, it's different. He's a Negro. You're a man like me, but we are different. From such different backgrounds."

"Then why did you invite me here, into your home? Into your life?" said Max.

"We have to agree on the disposition of Father's estate. I thought it could be done more expediently if you saw Given House and we became acquainted. Mary encouraged me to invite you and your wife here, but we'll never be kin."

"We could be friends, though. I'm not that bad. It's uncanny that we spent five years living together at school and were oblivious to the connection," said Max. They were both relaxed from the wine and the bourbon. Max asked the question he had inside him for so long. "Why did you despise me so much?"

"Hmm. I don't think I singled you out specifically, but I felt threatened by you."

"How? You had all the advantages. The pedigree, the money."

"My mother told me my destiny was to lead, and then she was gone. I didn't know how to do what she expected of me. As I got older, I saw myself more like my father, the man she dismissed as inconsequential. I wanted to live up to her expectations. I saw you—intelligent, handsome, and well-liked—as my competition. It didn't reconcile with my expectations of my birthright. I lashed out at you by attacking your heritage. Everyone talked disparagingly about the Germans and the Irish in Cincinnati. I didn't think much about it. Did it really bother you?"

Max said, "I was frustrated. I wanted to be like you and others and become successful. I believed that if I worked hard, I could achieve that. But you made me feel dirty and unworthy because of something I couldn't change. You weren't the only one. I saw it in the city. I knew what the natives thought of Germans. But you made it personal. I couldn't understand why someone like you, who had so much, felt the need to put me down. There was plenty of room for us both to succeed."

Aaron shrugged. "What can I say? We were boys."

CHAPTER 6

The next morning, after Martha served breakfast, Aaron and Mary gave a tour of the mansion. They finished in the front hallway.

Aaron pointed to a large oil painting, "That's William and Lydia, my father and mother. They had the portrait done for their wedding."

Annie said, "They're a handsome couple. Max, he looks like you. His high cheekbones and the way he's pressing his lips together, the way you do."

"Yes, and his eyes," said Mary. "I see both Max and Aaron in his eyes." She looked at the two men. "I see it now, the resemblance. You're brothers."

"We share a father," said Aaron sharply. "It's a fact. Why all the fuss about brothers?"

Mary said, "I'm sorry, darling. I don't mean to make a fuss. I know this whole revelation has been difficult for you."

Aaron said, "Let's show them the grounds," and walked to the front of the hall. They followed.

They donned their coats and went outside. Mary took Aaron's arm and patted his forearm, whispering to him.

Aaron described the farm's operations as they toured the summer kitchen, stable, and barn, and walked past the icehouse and smokehouse. They stood in the center of the outbuildings talking in the cool morning air.

Aaron pointed to a small cabin just past the barn. "That's the servants quarters, where the others besides John and

Martha live. The chicken coop is there." He pointed toward the front of the house and the Y in the front driveway. "Lyle's farm is down that other lane. His house is less grand than this one, but he has about the same acreage as Given House, about fifty acres."

"Do you grow cotton?" asked Annie.

"No, not much cotton in Kentucky. Most of our fields are hay and corn to feed livestock. We also grow wheat and barley," said Aaron. "The farms in central Kentucky either have grain and livestock as we do, or they grow hemp to make rope and bags for the cotton industry down south. Some raise thoroughbreds."

"We passed some horse farms on the trip here," said Annie. "The farm is beautiful. So peaceful."

"Nothing like it," said Aaron. "John and I used to ride for hours around the neighboring farms as boys. In summer, we'd be gone all day. We'd sneak berries or tomatoes from a garden or grab apples from the neighbor's orchard. There's a creek that runs through the back of the farm. We'd swim and catch crawdads and tadpoles. It was a great place to be a boy." Standing in the cool breeze, they admired the rolling hills surrounding the farm and the minor foothills of the Appalachian mountains to the east.

"Shall we go inside? Get down to business?" said Aaron.

"Yes. Thank you for the tour," said Max.

"Do you mind if I walk for a while?" asked Annie. "The fresh air will do me good."

"Of course," said Aaron. "I recommend you stay on the roads and paths. Will you be comfortable alone, or would you like me to have Martha accompany you?"

"Should I be worried? Any wild animals on the farm? Rabid cattle?" said Annie.

"You're safe. There are foxes, coyotes, and an occasional bear, but unless you're a small animal such as a chicken, they're not interested in you. Do watch for snakes. We have copperheads here," said Aaron.

"I'm sure I'll be safe alone. Thank you."

#

Max and Aaron went into the library and shut the door. Aaron spread out several sheets of paper on the desk. "Here's an inventory of the property in the estate. Let's start with Given House. I'm assuming you have no wish to own it?"

"No. Do you and Mary want to keep it?" said Max.

"No, Mary has no desire to live amongst the fields and trees. I will miss the familiar places of my youth, but I find it prudent to let it go and raise my family in the city. My uncle Lyle desires to purchase Given House and the land. He has always coveted the house my grandfather gave to my mother instead of him. I propose we sell it to him."

"Does he have the means to purchase it at a fair price?" asked Max.

"He doesn't have the cash, but with his land and share of the slaves as collateral, he should be able to secure a loan for the purchase."

"Then selling to him seems the logical disposition," said Max. "At a fair market price, of course."

"Of course," agreed Aaron. "I'll proceed with getting an appraisal."

"What about the possessions inside the house and the farm equipment?" asked Max.

"There are a few possessions I'd like to have. Here's the list Mary and I made. I want the painting of my parents, my mother's wedding ring, and some of her jewelry. I can have the jewelry appraised and deduct the cost from my portion of the estate proceeds. The painting has sentimental value to me but no real market value. Mary fancies the curio cabinet in the parlor and the crystal glassware, china, and silver. Again, we can deduct the value from our half of the estate if you agree."

"Yes, you should have anything you want," said Max.

"Is there anything that you'd like?" Aaron asked.

"I'd like his desk," Max said as he ran his hands across the smooth cherry desktop in front of them.

"You do? Why?"

"I'd like something of his. I didn't know him, but I'm of him. It's a beautiful piece of furniture."

"It's yours," said Aaron. "Anything else? Is there anything Annie would like?"

"I'll ask her. She's not one for decoration, but there are some beautiful items in the house. Is it all right if she makes a list?"

"Of course. We should offer anything you or I don't want to Lyle first and then sell at auction with the proceeds going to the estate. Mary can walk through the house with Annie to see if anything catches her eye."

"Thank you. That's helpful," said Max.

"Father's house on Fourth Street. You and I can visit there next week. There are a few things I want from there as well. They're listed on the third sheet," said Aaron.

Max looked at the list of items. "Does he have any papers? Journals or letters?"

"I didn't find a journal. There are some letters. Mostly correspondence with his brother in Connecticut and a smattering of business and personal acquaintances."

"Can I read those?"

"What are you looking for, Max?"

"I'd like to read them to understand him and who he was."

"I don't think they'll convey much. He was just a man who built his insurance business," said Aaron.

"I'd like to."

"If you're hoping to find anything of you or your mother in them, I don't think you will. I haven't read them all, but I didn't see any indication of it. Whatever he might have felt, he kept to himself," said Aaron.

"I understand, but still, may I?"

"It's your time to waste. You can go through them. I've already spoken to a real estate man about selling the house. Do you think four weeks will give you enough time to go through or remove what you want? While you're sorting through, would you be willing to sort out anything we should destroy before the auctioneer inventories the items to sell?"

"Yes, I can do that," said Max.

"Here is the inventory of his other properties. I believe I have everything with the approximate value as of last week. There are stocks in railroads and several companies. The estimated value of these is $33,000. I suggest we divide them equally between us. I've drawn up an allocation schedule. I attempted to apportion them without splitting up any investment for simplicity's sake."

"I'd like to review the list for equity purposes. Assess the assigned value and potential volatility of each?" said Max.

"Still the analytical one, I see."

"Don't take offense. I'm protecting my interests."

"It's within your rights," said Aaron, nodding. "The Negroes. John will be freed, and the $1,000 father willed him will be deducted from the estate. That leaves these eleven." He handed Max another sheet with the names of the slaves. Each had an assigned value next to their name, ranging from $400 to $1,200. "I consulted two slave traders to arrive at the values. Lyle has agreed to the figures. He wants to purchase our share of them, along with Given House."

They looked at the list together. Aaron said, "Harry is John's brother. He is probably the most skilled of them all. He's the blacksmith for the two farms. He oversees the animals, the horses, and the cattle and pigs. He's also the mechanical one who kept things running around the properties. He maintains the fences, main house, and buildings.

"You met Martha. She is John's sister. She keeps the house—cooks and cleans, and does the laundry. She also tends the vegetable garden and works in the fields during planting and harvesting."

"Is William also Harry and Martha's father? Their last name is Johnson too," said Max.

"No. Their father was sold shortly after they were born. Slaves don't need a last name. For convenience, slaves take on the surname of the plantation owner. The other three slaves in William's lot are George, Cecelia, and Charlie. They're priced based on their age, sex, and skills. George oversaw the farming for William. The other two are field hands. Sometimes they would help out on Lyle's farm."

"Are there any children?"

"There's one they call Little Nick over at Lyle's. He's a good worker but only nine years old, so he's not worth as much."

Max rubbed his hands through his hair in a combing motion. "Can we free them instead? What if I buy them with my proceeds?"

"They're needed to work the farm. The value of the farm diminishes to Lyle without the labor. Besides, he owns them jointly with Father's estate. He has to agree to whatever happens to them," said Aaron.

"What if I don't agree to sell my interest in them? In my half? Can we free half of them?" said Max.

"You don't want to pick that fight with Lyle. Law prohibits any new slave trade in Kentucky, so he must use the ones we have now and their offspring. No new slaves are being traded from Africa anymore. They're a valuable commodity that Lyle needs. Besides, they're better off staying together here on the farm. They've been treated well and have it pretty good. Lyle's a little tougher on them than William was, but they could have it far worse."

"What if I do want to pick that fight with Lyle?" said Max.

"Let it go. Don't stick your nose in something you don't understand. You might get bit."

"Is that a threat?"

"You are messing with the man's livelihood that he has worked for his whole life. He doesn't like you or me very much. You saw that. I can't say what he might do or how far he might go to protect his rights to his property. He's got a mean streak in him," said Aaron.

"What's he going to do, shoot me?"

"This isn't the North. I'm telling you to let this go."

"I don't know. Does this seem right to you?"

"We need to let things be as they are. We're not making things worse," said Aaron.

"That's the whole philosophy of the South, isn't it?" said Max. "They know slavery isn't right, but there's no easy answer to replacing all the labor if we free the slaves, so let's keep things the way they are. And the Northerners relented on abolishing slavery but compromised on an agreement that prevents the spread of it in order to keep the peace in the country. We all know we'll break the country if we push the issue too hard, so we're stuck."

"Sounds about right. It's an evil necessity for half the country's way of life. I don't have a better answer; do you?" said Aaron.

"I don't. God help us."

CHAPTER 7

Annie walked for an hour, staying on the paths worn by the horses and field workers. She stood at a distance and watched a group of four men and two women working in a field of tall hay. Two men moved down the field swinging large, multi-bladed curved scythes, cutting the golden grass, catching it on the blades, and laying it on the ground in heaps. Each man had a rhythm, starting with the tool high, swinging it into a patch and then turning the scythe at the bottom of his swing. They moved over and over, stopping every several minutes to rest their aching bodies. A man and woman followed each one and bent over to gather the stalks and tie them into bundles. Annie watched unobserved for twenty minutes.

She walked back toward the main house, down a path to the slave cabin and knocked on the door. Receiving no answer, she turned the knob and pushed the door open. She peered inside the windowless room. Daylight shined into the cabin from dozens of small gaps in the walls. It only took a moment to survey the entire room: the dirt floor swept clean; a table with two benches; an unlit fireplace with a single pot; a ladder leading up to a small loft; a few pieces of clothing hung on wooden pegs; a lantern, hairbrush, and Bible atop a single chest of drawers; a banjo against the wall next to a small drum. Annie pulled the door closed and walked toward the outbuildings. She followed the sound of water and scraping and found Martha washing laundry outside the summer kitchen.

"Hi, Martha," said Annie.

"Missus." Martha looked up from the washboard as she continued scrubbing.

"I want to thank you for your hospitality during our visit. We appreciate your efforts to make us comfortable during our stay."

"I do what I do. No matter whether there's two or four of you."

"Have things been quiet and less busy since Mr. Johnson passed away?" said Annie.

"No, ma'am. Master William hadn't been here much these last few years. We work over at Master Lyle's when we're not needed here. This is the end of harvest season. There's plenty to do."

"I see," said Annie. "Is that agreeable to you, working for Master Lyle?"

Martha looked at Annie, puzzled by the question. "Master William. He never beat us and wasn't a shouting man. Master Lyle, he's another kind."

"Does he beat you?"

"We all get the switch at times. You're from up north, ain't you?"

"Yes, I'm from Cincinnati."

"That's where Master Aaron lives now. Your husband, is he Master Aaron's kin?"

"Yes, they're related."

"He has the look of Master William. I see his eyes," said Martha.

Annie didn't want to divulge more than she should, so she said nothing.

Martha continued, "Your husband, will he be our new master? Come live at Given House?"

"No, we're staying in Cincinnati."

"I hear there're freedmen there. Negroes who free and have their own house," said Martha.

"Yes. Not too many, but there are some. Slavery is not legal in Ohio."

"Who are you?" said a man as he approached Annie.

"I'm Annie Mueller, a guest of the Johnson's. Who am I addressing?"

"You must be that Northern boy Max's wife."

"I am. Who are you?"

"I'm Lyle Reed."

"Ah. Mr. Reed," said Annie.

"You shouldn't be out here, filling Martha's head with Northern myths and lies. She don't need to hear that shit about some faraway place she'll never see. She's happy right here. Ain't that right, Martha?"

"Yes, sir."

"So, you go on back to the house then, Mrs. Mueller."

"I'm not quite ready to go inside just yet, thank you," said Annie.

Lyle stepped toward her, grabbed her upper arm, and squeezed firmly, "I think you are." He started pulling her toward the house.

Annie yanked her arm away with all she could muster, "Sir, you are hurting me."

"If you'll be on your way, I'll leave you be."

Annie started walking toward the house. Lyle followed her.

"I am quite capable of finding my way," said Annie.

"Stay away from my Negroes, and don't you be putting any of your Northern rubbish in their heads. They know their place and your kind of talk just puts dreams in their heads that make them even lazier than they are. If you Northerners want to live amongst the Negroes and talk nonsense to them about them being your equals, that's for you to do. Your cities will be the worse for it, but don't be polluting the minds of our Negroes and soiling what we have."

Annie wanted to protest but thought better of it. Lyle didn't seem like a man who wanted to argue with an abolitionist, especially a female one. She hurried up the steps of the main house and turned, "Mr. Reed." She saw hatred and determination in his face.

She found Mary working at the table in the kitchen.

"How was your walk?" asked Mary.

"The farm is serene and beautiful. I saw the workers in the field. I met Lyle."

"Where was Lyle?" said Mary.

"He came upon me when I was talking to Martha while she was washing. He wasn't happy with me."

"What did he say?"

"He told me not to fill Martha's head with ideas of freedom."

"You weren't doing that, were you?" said Mary.

"Well, she asked me about Negroes in Cincinnati. Lyle grabbed me and walked me back to the house."

"Are you all right?" said Mary.

"Yes, I'm fine. I was surprised to see such a violent reaction to such a small thing."

"It's not a small thing to these men in the South. It's not safe for you to challenge Lyle alone like that. The men here become increasingly agitated the longer the debate about slave versus free states continues. They talk all the time about leaving the United States and forming their own country, where their way of life and values won't be constantly challenged. They're losing patience. I've never liked Lyle. I don't think he likes Aaron either. He didn't respect William. I've never been comfortable spending time here."

"So you're not from the South—used to all this?" said Annie.

"No, my family came from Massachusetts. I don't have any desire to be a part of this world. I am sad for Aaron because it's his birthplace, and so it's home to him. He'll feel a sense of loss when he sells it."

"Is that what he's going to do?" said Annie.

"Yes, he's proposing to Max to sell it all to Lyle. There are a few things from the house that Aaron wants, and I've asked for the silver and crystal. Aaron asked me to see if there's anything you'd like for your new home. Anything we don't take will either go to Lyle or be auctioned off, so don't be shy."

"I can't shake the look on Lyle's face. He was enraged."

"I'm afraid of him too. I'll be glad when I don't have to come back here anymore," said Mary.

#

After dinner, Aaron summoned John to the library. "Come in, John. Please close the door. Have a seat." He pointed to the cushioned settee in front of the fireplace.

John flashed back to the conversation he had with Aaron's father in this same room on the morning his mother was sent away. He sat nervously and looked at the burning fire.

"John, we wanted to talk to you about my father's will. We have good news for you," said Aaron.

John relaxed slightly, smiled briefly with a slight nod, but continued to look at the fire.

"When Master William died, he left instructions in his will and revealed that he was Max's father. Max and I are related by blood then," Aaron said, pointing at Max. "William left half of his property to Max and the other half to me."

John said, "We saw the resemblance as soon as Mr. Mueller arrived. He looks like Master William and you. We're wondering if he'll be our new master?"

"No. We're going to sell Given House and all the property to Lyle," said Aaron.

"So, Master Lyle will be our new master?" said John.

"He'll be the others' new master, but not yours, John."

"You taking me with you, sir?"

"No, John. William made you a free man in his will. You don't have a master anymore."

John's eyes became glassy with tears as he continued to look at the fire. "Is that the truth? I'm free?"

"Yes, John, it is," said Aaron.

Tears streamed down John's face. He choked, then put his hands over his face and wept. "Praise the Lord. My Lord."

He cried for another minute. "I'm free." He wiped the tears from his face with the back of his hand.

Max teared up and had to look away.

Aaron let John compose himself before he continued. "There's something else. William wanted you to know. William was your father too."

John said. "I know that. I knew I had white blood in me. Look at me. My skin is light. My kin knew my daddy had to be white. Miss Clara, before she died, she told me who my daddy was. About him and Mammy. Told me I couldn't tell nobody. But if people pay attention, they can see my cheekbones and nose are like his. If they heard how he talked to me when we were alone, just the two of us, they would know just like I know. He treated me better than any white man I ever met. He never said it and couldn't let nobody see it, but I knew he was my daddy. Praise the Lord. He couldn't free me when he was alive, but he freed me in death. God bless Master William."

"One more thing," said Aaron. "William left you a sum of money in his will. One thousand dollars."

John whistled. "I never dreamed I'd have that much money. I'm a rich man." John was smiling now. "When am I free?"

"You're free now," said Aaron. "I have your papers. You'll need to keep them with you."

"What about Martha and Harry and the others? Master William free them too?"

"No, John, just you. He freed you because he was your father."

John nodded. "Can I go tell them now, about me being free?"

"You go on and tell them and say goodbye to them," said Aaron.

"What do you mean, say goodbye?"

"You can't stay here on the farm. Lyle won't allow it. You're free, and the rest are not. He won't have you here and talking about freedom to them. We'll take you with us on the train to Cincinnati tomorrow morning."

"What am I going to do in Cincinnati? This is my home. My family is here. That don't sound like freedom to me," said John. "You're still telling me what I can and can't do. You telling me I have to leave them tomorrow, just like that?"

"I'm sorry, John, that's how it's got to be," said Aaron. "You'll be safer in Ohio. Your freedom could be short-lived if you stay in Kentucky. Go to Cincinnati. Start a new life with the money William left you."

"I'll buy Martha and Harry's freedom from Master Lyle with my money. They can come with me."

"They're not for sale, John. Lyle is keeping them."

John's face tightened. "No, no. Master Lyle the only master now, and Master William isn't here to calm him. I don't want to leave them here with Master Lyle. I'm afraid for them."

"You must," said Aaron.

"It's not right. I'm free, and they're not. Just because of who my daddy was? It's not right. None of it is right. We all got the same daddy," he said, motioning to the three of them, "and look at where God put us. Same daddy, but different mammys, and different color of our skin. Why did God do that to us? None of it is right." He looked at his two half-brothers, who sat silently, unable to respond, then walked out of the library.

Aaron called after him, "We leave at seven tomorrow morning for the train station John. Pack your things. Tell Henry he's driving us, and he needs to get Lyle's carriage and another driver."

"He's not as happy as I thought he would be to hear the news," said Aaron. "He almost seemed ungrateful."

Max exhaled. He could hardly process all he had just witnessed. Meeting John and the other enslaved people, seeing John's emotions upon learning of his freedom, thinking of the implications of him having to leave his siblings behind, trying to understand what John thought of his condition versus Aaron and Max's, having to serve at Aaron's beck and call. Aaron's callousness. Being a slave. It was inhumane. "I imagine he's feeling a little lost right now. Leaving his family on such short notice. He feels injustice even in his freedom. It has to be overwhelming for him."

"He's free, no longer a servant. I can't believe William left $1,000 to a Negro!"

"He was his son," said Max.

"A bastard mulatto son," said Aaron

"Don't you feel any connection to him at all? For God's sake, you grew up with him."

"He was my butler. His place was to serve me and keep me company. He cleaned my clothes and polished my shoes. He's not the same as you and me and never will be."

"What's going to happen to him when he gets to Cincinnati?" asked Max.

"He's a free man. That's his to decide," said Aaron.

"But how's he going to get started? He doesn't know anyone or the city. Where's he going to live?"

"I'll take him to one of the boarding houses in Bucktown. I'll give him some of his money. He'll be with his people."

"A bumpkin like him shows up with a pocketful of money there. They'll rob him blind or worse," said Max.

"He's not my problem. He's a free man, so he needs to make it on his own like everyone else in this country."

"That's easy for you to say," said Max. "You were born into a place of status, with an education, money, and the right pedigree, not to mention white skin. He needs a little assistance until he gets a foothold."

"If you're so worried about him, then you take care of him. He shares as much blood with you as he does with me," said Aaron. "You always were soft. He's a Negro, for Christ's sake."

"It's called compassion," said Max.

"Do what you will."

"Any other business we need to talk about tonight?" said Max.

"No."
"Good. Do you have more bourbon?"
Aaron poured them each a healthy glass.
"To brothers," said Max, raising his glass.
Aaron shook his head, "To putting this all behind us."

CHAPTER 8

Five weeks later, John was employed as a barber on Third Street in William Watson's barbershop. Watson was a leader with significant wealth in the Cincinnati Negro community, owning two barbershops, several buildings, and 560 acres of land in northern Ohio. Max had been a customer of Watson's for years and brokered the introduction. John's education, neat and orderly appearance, and acquired skills of serving and grooming men qualified him to work in the shop. Barbering was a semi-skilled profession that Black men held exclusively in Cincinnati and paid more than manual labor or riverfront work.

John spoke little during his first few days of work. He observed the other barbers and how they interacted with their white clients to learn how to get along in his new profession. He knew how to play the humble servant of men and had polite manners, a calming voice, affable nature, and a broad smile. His relatively light skin put his customers at ease; some men requested John based on his appearance.

The customers would come in waves, heavier at lunchtime and the end of the day. John, Watson, and the other barbers conversed between customers.

"Where are you living?" asked Lewis, the barber who worked next to John, as he brushed the hair off his chair. A young boy moved between them, sweeping up the hair on the floor into a dustpan.

"I'm in a boarding house in Bucktown," answered John.

"Are you by yourself?"

"Yes, just me."

"You like it there?" asked Lewis.

"It's loud at night. I'm used to the quiet. City life is different."

"That's a rough part of town."

"A man put a knife to me and took my money the first week I was here. I was robbed again a few nights later. I've stopped carrying any money," said John.

"They see you coming. Know you're not wise to the ways of the city. Most white and Black folk in that part of town are down on their luck, and robbing, gambling, and whoring are the only means they have to make a living. You're an easy target in your nice clothes. You don't belong there."

"Any suggestions on where to live?" said John. "I didn't know where to go when I arrived in town. The white folk who brought me here told me that was the Black neighborhood."

"These rich white folk?" said Lewis.

"You know Mr. Mueller?" said John.

"The ironworks man?"

"Yes."

"He don't know where proper Black folks live, and he wouldn't be caught in Bucktown for anything. You need to get out of there," said Lewis.

"Where then?"

"The respectable Black families live in three or four neighborhoods. Some are in Over-the-Rhine with the Germans, some in Little Africa. Best to live in a neighborhood near your own kind. Until you figure that out, you move to a nice boarding house. Try the Dumas House on McAllister Street. It's owned by a Colored man, and respectable Coloreds stay there. You'll pay a little more, but it's safer and cleaner. You move there tonight, you hear me?"

"Sounds like a good idea."

"You need help moving your things, you ask Jimmy here, and he'll do it for a quarter. He'll bring a friend too," said Lewis.

The boy sweeping looked up at the men when he heard his name. "Yes, sir, I'm happy to earn a few after hours."

"Can you come with me after work, Jimmy?" said John.

"Yes, sir."

Lewis said, "You told me you left kin on that plantation in Kentucky. Do you know how they're doing?"

John said, "My sister had to move out to the fields after years of working in the house. She's not used to that kind of work every day. Master Lyle doesn't like my brother and sister 'cause they were part of Master William's plantation. I tell you, the day I left with my free papers, I was so happy until I got here and thought about them back in the fields. Why did the Lord free me and not them? I think of them every day."

John shook his head. "I heard Master Lyle is thinking of selling them down to Mississippi 'cause he needs the money. I'm afraid if they go down there, I'll never see them again, like my mammy. They sold her downriver when I was just a boy. When my master died, he willed me some money. I want to use that money to buy my sister and brother, but Master Lyle won't sell them to me. He insists on selling them down south. I'm fearful that if they go downriver, they'll be just as hard to find as her. I ain't given up on finding Mammy either. It wears on me every day."

Lewis lowered his voice even though there were no customers in the shop, "If your sister and brother can get across the river to Ohio, there are people that can help them."

"What do you mean?" said John.

"The railroad."

"What?"

"The Underground Railroad."

"Is that for real?" asked John. "We heard talk of that, but where is it?"

"There's stations here in Cincinnati. They aren't real railroad stations, just people who hide runaways or secretly take them to the next station. Then those people get them to the next place and so on. Most escaped slaves go to Canada."

"Why don't they stay here in Ohio? I thought Ohio was a free state?" said John.

"It is, but the Fugitive Slave Act is a national law allowing federal marshals to capture escaped slaves and return them to their masters, even if they're in free states. The law also makes it illegal for white or Black folks to assist a fugitive slave, and the marshals get a reward if they help return a slave to their master."

"So the only way for my sister and brother to be free is if I buy them?" said John.

"Or they go to Canada."

"How far is Canada?"

"Long way. A few days on a horse or a day on a train," said Lewis.

"What's Canada like? My brother and sister didn't learn to read like I did. How they going to get by?"

"It's got to be better than working on the plantation, right?"

"Maybe I could go with them. How do I get them to one of these stations?"

"You talk to Mr. Watson," said Lewis. "He knows some conductors on the railroad."

The front door opened, and Watson greeted a well-dressed man. The two came over to John's chair. "This is John. He specializes in younger men's cuts. He'll make you look real good," said Watson.

"Good morning, sir," said John smiling and pointing to his barber chair. The man sat, and John placed a towel around his neck. "How would you like it today?"

"Take plenty off the top. My wife says I'm looking shaggy. Trim the sideburns and shave the beard clean."

"Yes, sir," said John. "What's your business?"

"I'm a printer. We do specialty printing. Stock certificates, banknotes, all kinds of things, made to order. Lithograph printing of pictures is our specialty."

"How's business?" said John.

"Booming! With the railroads, I get orders from far corners of the south and the west. Louisville, Saint Louis, and Chicago have printers, but our reputation is unsurpassed. Most small towns can't support a full-time printing business like ours. Over half of my business is from Kentucky, Tennessee, and even Alabama. I, for one, am a friend of the Southerner. Who are we to tell them how to govern their states? It's anti-American. The states have the right to set the laws that work for them and their people. If they need slaves to farm their lands, that's their business. I'd never own a slave, but I'm no abolitionist. You hear me?"

"Uh-huh," said John.

As John pulled the razor up the man's neck, he applied a slight twist, nicking him.

"Ouch, watch it!" the man cried.

"I'm sorry, sir. You hold still now, and that won't happen."

The man remained calm and quiet for the remainder of his shave. John toweled him off, and he rose. He gave John a coin for his tip and nodded as he moved to the front of the shop to pay.

Lewis eyed him disapprovingly. "Don't you be taking your frustrations out on the paying customers. You smile and nod your head next time, you hear?"

John nodded, frustrated but understanding the need to satisfy their clients for his livelihood.

John's next customer was an elderly attorney who eyed John up and down and said, "I haven't seen you before. You're new, aren't you?"

"Yes, sir, been here just a few weeks," said John.

"You sound like you came from down south?"

"Yes, sir, Kentucky. Happy to be living in Ohio now."

"I'll bet you are. Damned Southerners continue to push this country apart with their insistence on going against the will of God and the Founding Fathers of this country. I agree that states have the right to set their own laws, but not if it codifies the immoral treatment of one human being over another, no sir. No man has the right to reap the earnings of another man's labor without compensation. Damned Democrat politicians use their elected positions to benefit themselves. Corrupt, the whole lot of them. You with me?"

"Yes, sir," said John, barely audibly, as he continued to cut.

The man became more vehement as he continued. "This damn *Dred Scott* decision in the Supreme Court is the last straw. Court Justices kowtow to the Democrats. Southerners claim this one ruling settles the slavery question once and for all. I say damn them and the cotton bales they sit and chew their tobacco on. They think this means they won. No, sir. It has strengthened the Northerners and the Republican party's resolve to kill slavery everywhere."

John nodded his head in agreement but remained silent.

Later in the morning, a tall red-haired man came into the shop. John overheard him say to Watson, "How about him? He looks like the most white of all of them."

John seated the man and wrapped him in a cape. "How are you this fine day, sir?"

"Yes, it is a fine day, thank you. You're a new barber. Where did you come from?" said the red-haired man.

"I used to live in Kentucky. Moved here several weeks ago," said John.

"Another Negro. Just what our city needs. Why did you come here?"

"I gained my freedom and came here where I could be paid for an honest day's work."

"Well, we'd just as soon your kind stay in Kentucky. I'm happy to let you give me a shave, but we don't need more Negroes in our city. You—you're working and supporting yourself, but too many of yours have come into this city and expect that the good citizens of Cincinnati will feed you and take care of you. Hell, most of you can't read or write, so you add to the vagrant numbers we have to support. We go freeing all the slaves, and you become our problem. We have enough problems with the poor Irish and other lowlifes we already support."

John took a slow breath and held his blade steady as he shaved the man.

"You have a wife?" asked the man.

"No, sir."

"You get yourself a Black wife. Leave the fair ladies of this city alone, you hear me?"

"Yes, sir," said John.

After the man left, John said to Watson and Lewis, "He was as hateful as the overseers on the plantations. I thought Northern men were more open-minded."

Watson said, "I think most men in Cincinnati think like that gentleman. They may talk politely to us and say they're anti-slavery, but they'd rather not see us at all. They wish we'd just go away."

"Mmm-hmm," said John. "Every day, I'm learning more about what freedom means to the Negro in the North."

"You a church-going man, John?" asked Watson.

"I read the Bible, and I used to attend church with the others from the plantation when Master Lyle took us. We stood in the back. I rarely found the preacher's words to be inspirational. His words often contradicted what I read in the Bible, so I haven't been to church since I came to Cincinnati. I still read the good book, though."

"It was a white preacher at this church?" said Watson.

"Yes."

"Why don't you to come to our church, the Baker Street Baptist Church. It's an African Union Baptist Church. A church for our people. I think you'll find it a more welcoming experience. The most upstanding Negro families in the city make up its congregation. Will you join us on Sunday?"

"All right. I'll give it a try," said John.

"Good. Nine on Sunday. It will do you good to be among people like yourself. Hearing these white men speak from their place of superiority every day can be disheartening. If that's all you hear, it's hard for a man to hold his head high, even if he is free."

CHAPTER 9

Annie opened the front door. "Good evening, John. Come in."

"Mrs. Mueller," said John, removing his hat and bowing slightly.

"John, you must call me Annie. We're practically brother and sister." She took his hand and led him into the hallway. "Come in, please. Max should be home from the shop any minute. Let me take your hat and coat."

Three-and-half-year-old Lizzie stood holding onto Annie's legs and eyed him curiously. "Lizzie, can you say hi to John?"

Lizzie took her thumb from her mouth. "Hi, John."

John squatted down on his haunches. "Hi, Lizzie," he said quietly, letting a smile break his stoic demeanor.

Lizzie stepped forward and hugged John.

John placed an arm around her and squeezed. "You're a friendly one."

"She's never met a stranger," said Annie. "Let's sit in the parlor."

Annie offered him a seat on the couch. She handed Lizzie a doll. "Lizzie, you play with Dolly while John and I talk."

"John, tell me how you're getting along in your new life."

"I'm finding my way. I moved to a new boarding house that is quieter and populated with a better class of Negroes."

"Where's that?"

"It's the Dumas House," said John.

"I've heard of it, yes. Do you think you'll be there long? Any prospects of renting a house with your inheritance?"

"I'm saving that money to buy Harry and Martha's freedom. That's what that money is for."

"I understand, John. How is your job at the barbershop going? Max said you gave him a haircut last week."

Marie came in from the kitchen and stood in the doorway, inspecting John.

Annie said, "Oh, this is Max's sister, Marie. Marie, this is our friend John. Marie lives with us and takes care of Lizzie and the house while I'm at work and attending to my obligations."

They exchanged nods and greetings.

Marie said, "Dinner is ready whenever you are, Annie."

"Thank you, Marie. We'll eat when Max arrives."

Marie retreated to the kitchen.

"Your job at the barbershop?" Annie asked.

"Mr. Watson is as fine a gentleman as I have met. He has been very kind to me, as have the other men in the shop. They've helped me navigate the city. The work itself is tedious but not strenuous or taxing."

"What are you doing with your free time?" said Annie.

"The time when I am not at the barbershop?"

"Yes, in the evenings, on the Sabbath?"

"It is a novelty for me—to have time to serve no one but myself. I walk about the city. I especially enjoy watching the boats on the riverfront."

"Have you made any friends?"

John didn't respond.

"Any acquaintances that you spend your free time with?"

"No, ma'am."

"Well, you're welcome to dine with us any evening you like. Just let us know so Marie can set another plate."

"Thank you, ma'am."

"Just call me Annie," she reminded him.

He nodded.

Lizzie waddled over to John and handed him her doll. He turned it to her and made voices, making Lizzie laugh. After a minute, she climbed up on the couch next to him and sat.

"It must be difficult. All alone in a new place, a city, after living all those years at Given House," said Annie.

"When I dreamed about freedom. I saw my family and friends on a farm—one that we owned. Working the fields in a house not so big as Given House, but a place where we felt safe. I never imagined living amongst so many people, especially white people."

"You never married?"

"No."

"Why didn't you? Were you allowed to marry?"

"The masters had to approve any marriages. Master Lyle wouldn't allow us to marry anyone from other plantations. He let us visit with other families on special occasions, but he didn't like us to have reason to visit other than that. A few on our farm married and had children. We'd have a marriage ceremony in the yard."

"But you never found anyone?"

"I wouldn't let myself get that close to anyone. I was too afraid that if Master Lyle became unhappy with me, he'd sell her away like they did my mammy. I couldn't face that. And I couldn't bear to see a woman I loved whipped or have to lay with one of the masters. And marriage leads to children, and a plantation is no place for a child," he said, looking down at Lizzie.

"That must have been very lonely. I'm sorry, John."

"What you sorry for, Annie?"

"For all of it. For the injustice."

"It's not your fault. You've been nothing but kind to me. Why are you so nice to me?"

"I was raised in a very well-to-do family in New York City. My father was a banker, and I grew up surrounded by refined things, servants, and education. Similar to how the ladies and gentlemen of Southern plantations grow up, I suppose. But I was different from most of the people around me. I wasn't interested in being part of society, having beautiful things, and being pampered. I wanted to go out in the world and be someone on my own. My family expected me to be a proper lady and wife and fall in line under a husband's rule.

"I wouldn't succumb to society's constraints on me as a woman. I wasn't permitted to do many things that boys and men do. The laws and proper ways of society prohibited me. My mother wouldn't support me, so I became estranged from her and my family. I started working to champion rights for women. I thought about becoming a speaker in the women's movement, like my father's cousin Elizabeth Cady Stanton, and Lucy Stone. But then I met Max, and he accepted me for who I was and supported me in wanting to have the same rights as men. I gave up on any chance of traveling the country as a women's movement advocate when we had Lizzie. I need to be a mother for her.

"Because of my experience being oppressed as a woman, I see the gross injustices that society places on the Negro. When I lived in New York City, I had several freedmen acquaintances that I came to know. It helped me recognize that people are born into their circumstances, and it's unjust to judge them because of that or to disrespect them or their right to live their lives like anyone else.

"That's a long answer to your question."

"You go out of your way to help me," said John. "No other white person ever done that."

"I see helping you as one small contribution I can make to help the cause against slavery and oppression of the Negro. I can't change the way things are, but I can do my small part."

"God bless you, Annie."

"May God bless you and your family. You miss them."

"I miss them every day. I'm sick for what they may be facing at the hand of Master Lyle. And I worry he's going to sell them downriver."

They heard the front door open and close.

Max entered the room, "John Johnson. Welcome to our home."

Lizzie jumped from John's side and ran to Max, "Papa, Papa." He picked her up and kissed and hugged her.

When Max put the girl down, the two men shook hands.

"How are you?" said Max.

"I am still free," said John

"Yes, you are. How does it feel?"

Annie shot Max an eye of disapproval for his question.

"I praise the Lord for what he has given me and that he might bring the same to Harry and Martha."

"We were just discussing them," said Annie. "What did you learn during your visit to Given House?"

"Did you see them?" asked John.

"No, we didn't have the opportunity," said Max. "They were working in the fields. Aaron and I were only there overnight to oversee packing the crates to be transported here."

"Did you hear of them? Are they in good health? Is Master Lyle going to sell them?" said John.

"So many questions. I think they're doing fine. They're working. Lyle needs them to finish bringing in the fall harvest. They're not going anywhere for now," said Max.

Annie asked, "Did you learn any more about his intentions?"

Max said, "He's having trouble coming up with the full amount due Aaron and me for the estate. He couldn't secure a loan from the bank for the full amount we agreed to. The banks in central Kentucky have limited capital available. We discussed options. One option is to sell off some of the assets on the property or part of the land. He didn't like that option. We agreed to set up a payment schedule over the next three years. He will pay us from the proceeds he earns from the farm."

Annie asked, "Can we buy Harry and Martha?"

John looked at Max expectantly.

"No," said Max. "I tried. I did. He's adamant now that he's going to sell them to relatives in Mississippi to generate some needed funds."

John emitted a low moan and placed his head in his hands.

Annie said, "Did you offer to pay more, whatever the slave traders in the South would give him?"

"Yes, but it's not just about the money. His family needs slaves badly. They lost several to a fever that spread through the slave quarters."

Annie rested her hand gently on John's shoulder.

"I have to save them before they're gone. Please help me." John knelt before Max and placed his hands at Max's feet.

Embarrassed by the gesture, Max said, "I'm sorry, John. I don't know how to save them. I tried. Please, sit." He placed his hand under John's upper arm, guiding him up.

Marie came in. "Max. Dinner is ready."

"Thank you. We'll be in, in a few minutes." He shook his head slightly at her, indicating she should leave.

Annie said, "Max, we have to try to save them."

Max ran his fingers through his hair, front to back, several times. "I wish there were a way, but we can't."

"The Underground Railroad," said Annie.

"It's too dangerous. Lyle will know it's us. He'll come after them. It would put us in danger, as well as the entire railroad operation in Cincinnati," said Max.

John looked up. "I know someone who knows conductors here in Cincinnati."

"You do?" said Annie surprised.

"Yes, someone at the barbershop."

Annie said, "Yes. I know who you mean. He could help us get them from Cincinnati to the next station, but we need to get them from Given House in Kentucky to Cincinnati."

John asked Annie, "Are you part of the railroad?"

"I can't say, John. You have to be very careful. You can't use anyone's names to anyone, do you understand?"

"Choo Choo," piped in Lizzie.

Max picked up Lizzie from the floor and took her into the kitchen. When he returned, he said, "Annie, you've got to stop. You're putting us all at risk—you, me, Lizzie. If we're arrested for aiding a runaway, we could go to prison, not to mention what the publicity would do to Miller Industries. One-third of our business comes from Southern customers."

Annie said, "I'm cautious. We have to do this for John, Martha, and Harry."

Max reddened in the face. He whispered, "You can't be part of this. Let the others do this one! Lyle will come after them. He'll know."

"How will he know? Why wouldn't Martha and Harry try to run away? Why would he suspect us?" said Annie.

"I don't like this," said Max.

"I know you don't. It's frightening, but we have to try," said Annie. "I promise, I'll hand this one off. They can get Calvin Fairbank to go to Given House and bring them north. He's gone even deeper south to rescue people."

"Annie, please. Let's let John initiate this. You said you have a contact, right, John?"

"Yes."

"Good. John can work with the railroad and tell them the best way to retrieve his brother and sister. He knows the routines at Given House. We must put our trust in the others and say our prayers."

John said, "I can go with them and show them the way. Harry and Martha may not go with someone besides me. They'll be too afraid."

"Too afraid to run for their freedom? Even if the alternative is being sold to a cotton plantation in Mississippi?" said Max.

John shook his head. "No slave has tried to run from Given House in a long time. It will take some convincing."

"Why are they so against running?" asked Annie.

"Well," John said hesitantly, "some years back, a field hand named Myron tried to run. He left at night. Didn't tell anyone where he was headed, but we knew he was running. When they discovered him missing in the morning, Lyle brought us all to the yard and asked where he had gone. None of us knew. He and the overseer, Wally, started hitting each of us with a spiked paddle, one by one, asking us where

Myron went. We knew nothing. He started with the men, and when no one told him anything, he began hitting the women. Then he hit the young'uns. There were only two children at the time. Little Sara, she screamed and screamed."

Annie took a deep breath as her eyes met Max's.

John went on. "Master Lyle, he screaming like a crazed man at all of us to tell him where Myron went, or he swore he'd keep hitting Sara. We all screaming and crying, and Lyle kept hitting Sara on the bottom, on the back. Sara's mama, she ran at Lyle and tried to grab the paddle. He swung at her and hit her right in the face with that paddle. She screamed bloody murder and fell to the ground. Lyle yells at her, saying, 'Tell me, tell me,' or he will kill Sara. We tried telling him we didn't know, but he killed her anyway. He swore at us and made us get one of Myron's shirts so the slave catcher's dogs could smell his scent.

"After they caught Myron, Master Lyle stripped him naked, tied him to a post in the yard and whipped him with a hundred lashes on his back. Made us all watch. He warned us that if one of us ran, we would be punished worse next time. After that, we all agreed that we won't run because we don't know what Master Lyle is capable of."

Annie pulled her handkerchief from her sleeve and wiped her eyes. Max sat with his head down and eyes closed. He took a deep breath and looked up. "Where was William when all this was happening?"

John said, "Master William, he was in Cincinnati. He wouldn't allow Lyle to do that, but when he was gone, Lyle was in charge."

"The devil himself," muttered Max, crossing himself. "I'm sorry, John."

"Do you think Martha and Harry will leave?" asked Annie. "I don't know what I would do in their shoes. My God. They're trapped."

John said, "They won't want to, but they got to. If they go downriver, their lives will be even worse than they are now. As much as it pains them, they got to do this for themselves.

The others, they'll understand why they're running. I pray that Master Lyle shows a little mercy on the rest of them."

"Not likely," said Max.

"He may," said Annie. "Things are getting tight. He can't afford to injure any of his labor. He's nothing if not a greedy businessman."

"You make sense. Let's hope," said Max. "John, I strongly advise against you going personally to retrieve them."

Annie said, "Max, you heard John. He has to go to convince them to leave. Otherwise, they may not run for fear for the others."

"It's too risky," said Max. "John, if you're caught, your punishment will be worse than prison. There's no telling what they'll do to you if they catch you. I don't think Lyle will leave it up to a judge to decide what to do with you. You have your freedom, don't give that up."

They all sat thinking.

Annie asked, "John, can your brother and sister read?"

"Martha can read a little, but not Harry."

"What if you wrote her a note?" said Annie.

"I don't think she'd trust it. I need to go myself."

"What if we sent a photograph of you? So she knows the message came from you. We can give your message to whoever goes to retrieve them. You write down whatever you think will make them leave. I'll help you write it."

"Annie's very good at persuasion," said Max. "She's helped me with speeches and proposals. Do you think it could work?"

"I don't have a photograph of me," said John.

"We can take care of that. James Ball, a friend of your boss, owns a daguerreotype studio. Why don't you talk to William about all this in confidence tomorrow?" said Max.

John agreed.

"Lyle will send slave catchers after them," said Max. "They'll come to find you, John, so the less you know about the plan or their whereabouts after the rescue, the better. It's probably best to let them be on their way to Canada on their own."

"You mean I can't see them when they here in Cincinnati?"

"I don't think it's a good idea," said Max.

"So, I'm gonna lose them like my mammy?"

"After a while, you can go see them in Canada. You're free. Once the heat is off, you can visit. This is probably best, for now, John."

"I reckon free in Canada is better than a slave in America."

"I know those don't seem like good options," said Annie.

"There's great risk for them to do this," said Max. "but it may be your best chance to save them. Think about it. Talk to Watson."

"Thank you both," said John, his face tired. "My heart is heavy with worry for Harry and Martha. I won't feel free until they are free too."

"We'll do what we can," said Annie.

Max reached out and embraced John, patting him on the back. John tentatively reciprocated.

CHAPTER 10

Calvin approached the cabin quietly and surveyed the surroundings. Five adults sat around a fire pit, eating and talking quietly. It was dark except for the small fire and lights from the windows of Given House, less than one hundred yards away. Crickets chirped in the surrounding fields.

Calvin walked toward the group and came into the light of the fire. "Good evening, y'all."

"Who are you?" asked the biggest of the men, standing.

"Don't be alarmed. My name is Joe," said Calvin in a hushed voice. "I've got business with Martha and Harry."

The group glanced between the main house and Calvin.

The big man asked, "What business?"

"It's a private matter. Can we go inside the cabin?"

The big man inspected Calvin up and down. He nodded at Harry and Martha. They stood and moved toward the man. Harry led them inside the cabin. Martha lit a candle. They left the door open.

Calvin spoke in a quiet voice, making eye contact with the two siblings. "Your brother John sent me from Cincinnati."

"John?" said Martha. "How is he? He still free?"

"Yes, he's in Cincinnati. He has a job working as a barber. He's worried about you. That's why he sent me. He heard that Lyle plans to sell you both downriver to Mississippi. He wants me to bring you north, to freedom."

"Oh my Lord. He sent for us," said Martha. "Praise Jesus."

"How you gonna do that?" said Harry.

"We have to hurry. I will take you to the Ohio River and across to Cincinnati. From there, the Underground Railroad will see you to Canada."

"Why we go to Canada?"

"You'll be safe in Canada. The slave catchers can't get you there. There are other Negroes there you can stay with."

"How we know John really sent you? This a trick?" asked Harry.

"No, it's no trick." He pulled the photo of John from his jacket pocket.

"It's him," said Martha, taking the daguerreotype from Calvin. "He looks fine. Look at his clothes." Smiling, she handed the photo to Harry.

Harry looked at the photo, then at Calvin, then Martha. "What about the slave catchers?"

"I brought some passes that look like they're from Master Lyle until we get out of the county. After that, we'll tell anyone you're my slaves, and we're going to sell some squash and pumpkins in Covington. I have a wagon full of vegetables waiting for us north of here."

Harry shook his head. "No, I don't wanna run. Master Lyle near kill us if he catch us."

Martha took Harry's forearm with both of her hands. "This our chance. We have to try. I don't want to be sold down the river. I want to be with John."

"You know what he gonna do to the others if we run," Harry said to Martha.

"You can't think about that," said Calvin. "You have to think about yourselves. John said what Martha said. Better risk what Lyle might do to them than be sold downriver. Besides, Lyle has fewer and fewer slaves. He won't risk killing any of them on account of two runaways. He needs them."

"He may not kill 'em, but he'll beat 'em," said Harry.

"You have to take the chance," said Calvin. "Come with me now. Don't talk to the others. Tell them nothing, so they don't know anything. Just leave."

"I don't like this," said Harry. "We just gonna ride all the way to Cincinnati then on to Canada, just like that? White people know we're slaves. They gonna send us back soon as they see us."

"You're with me. I've done this before. Rescues. Then the railroad. There are white and free Black people along the way that will hide you and take you there. I know it goes against everything you've experienced in your life to trust me, but you have to."

"Why should I trust any white man?" said Harry.

"John sent me. He trusts me."

"How we know John really sent you. You could be making a big lie, picture and all, to try and trap us."

"John told me that your mammy, Jenny, would want you to be free. Not end up down river like her. Your mammy used to sing you a song. 'Baby go to sleep, sleep baby sleep. Some day you wake up free, you and me.'"

"I remember that song. He tellin' the truth, Harry; we have to go," said Martha. "This is our chance."

"I'm afraid. I'm really afraid," said Harry, shaking his head.

"I am too, but we wasn't born lucky like John, so we have to take our freedom for ourselves. I'm going, and I want you with me," said Martha. She put her arms around him. "Please, Harry, please."

Harry relented. "I'll go."

Calvin said, "Good. Now, we're going to walk out of here. I'm going to tell your friends that I need to take you to the courthouse. You can say goodbye quickly like you're a little worried, but you'll see them tomorrow. That's it. You understand? Martha, Harry, you understand me? You say nothing else! You ready?"

They both nodded their heads.

"Wait," hissed Martha, stopping Calvin. She went to the dresser, pulled a small metal disc from a drawer, and put it in her shoe. She looked around the small cabin, the only home she knew. The three walked outside.

Calvin addressed the group, "I need to take Martha and Harry down to the courthouse for some official business. They'll be back in the morning. You all go on with your night, regular-like. No need to tell anyone in the house they're gone. That will just create more problems for them and you. You understand me?"

The big man looked suspiciously at Calvin, then at Martha and Harry. Martha nodded at him. He sat down and looked at the fire.

Martha went to the woman in the group and hugged her. "We'll be fine. I know we will," she whispered. Then she said to the men, "You boys look after each other."

Harry nodded to the group, then followed Calvin and Martha across the field.

Calvin spoke softly when they reached the road, "Tonight we walk north to Corinth County. The wagon and horses are waiting for us there. We'll ride tomorrow in the daylight. I have papers that say you belong to me. Anybody asks, your names are Adam and Mary, like in the Bible. I'm Master Joe. We're from Versailles, Kentucky, and we're taking our squash and pumpkins to sell in Covington and then buying some furniture and dry goods to bring back in the wagon. Can you remember that?"

"Yes, sir," they both said.

"Keep your eyes open and stay quiet. Tell me if you see anyone. If we can get to the wagon, we have a good cover story, but tonight, we have to get as far away as possible without anyone seeing us. If we see anyone on the road, we hide until they pass."

They walked in silence along the moonlit roads. Calvin led at a fast pace, with Martha and Harry close behind. As they approached the lights of a farmhouse, they heard a bark, then more barking.

"Shit," said Calvin.

"I don't like dogs." Harry's first words since they began walking. He squatted down and felt on the road for a rock.

"Is it bloodhounds?" whispered Martha.

"No, just a farm dog," said Calvin.

The barking grew more agitated and louder as the dog ran down the front field of the farm.

Martha crossed herself and whispered a prayer.

Calvin pulled a piece of dried meat from his satchel and tossed it to the beast as he approached. The dog grabbed the meat and ran back toward the farm, leaving them in peace. They watched the farmhouse, but no one came.

They continued on, the roads and scattered farmhouses indistinguishable from each other after a few hours. Later in the night, they passed through a small village where everything was quiet. They stopped once to relieve themselves and drank water from a stream. After several more hours, Martha said, "Master Joe, I need to rest my feet."

"All right, we'll rest a minute in those trees." They walked into the clump of trees and sat on the ground. Calvin removed some bread and dried meat from his satchel, and they ate. Martha pulled the silver disc from her shoe and rubbed her foot.

"What's that?" said Calvin.

"It's my charm." Martha rubbed the charm, feeling the pattern of lines and curves on the surface. "It brings the spirits of my father and his father and our people all the way back to Africa. They watch over me."

"So far, they're doing a pretty good job, but don't leave it in your shoe," said Calvin.

"How much farther?" Martha asked.

"Not sure, but we're making good time and should arrive early morning. Let's keep moving."

Martha put on her shoe, and they began their walk again. She had to step gingerly on her now blistered foot but made no complaint.

After sunrise, they increased their diligence. They moved more quickly in the daylight without fear of tripping, but they were more exposed. Now that they could see ahead, the road seemed to go on forever. They climbed rolling hills that winded them, then recovered as they walked down the backsides. At each crest, they could see the next one and tried not to think about the effort they'd need to summit each. Martha walked on the side of her foot to avoid her blister. They heard a horse and spied a mounted figure ahead on the next hill.

Calvin looked around. "Run for those trees," he said, pointing to a stand about thirty yards back down the road.

They took off running, broke through a line of bushes and dropped to the ground, panting. They watched the horseman approach, praying he hadn't seen them. He passed.

Back on the road, they reached a small cluster of houses and took a road west, away from the morning sun.

"It's just another hour or so," said Calvin.

They saw movement in a field ahead and took cover in some brush. A crew of five pulled plants out of the ground using shovels.

"Do you see an overseer?" whispered Calvin.

"No," said Harry. "They chained together. I think they working on their own."

"Keep looking. We have to be sure."

"They're alone. They ain't gonna bother us," said Harry.

"Stay on the road," said Calvin. "Say nothing to them."

They walked along the road. As they neared the crew, the workers looked up from digging and pulling and curiously observed the three. Harry and Martha couldn't help but look at them, in their chains, already at work, another day in bondage. Martha crossed herself as they moved on down the road.

As they approached a large farmhouse, Calvin pointed. "Hide in those bushes. Let me go make sure it's safe."

Harry and Martha sat on the ground out of sight.

"I never walked so far in my life," said Harry.

"Me neither, but I'll walk all the way to Cincinnati if I have to. This is our road to freedom." Martha took off her shoe and aired out her bloody foot.

"You gonna make it?" said Harry.

"Jesus endured nails through his feet and hands before his resurrection. I don't mind a raw foot for my freedom. Harry—we gonna be free. It really gonna happen."

"We're still a long way from the North. By now, Master Lyle knows we're running. May the Lord have mercy on George, Charlie, and Cecelia."

"Amen." She pulled the picture of John from her pocket. "My, look at those clothes he wearing. He looks free, don't he? That gonna be us soon. What you think it feel like, having a job where you get paid?"

"I don't know. How you find a job?" said Harry.

"I don't know, but John found a way. We'll find a way too. I can't wait to see him again."

"What you think Canada like? White people in Canada have better souls than white people in this country?"

"I suppose they the same. They all white," she said.

"Then why is Canada a better place to be?"

"Slavery not allowed in Canada. No slaves anywhere, and slave catchers don't have no power there. If we stay in the United States, we be running from Lyle the rest of our lives. Always looking over our shoulders for a slave catcher or somebody to turn us in for a reward."

"I wish I knew what it was going to be like. Maybe it will be worse," said Harry.

"We are going to be free. I don't see how that could be worse than being the white man's slave. I'm done being that."

Harry looked at the picture. "John doesn't look happy."

"No, but he looks free," said Martha. She laid back in the grass and closed her eyes.

CHAPTER 11

Calvin drove the horses with Martha and Harry amongst the wagonload of gourds and squash. They ate the food Calvin left in the back, then sprawled across the produce and slept. The trip took all day. They passed several farmers on horseback, carriages and multiple towns. No one paid any mind to them—just two slaves traveling with their master. As the sun set, they crested a large hill and saw a river in the distance.

Calvin turned to them, "That's the Ohio. Cincinnati is on the other side."

"Across that river is a free state?" said Martha.

"That's right," said Calvin.

Cincinnati filled the basin below them with buildings and houses, some streets already lit by gas lamps. Dozens of church steeples stood above the structures. A haze of dark smoke hung above the city, trapped by the surrounding hills. "I ain't never seen so many houses," said Martha. "Lotta Black people live there?"

"I read in the paper that there are over 3,000 Negroes in Cincinnati," said Calvin.

"All of them free?"

"Yes, slavery is illegal in Ohio."

"All we gotta do is cross that river, and we're free," said Martha.

Calvin took a road to the west into an area with fewer buildings. A brilliant orange sunset blazed on the horizon as they moved along the river. Calvin stopped the horses in front of an inn and tied them to a post.

"You two stay here. Anyone comes, you say nothing to them, Mary and Adam." Calvin went inside.

"What you think he doing now?" asked Martha.

"I don't know. We just do what we told," said Harry.

They looked beyond the inn to the Ohio River behind it. The current moved swiftly with an occasional branch floating downstream. A steamboat made its way up the river toward Cincinnati against the current, black smoke spewing from its smokestack.

"Look at that big boat," said Martha. "It looks like a county building on water. This place full of things we never seen. We're close, Harry. We almost free."

"I'm still afraid someone going to come along and take us back. What you think Lyle doing to the rest of them?"

"I'm not thinking about that. I'm done with that. We almost to the promised land on earth."

"You get yourself in trouble, ignoring the bad. The bad still with us," said Harry.

Calvin emerged from the inn with a man who nodded at the two of them before joining Calvin on the wagon's front seat. They set off down the road, the sunlight now almost gone. In less than a mile, Calvin pulled the wagon into a grassy area between the road and the river.

"Hop out now and go with him. He'll take you across," said Calvin.

Martha looked at Calvin. "You leaving us?"

"My part is done. He's a friend; you'll be safe."

"Where he taking us?" said Harry.

"He'll take you across the river to a safe place for the night. It's the first stop on the Underground Railroad. Go on now. It's all right."

They got down from the bed of the wagon. "Thank you, Joe," said Martha. She touched his trouser leg.

"God bless you both. Good luck to you," said Calvin, nodding to them. He shook the reins and drove the wagon back up to the road.

"This way," said the man, as he led them down a steep embankment. Martha slid and fell on her backside, sliding down the grass-covered bank for several feet before gaining control. The man took her by the hand and pulled her up. "Careful now."

Harry followed. It was almost dark. The man led them to a small rowboat tied to a tree. He steadied it and helped them step in, pointing to where they should sit.

He whispered, "Voices carry on the water, so we have to be quiet."

They nodded.

The man untied the boat and climbed in. He sat in the center seat and rowed. The current moved them downriver as he quickly rowed the boat the four hundred feet across it. As he rowed, he scanned both shores for any signs of people. He maneuvered to a spot on the Ohio side. "Can you jump out and hold the line?" he whispered to Harry.

Harry jumped out, splashing in the water and held the rope tied to the front of the rowboat. The man climbed out, pulled the boat up the bank, and helped Martha.

"My shoe! I lost my shoe," she whispered excitedly as the mud sucked her shoe from her foot.

"Leave it." The man pulled the craft further up the bank and started walking along the river in the dark. The two followed him. They came to a narrow path leading to the road above the river.

As they walked along the road, the countryside gave way to the city. First a few buildings and a sawmill, then small factories and finally rows of houses. They walked several blocks north, away from the river, into a neighborhood of two-story homes. The man led them up a front walk onto a porch. He knocked three times, paused, then twice more. A Black man opened the door, motioning for Harry and Martha to enter. He nodded at the man who had escorted them, then closed the door.

Harry and Martha took in the interior of the house. It was less grand than Given House but decorated with rugs, lamps, and carved furniture.

"You're safe here," said the man. "Call me Sam."

Martha's knees buckled under her, and she fell to the floor. Harry and Sam moved to assist her.

"Nan, bring some water," called Sam.

A large woman joined them in the foyer and handed Sam a wet cloth. She held a cup of water. Sam dabbed the cloth on Martha's face, reviving her back to consciousness.

Martha looked up at them from the floor.

"Easy now," said Sam. "You've had a long journey."

Nan handed her the water, and Martha drank.

Sam said, "Can you get up?"

"Yes, thank you."

"Come into the kitchen. You must be hungry," said Nan.

The men helped Martha up, and she hobbled into the kitchen. They sat on a bench, and Nan served them soup and bread. Martha and Harry began eating silently, unsure what to think of their hosts and what might be in store for them next.

"You can rest easy. You should be safe here. We have beds upstairs in the attic where you can sleep tonight. Tomorrow, we'll move you along to the next station in Hamilton," said Nan.

The two emptied their bowls quickly, and Nan ladled more soup for each of them.

"How are you feeling now?" Nan asked Martha.

"Oh, I'm all right. I don't know what came over me."

"You've been awake for nearly two days and nights, with little to eat and walked from hell to freedom," said Harry. "It's no wonder you fell to the floor. She got a bloody blister on her foot that needs tending to."

"I'm fine," said Martha. "My foot rubbed on my lucky charm. Then I lost my shoe in the muck."

"I'll draw you a bath. You can wash up and clean your foot. You don't want it to fester. You still have a ways to travel to Canada," said Nan. "What are your names?"

"I'm Martha, and this is my brother Harry."

"You were in Kentucky? Where?"

"Scott County. We lived at Given House plantation. Born there and spent our whole lives. Never been outside of the county until now."

"What made you decide to run?" said Nan.

"We didn't decide," explained Martha. "The Lord brought us a man, Mr. Joe, who showed up at supper and led us here. We didn't know nothing about how to go north to freedom. We's about to be sold downriver to Mississippi by our master. We'd be in the bowels of Hades if that happened. Our brother John sent us Mr. Joe. John, he's free now and lives here in Cincinnati."

"How did John come to be free?" asked Nan.

"His daddy not the same as ours. His daddy was Master William. Master William died and made John free in his will. Here's a picture of John."

"He's a handsome man," said Nan.

"Is this your house?" Martha asked Sam.

"Yes, it is."

"How you afford this finery?"

"We work for a wage. Sam is a whitewasher, and I do laundry."

"So you free?" said Martha.

"We were freed by our master some ten years ago. Came here and been working for ourselves ever since."

"Nobody have a claim to you?"

"Not anymore."

"Is Canada like this?"

"Canada is free for all men. You can earn your living there, like here. We help lots of folks get to Canada on the railroad."

"Any of them ever come back?" said Martha.

"Some do. Once they have papers proving they're freedmen, or if they buy their freedom," said Sam.

"Is it hard living on your own? Buying your house and your food? How do you know how to do that?" said Martha.

"It was hard at first. You'll have others to help you. There's a community of Colored in Canada. We didn't have all this when we were first free," said Nan motioning around the room. "Lived in a room in a house with some other families for a while until we saved some money."

"How long does it take to get to Canada?" said Martha.

"I don't know what route you'll take. From here, you'll go to Hamilton, then maybe Eaton or Paris. Eventually, you'll end up in Detroit, your last stop in the United States, before crossing the river into Canada. Probably six or seven days," said Nan.

"How do we know where to go?"

"The conductors will make sure you get to the next station. Sam and I have been doing this for about five years. Probably helped two hundred slaves make their way. The railroad tells us when you get here and where you go next. Sometimes, they put you on a real train above ground. That makes the journey much faster to Detroit. But you can't go that way since you're runaways. Your master will send someone after you.

"We have to be secret about everything. We won't tell you much about us in case they capture you and torture you to learn about the railroad. You can't tell what you don't know. Our real names aren't Sam and Nan. But don't you worry; the people on the railroad care about getting you safely to the next station. They're good people."

"Thank you for helping us," said Martha.

"You ever been caught?" asked Harry.

"No. Try not to worry. You'll only be here one night, two at the most. We keep things moving," said Sam.

Nan said, "You ready for a bath? Martha, you can use the water first, then Harry. Tomorrow we'll have some new clothes and shoes for you, now that we know your sizes. Sam will meet with the railroad coordinator tonight to arrange that, and he'll get instructions for your next station." Nan led

Harry up to the second floor. A ladder was propped into an opening on the second-floor landing that led to the attic. "Go on up and make yourself comfortable. I'll fix Martha's bath."

#

They sat at the table the following day, talking with Nan over a breakfast of griddle cakes, eggs, and bacon. Nan went to the front door to answer the same secret knock. They heard voices then a man and their brother John entered the kitchen.

Martha ran to him and fell in his arms, crying. "Oh Lord, my prayers are answered. I didn't think I'd ever lay my eyes on you again." She hugged him.

"Oh Martha, thank God you're here." John broke from Martha and hugged Harry in a tight embrace. "Brother, you're safe."

Harry cried into John's shoulders, finally letting the pressure of the last two days go.

John caught them up on his new life, and they told him of their adventure to freedom.

"I feel bad for what we done to the others," said Harry. "The Lord may punish us yet for what Master Lyle do to them."

John said, "No, Harry. The Lord won't bring his wrath on you. It's no sin to want to be free. His wrath will find Master Lyle on his judgment day. In the weeks since I've been free, I've come to see that the white man is born into his circumstances, just like we were. God didn't make us Negroes to serve the white man. Men like Master Lyle believe it is their place to keep the Black man in the dark and use him until there's nothing left. But God looks at all his people the same here on earth and on judgment day. If we are born unlucky, it is our right to try and put ourselves in a better position. So wanting to be free and in charge of your own life is no sin. We all got to help each other get there."

"John, you so smart, and now you free," said Martha. "You gonna come to Canada with us?"

"No, Martha. I'm sorry. I'm staying here. I think I can make a life here. I've found people like me. They're helping me. Living in the city is different, but I'm getting used to it. I'm still learning so much, and there's plenty of hate for the Negro here, but I won't run away. I deserve a place here in the United States. This is my home now. And I still need to find Mammy. I can't do that if I go to Canada."

"We stay here with you, then," said Martha.

"Yes, the three of us together," said Harry.

"I wish you could, both of you, but it's not safe. Lyle will come after you. Slave catchers may already be here. If they find you, they'll drag you back to Kentucky. He will be angry. You don't want any part of that. You have to go on to Canada. That's your best chance to stay free."

"Free. I can hardly believe it," said Martha. "I don't know what it supposed to feel like, but it feel good waking up this morning and not doing for somebody else. I don't know what I'm supposed to be doing. How you figure that out?"

"Right now, you just set yourself on getting to Canada, you hear me," said John. "Before you know it, being free will feel like the way it's supposed to be."

"Is that how you feel?" she said.

"Yes. It took me a while to get used to deciding what to do, not having someone else decide for me. But now, I feel like it's the natural way I was born to be. You'll see. The railroad people will get you to Canada, and you'll make a new life for yourselves there."

"Will you come to visit us?"

"I will. When I find Mammy and free her, I'll bring her to you."

"I'd like that," said Martha.

"I have to go now," said John. "I don't want to bring any attention to this house, and slave catchers may be following me. So we have to say goodbye for now. I'm happy you're free and on your way. I'll be praying for you."

"Let me look at you," said Martha. She rubbed his arms.

"Here, take this money," said John.

"You a real man with money now," laughed Martha. She hugged him tightly, then pulled back, tears in her eyes.

John and Harry embraced. "Take care of her," said John.

He took one last look at them, then let himself out the front door.

CHAPTER 12

Max stood on the sloped bank of Cincinnati's public landing about twenty yards from the Ohio River. Behind him, the shops and inns along Water Street were bustling with Cincinnatians and travelers from cities across the country. Max's employees loaded the second of two large, heavy pieces of equipment onto the steamboat, *The West Wind*. A small crowd watched as the men used casters, boards, pulleys, and horses to move the iron machines from the specially-built drays onto the landing, then up a ramp onto the front of the steamboat.

Max's brother Peter, a reporter for the *Cincinnati Commercial* newspaper, interviewed Max as the crew carefully loaded the cargo.

Peter stood with a pad and pencil, taking notes. "What are these two pieces of equipment?"

Max said, "At Miller Industries, we make custom machinery for all kinds of enterprises, using the highest quality iron, advanced design, and finest craftsmanship in the West. The machines being loaded onto the riverboat are for a farming customer in Louisiana. The first is a state-of-the-art threshing machine, and the second is a highly efficient flour mill, powered by the latest in short stroke, high-speed steam engines."

"Stop with the salesman bit. You know I won't print all that embellishment," Peter said. "What is the value of the equipment?"

"The total cost of both machines is around $6,000. We manufacture at a lower cost than the Philadelphia or other eastern manufacturers and deliver them in a shorter timeframe due to our efficient construction processes and closer proximity."

Peter shook his head. "Do you sell a large amount of equipment to customers in the South?"

"Yes, over half of our business is for southern and western customers, with the remaining here in Ohio and northern Kentucky," said Max.

"Are you concerned about the increasing talk of Southern secession over the slavery issue?"

"No, I think what you have on both sides is a lot of talk from politicians, catering to extremist views and newspapers, the *Commercial* excepted, trying to sell more papers."

Peter raised his eyebrows. "Then you think the debate over slavery will just blow over?"

"Once the presidential election is over, we can all go back to our business," said Max. "This country has too much dependent on our growing national markets. With the steamboats and now railroads, goods are sold across the nation. We'd be foolish to let an issue like slavery disrupt the markets and the opportunities they create for Americans. We've all found a way to get along with different points of view on slavery up until now. There's no need to push us to one extreme or the other."

"I see, but what would that do to your business if there were a disruption to the Southern markets?"

"Peter, can't you let it drop?"

"As a leading businessman in town, your perspective and the impact on your manufacturing concern is an indicator of what Southern market loss might mean to Cincinnati's economy. What would be the impact?"

"It would be devastating. I have almost 250 employees, up from 150 just five years ago. As I said, a significant portion of my business is in the South. If I lost those sales, I would have to let some of my workers go. Much of my factory machine business and the decorative ironwork business is centered in the north and west, but the farm machinery business would suffer a major loss."

"Does it bother you that plantation owners who employ slave labor use your farm equipment?" said Peter.

Max eyed his younger brother disapprovingly, but Peter waited for an answer.

"I don't judge my customers or tell them how to run their businesses. I could never own slaves myself; it goes against my morals. But I sleep fine selling to these plantation owners. In fact, by using the machines from my factory, less manual labor is required to generate more output on their farms. Anything else? I have to get home. Annie and I are hosting a dinner party this afternoon."

"No, I think I have everything I need. Thanks, Max. I appreciate the story."

Max said, "In your article, can you focus on Miller Industries, the machines, and the productivity they provide and downplay the Southern customers and slavery? Please?"

"I can't promise, but I'll try to ensure you don't come off sounding like a crass businessman who has put profits ahead of your moral beliefs."

"Peter!"

"Thanks, Max. See you Sunday," he said with a wave as he walked up the riverbank toward the city.

CHAPTER 13

Annie grew up in New York City in genteel surroundings but had little interest in most aspects of that life. Once she moved to Cincinnati, she abandoned polite society, its social etiquette, dinner parties, and calling practices and adopted the more plebian activities of Max's German family in Over-the-Rhine. She loved the casual Sunday afternoons spent at his family's saloon.

On the other hand, Max aspired to be part of the new monied aristocracy of Cincinnati. He knew he would never be part of the old money of Cincinnati's first families, but he felt that being recognized as a leader and contributor to bettering the city was a measure of his personal and professional success. His boarding school years at Saint Xavier exposed him to some of the upper class, and the Jesuits leaned toward a more elitist social outlook. Max now rubbed elbows with Cincinnati's professional elite at work and on the city council.

He had not had the opportunity to develop his entertaining skills, so he convinced Annie to help him evolve his standing in this area. He proposed a series of dinner parties, starting with a small group of close friends, that would be a safe environment to practice their hosting skills. Annie knew how to host a formal party but focused on making their guests comfortable in their home and facilitating an engaging conversation. Max insisted she purchase the essential entertaining silverware, china, and glassware for the occasion. She recruited Max's sisters, Marie and Helene, to cook and instructed them on how to serve a proper party.

The guest list included John; Mary Berry, a feminist schoolteacher friend of Annie's; Patrick Sweeney, Max's best friend from school, and his wife, Molly; Aaron and Mary Johnson. All the guests met the criteria for safe invitees, except Aaron and Mary. Their Southern, privileged heritage was a step above the rest socially, but Max included them to improve his relationship with his half-brother. Following proper etiquette, Annie had delivered formal written invitations for 4:00 PM.

Max dressed in his finest trousers, waistcoat and jacket. Annie refused to make a fuss for the occasion and wore a simple dress. Marie and Helene were busy in the kitchen preparing the food while Annie fed Lizzie. Max walked through the parlor and dining room, adjusting the placement of the furniture and candles. He opened a bottle of wine and arranged the glasses on the side table in the parlor.

Entering the kitchen, he said, "There are no flowers. I thought you would buy fresh flowers at the market today for the table?"

Annie said, "Max, relax. We agreed this would be a casual evening with friends. You'll make the guests uncomfortable if you don't stop fussing."

Max said to Annie, "You look beautiful. Are you sure you don't want to wear your dinner dress?"

"That would be too much for this occasion, and it's too full to be comfortable. I only wear that when I have to."

Marie and Helene smiled at each other knowingly. Helene said, "Did you invite the mayor? The president? I've never seen you so nervous about a meal, brother."

"I want everything to be just right. You two know what to do?" said Max.

Helene said, "We've been serving guests at the saloon since we were five. I don't think you need to worry."

"But this is different. This is more formal."

Helene rolled her eyes. "One more word, and I walk out. Annie has given us instructions on serving tonight, and we're not imbeciles. You be your congenial self and leave us to the dinner."

"All right. I relinquish control to the women."

"As it should be," said Annie.

A knock sounded on the front door.

Max said, "They're here. Marie, can you take Lizzie? Annie, come."

Annie stood, removed her apron, placed her hands on Max's shoulders and put her face to his, "Relax!" She gave him a quick kiss.

They opened the front door and greeted John, dressed in a new suit and hat.

"John, look at you. You look more handsome and comfortable in your city clothes every time I see you," said Annie. "Do come in."

Max shook hands with John, and they exchanged pleasantries. "Let me take your hat," Max said, placing it on the foyer table.

In the parlor, Max offered John a drink.

"No, thank you. I practice temperance and Godliness."

"Some apple juice then?" asked Annie.

"Yes, thank you."

"What's the news of Harry and Martha?" asked Max.

"I received word that they are safe in Canada."

"Oh, that's wonderful news," said Annie.

"I had a slave hunter inquire at the shop last week," said Max. "A man dressed in a fur hat carrying a rifle came into the shop and insisted on speaking to me. He asked whether I knew anything of their whereabouts. I answered all his questions, and he went on his way."

"He came to the barbershop as well," said John. "He poked his nose into the back room and rudely questioned the other barbers. Mr. Watson told him to leave us in peace, or he'd send for the constable. He left but told me he'd see me again."

"That sounds like he was threatening you," said Annie.

"You have nothing to fear, John," said Max. "You have the law on your side on this."

"Do I? even as a Black man?"

"You do, John. You took no active part in helping them run."

"I still have a sick feeling, standing up against any white man."

"You have the right to be free here in Ohio. He doesn't have the right to harass you," said Max. "Granted, you don't have the right to testify or defend yourself in a court of law as a Negro, but others can do it for you. Don't be afraid of him if he comes back."

"It's hard to unfeel the years of not being able to stand up for myself," said John. "I want to, but when I stand before a white man, he seems to tower above me as if God himself put him there."

"I pray over time that your confidence will increase," said Annie.

Max answered the door and led Mary Berry into the parlor. Mary wore a dress buttoned to her neck with her dark hair cut short and tucked behind her ears.

"The working woman herself," bellowed Mary as she embraced Annie.

"So good to see you," said Annie.

"Where's my little Lizzie? I brought her this," she said, holding up a copy of *The Riddle Book*.

"Thank you. She's in the kitchen with Marie. Please, take it back to her. She'll be thrilled to see you and the book."

Max escorted Patrick and Molly into the parlor.

Patrick surveyed the room, "Very nice for a lad from over the canal. I approve."

"Patrick and Molly Sweeney, this is John Johnson," said Max making introductions. "John is a friend of ours. He's new to Cincinnati and works at Watson & Barnett's barbershop. Patrick and I were best mates at school growing up. Patrick now manages the O'Neil Furniture Company."

Patrick hesitated, then shook John's hand. He looked at Max, then at John. "This is my wife, Molly."

"A pleasure to meet you both," said John.

Marie led Aaron and Mary into the room.

"Aaron, Mary, welcome to our home," said Max as he moved across the room to greet them, shaking Aaron's hand and taking Mary's lightly.

Annie greeted them. "What a lovely dress."

Mary wore a dress with a gold silk hoop skirt and lace sleeves, and a cashmere shawl. "Thank you. I may be overdressed, but I was delighted to receive your invitation and the opportunity to wear it. Thank you for including us. With the children, we don't get to socialize as much as we'd like."

Annie introduced, "Mary Berry, this is Mary and Aaron Johnson. Mary and I have worked on some women's causes together. She's a teacher. Aaron is an attorney here in town."

Max led them into the room, completed introductions, and offered wine and bourbon. Aaron introduced his wife, Mary, to Patrick. "Patrick, Max, and I all lived together at Saint Xavier. Five years. We practically grew up together."

"Like brothers then," said Mary Berry.

"Almost," said Patrick.

Aaron stopped when he noticed John.

"Hi, Aaron," said John.

"John, how are you getting along?" said Aaron.

"I'm fine, just fine, thank you. I'm barbering for William Watson and making my way. I found a more hospitable place to live for now."

"Oh, where's that?" said Aaron.

"The Dumas House. Do you know it?"

"I do. Glad you're getting along," said Aaron.

"You should come in for a cut or shave some time. Watson & Barnett's on Third Street. I'll treat you well."

"Maybe I'll do that sometime, thank you," said Aaron.

Max stepped into their conversation and whispered, "Do we all agree to keep our relationship in confidence?"

Aaron and John nodded in agreement.

Aaron whispered to Max, "This is a bit awkward, Mueller."

Patrick joined the three men and looked from one to the next. "It's a bit uncanny, isn't it?"

"What's that?" said Aaron.

"Both you and John with the same surname, Johnson," said Patrick.

"That is a coincidence," said Max.

"It's a common name," said Aaron, glaring at Max.

Patrick gave Max a quizzical look, then turned to John. "Where are you from, John?"

"I was raised on a plantation in Scott County in Kentucky. Born a slave, but now I'm a freedman," he said with pride in his voice.

"How did you manage that, if you don't mind sharing your story?" asked Patrick.

"It's not much of a story. My master died earlier this year, and in his will, he disclosed that he was my daddy and freed me. I came to Ohio to live, where a Black man can feel like he is somebody and earn a living."

Mary Berry said, "What was that like, being enslaved by your own father?"

"Once I learned he was my father, I questioned why God made a man, who was kind most of the time, pretend he couldn't see me as a person. He was right there in the same house with me, yet he kept me at a distance as if there were a blanket between us that neither the whites nor the Blacks were allowed to push through. I don't think he thought much about what happened on the Black side of that blanket, so he looked the other way when it was uncomfortable for him. That's just how it had always been on the plantation. As a boy, I longed for him to acknowledge me, but he never did when he was alive. I just had to be strong and accept my place."

The guests stood in quiet discomfort listening to John. Aaron stared into the fire, downed the remainder of his bourbon and swallowed hard. "Mueller, how about a refill before dinner?"

"That must have been very difficult," said Mary Berry. "I read *Uncle Tom's Cabin*. Did he whip you?"

"Mary," said Annie.

"It's all right, Annie," said John. "I don't mind telling people what it was like. I think folks need to know. I see all these people going on about their business in this city as if slavery is happening in some other world. If they know what it's like to be on that side of the blanket, maybe they'll help change things. Miss Berry, my daddy never beat me himself. Deep inside, he had a good heart. He let the other master on the plantation beat us when he wasn't happy with us. Master Lyle could whip a man until he was bleeding and passed out, and he made the rest of us watch him do it. Seeing and hearing that as a young boy made me afraid to do anything wrong."

Max said, "John, you're a strong man. And now, you're making your way on your own in a new city." He raised his glass, "To John's new life as a free man."

The guests toasted.

John looked at the ground shyly.

Aaron glared at Max.

Patrick cocked his head, thinking, a puzzled expression on his face.

"Shall we eat?" said Max, motioning toward the dining room.

CHAPTER 14

Annie and Max sat at the ends of the dining table. A half dozen candles lit the table, supplementing the dimmed lights of the gas chandelier. Max said, "Annie and I would like to thank all of you for coming tonight. We are grateful to have you all as friends to share an evening of the blessings that God has bestowed on us. Let us give thanks and enjoy this fine food prepared by Helene and Marie, the wine, and good conversation."

Marie held a soup tureen while Helene ladled into china bowls at each plate. When they reached John, he sat back, bowed, and thanked them.

"Terrapin soup," said Annie. "Enjoy."

The guests began slurping the soup with their spoons.

"Delicious," said Mary Berry.

"Where did you find the turtles, Annie? At the central market?" asked Molly.

Annie said, "Marie? Where did you find the turtles?"

"John Bates has a fancy grocery store on Sycamore Street," said Marie. "He had a special shipment of canned turtle soup."

"Marie is a wonderful cook and housekeeper. Max and I would be lost without her," said Annie.

"Your home is lovely, Annie. I love the paper on the walls in this room," said Mary.

Max said, "Annie and I are working with architects now to design a new home in Mount Auburn."

"That's quite a ways from the river," said Molly. "Will you keep a place here?"

"I don't know yet. A horsecar runs into the city daily, but it won't be as convenient as the ten-minute walk that Annie and I have to the shop today."

"I love your dining table and sideboard," said Mary. "Where did you acquire them?"

Patrick chimed in, "Finest hardwood table available from the O'Neil Furniture Company. When Max and Annie married, they needed to set up their home quickly. We outfitted them with this room, the parlor, and the bedrooms. I'm a bit biased, but we make some of the finest furniture in town at affordable prices."

"How much of your business is Southern customers now?" Max asked Patrick.

"Probably a third of it. We manufacture ready-made furniture and ship it west and south. About five years ago, Max helped us design special planers and jigs to make the pieces more quickly and allow for faster assembly. The new process doubled our output with the same number of men. That allowed us to expand outside of the local market. Why the question?"

"I was interviewed today by the *Cincinnati Commercial*. The story was supposed to be about the advanced machinery we build for farms, but my brother, Peter, the reporter, pushed me hard on the percentage of my sales that went to the South. He questioned me about the potential impact if this slavery issue leads to an interruption in Southern markets."

Aaron said, "That question seems to be at the forefront of many conversations in all circles these days."

Molly said with some concern in her voice, "The Southerners wouldn't stop buying from us, would they, Patrick? They need Northern products, don't they?"

"They do," said Patrick. "As long as we leave things in the North and South as they are and let the western states make up their own minds on the slavery issue, as is their right under our federal form of government, we can all coexist peacefully."

Mary Berry said, "So you support Stephen Douglas's outlandish Kansas-Nebraska Act that gives new territories the right to expand the peculiar institution? You support enslaving more men, women, and children in a country where all men and women are alleged to be equal?"

"As a proud Democrat, I do support the Kansas-Nebraska Act," said Patrick. "The states and territories of this nation have the right to manage their affairs, un-harassed by a central rule. That's what our republic stands for; our ability to self-govern. I hope to see Stephen Douglas as our next president."

"Slavery is wrong, and we must abolish it throughout America," said Mary Berry.

"If we start mandating the slavery laws of the states, what's next? We'll be right back to the dictators and tyrannical forms of government we see all across Europe," said Patrick.

Mary Berry pressed, "Is that your greatest concern? An oppressive federal government trampling on your rights as a man? Do you believe that if we prevent the spread of slavery to new territories, it will impact your position as a white man in this country? I don't think so. The Negroes and women are so relegated that your dominance will persevere, regardless."

"You don't know what you're talking about," said Patrick.

Max said, "I love the passionate discussion, but let's keep it polite, shall we?"

Annie said, "Aaron, as an attorney, what is your perspective on the *Dred Scott* decision handed down by Chief Justice Taney? From what I read in the papers, it seems like it was an abuse of power of his supreme court seat along political lines. The decision has inflamed the nation and fanned the slavery debate even more."

Max's sisters cleared the soup bowls and served the next course as the conversation continued. They brought carved roast beef, mashed potatoes, and beets. Max poured wine.

Aaron sat up in his chair and slipped into an air of a professor, explaining to his pupils, "Judge Taney's ruling argued that Dred Scott couldn't appeal to the supreme court because as a Black man, he wasn't a federal citizen. Taney angered much of the North by asserting that African Americans could never be citizens of the United States. The founders, in his opinion, did not consider African Americans to be part of the people who were guaranteed rights by the government.

"More importantly, in his ruling, he declared that the Missouri Compromise was unconstitutional, and the idea of popular sovereignty spelled out in the Kansas-Nebraska Act was also unconstitutional. Since then, the South has used Taney's ruling to justify the case for expanding slavery."

Aaron nodded at the attentive guests around the table. "Legal scholars continue to debate the ruling and the broader issue. It will take time to resolve it fully."

"You've quite a grasp on the law and politics," said Molly.

Mary Berry said, "We must not wait for time to resolve it. We, the people of this country, must act. We cannot stand for this abhorrent institution to continue."

Mary Johnson said, "It certainly has energized the anti-slavery factions. John Brown's rebellion and seizing the national arsenal at Harper's Ferry were disturbing to read about. Men leading armed insurrections against others is hardly a civil way to address the issue. Brown was a radical of the worst kind who stirred up a group of Negroes and tried to create a rebellion."

"I agree we can't have armed Negroes terrorizing the citizenship," said Aaron. "All the inhabitants of our nation must respect the laws of the states."

"I hate to see the violence break the peace and create disunion," said Max. "It threatens our ability to prosper as a nation."

"I think Mr. Abraham Lincoln agrees with you," said Annie. "In his debates with Mr. Douglas, he has suggested that preservation of the Union is paramount above all. He won't advocate for the full abolishment of slavery for fear of alienating the Southern states. Lincoln emphatically stated that he is not inclined to interfere with slavery where it exists today. He said the government doesn't have the power to do that. Did anyone hear his speech here in Cincinnati at the Fifth Street Market last month?"

"I went," said Aaron.

"I did," said Mary Berry.

Annie said, "Lincoln seems like an honest and sincere man and a wise leader. Even though he won't push for abolition, he believes that slavery is morally, socially, and politically wrong. He doesn't want to see it spread further and would like to see it gradually end in our country. Lincoln painted Douglas as a maneuvering politician who won't commit to a moral stand on slavery but is walking the line to appeal to both North and South."

Patrick said, "All politicians have to do that. That's how they get elected. Max had to do that to become a councilman."

Annie said, "I would suggest that the issue of slavery and Douglas's stated moral position is far different from the compromises Max makes as a city councilman."

Mary Berry said, "I'd like to see Governor Chase be the Republican nominee for president. He has proven he's a true abolitionist. He has taken on legal cases for Negroes to help them sue for their freedom and rights. That is the kind of moral leadership we need in this country!"

"I agree he has been as strong a defender of the Negro as any white man, but I think his positions are too extreme to appeal to many Northern voters," said Annie. "Most Northerners and Southerners, for that matter, fear that if slaves were all liberated, they would create social unrest across the nation. Salmon Chase couldn't garner enough support to win the election."

Max said, "There is a practicality question of immediate emancipation. That's what makes the problem so difficult to resolve."

"I agree," said Aaron. "If all the slaves are freed, where would they go? How would they support themselves? How would the plantation owners be compensated for the loss of property and labor to work their farms?"

Mary Berry said, "If there's a cost, then society needs to pay it. Face the music, as they say."

"What's the price of that?" asked Patrick. "Are you suggesting our taxes pay for Southern plantation owners' slaves or labor? I'll take up arms myself before handing over my hard-earned money to line the pockets of the Southern aristocrats or support millions of freed, uneducated Negroes. Jesus, why don't they go back to where they came from?"

Annie glanced at John, who was silently staring at the table. "Patrick, most of the Negroes were born in this country, same as you. Secondly, it's not like the Africans chose to come to this country. The African slave trade preceded the Declaration of Independence. Those people were captured, brought to this country, and forced to help settle America against their will. They've been suppressed in chains and worse. They've been prevented from being educated and given none of the rights needed to assert for themselves life, liberty, or the pursuit of happiness. Is that fair?"

"The world isn't fair," said Patrick. "Look at Max, born a German, or me Irish. I wasn't born with the same position in the world as you, of Anglican birth."

"Whoa, wait a minute. You want to talk about fair? I was born a woman. I don't have half the rights you do," said Annie.

Now red in the face, Patrick said, "That's the natural order of things. Men, women, Negroes. God gave us all different abilities. We're not all the same."

"I think the wine and whiskey may be loosening our inhibitions more than is polite," said Max. "I apologize if our spirited debate is cause for discomfort to any of our guests."

Several at the table looked embarrassingly at John. He met their eyes, then returned his gaze to the table. Patrick looked back and forth to the others seeking affirmation, oblivious to his affront. An uncomfortable silence lingered in the room.

"Let me see to our dessert," said Annie.

Mary Johnson said, "I appreciate being part of the discussion. Thank you all for sharing your perspectives. I fear our world is changing around us. The newspapers are so full of editors' opinions and commentary that it's hard to know what's real and what's hyperbole. Thank you, Max and Annie, for allowing us to discourse on these topics civilly."

"Here, here," said Mary Berry. "We need more willingness to discuss like this openly. Here's to two of my favorite people, Max and Annie."

"Thank you, Mary," said Annie. "Thank you to Marie and Helene for the delicious meal. And now, dessert." Helene and Marie served an apple tart around the table.

"Has anyone been to the new Pike's Opera house yet?" said Annie.

Mary said, "Yes, Aaron and I attended the opening night gala. It's a beautiful theater. The black and white marble tiles in the lobby are stunning—and the staircase. It's magnificent."

"We saw the opera *Martha* there," said Molly. "The auditorium is enormous; three tiers of seats. The opera was beautiful. I didn't understand a word of it, but the music was moving. I loved the French horns. Their sound resonates to my bones."

"How poetic of you, my dear. I didn't realize you were such a music lover," said Patrick, leaning into Molly and trying to kiss her.

"I can see right through that whiskey-induced siren you've turned on. You've had too much to drink tonight, Paddy. Don't try charming me at this hour."

They finished their meals and conversed in the parlor over after-dinner drinks. Max and Annie said goodnight at the door as the guests made their way to the foyer.

Annie spoke with Mary Johnson as Max and Aaron conversed privately.

"An interesting evening," said Aaron.

"I hope we can see more of each other. I want to get to know you," said Max.

"Let's dine some evening, just you and me. I like you, Mueller, but I didn't appreciate being blindsided by the appearance of John tonight. He and I have a history that I think we both would prefer to leave in the past, especially given the current national discourse. Can you respect that?"

"I'm sorry if it made you uncomfortable," said Max.

"Well, thank you for the invitation. Mary had a nice time. You and your wife have an inviting home."

"Good night."

"My goodness, it was an exciting evening," said Mary Berry. "Thank you for including me. We have to get together soon. I want to tell you all about the Women's Rights Convention in New York. It was fabulous. There was so much restlessness in the crowd that it made tonight look like a bedtime story. Let's set a date."

"Yes, we must, dear," said Annie.

"Kiss little Lizzie for me. She's turning into quite a beautiful girl."

"Good night."

"John, thank you for coming," said Annie. "I hope the conversation didn't upset you?"

John said, "As a servant at Given House, I heard most of the attitudes expressed tonight. I have had much practice at biting my tongue. It is encouraging, though, to learn more about the political activities that may impact the future of the country and the condition of the Negro. Your friend Mary Berry—I like her. She is a direct, principled, and fearless woman."

"That she is," said Annie.

"Good night, John," said Max, shaking his hand. It was nice to have you here. I'm sorry for Patrick's outbursts."

"Thank you, Max."

Molly and Annie conversed in the hall while Max and Patrick remained in the parlor.

"One more whiskey?" said Patrick.

Max poured them both a short one.

"Where did you get this?" said Patrick.

"Aaron introduced me to it. It came from Kentucky, down near Lexington."

"Smooth."

"I'm glad you enjoyed it."

"What's up with you and him?" asked Patrick

"What do you mean?"

"You never liked him. Now, he's here in your home."

"We had some business dealings and have become reacquainted. I have a new perspective on him."

"Interesting. And John? Where'd you find him?" said Patrick.

Max lowered his voice. "You're my best friend. I trust you with my life, so I'll tell you this. He's sort of a relation to the family."

"Christ, I knew it."

"Knew what?"

"I knew there was something strange. It struck me when you introduced him, and then I saw Aaron. I watched the three of you during dinner. I knew something was amiss. All three of you were watching each other. Then I looked more closely. You bloody look like cousins, the lot of you!"

"Are you a psychic? You see it?" said Max.

"Max, I know you, and I see it in them. What the hell? A Colored?"

"Keep your voice down. My sisters don't know anything. Annie does. It turns out John, Aaron, and I all had the same father, William—the plantation owner that freed John."

"God the Father, Son, and Holy Ghost. How can that be?"

"I was more surprised than you to discover it. Long story. Very long story that I'll tell you about over a beer soon."

"Whiskey?" Patrick raised his glass and turned it upside to show it was empty, then pushed it forward to refill.

"I think you've had enough for tonight. Molly won't be happy with me if I give you more fuel to stoke that fire. Let's get together then, over whiskey. Keep this to yourself?"

"Your secrets have always been safe with me, but Christ— A Negro?" said Patrick.

"It's all right, I promise. You could have been a little more diplomatic tonight about your opinions of Negroes. John was sitting right across the table from you."

"I don't think I was out of line with most men's opinions. I'm sure he's heard it before," said Patrick.

"You were rude. It was ungentlemanly."

"I'm sorry. I forgot I was sitting at Father Max's table."

"Please just try to be a little more considerate next time?" said Max.

"For you… It means that much to you. I will."

"Thank you."

The two embraced and walked arm in arm to the foyer.

"He's all yours, Molly," said Max.

"I thank you for the lovely evening and forgive you for the condition of my husband."

Max kissed Molly's cheek. "Good night."

Annie and Max helped clean up, sent Helene home, then went upstairs. They lay in bed talking.

"I think it was a successful first dinner party," said Max.

"Do you? Marie and Helene were wonderful, but I think we may want to more carefully choose the makeup of the guest list in the future," said Annie.

"It started a little rough but smoothed out after a while," said Max.

"It was spirited debate. You did a nice job mediating."

"Aaron was not happy that I surprised him by inviting John. He did say that he liked me as he was leaving."

"Did he?"

"That's progress. I don't think we'll ever be close as brothers, but I feel a connection to him. I want to know him," said Max.

"And John?"

"I see the difficulties he faces every day, even in freedom. Tonight, for example. It was unsettling, and I am sorry for all he's been through. I don't feel a connection to him, though."

"Give it time. You need to get to know him as a person, and John is still adjusting to an entirely new life. John's comments about William tonight…you're like William in a way."

"In what way?" said Max.

"You ignore the things that make you uncomfortable about John or are inconvenient for you."

"I don't ignore them."

"You don't do anything to change them."

"What can I do? Slavery is woven into the fabric of the American South," said Max.

"It's not right, and it needs to be eliminated. You're a councilman. You can influence. You can do more to help John and others like him."

"I've helped him plenty," said Max. "We helped him get settled here. We invited him into our home. We helped him rescue his brother and sister."

"Did you?" said Annie. "If I recall, you insisted we couldn't get involved in that."

"We supported him. We have to think of Lizzie's well-being."

"Max, I love you, and you have a kind heart and a Christian soul. I think about John and what he must think of you. You and he were both bastard sons of William. You get half his fortune, and John gets a few dollars and papers that are an entry ticket to the bottom of the American ladder that you and I take for granted. Sometimes I wish you'd look into your soul and be more active."

"I'm uncomfortable being an activist like you. I have my reputation. Our livelihood depends on it."

CHAPTER 15

October 1860 – One Year Later

Max and Aaron sat at a table in the saloon on Vine Street, in the heart of the business district.

"Are you sure you want to invest in this enterprise?" asked Aaron.

"Yes, Annie and I believe that we must help John, both because he's my blood relative and because it's a way to assist the Negro cause tangibly, beyond rhetoric. Helping John establish his own business will set him on the road to supporting himself and his future family."

"Many businesses fail. You could lose your investment."

"I accept the risk. I plan to advise him and encourage you to do the same in legal matters. Can you do that for him?" said Max.

"I will take on the role of trustee for the business as you ask, but as I've told you, John and my history growing up together under the circumstances that we did, prevent us from having a peer relationship. I was raised differently than you were. I had the same religious education as you at Saint Xavier, and I see the wrong in slavery, but I don't see the Negro as equal to us. They are a different breed. And I worry that the emancipation talk in the North may lead to consequences that will disappoint Northerners if the Negro population is free to infiltrate their lives."

"Well, maybe your trustee relationship will allow you to see John in a different light," said Max. "I know I have benefitted from knowing him personally. Before knowing him, I never had the opportunity to get to know a Colored person man to man."

"I grew up with John, in the same house. I don't need to get to know him personally," said Aaron.

"All right then. Be the trustee for his business, then. That will be a great help to him."

"Lyle is still behind in his payments to us for Given House. With two of his slaves running away, he had to hire additional labor to work his fields this year. I fear we may wait a long time for the remainder of our payments from him."

"I want to go ahead with this. I want to believe Lyle is good for his debt," said Max.

"It's your capital to waste. Let me know when you find a barbershop and need me to help with the purchase."

"Thank you."

Patrick entered the saloon and joined them at their table. "Can I bring either of you a drink from the bar?"

"Beer for me," said Max.

"Whiskey," said Aaron.

"On the eve of this election, I'm afraid that Mr. Lincoln is going to win and start a series of events that will take our country down a path from which there is no return," said Max.

"On this, we all agree," said Aaron. "The Northern Republicans are solidly behind Lincoln, while the Democrats have split their support between the North's candidate Stephen Douglas and the South's candidate John Breckinridge. The Democratic conventions were a fiasco. How do they expect to win a presidential election if they can't agree on a platform, let alone a candidate?"

Patrick said, "Yes, they let themselves get caught up in the slavery question. By not compromising, they have backed a pro-slavery position that most Northerners cannot accept. They're shooting themselves in the foot."

Aaron said, "I understand the Southerner's position. Anything stronger than a popular sovereignty position, where the territories decide their fate, is a continued attack on the South's way of life. They fear a Northern hijacking of the country and will secede if Lincoln wins."

"Well, that's what's going to happen. Lincoln is going to win. I pray for our country," said Max.

"There is strong support for Douglas in this town," said Aaron. "Why so fatalistic, Max?"

"This town is filled with people like us. Our commerce is tied to the South, but we cannot be blind to the national landscape," said Max.

"I am encouraged by the newspaper accounts I read," said Aaron.

"What paper?"

"The *Daily Enquirer*."

"You are reading the paper aligned with your politics," said Max. "The editors write to their audience to sell more newspapers. Read the *Gazette* or the *Cincinnati Commercial*, which supports the Republican perspective, and you will see the other side. The national vote will elect Lincoln. The only question is, what will be the response of Southern Democrats? Likely secession, but whatever it is, it won't be good. Our national stability and associated prosperity are about to be upset."

"Secession will devastate my business," said Patrick.

"Mine too," said Max. "I'm even more concerned about what the Northern response to secession will be. Do the Southern states want to set up a separate republic that competes rather than aligns with the North? Are they willing to go to war to achieve that?"

Aaron said, "The Northern abolitionists are radicals ruining this country."

"I'm so saddened to see it," said Max. "Do the men pushing these positions see the implications of what they're advocating? Do they want a war with all its violence?"

Aaron said, "I think the leaders in the South welcome the opportunity to be rid of a strengthening Northern influence. They'll proudly take up arms for their beliefs and independence. They see it as a worthy and glorious cause."

Max said, "The aristocrats in the South have decided that they would rather become a separate nation to retain the power to preserve their way of life, but what about the majority? It is a small percentage of the Southerners that own slaves. Do the masses in the South believe it's a noble cause to kill for?"

Aaron said, "They have pride in their states and their rights as free men and are weary of Northern arrogance and a strengthening federal government against them."

"I don't understand how it has come to this," said Max. "What do they hope to gain by secession? It will lead to economic ruin for the South, even more than for the North. I am struggling to support any position that leads to violence of Americans against Americans. That's not a fight for which I can offer support or personally take up arms."

"Always the pacifist," said Patrick. "If it comes to it, I'll gladly fight to preserve the union of the states and our way of life. What about you, Aaron? Where do you stand on this?"

"I understand the Southern man's position and sympathize with it, but I no longer have a dog in that hunt," said Aaron.

"If it comes to fighting, will you fight for the Union?" Patrick asked Aaron.

"I'll support the Union. That is my future and my family's future."

"I think you are with the majority of men. What about you, Max?"

"I am deeply conflicted," said Max. "I love this country and abhor the evils of slavery, but my conscience will not allow me to wage war against another man. There has to be another way!"

"But would you fight?" said Patrick. "Will you take up arms to defend the Union that our forefathers fought to create? Do for our children what they did for us? Or will you run from the fight?"

"It shouldn't have to come to this. It's unnecessary," stated Max.

"In your mind's ordered, rational world, that is so, but we don't live in that world. We inhabit the democracy we created that allows the menagerie of men's wills to evolve our government," said Patrick. "I think you need to steel yourself for what's to come."

#

April 1861

Max and Annie sat in their parlor reading the newspapers with Lizzie playing with her dolls on the couch next to Max.

"How could things have deteriorated so rapidly since Lincoln's election?" said Max. "First, South Carolina secedes, and now most Southern states have joined them. They're setting up a whole government with their own president. They started a war by attacking Fort Sumter. Today, the papers say Lincoln has called for 75,000 volunteers to put down the insurrection. 75,000 soldiers! My God, Annie, 75,000 men to fight a war." Max closed his eyes and prayed to himself.

"Papa, sleeping?" said Lizzie, climbing on his lap and touching his closed eyelids.

Max opened his eyes which were moist with repressed tears. "No, darling, Papa is praying to God for peace." He hugged his daughter.

Annie said, "Signs of the conflict are all over the papers. Southern sympathizers at a speech at the Fifth Street market had eggs thrown at them. Students at Miami University are leaving in droves to go home to the South to sign up for the Confederate army. It's affecting things big and small now."

"Today, it's eggs on our streets. Tomorrow, will it be bullets?" said Max. "How do we have a war where neighbors take sides based on their viewpoints? This isn't as simple as North versus South. I don't understand how a group of people can be willing to kill their fellow countrymen to preserve their right to hold slaves. It's incomprehensible to me."

"I know, dear, but the South has initiated a war against us. We must defend ourselves and our nation. We can't let a group of radicals set this country back further from the founders' ideals. From liberty for all people. Our futures and Lizzie's are at stake."

"Yesterday at city council, we debated, but in the end, there was unanimous support for Lincoln's call up. We agreed to organize volunteer enlistment by ward to meet the request for soldiers. They are asking for three-month enlistments. The war shouldn't last much longer than that if the Union can organize quickly and put down the rebellion."

"Max, I know your pacifist nature, but as a councilman, people will be watching you and expect patriotism."

"I know that. I need to find my role in this nightmare. I'm going to the meeting at Turner Hall today for German volunteers. My brother, Albert, and Marie's boyfriend, Hugo, are joining me. Hugo has been part of the standing German militia in Over-the-Rhine for years. Oskar wants to go, but I've forbidden him; he's only sixteen. He needs to finish school."

Annie said, "Why are you going to the German enlistment meeting and not one of the others in the city?"

"My brother and family friends will be part of that regiment. I feel like that is where I belong today."

"I understand how that might feel more comfortable in this situation, but I'm surprised. You've tried to distance yourself from your German heritage publicly. Are you considering signing up? Can you take up arms?"

"I don't think I can, no. I can't take the life of another man, but I need to do my part. I will contribute to the war in a non-combat way. The war effort will require iron-made equipment. I propose to offer Miller Industries help to supply the armies."

"Supplying the equipment to wage war. Isn't that just as bad as waging war yourself?"

"What choice do I have?" said Max.

"This is so awful. Why have these rebels insisted on war to resolve this?" she said.

"I don't know. I wish there were another way, but I'm afraid there's no going back."

#

As Max walked through the city streets north into the German neighborhood, he observed a host of changes. American flags hung from buildings and houses. Groups of people assembled, listening to ad-hoc speeches supporting taking up arms to defend the Union. There was excitement across the city, driving men to sign up. He didn't understand their enthusiasm and remained somber, praying to himself for strength and guidance to face his fears and convictions.

As he approached Turner Hall, a crowd of men lingered outside. A row of militiamen stood guard across the front of the building. Max greeted acquaintances as he entered the meeting hall. He found his brothers Albert, Peter, and Oskar.

"Oskar, what are you doing here?" Max demanded. "Go home."

"I want to hear. I'm not enlisting," said Oskar.

Peter said, "He has a right to be here. Let him be, Max."

Max took a deep breath and pressed his lips tightly. Oskar moved away from Max to the other side of Peter as the meeting was called to order by Gustav Tafel, a leader of the Turner Society. Tafel began in German, then switched to English. Peter took notes for his newspaper. Tafel stood before the men and summarized the sentiment of most of those in attendance.

"My fellow citizens, it is time for us to put the evils of the Southern slavocracy to its death and replace them with freedom for all men. I call on you to enlist to support our president's request for capable men to win this fight. Those who have proven yourself, either in the conflicts in our homeland or in the militia, step forward to defend our freedoms."

Several men made speeches, then Tafel introduced the regiment leader, Robert McCook, a Scotch-Irish lawyer who had defended the Turners in the Cincinnati riots a decade earlier. Although not a German, McCook had political connections in the state capital and Washington that would help establish and arm the unit. The men lined up to sign on to the *Die Neuner*—the 9th–Regiment Ohio Volunteer Infantry, composed of ten companies of Germans.

The group elected General August von Willich as their drillmaster. As a former Prussian artillery officer, Willich knew military formations and had experience in drill instruction. He announced that the men should report to the Orphan Grounds on Monday to begin their service.

The room buzzed with excitement. While the men waited in line to sign up, speakers took the podium to support the cause and appeal to the men's patriotism and sense of duty. A band played music in between speeches. Men filled mugs with beer from several kegs. The camaraderie and thrill of fighting were contagious, appealing to the masculine American virtues that put George Washington and other military men as role models. Albert, and Marie's boyfriend, Hugo, who was Gustav's brother, moved to the line to sign up.

Oskar made another plea to Max to allow him to volunteer. "I'll volunteer to be a bugler or a clerk. Please, Max. I want to do my part."

"No. You're too young. I know you want to serve, but you have to wait. Finish your education."

"Some of my classmates have signed up with other regiments. I'm not too young. You may be afraid, but I'm not."

"Oskar, you should be afraid. This is not a game. Men will die."

"I am willing to die for my country," said Oskar.

"I commend you for your bravery, but I can't allow it."

"Let me be my own man."

"When you are of age, you can decide for yourself. Until then, you must find another way to serve."

"You're a coward," said Oskar.

"Go home," said Max.

"I used to look up to you. I can't anymore," said Oskar.

"I'm sorry you feel that way. I have always followed my conscience and what I believe God instructs me to do. I ask that you respect that."

"I can't respect you now." Oskar moved through the crowded room to join Albert.

Max stood alone in agony. He felt like an outsider. He was torn between his sense of duty to his country and his anti-violence stance. Without further thinking, he moved to the line.

When he reached the table, the experienced military leaders, men he knew, greeted him and looked at him expectantly. Max said, "I want to serve, but I cannot take up arms. Give me a role that supports the men who will fight."

The lead officer responded. "Max, we appreciate your offer and sense of duty, but this is an infantry regiment. We are only taking the most experienced and qualified men who have previously fought in battle or drilled with our militias. I'm sorry. There may be a place for you in waging this war, but it is not with us."

Max was stunned by the outright rejection. He contemplated an argument, but before he could vocalize it, the officer asked him to step aside for the next man in the long line. He looked around the room. Were the men looking at him, judging him? Did they think he was unmanly? Not a patriot? He felt embarrassed, ashamed. What was his duty? What should he do now? Max moved through the boisterous crowd and left the hall.

CHAPTER 16

The following week, Annie, Max, and Lizzie accompanied Marie to watch the newly recruited German regiment march in their first public parade. They stood at the edge of the Orphan's Asylum grounds at Fourteenth and Elm Street in the Over-the-Rhine neighborhood. The yard had been turned into a makeshift assembly point and training base for the army. At one end of the block, stacks of lumber lay for the planned barracks. Several cannons rested ominously on the grass. Hundreds of families and supporters stood along the street, waving American flags and cheering. The Turner band played a march as General Willich led the men down Elm Street and onto the open field.

The men did not yet have their Union army uniforms, but marched in straight lines, with stiff backs in the German style taught by Willich. They marched close together, moved their legs with unbent knees, holding their bayonet rifles on their left shoulders. A drummer tapped continuously to keep them in step.

"There's Hugo," said Marie. "He looks so handsome. He's talked about nothing but the war since last week. I was just getting used to spending time with him, and now, he's off to God knows where and I don't know when or if I'll ever see him again."

"He's a brave man, Marie. He fought in Germany. I'm sure he knows how to look after himself," said Annie.

Oskar joined them along the edge of the crowd.

"Why aren't you in school?" asked Max.

"They won't miss me. Dozens of boys have left to sign up to fight. Even some of my teachers have left."

"You need to be in class. Your education is important. Don't be daft," said Max.

"I'll go after this. I wanted to be here to support Albert. Won't you at least allow me that?" said Oskar.

"Then off to class."

"Look, there he is," said Oskar, pointing. He laughed. "He's out of step."

"He doesn't have the experience that Hugo and some of the veterans have. He's only been drilling with the Turner militia for a few months. You can't expect him to know all the drills already," said Max.

"I'm envious he's been a part of the Turner militia. I've only been able to participate in the Turner gym activities," said Oskar. "Had you allowed me to join the Turner militia last year, like Albert, I could be there with him."

"Enough, Oskar!" said Max. "When you are of age, you may do as you please."

Once the men were on the field, they marched into a square around the perimeter of the block, looking inward. Officers stood before the ten companies of the regiment and inspected their men. Each company took its turn; the officers gave commands in German, directing the inspection.

"They're an impressive army," said Marie. "They'll teach the Rebels to challenge the United States military."

"When do they leave?" asked Max.

"Hugo said they are marching to Camp Harrison tomorrow morning."

"Where's that?" asked Oskar.

Marie said, "It's just north of town. They've created a temporary camp on the grounds of the Cincinnati Trotting park up by the Spring Grove Cemetery. Hugo rode up there. He said there are just a few shacks set up. They're awaiting tents and proper equipment. The men will be mustered into the army officially and await their orders as to where they'll go next. It sounds cold and uncomfortable."

"Do you want to go and see him off?" asked Annie.

"Yes. It may be the last time I see his face for a while."

"You go. I'll stay home with Lizzie. It's important you're there for him."

"Thank you. What do you hear of your brothers? Have they signed up?" asked Marie.

"My brother Caleb, who went to West Point, is already deployed as an officer in the Quartermaster Corps. He is in Washington but will likely be deployed to help supply one of the regional armies. I've no word of my brothers Anthony and John or whether they have signed up as of yet."

"I read that more than the requested 75,000 men have already volunteered across the North," said Oskar. "So you're off the hook, Max. There are plenty of brave men stepping up to fight."

"There are other ways to serve our country and the war effort, Oskar," said Max. "I've already spoken to an army representative about contracts to fit steamboats with iron reinforcements for use in the war. Our brother Peter will travel with infantry companies to report on the war firsthand from the front."

"They sound like milksop contributions to me," said Oskar.

Annie said, "Oskar, the war department is rushing to put together an army to combat the Southern forces. In addition to soldiers, the army needs munitions, supplies, medical care, and an organization to support the troops. There are plenty of noble ways to contribute to the cause besides fighting with arms. Can you please show a little more respect to your brother, who has been so good to you?"

"I'm appreciative of all Max has done for me, but I've already told him I can't respect him, given his position on the war."

"Oskar," said Annie.

"It's all right, Annie," said Max. "He's entitled to his opinion and not alone in it. Even my friend Patrick has questioned my patriotism and valor."

"What is Patrick's status?" asked Annie.

"He has enlisted in the 1st Ohio Infantry."

"It seems everyone we know is deploying. They're going in so many different directions," said Annie.

"The other thing we can do is pray for all of them," said Max.

After watching for another twenty minutes, he said, "I need to get to the shop. I've already had eight men leave work for the army, and I'm afraid I will lose even more. I need to get there to help out."

Annie kissed him. "You're a good man, Max Mueller. Try not to be so hard on yourself."

Max nodded at her, ignoring her attempt to console him, then stooped down to kiss Lizzie on the top of her head. He pushed his way through the crowd and started back downtown toward his shop.

As he walked through the streets toward downtown, he passed dozens of men walking along the canal, headed toward the new Camp Harrison and the other new nearby camps, Camp Colerain and Camp Clay. When he walked past the train station, men stood in lines, waiting to board the train for Camp Chase in the state capital of Columbus. Hundreds of men who had arrived by steamship were passing through Cincinnati on their way to their camps. They milled about the central market at Fifth Street. Some men lay on the ground or sat propped against the market building, with nowhere else to sleep. Women staffed tables, serving sandwiches and ladling from a kettle of soup warming over a fire. Many of the storefronts were dark. A sign on one read "CLOSED— Gone to fight."

Max reached his shop yard to find two employees standing beside a dray arguing.

"Take it back. Put it on the next steamship, then," his foreman, Jim, was shouting at one of the younger workers.

"What's the problem?" asked Max.

"This one allowed a ship captain to bully him around. It's what happens when you send a boy to do a man's job," said Jim.

"It's not my fault," said the young man. "He wouldn't let me put the machine on board."

"Tell me what happened," said Max.

"I tried to deliver this threshing machine onto the steamboat bound for New Orleans, but the ship's captain refused to accept it."

"Why?" asked Max.

"He said the new Secretary of the Treasury, Salmon Chase, has ordered that no goods may be shipped to the South which might aid the Rebel cause."

"Did you explain what the machine was? It's used for food and feed production, not waging war," said Max.

"I told him, but he said it would aid in feeding their armies and wouldn't be allowed. Other men shouted at me—calling me a traitor for supplying the Rebs."

"Bloody hell," said Jim. "How are we supposed to go on making a living if we can't deliver the goods to our paying customers?"

Max said, "I understand what they're trying to do, but you're right, Jim. Do they want the people of the South to starve to death? Will they cut off the supply of everything to the South?"

"He threatened to confiscate the machine if I tried to load it on his ship," said the young worker.

"All right," said Max. "Put it in the back of the shop. I'll go down to the riverfront and see if there's any leeway. Maybe we'll have better luck with another captain."

"Soldiers were patrolling on the riverfront, Max. They mean business."

"What are we to do with the orders we are finishing in the shop? Just let them sit until this conflict gets resolved? It could be months," shouted Max in frustration.

"I need to speak with you," Jim said to Max.

"Let's go into the office."

"Eleven more men came in this morning to tell me they have enlisted and won't be coming to work. Another twenty or so simply didn't show up. That's over fifty men, almost a quarter of our workforce gone," said Jim.

"Any critical jobs that can't be covered by other men?" said Max.

"Not yet. I'm worried about the draftsmen and men who design the machines. If we lose them, we're sunk. We can hire laborers to replace those who leave, but if we don't have the plans on what to make, the men can't work."

"I'm afraid even hiring laborers will become a problem," Max said. "Men are walking away from their jobs in droves."

"Should we have Annie place an ad in the newspaper?" asked Jim.

"I don't think that will help. Let's wait a couple of days."

"There's another thing," said Jim.

"What's that?"

"We've had some order cancellations. The iron railings for the house on Milton Street. They said to stop working on those. They have no men to work on the construction, so they put the project on hold."

"Any more besides that one?" said Max.

"Yes, several more jobs that we haven't started. We received letters to cancel them too."

"Sounds like we may not need all the men because we won't have the work for them to do," said Max. "When Annie comes in today, she'll go through everything and lay out a revised schedule. Did you put the letters on her desk?"

"Yes."

"When she gets here, tell her everything you know about so far, both the men leaving and the canceled orders."

"Right."

"She'll also go through the orders and pull all the ones for Southern customers. What about Kentucky? Is the Secretary allowing us to do business with our customers there? They've declared they're neutral in this."

"It's unclear. No official word that I've heard. I'm suspicious of their allegiance to the Union," said Jim.

"I suppose it depends on who in Kentucky we're dealing with. Most of the people in the northern Kentucky cities align with us, but further south, I imagine their interests more closely align with the Confederates. Let's meet this afternoon after Annie has assessed the impact. In addition to modifying the schedule, we'll need to decide our position on Kentucky and with whom we'll do business. I don't want to be part of supporting the Rebels or perpetuating the conflict."

#

May 1861

Max, Annie, and Marie walked with a crowd of civilians and soldiers from the train station to Camp Dennison. The camp had been quickly built several miles north of Cincinnati along the banks of the Little Miami River. Named after Ohio's governor, William Dennison, the camp could house up to 15,000 men. Camp Dennison was a transitory camp established to house regiments until their ranks were complete and they could be officially mustered into the army.

They bought some food and drinks from the vendors along the muddy road and then found seats in the stands in front of the main parade ground. The Ohio 9th Regiment's ten companies marched proudly onto the grounds in their uniforms. Their band played music, and the color guard carried the 9th's flag. A group of women from Over-the-Rhine had made the flag from blue silk, with the name of the regiment and thirteen gold stars embroidered upon it. Streamers with German slogans flew from flagpoles. The men marched into a square formation with the officers in front. After several speeches by military leaders, the band played "Hail Columbia" and "The Star-Spangled Banner." The regiment was sworn in for three years in response to the army's call for longer enlistments than the initial optimistic three-month commitment. After the ceremony, Hugo and Albert found them, and they walked across the road to the lawn of a church. Annie and Max spread a blanket on the ground and sat with Albert while Marie and Hugo took a walk.

"You look very gallant in your uniform, Albert," said Annie.

"The ladies will be even more interested in you now," said Max.

"I look forward to when I can sit with ladies again. I've grown tired of the company of men in the army," said Albert.

"How is it, candidly?" asked Max.

"The camp is much better now. When we arrived a few weeks ago, we had only tents. The new barracks are small and have no heat, but at least we're protected from the rain and have cots to sleep on. They've also figured out how to feed us. We didn't have regular meals until last week. They're nothing like Marie's cooking, but my stomach no longer aches for food.

"I am ready to move out. We all want to do what we signed up to: fight the Rebels and end the revolution. We're tired of marching and target practice. Most of the days, we sit and wait. Major von Willich has forbidden alcohol, but we found some men from Cincinnati that sell lager beer in the woods. It helps to deal with the boredom. I'm ready to fight."

"The army has taught you to shoot?" asked Max.

"Yes, we've only had a few turns on the firing range, but I didn't do too badly last time out. We've also learned to use the bayonet."

"You're ready for that?" asked Max.

"If it's what must be done, I'll do it," said Albert. "If it's a gutless traitor's life or my own, I know which one will win."

"God be with you if it comes to that," said Max.

"When do you expect to leave?" asked Annie.

"We're still waiting on more guns. The men with the standing militia have their weapons, but the army will supply the rest of us. Within a month, this camp will be empty. By the end of June, we expect to be somewhere in Western Virginia, under General McClellan's command."

"McClellan, he leads the Ohio militia?" said Max.

"Yes. He's addressed the troops, but we don't see him much around camp. His headquarters are in Cincinnati, where he can communicate better with all the troops. He's led the rapid formation of the army."

Max said, "He has an impressive military background from the war with Mexico. He's been successful in commerce as well. He stepped away from being president of the Ohio and Mississippi Railroad to serve in this role. It's reassuring to have men with his experience leading our forces."

"How is everyone at home? Mother?" asked Albert.

"She's well. She's proud of you and prays for you," said Max.

"She's happy to be spending today with Lizzie," said Annie.

"And how is business at the Eichen Garten?"

"The crowds are smaller with so many men gone. Helene let the hired help go. She and mother will manage, and Oskar will help out on Sundays. They have been cooking food to feed the soldiers who camp at the Orphanage Grounds," said Max.

Marie and Hugo joined them and sat on the blanket. "Shall we eat?" said Marie. She took the picnic lunch she had prepared from a basket.

"It is wonderful to have your home-cooked food again, Marie. The meals here are a break from the monotony of drilling and sitting around, but I've had enough of boiled potatoes and salted meat," said Albert.

Marie handed each of the men a piece of apple strudel.

Hugo took a bite and closed his eyes. "Oh, my love, that tastes like heaven itself. I'll carry the memory across the miles and recall it when I need a reminder of what we're fighting for."

"It's just strudel," said Marie.

"It's *your* strudel," said Hugo.

After they finished eating, Marie said, "I'll meet you at the station." Hugo said his goodbyes, and he and Marie walked off to have a private farewell.

Max gripped Albert's shoulder. "Papa would be proud of you, Albert. You are representing your family and your people bravely. We all will pray for your safe return and a victory that will restore peace and prosperity for our nation." He put his arms around Albert and pulled him close, eyes tearing. "Stay safe." They patted each other's backs.

Annie took Albert's hands. "You are fighting a noble fight for all of us. For Max, me, Lizzie, your family and friends. For all Americans who should have the right to pursue their lives unencumbered by those who abuse power over others." She kissed his cheeks. "We love you, Albert."

Albert stepped back, forced a smile, then turned and walked toward the camp.

Max put his arm around Annie's waist as they watched him until he was lost in the crowd of soldiers amongst the barracks.

"He's so brave," said Annie.

"He doesn't know what's in store for him. I'm fearful. Fighting a war against our countrymen. How do you win this war?" said Max.

"I don't know, but I'm thankful for all the brave men like him. We're at war, and we can't stop it. I don't advocate violence, but we have to defend ourselves. We were attacked. They mean to replace our free society with a government controlled by a small group of men who wield power over others. We can't stand by and let this happen."

"My intellect tells me you are right, but my heart is overwhelmed by the course of the struggle. I was so hopeful for our city and our country. Now I feel we are lost," said Max.

They stood in the gray afternoon looking at the vast camp, with rows of small barracks and hundreds of men moving about the muddy ground. The smell of the cooking fires mixed with latrine odors contributed to the depressing atmosphere.

"We may never see him again. Is it worth it for the cause?" said Max.

She took his hand and tried to look him in the eyes, but he wouldn't look at her. "We'll get through it. We have each other."

CHAPTER 17

October 1861

Hundreds of men and a few women filled the Ohio Mechanics Institute hall. The Institute had invited business leaders and city council members to meet to address the growing concerns of business enterprises due to the war.

Leonard Fernwood of the Institute, chair of the meeting, made introductory comments, "The committee report was distributed to Institute members last week. If you want the details, read the report. The key findings include the following impacts of Congress's order preventing the shipment of any goods to the South, including Kentucky. Hundreds of pounds of pork from the slaughterhouses and other food in warehouses have spoiled. Iron and lumber businesses have been significantly impacted. Furniture manufacturers have halted production and have furniture stockpiles unable to be shipped. The sales of liquor, shoes, dry goods, and manufactured goods have dropped dramatically. Merchants are distressed, and many face bankruptcy due to the inability to collect debts owed by parties in the Confederate States."

Fernwood continued, "These impacts have decreased steamboat shipping of cargo and waterfront commerce activity, reduced employment within the impacted industries, and increased financial hardship on business owners in Cincinnati. A severe labor shortage due to the enlistment of men in the army has further hampered commerce across all industries in the city.

"Tonight, we'd like to discuss the report's recommendations and gain feedback from the members present." Mr. Fernwood pointed to the people on the stage as he continued. "I'd like to thank the authors from the committee and government officials seated here: Evan Mitchell and Arthur Stewart from the Institute; Howard Schlitz from the mayor's office; Max Mueller, city councilman, and his wife Mrs. Bennett Mueller, who penned the document on behalf of the authors. We'll take feedback from today and draft an official recommendation letter to take to city council for consideration. We also plan to prepare letters to the Ohio State Governor's office, Secretary of War, Secretary of the Navy, and Secretary of Treasury, as appropriate. Our objective is to recommend the most impactful ways we, as members of the Institute, believe we can mitigate the detrimental impact of the war on the Queen City. Any questions on procedure for this evening?

"I now open the floor for comments or questions." Fernwood nodded to a man seated near the front.

"Thank you—Tim Mullard, from the *Enquirer* newspaper. The Lincoln administration and Secretary Chase usurped states' and cities' authority by declaring a blanket embargo on the shipment of goods to the South. Not only is this unconstitutional, but an injustice to the innocent citizens of the South who will, in time, incur severe hardships in their personal lives."

Mr. Fernwood responded. "Thank you for that opinion. Our purpose here tonight is not to debate the government's policies nor comment on their constitutionality but rather to review the report's specific recommendations in order to finalize the report. Do you have specific feedback?"

"Is the committee open to additional recommendations?" asked the newspaperman.

"We're open to them, but we are not going to take time to discuss or debate them this evening. Do you have one?"

"Petition the Secretary for repeal of the order."

A man from the audience stood. "That's not going to happen. We are at war. The Secretary and President have special powers during wartime to protect the country. What we should do is have the mayor petition the Secretary for an exemption for Cincinnati. Due to our proximity to Kentucky and its declaration of neutrality, commerce should not be interrupted."

Another man stood, "The governor of Kentucky has declared neutrality, but many Kentuckians are friends of the Confederacy and support slavery. Goods are slipping from Kentucky to the South. I am not in favor of trusting the whole commonwealth."

Max stood on the stage, "Gentlemen, we will take the embargo issue back to the committee and the city solicitor and see if there's a legal remedy or recommendation we can include. Let's move on."

Fernwood said, "Thank you, Mr. Mueller. Gentlemen, I ask that you ask to be recognized by me before speaking." He pointed to a man, "Mr. Jeffries."

Jeffries stood and said, "I want to take exception to the recommendation that a special office for the employment of Negroes and women be established to aid in the city's labor shortages. We don't need taxpayer money going to educating or employing Negroes and ladies in how to do men's jobs. This is a temporary problem that will resolve itself as soon as our armies whoop the Rebels." Voices of agreement rose from the crowd.

Fernwood again recognized Max. "Hal, I'd like to believe that our soldiers will be home and back at work soon, believe me. My business has lost over 50 percent of its workers. Unless you know something I don't, we are in for a long haul. Men have enlisted for three years, and it may take a good part of that to resolve our differences. In the meantime, employing women and Negroes does two things for us. One: it provides those businesses that are willing to employ them with critical labor. Two: it provides those women and

Negroes an income that they need to feed their families. It doesn't solve our city's growing indigent care problem, but it could help."

The crowd erupted with shouts of "Not for Negroes," and "Women can't do the jobs."

"You're a radical," another man shouted.

Fernwood banged his gavel. "Quiet, please, quiet."

Max said, "Does anyone support this recommendation in any form?"

Only a few hands went up.

"We have your feedback on this one. We'll remove this recommendation from the report, but some of you business owners may decide on your own to employ women and Negroes in the coming days. The committee is only looking to assist you in weathering this storm." Max looked at Annie, signaling his acknowledgment of her disappointment.

"The recommendation that the city suspend collection of tax payments to distressed businesses. Why not all businesses?" asked a man.

Max answered, "The city has limited finances and ability to borrow money should a tax shortfall not cover city expenses. We can look at other options, but businesses that can pay need to do their part during this crisis."

Another man was recognized, "What about simplifying the government contracting process? What can the city do to help us there? Right now, it seems like there are a few men that are benefitting disproportionally due to the war efforts. Procter & Gamble received a contract to supply all the candles and soap for the entire army. Springer & Whiteman was awarded a contract for supplying rations. Mr. Mueller, I hear your company is helping the army build gunboats. Today, a few benefit greatly, while the rest of us starve for business."

Shouts of agreement came from the crowd.

"Why can't the city streamline the procurement process and make it fairer?"

Evan from the committee answered, "There may be something there. We can look at it. I would like to point out that Procter & Gamble is not supplying the entire United States Army, but I understand they were awarded a contract for the western armies. That is part of the problem. We're not dealing with one army. Each state and the federal Department of War outfit their own armies."

Another man stood. "Number six. The recommendation to fund family relief for soldiers' families from city funds. That sounds to me like the work of the churches and charitable societies."

A man in the rear shouted above the other voices. "Lincoln should fund that by paying the soldiers more. Non-officers are only paid $13 a month; so far, my son hasn't seen a paycheck yet. They need to pay them more and pay them every two months like promised."

Fernwood silenced the crowd with his gavel.

Evan said, "We'll include a comment on that in our letter to the Secretary of War. It can't hurt to throw in our support."

A man raised his hand and was acknowledged. "What about a city-funded enlistment bounty to supplement the $100 federal bounty for men who enlist?"

Evan responded, "We can look at that also. There are reports of bounty brokers abusing the system by recruiting some men who take the bounty payment and then desert or re-enlist in other localities. We don't want to encourage further abuse by making the broker business more profitable, but we see the merits in providing more compensation to entice soldiers."

The meeting went on for over two hours. Fernwood said, "Gentlemen, unfortunately, we are out of time. Thank you to the committee, Mr. Schlitz, councilman Mueller, and all of you for your thoughtful feedback. Please address any written comments to Mr. Evan Mitchell, the committee chair, by the week's close. He has informed me that they will draft the final recommendations by the end of next week. May God bless the United States of America. Goodnight."

Max spoke with several members who approached him while Annie conversed with the committee members. They left the hall together, stepping into the cool night air.

"I think it was a successful meeting," said Annie. "We didn't have anything thrown at us."

"The men of the Mechanics Institute tend to be reasonable on the whole," said Max. "We're all trying to make our enterprises succeed and face similar problems. It's one of the few institutions I participate in with a cooperative rather than competitive focus. I'm sorry about the women and Negro workers recommendation."

"Well, we tried. It's not the first time one of my efforts to advance the position of women has been stifled. You're right, though; if the war lingers, they'll have no choice but to hire women," said Annie.

"Thank you for all your work in drafting the recommendations. Once again, your writing and persuasive skills shine," said Max.

"It was good to see you so forthright when you spoke tonight. Your mood has been depressed lately," she said.

"It's the war, the uncertainty—for the business, for the nation, for us."

They approached a group of men gathered under a streetlamp. Some were in uniforms, with firearms, others in street clothes. As they neared, one of the men stumbled toward Annie, "Hey lady, we're from Indiana on our way to Camp Dennison. Might you share your company with us tonight before we take up arms to defend the Union?"

Max stepped in front of Annie, "Step back, sir or I'll have the constable arrest you for public drunkenness. Uniform or not, you've no right to address a lady that way."

The man's comrades pulled him away and apologized. Several laughed as they pushed the man, and he fell to the ground.

"The price we pay for being a border city funneling the armies to the front. We have to host every lowly cretin that's itching to shoot a Rebel. Are you all right?" said Max.

"I'm fine. I appreciate your gallantry, but you should be careful. Those men were armed," said Annie.

"I didn't think. I just reacted. I should exercise more caution. A man in that state could shoot unintentionally."

"Max, you defended me reflexively. If pushed, all men would do the same for something they love. I have to believe that it's a similar reaction for many soldiers. I know you've been struggling with the decision on whether to enlist. Do you think you would defend yourself in the face of death in a kill or be killed situation?"

"Well, if those are the circumstances, I think I would, without thinking. The problem for me comes in thinking. The politicians of this country have created a situation where we are forced to go to war. In my mind, it's unnecessary. And those politicians now ask the men of this country to wage war with their lives and take the lives of their fellow countrymen to achieve their objectives. I cannot place myself in a position with a weapon where the only choices are kill or be killed. It is immoral to me and a tragedy."

She put her arm in his. "Part of why I fell in love with you is your morality. I know this is hard for you as a man. Men are expected to take up arms and fight. Know that I support you. I don't know what I would do if I were in your position. This is one time when I am glad to be a woman."

CHAPTER 18

Max and Aaron sat at a table in the Armleder Saloon, just south of the canal.

"Your family has a saloon in Over-the-Rhine, don't they, Mueller?" said Aaron.

"Yes, remember, you embarrassed me in my first city council race by calling that fact out to the audience and suggesting I was a criminal for flouting the Sunday temperance laws. No one seems as concerned with those things these days. War tends to change people's priorities."

Aaron said, "With all the soldiers passing through town, public drunkenness has become a sport, it seems. This place is all right. Seems like a mixed crowd of Dutch, non-Dutch, and soldiers. How's the food here?"

"It's good. I recommend the sausages. A butcher up Over-the-Rhine makes them. Try them. You might find that German food is not as offensive as you think. The lager is from the Hauck brewery and is as good as any in the city."

"I'll try the sausage, but I'll stick to whiskey, thanks. How is your business faring?"

"Not well," said Max. "I've lost all my Southern business and half my employees. We're still trying to get a handle on our sales forecast. I did pick up supplying the iron plates for converting three steamboats into war-ready tinclads. We're working for Joseph Brown at the Cincinnati Marine Railway, who has the contract with the Navy. That will keep five or six of my men busy for weeks. I hope to get more war-related contracts, but I have stiff competition. Miles Greenwood at Eagle Iron Works has secured a number of them. He's well connected. I've heard he's building cannons and has a contract to convert 4,000 old muskets into more modern rifles for Ohio's military. They're calling them Greenwood Rifles. He's an innovator. I respect him, but the devil has hired several of my men."

"He's a shrewd businessman and familiar with influential men in town. Have you considered partnering with him?" said Aaron.

"Greenwood?"

"Yes."

"He's been my main competition for years. That would be like admitting defeat."

"I didn't think you were so vain, Mueller. Not part of your makeup. Am I wrong?"

"No, I… It's a thought. Might be something there."

"I'm not as stupid as you think. You need to use this war to your advantage. Speaking of stupid, what do you hear of Patrick?" asked Aaron.

"I spoke to his wife last week. She received a letter from him. His battalion is in Kentucky, trying to keep the state from going to the Confederacy. Did you see the governor there declared they're neutral? I admire that. Too bad the whole country couldn't do that."

"The governor didn't do it to be admired. He's trying to do what's most advantageous to his citizens and himself. Neutrality allows them to continue their way of life with slave labor, un-harassed by the abolitionists. Kentucky is a confusing place right now—half Yankee, half Rebel."

"You haven't enlisted yet. Are you going to?" Max asked.

Aaron poured whiskey from the bottle on the table into his glass. "My mother, if she were alive today, would have celebrated to see me off to war to put down the North. My father wouldn't have condoned me taking up arms to defend the Southern social and labor system."

Max took a sip of his beer and peered through the side of the glass. "And you?"

"I don't feel like I fully belong in either world," said Aaron.

"I know how that feels. I felt that way as a German boy at school with all the native-born Americans. I still struggle with it. Depending on where I am and who I am with, half of me has its advantages or detriments."

"Maybe I should wait and see who wins to decide where my allegiance lies," pondered Aaron with a chuckle.

"Your allegiance is undecided?" said Max.

"No. I told you before. I don't care one way or another about Southern slavery, but my future is in the Union."

"Are you going to enlist then?"

"No. I can't do that. It would be like waging war against her. I'm like Kentucky, I guess. I declare neutrality," said Aaron.

"My conscience won't allow me to enlist either."

"That figures. That's who you've always been."

"Are you concerned with what people will think of you, not enlisting?" said Max.

"Sure, but it's a pointless war. My parents couldn't agree on which side was God's side. I don't think the men fighting this war will resolve the question. Christ, Mueller, why do I allow you to drag me into these introspective conversations? No one else does that. You remind me of school and the Jesuit priests."

"Sorry. I appreciate the ear. Most men don't understand. They can't look inside themselves like we were taught."

Aaron shrugged.

Max said, "Patrick's wife said his furniture factory has closed. Most of their business was in the South. They can't even ship what's already been made. She had expected to receive money from the company while he was gone, but now she's worried. They have three children. I told her I would help if she needed it."

"It's endless," sighed Aaron.

"What is?"

"The line of people holding their hand out for help."

"It's Patrick's family. I can't leave her to fend for herself," said Max.

"I don't see why you feel such allegiance to him. The last time we saw him, he was practically drooling like a rabid dog to fight and insinuated that your pacifist nature was cowardly."

"He's one of my best friends. We have differences of opinions, but that doesn't mean I should abandon him or his family in time of need. We can't let disagreements about the war destroy years of friendship."

"He saw what was coming. He should have better prepared financially," said Aaron.

"Easy for you to say, you were born of money. Patrick and I have had to work for ours."

"Says the man who took half of the inheritance I was due! What did you do to earn that money? You didn't even know the man," said Aaron.

"I'm not talking about that. Patrick and I started with nothing and built our businesses."

"Well, it looks like the jury is still out on the success of those."

"Are you devoid of compassion for anyone?" said Max. "I believe that if I have the means to help, I should. You don't need to disparage me for it."

"Christ—you're so sensitive," said Aaron. "Speaking of our inheritance, I received a letter from Lyle this week. It wasn't good. He said he wouldn't be making the remainder of the payments he owes us. He considers the debt eliminated with the declaration of war and the embargo against the South."

"What the bloody hell?" said Max. "Kentucky is neutral. We're not at war with Kentucky. Can he legally do that?"

"Nothing in the contract we signed with him addresses this situation. We'll have to wait until the war is over to resolve it. Jurisdiction is a problem right now."

"This is criminal. He owes us," said Max.

"Even if we could win a court judgment, he doesn't have the money to pay us. He was an incompetent farm manager to begin with, and now with the loss of some of his slaves and reduced markets, his prospects look grim. All this disruption must be even more depressing for him than for us. I have no affection or respect for the man, but I understand the dire feelings seeing Given House decline and not being able to do anything about it.

"Central Kentucky is in a war within its borders. Confederate supporters are attacking Union loyalists on the streets. Last week, Confederate sympathizers cut down most of the apple trees in the orchard of one of Lyle's neighbors. More slaves are running away, reportedly encouraged by abolitionist-minded neighbors."

Max let out a large sigh. "It's senseless. Between the drop-off in my business and now this news, I'm going to have to tell John that I can't help him buy his barbershop right now. We finally found a shop to buy. I hate to disappoint him," said Max.

"John's impacted like the rest of us now. It's as much his war."

"I'm also going to have to delay construction of our new house. I probably couldn't find the men to work on it anyway," said Max. "How about you? Will you be financially sound if the war drags on?"

"I'll manage. Our law practice has slowed with the reduction in commerce, but I still have some cases for now. I may have to pursue other business opportunities to get through this period. Mary and I will make adjustments in our spending, like everyone."

"I don't understand how some people are so encouraged by the war," said Max. "They're enthusiastic that the North will prevail, and the country will be better afterward. How can they feel confident? What is there to be excited about? There are already hundreds of men dead and wounded on both sides. The battle at Bull Run was an embarrassment for the Union armies. They thought the Confederate army would fold at the first attack, and it's clear nothing of the sort is going to happen!"

"You and I both fell from that same part of the tree. We look at the world through a critical, realistic lens. I, like you, struggle to find hope right now." He poured another glass of whiskey for himself and then poured whiskey into Max's beer glass.

A group of soldiers erupted in shouts, pushing against them as they spread out to watch two men swing at each other. One decked the other, and the men cheered as they pulled him off the floor.

Max and Aaron stepped back, Aaron grabbing the whiskey bottle. They let the commotion die down, then returned to their seats.

"We can't even have a drink in peace," Aaron muttered. "Bloody war."

#

Max sat in the barber's chair, a cloth wrapped around his neck, as John used the straight razor to shave him. "How are you faring, John?"

"I'm doing the best I can, earning my wage. I miss my family. Wonder about the ones left at Given House."

"Have you heard from your brother and sister?"

"They have a friend who wrote a letter for them. They both are working for wages. They're living with some Colored folk. I think they're all right. There are days I wish they could come and live with me here, but now with this war on, they're better off staying put in Canada."

"I think you're right, John. Although the Union won't likely enforce the Fugitive Slave law during the war, there's still the risk that if they were caught and taken back to Kentucky, Lyle could re-enslave them."

"What do you think is going to happen with this war?" said John.

"I don't know. Both sides are dug in. I think it's going to take a while to resolve it."

"I tried to enlist at one of the meetings," said John.

"Which one?"

"I went to the recruiting office for the Third Ward. Saw in the paper they were having trouble filling their ranks. They were offering a hundred dollars just to join. But they said they weren't taking Colored men."

"Why did you want to enlist?"

"The way I see it, the Southern way of life is no way of life for the Colored. I thank the Lord every day to be free of it. But it's still there, holding a grip on plenty of men and women and trying to grow west. Pieces of it are here in the North too. I'm free but still not equal. The abolitionist cause is working to right that. I have more reason to fight the South than any white man in the army. I don't know why those recruiters don't see that."

"That's very noble of you, John. It's not the recruiters. The army doesn't allow Black men."

"I have a burning inside me that I've been holding back all my life. Fighting against those men in the army would make me feel like a full man in control of my destiny. I've been denied that too."

"I'm sorry they won't take you," said Max.

"I've been helping out with the railroad in the meantime. We've had more passengers since the war started. I still pray that my mammy might someday cross that river. I think about her every day."

After a moment of silence John asked, "Are you enlisting?"

Max sighed. "No, I'm not. I believe in the Union and our principles and denounce slavery, but as a Christian, I can't fight and kill another man. I'm supporting the war effort in other ways."

"I see you. You're closer to what the preacher says a Christian supposed to be than most men, but let me tell you, I've seen all kinds of Christians. In Kentucky, we went to the white church and those people saying all the right things about being Christians. They walk out of the church, and it's like they're different people, you hear me?" said John.

"I do."

John wiped the remnants of the shaving soap from Max's face with a towel. "You want the boy to black your shoes today?"

"No, they're fine, thanks. I have some bad news, John. It's about the barbershop and the money I promised you to help you buy it. I'm not going to be able to help you right now. Lyle owes Aaron and me money for Given House. Now with the war, he said he won't pay us the money. And my shop's business is way down too, so I don't have the money to give you. All the Southern orders have been canceled. When this is over, I hope to help you with it. I'm sorry."

"I don't feel like I lost it because I never had it. You and Miss Annie have been kind to me. I don't think this is the right time to open a new barbershop. Most of these chairs in here are empty more than filled these days. All the men have gone off to fight, and the ones still in the city are not getting a shave or a cut so often," said John. "Aaron, he isn't getting his money either?"

"No, he's not."

"Looks like we all three been cheated out of something by Lyle, then," said John.

CHAPTER 19

Annie and a dozen ladies sat on chairs in the basement of Saint Xavier Church. Annie had recruited Mary Berry, Aaron's wife, Mary Johnson, and several other acquaintances to join her Soldiers' Relief Circle. After they socialized for several minutes, Annie called the meeting to order.

"Ladies, thank you all for the work you did over the last two weeks to collect the items requested for the soldiers in Louisville. The crates were packed and shipped by steamer yesterday. Thank you to Lavinia Mitchell for coordinating this shipment."

The ladies politely applauded.

"I wanted to share with you a resolution that we, the representatives of all the Ladies Circles, drafted and sent to our state legislators, asking each of them to donate one day's salary to the Commission to aid in the procurement of soldier necessities."

"That is wonderful," said one of the women. "They can afford it."

"Anything we can do to increase our donations is a godsend," said Annie. "We haven't heard back from them yet, but we're hoping some will donate and that peer pressure might work to our advantage. At our meeting, we also discussed holding a major fair in Cincinnati to raise funds. No specifics yet, but the idea would be to hold it in a large hall and have exhibits, salvage and donated goods for sale, entertainment, lectures, and even dining. Make it a grand event that people want to come to and get something in return for the money they donate. Mr. Burnet, the commission president, supported the idea and will help us form a committee of prominent men in the city to assist the effort and lead the fundraising. He was talking about people like the mayor and one of the Ohio generals."

"That sounds like an ambitious project. Are you going to be involved in organizing it?" asked one of the ladies.

"I don't know yet," said Annie. "This was our first discussion, and many details must be thought through. The soonest we could hold it would be year-end, maybe tie it in with the Christmas season. I'll provide more information once I know more. I wanted you all to be aware, and if you have suggestions, let me know. I also wanted you to hear how supportive the committee is of your work, ladies. Mr. Burnet assured us that the army brass knows who we are and respects us as a vital part of the military's effort. The men are counting on us."

The women chatted. "Has anyone else noticed that things seem quieter in the city?"

"Yes, I have, too. The soldiers seem to have all gone off now. Very few marching in the streets anymore."

"I saw a cavalry unit from central Ohio passing through yesterday. There's still a trickle of soldiers in town. They're still feeding men at the central market every day."

"I took the train through Camp Dennison last week. It's nearly deserted."

"So many of our soldiers are in the South now, from the east coast to the Mississippi."

"It's difficult to know how the war is going. There's so little information in the newspapers. It comes in small morsels, and things change from one day to the next. I never know what to believe."

"I have received several letters from my husband as of late. He doesn't shed much light on the army's strategies or positions, but it's reassuring to have word directly from him."

"Where is he now?"

"He's with the 1st Ohio Infantry somewhere near Louisville. They're guarding Kentucky against the Confederates in Tennessee. So far, he said they've only had minor skirmishes with secessionist troops, but no major battles."

"My husband is in the 5th Ohio Infantry Regiment in Virginia. I can hardly read the newspapers. Some of the worst fighting has been in the east."

"He's so far away. I didn't realize Ohio regiments were fighting so far east."

Annie said, "Ladies, thank you all for your sacrifices at home and your work for the Soldiers' Aid Society. Your patriotism is inspiring. For those alone without your husbands, please let us know if we can assist you with anything. We are here to support each other.

"Our final topic for today is our next request. We have been asked to acquire donations for a military hospital in Nashville, Tennessee. Most items are bedding-related: quilts, sheets, blankets and pillowcases. There are also dining items, including bowls, plates, cups and saucers, spoons, and tumblers. I have the list of the requested quantities. Would someone like to take the lead on this one? You'll need to coordinate collection at your house and arrange the shipment. Many of the railroads provide shipping at half price for Sanitary Commission shipments. The crates just need to be properly labeled."

"I'll be happy to do this one," said a woman.

"No, please, let me," said Mary Johnson.

"Oh well, that's wonderful. We have two volunteers. Would you like to work together?" said Annie.

"No, I want to do it," said Mary. "I don't feel I've done my part yet. My husband offered to fund the next request in full. I will buy all the necessary supplies and arrange for shipping them."

"Well, of course," said the other volunteer, somewhat startled by Mary's rebuff.

"Well, that's very generous of you and Aaron," said Annie. "Let's show our appreciation to the Johnsons." The ladies applauded.

"Mary, here's the list of items and the instructions for packing and shipping. This is so wonderful of you."

Mary took the paper. "I think I can arrange for it all."

"Don't you want to review it?" said Annie.

"No, thank you." She folded the paper, tucked it in her bag, and headed for the stairs.

"Please let us know if you have trouble securing any items or need assistance," called Annie after her.

"She seemed in a hurry," said one of the women.

CHAPTER 20

Annie sat working at her desk in the office on the upper level, overlooking the Miller Industries' factory floor.

Max came in and took off his coat, covered in a light dusting of snow. "Maybe we'll have a white Christmas tomorrow."

"How is work on the gunboats progressing?" Annie asked.

"The two promised should be ready by year-end, but I'm worried about the work that Brown's team is doing. Some of their workmanship is shoddy. He's under tremendous pressure to deliver them by the promised dates. I have my foreman watching them like a hawk, but they disregard his comments and suggestions. I have to go myself and reason with Brown to correct things. It's not only his reputation on the line but could be the lives of men on those boats," said Max. "How were things here this morning?"

"The men are in good spirits. With the long hours they've been working, they're looking forward to the day off tomorrow. We received this message from the mayor's office." She handed him a letter. "Eads & Nelson, a firm in Saint Louis, is contracted to build gunboats for the army. They are behind schedule and subject to penalties of $200 per day for every day they're late. They're looking for qualified mechanics to work for them for thirty days. They inquired if we had any men we could spare."

Max said, "I understand the pressure. We're feeling it too. Do you think we could get by without one of the men working on the boats?"

"We've plenty of work, but we could move a man over from the machinery group. Our work shouldn't be impacted as long as we have enough men who know what they're doing," she said.

"Then let's see if anyone would be willing to go. We can ask at the party at the end of the day. Anything else?"

"This came in as well," said Annie. "It is a request to bid on building iron reinforcement structures for the city defenses. They're placing guns at Price Hill, Mount Adams, Fort Mitchel, and two other locations across the river in Kentucky. The cannons are already in place."

"When are the bids due?"

"December 31st."

"I'll take one of the mechanics with me the day after Christmas to look at them. Is that it?"

"Did you see this?" Annie handed him a newspaper folded with an article circled. "Eagle Iron Works had a fire last night. The second one since the war started. It's suspected arson by Confederate sympathizers."

"Damn. Do you think we need to hire a watchman for the shop?"

"That's not where I was going with this," said Annie. "This is your opportunity to approach Greenwood. Go to him and offer our help. He can use the excess capacity in our foundry and our men. If you can help him in his time of need, maybe it's our chance to partner with him—become overflow capacity for him. He's got deadlines he needs to meet as well. He would welcome the help or at least the gesture."

Max ran his hands through his hair.

"Max, the man is not a deity. Why are you afraid to approach him? Go! Now. He's probably scrambling for what to do the day before Christmas."

"Fine." He took his coat off the back of his chair and put it on. "I'll be back in time to address the men at the end of the day."

#

Max, Annie, and their foreman, Jim, stood on the upper level looking down on the one hundred twenty employees on the shop floor.

Max said, "Annie, Jim, and I want to thank you all for all of the hard work that you've done this year. I know that we've asked much of you, as many of your co-workers have gone off to war, to fight for the freedoms and opportunities we are blessed to have as Americans. Our prayers are with these men and their families.

"A few pieces of good news. We received contracts to work on two more tinclads and supply iron fixtures for new gunboats. We have been asked to bid on making the reinforcements for the city defenses, and I just met with Miles Greenwood. We will be assisting Eagle Iron Works with fulfilling their government contracts to build cannons. We've also received an inquiry to supply one mechanic to assist a factory in Saint Louis in building armor for gunboats there. Please see me if you are interested and can travel to Saint Louis.

"We are blessed to have work when other businesses are struggling. I appreciate your willingness to take on new jobs and work the extra hours required to complete our jobs on time. Please take stock of your blessings and enjoy the day off with your families tomorrow. On Friday, in addition to your regular wages, Annie will add a $10 bonus for each of you. Remember that the work you are doing is important for the defense of the Union."

Cheers from the crowd.

Max continued, "If you would like to donate to the families of your co-workers who have gone off to war, please place it in the bucket on the table. I'm sure their wives and children will appreciate your generosity. Now, enjoy a beer and some food; Merry Christmas to you all."

The men applauded and then rushed to the keg of beer and food.

Max turned to Jim and shook hands. "Thank you, Jim. I am blessed to have you in charge. Let's go downstairs and join them," he said with a smile.

#

Max, Annie, Lizzie, Marie, and Oskar rose early on Christmas day and attended mass at Saint Xavier. After mass, they stopped at home to retrieve the food Marie had prepared and took it to the Fifth Street market. There was already a line of soldiers wrapped around the block.

"Muellers!" said Mary Berry as she greeted them. "What have you brought?"

"It's Marie's apple strudel," said Annie. "She's been baking for a solid day."

"They look delicious. Can you put them on the table at the end with the other sweets?"

Annie said, "I wasn't expecting so many. Where did they come from?"

"Most are part of regiments that are forming at Camp Dennison."

"Where did they all sleep last night?"

"They slept in hotels, the barracks at the Orphans' ground, or in the rooms here in the back of the market. Some residents have opened their houses to men passing through. Quite a few were sleeping outside here under the eaves when we arrived to set up this morning. They were so grateful to have hot coffee."

"They must be cold," said Annie. "What do you want me to do?"

"Why don't you and Lizzie serve the bread," said Mary. "Marie, can you go into the kitchen and see if they need help?"

"What can I do?" asked Oskar.

"See if they need help with beer. They could probably use your strength to roll the kegs."

"That I know how to do. It looks like my brother is doing what he does best. Standing around and talking." Max had already approached the men in line and was chatting them up.

Annie cut the bread and placed the slices in a basket. As the men moved along the food line, Lizzie handed each of them a piece.

"Well, look at this young patriot," said a man bundled in a coat and hat, gloveless and red in the face.

"Merry Christmas," said Annie.

"Merry Christmas," said Lizzie as she put the bread on the man's plate.

"God bless you, ladies," said the man.

"Where are you from, sir?" asked Annie.

"I'm from Danville. Kentucky hasn't allowed men to enlist for either side yet, so a group of us, we're forming a regiment of Kentuckians here in Ohio." He looked at Lizzie, "She's a doll baby. She reminds me of my little girl at home."

"God bless you, sir," said Annie.

The next man in line asked, "Can I have a second piece, little lady? I haven't eaten in two days."

Lizzie looked at her mother, who nodded.

"Thank you, ma'am. Your kindness is appreciated."

The next man said, "We appreciate your being here, ladies. Feeding us one of our last good meals, I'm afraid. We hear the food in camps is barely tolerable."

"Lizzie, you stay here and give the men bread. I'll be right back."

Annie found Oskar laughing with the men at the beer keg. "Oskar, we're almost out of bread. Can you go around to the bakers and see if they've any to spare? Take anything they can give. Pastries too. If you don't have any luck there, go up to the Orphan's lot where they're serving food and see if they have any extra."

"Right. Hal, help me out. I'll cover the Fifth Street bakers. You go Sixth Street and north?'

"Right," said Hal as they both set off.

The soldiers followed the food line, one of many lines that would make up their lives for the foreseeable future. A few were chatty, and some were outwardly patriotic. All were grateful for the kindness and the meal.

Several hours later, the line finally ended. They offered the remaining food to the soldiers sitting around the market and cleaned up.

Annie said, "Mary, will you come back to our house and have Christmas dinner with us?"

"Yes, thank you. I'd like that. You sure you don't mind me intruding on your family?"

"Of course not; you're practically family."

"Max won't mind?"

"He'll be happy to have you."

They walked to their house on Eighth Street, leaving Max to talk with one of the other councilmen.

"Oskar, will you please stoke the furnace? Add coal if needed," said Annie.

"That smells delicious," said Mary. "What is that I smell?"

Marie said, "Roast pork."

"You are a wonder," said Mary. "I wish I had your culinary talents. Where did you learn to cook, Marie?"

"My mother. She taught us girls all the recipes from her family. We not only cooked for the family but had to cook on Sundays for the crowds at the saloon."

"What can I do to help you in the kitchen? I don't know how to cook, but I can follow instructions," said Mary.

"There's plenty to do still. How about peeling potatoes?"

"Great. Oh, my word, look at that," she said as she spied the Christmas tree in the parlor.

"Auntie Mary Berry, come see our Christmas tree," said Lizzie, pulling her into the room. The nine-foot tree filled the corner of the room and was adorned with strings of popcorn and berries, blown-glass ornaments, bird feathers and other hand-made decorations.

"It's beautiful. Where did you get these?" she said, pointing to the glass ornaments.

"From Oma's house. They're from Germany," said Lizzie.

"So delicate."

"I made this one, and this one," said Lizzie pointing to several paper ornaments.

"They're beautiful. What's this one?"

"That's baby Jesus."

"I see, yes."

"Papa said we'll light the candles on the tree tonight to celebrate his birthday."

"I've never seen a tree with candles. That will be spectacular," said Mary.

"Mamma, can we light them now?" Lizzie ran into the kitchen.

"No, we must wait for Oma and your aunties and uncles. Sit here and help me shell these pecans. I'll crack them, and you use this pick to remove the meat. Like this." Annie showed Lizzie.

"Mary, how goes your nurse's training?"

"It's been a whirlwind. The lead instructor is an Irish nun from the Sisters of Charity, Sister Anthony O'Connell. She's an excellent teacher and a delightful person. We've done some hands-on at Saint John's hospital."

"I think it's admirable that you have dedicated yourself to nursing our soldiers. Your students will miss you, but this is such important work," said Annie.

"Preserving the Union and our representative government is so important. The rights of Negroes and women can only be elevated if we overcome this attempt by the Southern politicians to put down the people's voice. This is the best way I know how to contribute to that right now."

"You do so much. You make me feel inadequate."

"Annie, I've told you before. What you do—working at Miller Industries to manage the accounts and all—showing that a woman can be as effective as a man—and simultaneously raising Lizzie? That is doing as much to lead the fight for women's rights as any of my campaigns or rallies."

"Oh, you're too kind." She embraced Mary. "I question if it is enough."

The family sat around the dining table. In addition to Max, Annie, Lizzie, Oskar, Marie and Mary Berry, Max's mother Katharina, sister Helene, and brother Peter joined them.

Marie, Mary, and Helene placed plates of food on the table, which was set with china and crystal and lit by candlelight.

They folded their hands and bowed their heads as Max said, "Father, we thank you for your blessings of family, of freedom, of good fortune, and the bounty of food we enjoy today. We ask you to be with our loved ones who could not be with us today, especially Albert and Hugo, who are away defending our great country. Please be with all the Union and Confederate soldiers and bring a quick resolution to the war, returning peace and prosperity to the land. We ask this in your name. Amen."

They began passing the dishes of food, filling their plates.

"Prayers for Confederate soldiers, Max?" said Oskar.

"That's what you took from that prayer?" said Max. "What are they teaching at that school these days? Yes, Oskar, God loves the Confederate soldiers too, and they deserve his blessing."

"I don't think so," said Oskar. "They have waged war on the Union in the name of enslaving men and women."

"I pray for all the men fighting in the hope that as few lives will be lost as possible. Trust me, most soldiers fighting don't have hate in their hearts. They are doing their duty, following along because common sentiment says it's what they should do. Most don't want to kill in the name of their cause—either Union or Rebel."

Oskar said, "If it were up to you, we would have continued to argue about slavery for the rest of eternity, and nothing would be resolved. You're all talk and no action."

"Enough!" Max said, pounding his fists on the table. "I've had enough of your childish bravado."

"Boys, please," said their mother. "It's Christmas. Can we set our differences aside for this evening?"

"Yes, Mother," said Max respectfully.

"Yes, ma'am," said Oskar reluctantly, with a scowl directed at Max.

"I am happy to be with my children on this most blessed of nights. We have so much to be thankful for. Although war is around us, we can have peace in our homes. Max and Annie, thank you for inviting us into yours. I wish your father could be here with us. He would be proud of you all for doing your part in service to your community. How did it go at the market this morning?"

"It was a large crowd. We probably served Christmas dinner to over a thousand men," said Annie. "They were so grateful."

Helene said, "We had a similar crowd at the Orphan's grounds. It does a heart good to assist."

"I wish the men would let us women do more," said Annie. "I tried to volunteer my services to the new Sanitary Commission. The Cincinnati branch has recently been established. I approached its president, Mr. Burnet, and offered to help with coordination and scheduling, but he wouldn't even entertain my assistance. He suggested I form a circle for the Ladies Soldiers' Society. He wouldn't even talk to me about helping with the administration of the office. He handed me a pamphlet describing the steps for creating a Ladies Circle."

"What is the Sanitary Commission?" asked Helene.

"The government formed it to look after the conditions of the military camps and hospitals and provide assistance through the efforts of the public. They are part watchdog and part volunteer to assist with non-combat efforts."

"What do you mean by 'watchdog'?"

"They've been tasked with inspecting the camps, the prisons and the hospitals and reporting to the army on conditions that need attention. In the report from the first inspection of Camp Dennison, they found that the health conditions were atrocious. There was sewage throughout the camp, leading to men getting sick. The army took the report to heart, dug some drains, and repositioned the latrines in the camp."

"What other kinds of things do they do?" said Helene.

"They also provide supplies and assistance to the men throughout the armies. That's where the Soldiers' Aid Societies come into play. If the Sanitary Commission learns of a need, say for additional supplies at a field hospital, the Societies raise funds or solicit donations to send to the troops. Things like medical supplies or simple items such as checkers or pen and paper for soldiers to write letters. Although I felt put off by the Sanitary Commission's rebuff of my offer of assistance, I took their suggestion to heart and formed a ladies' circle. We meet weekly to review what's needed and work through our communities and churches to respond. It's an action-oriented organization, unlike many of the ladies' volunteer committees that do little but meet and gossip."

"Good for you, Annie. We can't do enough for our men at war."

Annie said, "Max has been quite busy, himself in aid to the war. Miller Industries built some iron reinforcements for the city defense on Mount Adams and Price Hill. They're also building armor for the army's new gunboats. They'll be quite instrumental in the blockade that Mr. Lincoln has ordered around all the Southern ports and along the rivers."

"There's so many miles of coastline to patrol. Can they keep boats from bringing goods to the South?" asked Helene.

Max said, "It's as much about keeping the South from sending cotton and other goods to Europe as it is about keeping supplies out of the South. If we can shut off the

South's sources of income and supplies, we'll force them to admit they need the North. The South is already lobbying France and England to recognize the Confederate States of America as a sovereign nation, using the supply of cotton to the English mills as a lever. Sure, supplies will get through, but the blockade is another pressure point on the South designed to wear down their resolve."

"It is becoming obvious that the war will last longer than we originally thought," said Peter. "The North and the South are building large armies and industries to support them and provide a constant supply of war munitions."

"It is such a waste of resources. All that money and debt we're incurring for what? To kill each other?" said Max.

"What would you have us do?" said Oskar. "Sit by and let the Rebs outgun us?"

"I'm not suggesting that," said Max. "I realize that since the war has started, we have to defend ourselves and put down the rebellion. But the war money could be spent in factories for things that help people rather than kill them. It's such a waste."

"It's not a waste!" said Oskar. "Our brother, Albert, is bravely fighting for our way of life. You do him dishonor with your yellow talk."

"Oskar," said Annie.

Marie got up from the table and ran to the kitchen crying. Helene followed her. "You two."

"What?" said Oskar. "He does. Albert and Hugo are bravely doing their duty. Max talks as if there's shame in what they're doing."

Peter said, "No, no shame. The men I've met in the camps are brave and proud to fight for the Union.

"The 9th regiment is likely to see more intense fighting soon. The Confederate forces are aiming at taking Kentucky. They have a better chance of winning if they can win the border states and cement sentiment and forces against the Union."

"Poor Marie," said Annie. "She's been so sullen since Hugo left. She's put her dreams of marriage on hold. She wears a smile every day but is terrified by the constant talk of war, the daily reminders of soldiers in the streets, and the lists of the dead and wounded in the paper. She's not sleeping well. She's had nightmares."

After dinner, they retired to the parlor. Annie offered warm mugs of mulled wine. Marie served pieces of stollen cake, a family tradition.

"Annie, can you play some carols for us?" asked Max.

"I'm a bit rusty, but I can play a few."

Mary Berry said, "When did you acquire a piano?"

"Max bought it for me as a Christmas present. I told him I didn't want it. We could give the money to a better cause, but he insisted."

"I want Lizzie to have the opportunity to learn to play," said Max. "Annie learned as a girl. To have the ability to play brings joy throughout life. I love to hear Annie play."

Annie played several Christmas carols, and they sang along.

"Mother, I asked Annie to learn one of your favorites," said Max.

Annie slowly played "Silent Night." The family sang *Stille Nacht* in German. When they finished, they sat silently, enjoying the flickering candles on the tree.

"Your father loved Christmas time," said Katharina.

Helene rubbed her arm. "He was especially cheerful this time of year, wasn't he?"

"No matter what else was going on in our lives, he seemed to be able to put that all aside and focus on the people around him. He was a lover of people."

"What would Papa have thought of the war, Mother?" asked Oskar.

"Your father loved what this country stood for. We left our homeland because the working man was oppressed, and he and his father were persecuted for their political positions. He thought human slavery was a horrible sin of society and would have supported the Union's cause to repel the Southern aristocracy's abuses. He would have mourned the war and been deeply discouraged by the killing, but he would have been proud of his sons and the German militia's response to the call to arms."

"Would he have signed up to fight?" said Oskar.

Katharina said, "I can't know what would be in his heart if he were alive today, Oskar. But I would have respected his decision, whatever it was. Putting your life on the line for a cause is serious and should be a personal choice, guided by your conscience."

After everyone had left and they cleaned up, Annie and Max lay in bed.

"It was a lovely evening. Your family has some beautiful traditions," said Annie. "The whole day was a nice break from the war."

"Yes, it was peaceful here in Cincinnati today. Other places across the South are not so fortunate. The war is destroying homes and property, in addition to taking soldiers' lives. I pray for our countrymen whose families have been devastated."

"Oskar is so confrontational with you. Why is he like that? He didn't use to be that way."

"He's at that age," said Max. "He's searching for his own identity and definition of who he is as a man. I went through the same thing with Papa. I felt he didn't know anything. Since he died, I've played the role of Oskar's father. I guess the rebellion against me comes with the role. I have to keep reminding myself not to let him upset me. I just wish he weren't coming of age during wartime. I worry he will enlist if the war continues when he turns eighteen. He has no idea what it means."

"You have two years before you have to worry about that. This war will be long over by then," said Annie.

"I pray that will be so, but I fear not."

"That's two years from now. We can't go on like this."

"I don't know. Both sides seem to be settling into a war mentality."

She snuggled further into him and moved her fingers across his chest. "Hearing your mother talk about your father and what his perspective on the war would be. He sounded like you."

"Me? Heavens no. You knew him. I'm nothing like him."

"I realize you're not of his blood, but don't you think he influenced you when you were young? I mean, you grew up in his house."

"I didn't know he wasn't my father at the time, but we were never close. He drank and was barely there. He knew I wasn't his son and avoided me, I think. It was too painful for him to see me, a bastard, fathered by a man who forced himself on my mother. He married her to save her from shame. He wanted little to do with me. At the same time, I was embarrassed by his German customs and wanted to be free of that heritage. When I went away to boarding school at the age of twelve, I never looked back."

"It sounds like Papa was a pacifist, too, like you," said Annie.

"I don't think he was a pacifist. He just avoided anything that made him uncomfortable."

She let it drop. "My heart goes out to Marie. Tonight was so difficult for her. I wish there were something we could do for her," said Annie.

"You're so worried about everyone else. Did you miss your family today?" asked Max.

"I don't have fond memories of past Christmases with them, but I miss my father sometimes. I wish he could have known you and Lizzie."

She burrowed into his chest, kissing it. He moved his hand along her side and back, and they kissed. Without words, they enjoyed the familiar progression of comfort to passion, making love before falling asleep in each other's arms.

CHAPTER 21

January 1862

Annie and Max sat in the parlor, reading the day's newspapers by the gas lamps on the walls and table.

"Finally, some good news for our troops," said Annie.

"What's that?" said Max.

"A major victory in Mill Springs, Kentucky yesterday. The Union defeated Confederate troops and pushed them back into Tennessee."

"Mill Springs. That's where Hugo and Albert are with the 9th. The Confederates have been camped there protecting Tennessee, but the fear is they'll move north through Kentucky. They know, like we do, how important winning over the border states is. Does it say anything about casualties?" said Max.

"It says casualties were light. Initial reports are that thirty were killed and 200 wounded. The Confederates lost 125 men and another couple hundred wounded or missing. No names listed."

"That's good. Few casualties."

"We're becoming numb to the war. Thirty dead is good news. They're just numbers now, not men. It says that the 9th played a decisive role by leading a bayonet charge to force the Confederates to retreat," said Annie.

"Bayonets. I can't imagine. Hand-to-hand fighting at such close range," said Max.

"I'm sure both Hugo and Albert are fine."

"We should tell Marie about the battle before she hears it from someone else."

"Did you hear about the ruckus at the Pike's Opera House?" said Annie, reading from the newspaper.

"No, what happened?"

"Wendell Phillips, the abolitionist, spoke there. I remember him from the women's rights conventions. He is a champion for antislavery and for women. It says here, 'A few minutes into his speech, the crowd started heckling him and throwing eggs. Cheers and boos interrupted him as he spoke. A fight broke out in the crowd, and then some started to get rowdy, pushing toward the stage. Other men in the audience threw stools and canes at them to push them back. Mr. Pike tried to restore order, but the mob rushed the stage. Mr. Pike had to rush Wendell Phillips out the back door.'"

Max said, "Clearly, there continue to be strong feelings on both sides of the slavery issue in this city. It's a shame to see civil discussions escalate into violence. It's hardly safe to express your opinions anywhere these days.

"Everything is being diverted toward the war. Today, when I was down at the waterfront, checking the progress on the steamers, I met a man in town looking to buy steamships. The Navy has hired Charles Ellet to create a fleet of ramming ships from steamboats."

"Who is Charles Ellet?" asked Annie.

"He's an engineer who designed some of the country's suspension bridges, including the one at Niagara Falls and one over the Ohio at Wheeling. Anyway, he learned about ramming ships in the Crimean conflict in Russia. He's sent men to buy nine or ten of the fastest steamships so he can convert them into ramming ships for the navy. Guess which steamship they bought?"

"I don't know?" said Annie.

"*The Buckeye State.*"

"Oh, Max. We met on that steamboat. I hate to see it converted to a warship. How sad."

"It will be hard to think of it in the same way ever again. The man I met said that the owners of these boats have raised their sale prices to exorbitant figures. They're profiting from the war, milking the government for all they can get.

"The government will pay their prices because ships take too long to build from the ground up. Building a profit into government contracts is only fair, but this sounds criminal. The government is moving so quickly to arm the navy that they don't have time to follow sound procurement processes. The whole situation is ripe for corruption. If you recall, we got a question at the session we did last year at the Mechanics Institute on whether a few businesses were profiting over more fair distribution of contracts."

"I remember," said Annie. "Have you had any direct accusations or inquiries since?"

"No, but I had a heated conversation with a citizen after one of the council meetings. He accused me of being disingenuous, refusing to fight in the war personally, while at the same time profiting from government contracts to equip the armies."

"How did you respond?"

"I struggled. I told him that I believed in the causes of the war, but I would have preferred to see us resolve our political and moral differences without fighting. Since the war is underway, I am compelled to do my part to support the Union. I tried to explain my religious beliefs, but he wasn't interested. He called me a morally bankrupt opportunist and an elite capitalist."

"Ouch. This man knows just the things to say to hurt you most," said Annie.

"I feel like a hypocrite, but I can't sit and do nothing. If I enlist for a non-combat role, I would feel less like a coward."

"You don't need to do that. You're doing more for the cause staying at the helm of Miller Industries than if you enlisted. You're commanding a hundred men in work to support the armies. They need you. Who would lead them if you weren't here? You're guiding important work and helping those men provide for their families."

"If I were gone, you could lead them. You know enough about the business now. I'm sure you could do it," said Max.

"That's very encouraging to hear you say. I appreciate it. I believe I could do the work, but as a woman, I would not be respected by the government contractors or some of the men in the shop."

"If you had to, you could do it, Annie."

"Well, let's just pray that we never have to test your belief. Besides, I'm busy enough leading my soldiers' relief circle."

#

Katharina stood at the butcher's stand in the market off of Findlay Street, ordering her meats for the Eichen Garten's Sunday meal. She spoke in German, negotiating tradeoffs in response to shortages due to the war. Lizzie wandered from her grandmother to a cluster of children playing in puddles in the street. Katharina thanked the butcher and turned to retrieve Lizzie. A tall, gray-haired woman approached.

"*Guten Morgen*, Katharina."

"*Guten Morgen*, Lissa. How is your family?"

They conversed in German.

"I was so saddened to hear of the death of Hugo. How is Marie?" said Lissa.

"What? What are you saying?" said Katharina, confused.

"You haven't heard? It was in the newspaper—the list of casualties from the battle in Kentucky. Hugo was among them. I'm so sorry."

"Are you sure? Hugo?"

"Yes, his name was on the list of the killed."

"No." Her hand went to her mouth. "Others. My Albert?" said Katharina.

"No, he wasn't on the list." Lissa shook her head.

Katharina pressed her hand to her chest, closed her eyes and said a brief prayer. "His brother, Gustav?"

"No, Henry Lange was also killed. I didn't know the others. I'm sorry, Katharina. For Marie."

"Oh, Thank you."

Lissa touched her arm, "Let me know if you need anything. I will pray for her."

"Lizzie," called Katharina.

"Yes, Oma."

"We must go now. Say goodbye to the children."

Katharina bought a German newspaper from the newsstand and found the article summarizing the battle and listing the casualties. She leaned back against a post and closed her eyes.

"Oma. What is the matter?" said Lizzie.

"Sad news, child. Hugo is lost."

"Where is Hugo?"

"The war has taken him."

"Where?"

"To heaven. Let's go home." She sighed and took the girl's hand.

#

Marie came up the stairs into the apartment above the saloon. Katharina sat at the kitchen table with Lizzie, pointing to objects around the room and teaching her the German words.

"Max won't be happy if he learns you're trying to make a *Fräulein* out of her," said Marie.

"Teaching her a few words hardly makes her German. It won't hurt her to be able to speak our language. He has benefitted from knowing the ways of both Germany and America," said Katharina. "How many men did you feed today?"

"Smaller crowd. Maybe one hundred. There were only six women today helping. I think some of the ladies are growing weary of the war. I only need to think of Hugo, and I'll gladly cook the same strudel and serve the same soup every day until he comes home."

"Sit down, daughter."

"Lizzie and I should be going. I have laundry today."

"Marie, I must tell you something. Sit," said Katharina. "Lizzie, go into the other room and play with the dolls. Go on," said Oma.

Marie sat on the bench next to her mother. "What is it?"

"I learned sad news. It's in the newspaper."

"What? Tell me."

"It's Hugo. He was one of those killed in the charge in the battle."

"No, there were very few casualties. Hugo is an experienced soldier," said Marie.

"Yes, my dear. His name is in the newspaper."

Marie's eyes filled with tears. "No, not Hugo. My Hugo." She shook her head.

Katharina touched her daughter's shoulder.

"No!" Marie moaned. She wept into her hands.

"I'm sorry."

"What am I going to do now? Without him…"

Katharina patted Marie's shoulder. She went downstairs to the saloon and returned with a bottle of whiskey. She took a glass from the shelf, poured and set it in front of Marie. "Drink it."

Marie took a drink from the glass. "I can't believe he's not coming back. Why him? This wretched war!" She sobbed quietly. "What of Albert?"

"He's not on the list. Here." She pushed the folded back newspaper toward Marie.

Marie read and sniffled. "It says the 9th bravely led the charge with their bayonets. The victory pushed the Rebels back across the river toward Tennessee." She thought of how handsome Hugo looked in the tintype photo in his uniform, holding his rifle. She imagined him with his uniform muddy, his hair disheveled, sweating and running with the bayonet-tipped rifle up a hill, charging at men. "Oh, God." She broke down crying again.

"You go lie down. I'll look after Lizzie."

Marie went into the bedroom at the front of the house and pulled the curtain to darken the room. She lay down on the bed and cried herself to sleep.

CHAPTER 22

April 1862

After Union victories at Fort Henry and Fort Donelson in February 1862, the Union held western Kentucky and parts of Tennessee. The battle at Pittsburg Landing in southern Tennessee, known as the Battle of Shiloh, matched 45,000 Confederates against 62,000 Union troops in two days of fighting. The Union victory set the stage for their advance into Mississippi. Casualties were the greatest of any battle to this point in the war and dealt a significant blow to Confederate morale. Over 10,000 Confederate men were killed, wounded, captured, or missing. More than 13,000 Union soldiers were casualties. As reports of the battle and the large numbers of wounded spread across America by telegraph, Cincinnati joined other cities in mobilizing to care for the injured.

Annie stood with the other ladies who led their ladies' circles for the Soldiers' Aid Society in the crowded room at the Mechanics Institute.

Mr. Thomas banged his gavel, quieting the room. "Ladies and gentlemen, thank you for coming on such short notice. Today, our objective is to share with you the plan to respond to the need for caring for the wounded that will be coming from Pittsburg Landing. It will take all of you, plus your hundreds of volunteers within your circles, to meet the needs of our brave men who were injured in the triumph at Shiloh.

"After the battle at Fort Donelson in February, we took steps to treat nearly five hundred men who were transported by steamship to Cincinnati. We opened two new military hospitals, and your volunteers responded quickly to care for the sick and wounded. We once again need your help. Unfortunately, this time there are even more needing hospital care.

"We have already received donations to fund the hiring and outfitting of two steamships to travel down the Ohio River to Paducah, Kentucky and then navigate south on the Tennessee River to Pittsburg Landing. Surgeons and nurses have staffed these makeshift floating hospitals to care for the wounded on their journey back to Cincinnati, where they will be transferred to our hospitals. Dr. Comegys was appointed chief surgeon on the steamer *Monarch*. Dr. Mendenhall will lead the relief efforts on the *Tycoon*. We thank these men, and the other doctors and nurses who dropped what they were doing to board the steamers earlier this week. Our prayers are with them. We are also grateful to the Ohio legislature for their donation of $3,000 and the Cincinnati City Council for contributing $2,000 toward the cost of these boat rentals. We are seeking donations to defray the expenses of the steamboats and supplies. Appeals for funds have been placed with the local newspapers.

"We anticipate that the steamers will arrive the day after tomorrow. Once it is known, we will post the expected arrival time here at the Mechanics Institute. We ask that you develop a schedule of volunteers to support your assigned hospitals. Start with a two-week schedule. We'll meet daily and monitor the needs of each hospital beyond that. I have your assignments and requested number of volunteers to cover the round-the-clock shifts. I also have a list of more than three hundred names of women who have volunteered to assist if you have any trouble securing coverage from your regular volunteers. You and your volunteers will report to the head nurse at your respective hospital and take direction from her.

"Please see Mr. White or me for your assignments. Thank you, ladies."

There was a rush of conversation as the women lined up.

Annie stepped up to Mr. Thomas. "Mrs. Mueller. I have your assignment here."

"It's Bennett Mueller," said Annie.

"I'm sorry?"

"I'm Mrs. Bennett Mueller."

"I see," said Mr. Thomas. "Well, your volunteers will provide staffing at the new military hospital at Camp Dennison. The army has converted several barracks into hospital wards. These will be the less severe cases. The most critically wounded will go to the hospitals here in the city. Sister Anthony will direct the nurses there. She is on the steamship to Pittsburg Landing with six of her fellow sisters. How many volunteers do you have?"

"Twenty-two," said Annie.

"See if you can get more. We're counting on you for twenty-five."

"That shouldn't be a problem."

"Thank you. Oh, something else—the shipment you sent to the Nashville Hospital?"

"Yes. What about it?"

"It never made it there. It is believed to have been stolen during the transfer from the steamship to the railroad in Louisville."

"That's terrible. Who would steal relief supplies? The crates were marked as Sanitary Commission shipments," said Annie.

"That is unknown. In that part of the country, it could have been Rebel sympathizers. I hate to ask this on top of everything else, but can you coordinate a replacement shipment? They're still in need. Ship the same items."

"Of course. We'll get working on that right away," said Annie.

"Thank you, ma'am. Next."

#

As the steamships approached Pittsburg Landing, Mary Berry stood on the deck of the *Tycoon*, talking with Sister Anne. They spent most of the journey from Cincinnati preparing the hospital cots and supplies and reviewing instructions with the head nurses. By the time they arrived, Mary was well acquainted with the sisters.

"There must be twenty or twenty-five steamships," said Mary. "What are they all doing here?"

"Most fly the yellow flag of the Sanitary Commission. I guess they're all here to treat the wounded, like us," said Sister Anne.

"Where are we going to dock? There's no room."

The two boats from Cincinnati cruised up and down the river for more than two hours, looking for a spot to land. Finally, a ship left, making room for them. The captains squeezed the vessels into the opening, and the nurses ran onto the shore behind doctors Mendenhall and Comegys. Once on land, they weren't sure where to go, so they made several passes along the nearly half-mile of shoreline, Dr. Mendenhall in the lead, several doctors following, and six nuns with their white habits trailing like a flock of seagulls. Mary joined the procession.

Dr. Mendenhall asked a shoreman, "Excuse me, can you direct me to who's in charge?"

"Don't know, sir," he said, rushing on his way.

They spied a tent with the Union flag flying and hustled toward it along the muddy bank. They repeatedly stepped out of the way of men and women rushing toward them. They respectfully stood aside as soldiers carrying stretchers blocked their progress. It was slow going. They passed scores of wounded soldiers sitting on the ground. Some were bandaged, but many had not yet been treated. Men moaned in pain, and some were crying.

As they passed a man lying on the ground, a tourniquet around his thigh and bloody flesh protruding below it, he reached and grabbed Sister Anne's tunic. "Please, sister. Can you give me something for the pain? Please."

Sister Anne and Mary stopped while the rest of them marched on. "Has a doctor treated you?" said Sister Anne.

"I saw a medic yesterday. He put this on," he said, pointing to the tourniquet. "He gave me morphine, but it's worn off," he said in a strained, quiet voice. "If you could just give me something. Please? I need relief."

"Has anyone checked on you since then?"

"No."

"No one?" Sister Anne looked at Mary, then looked around, unsure where to turn for help.

"I'm sorry. I don't have anything with me," said Sister Anne.

Mary said, "Stay here with him. I'll be back." Mary walked up the gangplank of the nearest ship.

A doctor stopped her from stepping onto the deck. "Who are you?"

"I'm Mary. I'm a nurse from Cincinnati. We just arrived. There's a man down there. His leg's been badly damaged and has a tourniquet on it. He needs medical attention right away."

The doctor said, "Lady, there are thousands of men here that need medical attention. You say this one's got a tourniquet?"

"Yes."

"Sounds like he's received medical attention. He'll have to wait. Others need attention more urgently than he does."

"No, you don't understand," said Mary. "He's bleeding badly. He can hardly talk. He needs something for the pain. He hasn't seen a doctor since yesterday."

"Ma'am, he's not my patient. I can't be treating every regiment's wounded. Please step out of the way."

Mary rushed down the gangplank and started up the next boat's. She stopped and retreated to the shore to allow two soldiers to carry a man down the gangplank. "What are you doing? Why are you bringing him back?" she yelled.

As the men moved by her, she saw the man's bloodstained coat, which had been ripped open, exposing his shredded chest stuffed with dark, bloodstained rags. Then she noticed the open, staring eyes. Mary watched the men push past the men lying along the bank. When they reached the top of the hill, they dumped the man from the stretcher into a clump of grass. One carried the stretcher and slid down the bank, the other following. She lost sight of them as they made their way along the riverfront path.

Mary approached the triage nurse at the top of the gangplank. "Please, ma'am, I have a soldier who needs morphine for the pain. He's on the shore waiting to be treated. He's desperate."

She looked at Mary.

"Please," Mary pleaded.

"We don't have any morphine to spare. We need it for our patients. You'll need to get it from your ship."

Mary ran back down and started toward the *Tycoon*. Above the din of the crying and screaming men, soldiers and doctors shouting directions to one another, she heard a man holding one end of a stretcher screaming on the next ship's gangplank. "We were told to bring him here. He needs a doctor now."

The man in charge at the top of the plank screamed back at him, "We aren't treating Confederates, no matter what their condition. I won't let loyal American men die because some secessionist Rebel managed to get ahead of them in line."

"What are we supposed to do with him?" asked the man with the stretcher.

"I don't care, but he's not coming onto my ship."

Mary started running. She slipped in the mud and fell. She hoisted herself up, now covered in mud. She wiped her face with her sleeve and continued. Finally, she reached the *Tycoon*.

The triage nurse greeted her. "Mary, are you all right? What happened? Where are the others?"

"I don't know. Sister Anne and I stopped to help a man. He has a tourniquet on his leg and needs morphine. I came to get some."

"We can't give it to men who aren't our patients. We need to save it for our surgery patients."

"He needs it."

"Mary, that's not protocol."

"To hell with protocol," said Mary. She ran into the surgery area, found the medications, opened the bottle of morphine pills and took two. She grabbed a tin cup and filled it with water from a large barrel.

The triage nurse said, "Mary, you shouldn't do that."

Mary hurried past her and back onto the bank. She oriented herself and then ran, dodging men until she saw the white of Sister Anne's habit bent over the man. Breathing heavily, Mary squatted down next to her, thrusting the two pills and now half-empty cup of water toward the man. She heard Sister Anne praying, realization dawning on her as she looked at the man's closed eyes.

"Oh, God, I'm so sorry," said Mary.

Sister Anne embraced Mary as she broke down in tears. The men continued to move past them, unaffected by this scene or the dozens of others happening along the shore.

CHAPTER 23

Annie knocked on the conference room door at the Cincinnati Sanitary Commission headquarters. Mr. Burnet, the president of the commission, greeted her. "Mrs. Mueller."

"Mr. Burnet. It's Mrs. Bennett Mueller. They said you wanted to speak with me?"

"Yes. First, thank you for all your service to the commission. Your organization and responsiveness have been among the most admirable of all the Ladies' Circles. Our country is blessed to have women of your capacity in their service."

"Thank you, sir."

"But that's not why I wanted to see you." He got up from the conference table and shut the door. "I need to speak to you about a most alarming irregularity we discovered with one of your team's shipments."

"Sir?" said Annie.

"You're aware of the shipment of supplies to the Tennessee hospital?"

"The one that was lost in transit?"

"Right."

"We've already assembled another set of crates. They will be shipped this week," said Annie.

"That's the efficiency I've heard of. Very good. The original shipment crates were recovered in a riverfront warehouse in Louisville."

"Oh, they found them. Good. Can they still use the second shipment?"

"They didn't find the goods, just the crates," said Mr. Burnet. "It appears that the crates contained only some of the requested plates, silver, and such, and instead contained guns and ammunition for the Rebel cause."

"What?"

"A night watchman was patrolling the warehouse and came upon some men, prying the crates open. The men ran off, taking a handful of the munitions, but the guard discovered that the remainder of the unopened crates contained a dozen guns and hundreds of rounds of ammunition."

"My word. How did they get in there?" said Annie.

"That is my question to you." he said.

"Why sir, I have no idea. I gave instructions to the ladies of my circle, who packed and sent them. To date, none have given me any reason to suspect that they would be involved in a traitorous affair such as this, so I have no idea who would have placed those items in the shipment."

"Be assured, Mrs. Mueller. I am not questioning your loyalty or honesty. You and your husband's reputations as upstanding citizens are secure in this town. But I need to ask about the ladies in your group that assist you."

"I do not believe any would betray the Union cause and do such a thing," said Annie.

"Are all the ladies well known to you?"

"Some more than others. I suppose someone may harbor Southern sympathies, but they all seem sincere and dedicated to the Union."

"Yes, well, often these things are motivated by money, as much as allegiance to a cause."

"Sir?"

"There's a large profit to be made from gun-running. The Confederates receive arms from European sources by gun-runner ships on the east coast. The navy is sealing up that avenue, so the connivers are resorting to more devious paths to get badly needed arms to their armies."

"I see," she said.

"It may be that one of your ladies was convinced to assist someone to do this for a price. She's not the mastermind behind it. Our shipments, labeled as relief supplies, are not carefully inspected by shore agents. It was quite a brilliant plan if that is what happened. I will report your response to the army. A military representative will want to speak with you."

"Of course."

"Say nothing of this to any of the ladies."

"Yes, sir."

"I appreciate your confidence and, as I said, all you are doing for the war effort."

"Thank you."

"How are the shifts at your hospital going?"

"They just started today," said Annie. "I'll be checking in at Camp Dennison, where we were assigned."

"Very good. I understand the governor's chartered boat arrived this morning with several hundred wounded. The *Magnolia* arrived last night with 220 aboard. The *Tycoon* is due this afternoon at half-past five with another two hundred or so. The most critically wounded will be taken immediately to the hospitals in the city. The rest will be taken by railroad to Camp Dennison. Your ladies will have their hands full."

"I never imagined there would be so many."

"I don't think anyone did. Thank you for coming in, Mrs. Mueller."

"Of course. Again, it's Bennett Mueller, if you please."

"Yes, Mrs. Bennett Mueller."

CHAPTER 24

Annie stepped into the dark train car. The odors immediately assaulted her—sweat, urine, feces, vomit, rotting flesh, and gunpowder. The windows were open, but the trickle of April night air flowing through the car was no match for the stench. More than twenty men sat in the car, and a half dozen lay on gurneys in the aisles and atop several rows of seats. Most were asleep, but several looked at her as she entered the car. A baby-faced young man sat in the first seat. His face was coated with sweat and dirt; the whites of his eyes were his most prominent feature in the dark car. She forced a smile and a nod. His head swayed in response, and he closed his eyes.

She looked at the shirtless man next to him. His arm was in a sling stained with blackened, dried blood. She saw patches of white moving in the flesh of his arm—maggots. She forced another smile.

A man in the second row stood and motioned for her to sit down. She shook her head. "No, thank you. Rest yourself." She took a deep breath and forced herself to pat him on the shoulder as she squeezed by him. He swayed as the train car started moving and dropped back into his seat.

Annie eyed an open space at the rear of the car. She wanted to move to that spot and become invisible but realized the stretchers in the aisle would prevent her from passing. She bit her lip and surveyed the car in front and behind her, realizing there was no room for her to move. All the open eyes watched her. She was hot and sweating, feeling a trickle run down her back. She pulled her handkerchief from her pocket and dabbed her brow. A soldier halfway back in the car jerked and vomited onto the front of his uniform jacket. The smell overtook the other odors in the car. Annie breathed into her handkerchief. Another man across the aisle vomited in reaction, and then a third. Annie stood frozen. She felt unequipped to help them; she had no supplies, but more so, she didn't know what to do or even what to say to bring comfort or relief to the men. She closed her eyes, took deep breaths, and told herself she had to be strong for these men. They had no one else. Her discomfort was trivial compared to their suffering.

She opened her eyes. "I'm sorry, I don't have anything on board to help you. We should be at Camp Dennison in less than half an hour. Nurses and doctors are waiting to help you. It's not far now."

"Are you a nurse?" said one of the soldiers.

"No, but I help organize some of the Soldiers' Aid Society nurses. I'm Annie."

"Annie. Thank you for being here."

"Oh, I'm not doing anything. I'm just riding the train to Camp Dennison to help out. I wish there were something I could do."

"It's nice to hear a soft voice," said a man from the back of the train.

Annie forced a smile and fought back her tears. They rode in silence the rest of the way.

When they arrived at camp, Annie helped each row of men stand and start walking down the aisle, patting shoulders and taking arms. She looked each man in the eyes and smiled. When the orderlies came on board to move the stretchers out, she touched each man and reassured him. She followed the last stretcher out of the car and across the yard toward the barracks.

She found the volunteer from her circle. "Sharon, thank you for being here. Remind me, what's your shift?"

"I'm 7:00 PM to 7:00 AM."

"God bless you," said Annie. "Who's the in-charge nurse?"

"That one, Miss Stephanie."

Annie walked over and introduced herself. "I came to check on my volunteers, but I'm here. I'm not trained in nursing, but how can I help?"

"Tonight, it's about getting these new men settled. The ones in this barrack are not critically wounded. But they all need to be fed, cleaned up, and given clean clothes. The ones that can walk can go to mess, but the rest will need to be fed in bed. The food is over there. The pitchers, basins, soap, and rags for bathing are over there. Clothes are over there. Put the dirty ones outside in a pile—it keeps the lice population down. If they have dressings or wounds that need to be treated, leave that to one of the nurses. Pick a man and get started. We can use you as long as you can stand. Thank you." The in-charge nurse moved on and spoke to a nurse at a nearby bedside.

Annie watched several women attending to soldiers to understand what to do. The man in the bed next to her was sleeping. A young man with intense dark eyes sat upright in the bed beside him, watching the nurses in action. She took a deep breath and moved to the side of his bed.

"I'm Annie," she said smiling.

"I'm Elliot," he shouted, returning her smile.

"I'm here to help clean you up, if you're amenable to it?"

"What?" the man shouted.

"Would you like something to eat?"

He looked at her, not understanding. "It's my hearing. I can't hear. There was an explosion. I felt the wind from it, but not a nick on me. Except now my hearing's bad."

She moved closer to his ear. "Can you hear me now?"

"A little."

"Watch my lips," she said, pointing. "Are you hungry?"

"No, I ate in the mess tent."

"Do you want to wash?"

"What?" he said.

She brought a pitcher, bowl, washcloth, and soap over and sat them on the stand. She motioned for him to wash. She poured some water into the bowl and soaped the washcloth.

She motioned for him to remove his shirt. He took the washcloth and washed his face, arms, and chest. She rinsed the washrag and soaped it again for him. She motioned to his pants. He took them off, leaving his drawers on, and washed his legs. She handed him back the washcloth and pointed to his drawers. She went to get him some clean clothes. When she returned, he pulled the sheet over himself and handed her the washcloth. She gave him the clothes.

"Anything else you need?" she shouted.

"No, thank you."

"Get some sleep." She touched his shoulder.

"Thank you," he said.

She discarded his dirty clothes outside. She stood in the night air for a moment before going back in.

#

Annie sat on the early morning train riding back into the city. She didn't want to leave, as there were still men who needed baths and clothes, but she had to go to the shop and let Max know where she was. She was exhausted. She hadn't intended to become part of the corps of women attending to the soldiers, but it was the only thing to do, given the situation. She was lost at first, but she began to feel comfortable performing the work by the end of the shift. She knew she would return as long as men needed comfort.

She thought about the war. To her, it was a fight for all people's rights. Northerners, Negroes, women, immigrants, Indians. Abolishing slavery had been the cause that created the rift, and it had to be eliminated now, or there would be no rights for any of them. This war had turned the nation into a war machine. It seemed everything had been turned on its side in support of the war. Everything. And the causes of abolition of slavery and protecting the Constitution now translated into thousands of men's lives impacted—dead or wounded. She questioned how all this killing and maiming would lead to a resolution.

Annie walked home from the train station.

"Mamma!" Lizzie ran to her in the foyer.

"Good morning, my darling." She hugged her.

"Where were you?" asked Marie.

"I was at the hospital helping the soldiers who are hurt."

Marie said, "Are you all right?"

"Yes, I'm fine. Tired."

"Max was worried when you didn't come home. He didn't sleep."

"Is he at the shop?"

"Yes."

"I went to Camp Dennison to check on the volunteers. They needed more hands. I worked all night helping with a steamship's load of injured soldiers. I'm going to wash up and go to the shop."

"I'll cook you some breakfast, some bacon and eggs."

"That would be wonderful, thank you."

"Lizzie, come and talk to me while I clean up."

After cleaning up, Annie sat at the table in the dining room. Marie served her breakfast and coffee.

"This tastes wonderful. Thank you."

"How was it up there?" Marie asked Annie.

"It's heartbreaking. We took in more than three hundred soldiers yesterday. More steamships from the Tennessee River are due today. Some of the wounds are severe; missing arms or legs, bad burns. Many have gunshot wounds. They're so grateful for the attention. I've never done anything that made me feel so important—so needed." Annie sensed Marie was thinking of Hugo as she listened to her description. "I'm sorry, Marie."

"No, I asked. I wanted to hear. I only hope that Hugo and his regiment had similar charity supporting them—women as strong and kind as you."

Annie winced in pain and closed her eyes.

"Are you unwell?" said Marie.

"No, just a little tired. Your breakfast helped. I should go. Max is probably still concerned."

#

Max rushed over to Annie as she entered the shop. "Are you all right?"

"Yes, I'm fine."

They embraced.

"Where were you? I was going out of my mind," said Max.

"I was at Camp Dennison."

"All night? Why?"

"I was tending to injured soldiers."

"We had no idea where you were. I didn't sleep all night," said Max angrily.

"I didn't either. For God's sake, hundreds of injured men from the battle at Pittsburg arrived by steamship yesterday. More are coming today. They needed every hand they could get. I couldn't just leave them."

"Are you an army nurse now, too?" he said bitterly.

"No, but I helped tend to the men."

"What could you do? You've no training," said Max.

"I fed them, bathed them, comforted them. Whatever they needed."

"You bathed them?"

"Oh, Max. Please."

"No, I want to know."

"What do you want to know? Can I tell you about the man who came in with one arm cut off and one of his legs rotten with pus and infested with maggots? I had to cut his clothes off because they were so blood-soaked, and he screamed in pain if I moved him too much. He threw up the food I tried to feed him, and I had to clean that up. The doctor gave him some morphine, and as he slept, I washed days of mud and sweat off him. What else do you want to know?" She was screaming at him.

He shouted back, "Why were you even there? That's not your job."

"It's a bloody war! There are no jobs. We do what we have to!"

The men in the shop had stopped what they were doing and were watching them.

Annie pushed past Max and went up the stairs and into the office. As she entered, the clerk, Tommy, quickly got up and left as Max followed her into the room. They spoke in lowered voices to prevent their argument from carrying onto the floor.

"Annie, it's just, you're doing too much. Working here, the Soldiers' Aid Society. Now you're adding nursing soldiers."

"Nursing is part of the aid society."

"What about Lizzie?"

"I saw her this morning. She's with Marie."

"You know what I mean," he said.

"Say it. Go ahead. You're thinking it. You think I'm neglecting my motherly responsibilities."

"You said it, not me."

"No, I said *you* think I'm neglecting them," said Annie.

"I do. Can you honestly say you think this situation is right? You're never home. You leave her with my poor sister, who lost her future husband and is in mourning, and then you disappear for a day, and Lizzie wonders where you are and if you're ever coming back."

"Were you home with her last night?" said Annie.

"Of course."

"Was she fed? Did you kiss her goodnight and reassure her?"

"Yes," said Max.

"What physical harm threatened our daughter last night?"

"She was in no danger, I agree, but last night is not the entire point."

"What is the point, Max?"

"We agreed that you would put Lizzie first. You could do your women's movement activities, work at the shop, and be a progressive woman, but you would make sure Lizzie is taken care of."

"She is taken care of. It may not be what you or I had as children—not that either of those situations is what we want for Lizzie—but she is looked after by three people who love her dearly—you, me, and Marie."

"This is not how I thought it would be."

She shouted again, "Well, too bad, Max. It's not only about what you want. We agreed I have a say too. We're equals, remember?" She continued more calmly, "The world may not see us that way, but we agreed we would be equal in our marriage."

They stood looking at each other in a standoff, each taking stock in their minds. The tension slowly drained from their postures.

"Annie, I'm tired. I was thinking about all kinds of things that might have happened to you when you didn't come home last night. You should have let me know you were going to Camp Dennison and wouldn't be home. I'm sorry I shouted."

"I didn't know I'd be there all night. I didn't intend to worry you. I went there to check on the volunteers. When I saw the hundreds of men, and they needed help getting them all settled, I just couldn't walk away. Oh, Max, it was awful."

He embraced her. "I was frightened for you."

"You still think I'm a dainty that needs to be taken care of? After six years of marriage."

"It's just…there are so many men in the city. Soldiers from all parts of the country. Who knows what could happen?"

"You have plenty else to worry about. I can take care of myself. You should have seen me last night."

She told him about her train ride and her evening. "I can't change the war's outcome, but I can do my part to ease the suffering of the men who end up in Cincinnati. I'm going back tonight. More steamships are arriving today. I have to."

"I know you do. I wish you didn't, but I know you do."

"We're both tired. We'll get through this war together."

Max took her hand and smiled but refrained from kissing her in the open office.

"Now, I need to work on the schedule," said Annie, stepping back.

"Two new orders were dropped off for custom jobs. They're there on your desk," he said.

"I almost forgot. Something else happened yesterday," she said.

"What's that?"

"Mr. Burnet from the Sanitary Commission called me to his office. One of the relief shipments we sent to Nashville never made it there. The police in Louisville found the crates in a warehouse with guns and ammunition in them."

"Someone tried to smuggle arms into the South in the crates?" he said.

"Yes, he said someone from the army would be investigating. He told me not to discuss it with any of the ladies."

"They think one of the ladies did this?"

"Possibly. Max, Mary Johnson handled that shipment. She insisted that Aaron donate the money to buy the supplies, and she took care of the entire shipment. I thought they were very generous, but now I'm unsure what to think."

"Do you think Mary and Aaron could have done this?" asked Max.

"I find Aaron unpleasant, but she's so sweet. I found it odd that she didn't want any help. It was unusual for someone to fund an entire request like that. I just let her handle it."

"Did you tell Mr. Burnet this?"

"No. I didn't want to raise suspicion unjustly. Maybe there's a simple explanation."

"Well, you must tell the army investigator," said Max.

"I know. Should we ask Aaron or Mary?"

"This is serious. It's treason to smuggle arms to the Confederates. I don't think we should. Let the army handle this. Stay out of it."

"Do you believe they are Rebel sympathizers?" said Annie.

"I don't know. It's hard to know where anyone truly stands on this war. What people say may not be what they're thinking. Given his position in his law firm, he couldn't come out and say he supported the secessionists, but given his upbringing and his mother's Southern roots, I think it's possible."

"What do I do? She's at our meeting every week."

"You don't do anything. Just keep an eye on her."

"It's awful to think that neighbors or people you see on the street could be actively supporting the rebellion."

Max said, "They're in the minority in this town, but they're here. Even if people support the Union, many object to including the fight against slavery as an objective of the war. It's a very polarizing topic that sets people off. The Democrats can't accept Lincoln's aspiration to create opportunities for all men. Most seem to want to limit access to success to those who already have it. I hesitate to bring up the war in polite conversation. Most can't have a rational discussion about it."

CHAPTER 25

As the war escalated, both armies incurred significant casualties. In the west, General Ulysses Grant kept the Confederate troops at bay. The Union took New Orleans and captured Memphis, giving it total control of the Mississippi River except for a stretch south of Vicksburg, Mississippi.

Confederate General Braxton Bragg advanced into Kentucky and headed toward Louisville. Meanwhile, General Edmund Kirby Smith moved into central Kentucky toward Lexington, looking to win over Kentucky for the Confederacy and advance toward Cincinnati.

#

July 1862

John swiped the razor up Max's neck. "How are Miss Annie and Lizzie?"

"They're good. Annie spends several days a week at Camp Dennison, tending to the injured soldiers. She says there's no shortage of men who need comfort."

"I see the ships come in daily, unloading more injured men," said John. "Only a few weeks ago, we were putting men on those boats to go to war. Now they're bringing them back on stretchers, all torn up. I saw a stack of coffins down by the riverfront, waiting to be filled with the dead. It seems like there's an endless supply of men."

The man in the chair beside Max butted in, "Lincoln's war needs to be stopped. The man has already cost the treasury 200 million dollars and the lives of too many good men."

"Mmm-hmm," said John, then turned his attention back to Max. "Your brother is off fighting, isn't he?"

"Yes, Albert. Last we heard, he was at Pittsburg Landing. We haven't heard from him in a few weeks. I don't know where he is now."

"It's hard to keep track of all the fighting. I read the papers, but they never have the whole story. And I never heard of many of the places they're fighting. This country's big."

The man piped up again, "Lincoln will be removed from office in disgrace. Starting this war to free a bunch of Blackies."

Max said, "Sir, if you please, I'd like to enjoy my shave in peace. A man gets little respite these days."

The man grunted.

John flashed a sign of appreciation to Max with his eyes in the mirror.

Max asked, "How have you and your friends fared with all the unrest in town over the last week? You had any trouble?"

"I've been staying clear of the riverfront and Bucktown. I know people living there. Some of them have left town until things settle down. They went up to Mercer County. Mr. Watson has a farm with a place to camp for anyone who wants to get out of the city. We're in a war against the South, and instead of fighting the Rebels, these boys are fighting each other."

Max said, "I heard the mob was pretty violent last night."

"I'm hearing that was the case," agreed John.

"I attended a meeting on Monday with Mayor Hatch and the committee he formed to address the rioting. He swore in thirty men to be a special police force to put down the violence."

"From what I hear, there weren't any policemen to be found," said John. "An Irish mob attacked two Black men walking home from their shift on the levee. Men angry at them for being Black and trying to earn a living."

"It's difficult for the police. We sent 120 of our regular police force down to Kentucky to fight against Morgan's troops approaching Lexington."

"Why are they sending police to do the army's job?" asked John.

"Well, we debated it at the city council meeting. With the Rebel forces threatening Lexington, Cincinnati could be next if they advance. We wanted to do our part."

"Seems like you are creating new problems by trying to solve another one. Are those policemen really the best at soldiering?" said John.

"It seemed like the best course of action at the time. In hindsight, you're probably right."

"I hope this special force you're talking about can keep things more peaceful. Last night, the group of Irishmen went and tore up houses in Bucktown. They threw rocks through windows and shot at houses. They set one of the whore houses on fire. Beat up any Colored man that was on the street. It doesn't seem like the police are too worried about what goes on down there. Crowds busted out all the windows in the African Methodist Church."

"I know the police arrested about eight white men," said Max. "It's no excuse, but the rioters were drunk. The mayor will probably swear in more police as soon as he can find men to take the job."

"You think more police is the answer?"

"It can help prevent more destruction of property. We can't have people afraid to walk on the streets."

"What do you think those white men are so angry about? Why do they need to beat up men who are just going about their business?" asked John.

"There's a history here in Cincinnati between the Irish and the Negroes. They all want the jobs on the riverfront working as stevedores and roustabouts. We had another clash back in June. Traffic was already declining on the riverboats due to the railroads, and now the war has reduced it even further. The result is fewer jobs. The Negroes are willing to work for lower wages than the Irish, so some of these men think the best solution is to run the Negroes out of town."

"What else can the Negro do for work? Most of them don't know how to do anything else except work in the fields," said John.

"It's a problem, for sure. I don't know what the answer is."

"Seems like we are on our own. Too many of us can't read and write. The Negro churches—we're teaching men and the young ones as best we can, running our own schools. If we're going to live in cities among the whites, we have to educate ourselves. The only other choice I see is to move out to places like Mr. Watson's farm and be farmers. Those the choices."

"You doing all right, John? Is the barbershop busy enough to pay you to live?"

"Things been all right. I've cut and shaved a lot of soldiers passing through town. They aren't regular customers, but they pay just the same."

"Will you come to dinner?" asked Max.

"Thank you, but I'd rather stay close to home. With all these angry men on the streets, I prefer not to walk the streets at night."

"You heard from your brother and sister?"

"Martha sent me a letter from Canada. They don't have all this war commotion up there. I'm glad they're there for now. I'm still worried about my mammy, though. God only knows what's happening in Mississippi. Union armies were tearing through there too. I hope God is watching over her. If the Union wins this war, maybe she'll be freed."

"I'm beginning to think that could happen," said Max. "When this war started, I thought it was only a political fight about how this country would be governed, but the longer it goes on, I see more hope that a Union victory will end slavery once and for all."

"That's what I'm praying for every day," said John.

#

Max sat at his desk, looking at the list of orders. He was encouraged. He now had enough war-related orders to keep all of his men busy for the foreseeable future.

One of the shop boys knocked on the office doorway. "Max, there's a Mr. Johnson to see you downstairs?"

"John Johnson? A Black man?" said Max.

"No, a gentleman. Says he's a Mr. Aaron Johnson."

"Right. Please send him up."

Max stood as Aaron entered the office. "What brings you here?" asked Max.

"A business matter. One of my clients asked me to seek your assistance," said Aaron.

"How can I be of assistance to an attorney's client?"

"It's a bit of a delicate matter. May I speak confidentially?"

"Of course," said Max.

"I have a client in Alabama who you previously made machinery for his flour mill. He desperately needs repairs and some replacement parts for the mill. It is out of commission, and he is losing income daily, and with the interruption in shipments to the South, his mill is of critical importance to his community."

"I'm sorry, but I can't supply machinery to Southern customers while we are at war. It would be a violation of Union orders."

"The man is not looking to get you into trouble, and he is not asking for new equipment, but he needs some parts."

"Is this for Harold Taylor?" said Max.

"I'm not at liberty to confirm my client."

"I'm sure it is. I've already manufactured the parts, but I can't ship them. I'm sorry."

"Max, I respect your strict adherence to the embargo, and I understand the damage violation of it could do to your reputation. You are a man of honor."

"I appreciate your understanding," said Max. "How did Mr. Taylor come to you with this request?"

"It's a long story but unimportant. Since you've already manufactured the parts, might you do me the favor of selling them to me? I'd be willing to pay you a premium for them."

"I can't do that, knowing you would turn around and deliver them to Taylor."

"It needn't be your concern what happens to them. They're taking up room in your shop. I'm sure you could use the income. I will pay double or triple the price. No record of the transaction need be made," said Aaron.

"I'm sorry, I don't work that way."

"What if they were stolen from your shop, and you could report them as such?"

"That would be dishonest, and I won't commit such a disloyal act against my country. I'm surprised that you would. You also have your reputation to uphold."

"I am a man of business, like you. I serve at the direction of my clients. During these uncertain times, I have to be a little more creative in the range of services I provide," said Aaron.

"I'm surprised you have retained Southern clients at all. We are at war."

"Indeed, we are. And the war has inflicted inconveniences on many. As I said, the nature of my relationship with this client is complicated and beyond what I am at liberty to discuss. Please forgive me if I have offended your loyalties. Forget I asked. How are Annie and Lizzie?"

"They're well, thank you. And Mary and your children?"

"All healthy and doing what they can to sustain as normal a life as they can. I know Mary and Annie see one another regularly in their work together to support our troops."

"Yes, they and the other ladies have made quite an impact. I've been impressed," said Max.

"Mary tells me your wife has a *manly* set of qualities that serve her well in her position."

"I'll pass that compliment along to her."

Aaron smirked. "Very well then, I'll be off. Thank you for the time."

CHAPTER 26

September 1862

The Union forces were defeated near Richmond, Kentucky, just over 100 miles from Cincinnati. The Union suffered more than 5,000 casualties, including 4,000 missing or captured. The Confederate army moved north toward Lexington and Frankfort. Cincinnati, a key supply depot for the military and a major city in the West, was also a prime target. Newspapers reported the Confederate progress into Kentucky, and Cincinnatians read with increasing nervousness as the war moved closer to the Queen City.

#

Monday

Max stood among his fellow city councilmen in the back of the crowded room in the Burnet House Hotel. The mayor had called the emergency meeting with the newly appointed Union general protecting the region to determine the course of action to address the advancing Confederate troops. As the mayor and General Lew Wallace spoke, Max conversed quietly with the other Fifth Ward councilman, Benjamin Eggleston.

Eggleston, a more senior politician and businessman, whispered, "I'm shocked that the army has put General

Wallace in charge of the defense of Cincinnati. His regiment was caught behind Confederate lines and suffered many casualties at Shiloh. Grant removed him from his command."

Max whispered, "I heard it wasn't his fault, but it was due to a miscommunication. He was instrumental in the victory at Fort Donelson. He seems very sharp and is steamrolling mayor Hatch."

Eggleston said, "Well, maybe he should be. Yesterday, Mayor Hatch was talking of surrendering the city."

"I think it is worth discussing," said Max. "Our Union forces at Richmond are newly enlisted and inexperienced. I hate to think of the devastation a determined Confederate army would inflict on our city if our only defense is this inexperienced army."

"You can't be serious. Do you endorse letting the Rebels take the city? Kentucky is already occupied, and Cincinnati is now seriously at risk of falling into Confederate hands."

"Well, if it's occupation versus the destruction of our factories, homes, and churches, then yes," said Max.

"You're in the minority, so I don't recommend you even bring it up as a course of action. It's too late for that. We must now focus on the defense of our citizens and property."

The men in the room quieted as General Wallace spoke, "Gentlemen, your citizens must be made aware that they are threatened by a daring and powerful enemy, but Cincinnati and its neighbors just across the river, Covington and Newport, must be defended. I call on all citizens to actively assist in preparation. Patriotism, duty, honor, and self-preservation call them, and all classes must respond. I order that one—all business be suspended at nine o'clock today. Every business house must be closed. Two—under the direction of the mayor, citizens should assemble in their local public places at ten o'clock, ready to assist. As soon as possible, they will then be assigned their work. This labor ought to be that of love; it must be done. The willing shall be properly credited, and the unwilling promptly visited. The principle adopted is — citizens will provide the labor while soldiers will conduct the battle. Thirdly—ferry boats will cease operation in the river until further notice. Martial law is hereby proclaimed in the three cities, but until they can be relieved by the military, the injunction of this proclamation will be executed by the police."

Council then voted and approved a resolution in support of Wallace's orders. They appointed a committee of three men to coordinate the city's defenses with Wallace's command. Wallace set up his headquarters in a room at the Burnet House. The mayor drafted an order and distributed it to the papers, ordering that all men, citizens or not, should assemble at their voting places to assist in preparing for the defense of the city.

#

Tuesday

John stood with twenty Black men in front of the schoolhouse.

James, a boarding house owner, shook the door handles. "Damn doors are locked. I spoke to the principal this afternoon. He said we could meet in the schoolhouse to organize our home guard unit. I don't know why they're locking us out." He knocked on the door.

"Bang louder," said one of the men.

"There's nobody in there," said John.

"Well, where are we going to meet then? We spread the word to men who wanted to fight to show up here. Now, what do we do?" said James.

"Can I help you, fellas?" a policeman approached with a gun in hand. "The mayor and General Wallace have said, nobody on the streets. What are you all doing here?"

"Officer, we are supposed to be meeting in the school to organize our home guard unit to help with the war," said James.

"A Colored unit?" said the policeman.

"Yes, sir, we want to do our part to defend the city," said James.

"No, no, no. You can't fight for the Union. This is a white man's war. Go on home!" said the officer.

"Sir, I read in the paper. The mayor called for all citizens and aliens," said John.

"Oh, you read in the paper. Aren't you a smart one? Get the hell out of here. He didn't mean you."

"But sir, we just want to do our part."

"Last thing we're going to do is arm a bunch of your kind with guns. Next thing you know, we'd have another riot on our hands. Now get, unless you want to spend the night in jail."

"Let's go," said James.

The men left the schoolyard. "What do we do now?"

"What can we do? It sounds like they don't want us helping the army," said James.

"I'd sure like to do whatever I can to win this war," said John. "This is as close as we've ever come in this country to having white people talking about doing away with slaving. We've got to seize this opportunity before it gets away from us. The abolitionists are being noticed. If the North wins the war, we have a chance at something."

"I don't know what that something is, but I'll fight to see it," said one of the men.

"Me too," said another.

"Problem is, General Wallace put the Cincinnati police in charge of keeping order, and I ain't never met a Cincinnati policeman who was a friend of the Black man," said one.

"You got that right."

"We best be getting home tonight then. Maybe tomorrow we can go to the army headquarters?"

"Yeah, yeah."

"All right. You all be careful."

John and James headed toward their neighborhood. As they crossed a street, two policemen came around the corner and pulled their guns on them.

"Stop right there. Where are you two going?" demanded one of the policemen.

"We're going home. We don't want any trouble, just want to go home," said John.

"No, you're not going home. You're coming with us. Turn around." They pointed their guns. One of the officers tied John's and James's wrists behind their backs with rope.

"Where are you taking us?" asked John.

"Shut up." The officer hit John on the head with his handgun and pushed him down the street.

When they came to a horse stable across from the Catholic Cathedral on Plum Street, the officer opened the gate and shoved the two men inside the stable. John fell to the ground. Twenty Black men were already in the outdoor horse yard. One reached to help him up and untied his hands.

"What is this?" said James. The fenced yard was adjacent to a small barn with stalls for horses. The yard was muddy with a thick layer of straw. Water and feed troughs stood at one end.

"Horse stable yard," said a man inside the yard.

"What are they going to do with us?" asked James.

"Policeman said we're going to work for the army."

"We tried to join the army. They told us the army didn't want Black men," said James.

"He said they'll be taking us to support the troops in the morning."

"These white men are crazy," said John.

"They're mad with war."

"One minute, they told us to go home. We walked around the corner, and another police officer grabbed us and brought us here. How did you get here?" James asked one of the men.

"I was sitting at home, eating my dinner. Policemen busted through my front door, shouting at me. Said I needed to fight for the Union, or they'd shoot me as a Rebel sympathizer. Pulled me out of my house in front of my wife and children. My wife was crying; babies was crying. I said I'll go, just let me get my boots and coat. They said I didn't need boots. I wouldn't be soldiering, just serving the troops. I don't know what that means, but it sounds like I'm right back where I was a few years ago, a slave in Virginia, serving a master."

"I don't understand. The North is free. Why are they doing this?" said John.

"Depends on who you talk to in the North, I guess. Some of the white men hate us as much as the plantation masters of the South. This war is making everything get turned upside down."

John paced along the fence, looking out between the boards at the group of policemen patrolling the street. "No, no, this can't be happening. I'm free. I have my free papers."

"Calm down," said one of the older men.

"I can't be calm," said John. "What are these crazy white men going to do to us? I don't know if they will shoot us or sell us back to somebody in the South. I wanted to help defeat the Confederates, but these men make me wonder what I'm fighting for. Trade one master for another one?"

"Stop your chattering. Nothing we can do about it," said the old man.

The men talked for a while longer, then quieted as night fell. Most stood, leaning against the fence. They designated the far corner as their latrine. John and several others sat on some wooden blocks.

Several hours after dark, two of the policemen opened the gate and stepped inside, guns held against their chests. The men became alert, preparing themselves for the unknown.

"What are you doing?" said one of the officers, looking at John.

"What?" said John.

"Who said you could sit?" The man approached John and kicked the block as John stood to avoid his boot. The other men sitting rose and stepped to the edges of the pen. The officer picked up the blocks and heaved them over the fence. "All of you, squat!"

They looked at the officer.

"I said squat." He cocked his gun, pointing it at them.

The men lowered themselves to a squat position.

"That's better. It's bedtime. This is how you're going to spend the night. I don't want to hear any more talking and no more moving around. Mike, any of 'em stands up, you shoot 'em. We don't need troublemakers in the army. Mike's going to be right outside. Let's have a peaceful night."

The officers left the pen, locking the gate behind them.

John's legs started to burn. He tried shifting his position slightly and flexing his muscles to relieve the pain. He suppressed his groans. He closed his eyes, and his mind raced back to the plantation. He was serving master William in the house; then, he was in Canada with his brother and sister. He imagined a lush hillside, sharing a meal surrounded by smiling friends and family. He tried to stay there in his mind.

CHAPTER 27

Wednesday

Annie, Max, and Marie sat at the dining room table, drinking coffee and poring over the morning newspapers.

Marie said, "It says that General Kirby Smith is marching toward Cincinnati and expects to have 25,000 men by the time he reaches here. Other Confederate forces will join his cavalry on their march northward. Meanwhile, another 15,000 men are moving toward Louisville. My God, what if we don't stop him?"

Max said, "In the two days since Mayor Hatch called for men, 14,000 have already volunteered. Men are coming into the city from all across the North. They know how important Cincinnati is to the Union. General Wallace is working on a defense plan to keep the city protected. He's called for building out defenses all across northern Kentucky. The Confederates will not cross the Ohio River."

"How can you be so sure?" said Marie. "I hear there are troops throughout Kentucky, and as they march north, more Kentuckians aligned with the South are signing up to fight us."

"We will defend the city, Marie. Try not to worry."

"I don't count on anything anymore. This war indiscriminately takes. It took my Hugo. We don't know where Albert is; we haven't received word of him in weeks. He could be dead or captured."

"Or maybe his letters were lost in the mail. Until we know something, try not to think the worst about Albert."

"We're not immune to the war," said Marie. "People here think we are. They read the newspaper reports and casualties lists and talk about numbers like there aren't real men behind the names of those killed or injured. I'm tired of this war and its killing. What's it getting us?"

Annie said, "I know they're real, Marie. I see them in the hospitals. I think people are starting to understand the hard truth. And for those that haven't, this threat to Cincinnati can't be ignored." She started to get up but doubled forward in pain, sitting back in her chair.

"Annie, are you feeling unwell?" asked Max.

"I, uh. No." She took some slow, deep breaths. "Give me a minute."

Max and Marie eyed each other.

Max said, "Annie, why don't you go lie down? You've been running yourself ragged. With the declaration of martial law, the shop is closed today, like all the other businesses. The trains aren't running either, so you can't be expected to go to Camp Dennison."

"I can hire a carriage. The hospitals aren't closing. I need to go."

"Annie, please."

She waved him off and tried to stand again, then sat, crying out in pain.

"You're not going anywhere. Let's get you upstairs."

Max helped her stand and slowly climb the stairs. "What is it?"

"It's cramps. My courses have been delayed, and now they're coming on with a vengeance."

He helped her remove her dress and put on her nightshirt.

"I've started bleeding. Can you get me a rag from the drawer?"

Max handed it to her, then turned away as she put it in place. "I'll ask Marie to bring you some hot tea. She'll check on you. I must go to the firehouse and sign up for the defense militia."

"You're going to fight?" she said.

"Annie, whether I want to or not, I must in this circumstance. It is my duty to protect you, Lizzie, our home, our city."

"Are you sure? Aren't there other things you could do? You're not a soldier."

"I will find a way to contribute without taking up arms, but we need every able-bodied man."

"What will you do, then?" she said.

"I don't know. Whatever they tell me."

"All right. I love you."

She laid her head back and closed her eyes. Max kissed her forehead, then stood until she drifted to sleep.

Max went downstairs and asked Marie to look after Annie.

"I hear some families are leaving the city," said Marie.

"Some with places to go are sending the children and women. Annie wouldn't consider leaving. Do you want to leave?" said Max.

"No, I'll stay to tend to Lizzie and Annie. I can still cook and help feed the soldiers. They're going to need even more. Men are forming militias on every open lot and public space. Even the schoolyards have been commandeered. I've never seen so many men in the streets."

"Thank you, Marie. Hugo would have been proud of you."

#

Max returned home in the early evening. "How's Annie?"

Marie said, "She's getting worse. She mostly slept. I gave her some tea, but she won't eat anything. She has a fever, and the bleeding is heavier."

"Is that normal?" he asked.

"No, it's not normal. Your friend Patrick's wife, Molly, stopped by and went up to talk with her. She told me she thinks that Annie may be miscarrying a baby. She said it has happened to her, and she had the same pains and bleeding."

"No, that's not possible. The doctor told Annie she could never have more children."

"I only know what Molly said."

Max rubbed his hands on his forehead, then back through his hair several times. He closed his eyes.

"Do you want something to eat? I'm going to feed Lizzie," said Marie.

"Yes, thank you. I'll see to Annie."

He entered their bedroom quietly and sat on the bed, watching her sleep. She stirred, moaned, and then opened her eyes.

"Max," said Annie.

"Hi." He gently pushed her curls from her face and rubbed her cheek gently with his thumb.

"How did it go? Are you in the army now?"

"Sort of. I will be tomorrow."

"You'll do the right thing, whatever needs to be done."

"Just like you do," he said.

"I'm not going to be able to go to the hospital."

"You should rest. Someone else will look after the men. You need to take care of yourself. Marie told me what Molly said—that you might be miscarrying a child?"

"I think so, yes," said Annie.

"Did you suspect you were pregnant?"

"Yes, for a few weeks now."

Max thought for a moment. "You should have rested more. All this running back and forth to the hospital and your meetings…"

"I didn't want it to get in the way of what I needed to do. So many men have given so much, so many have given their lives," she said.

"Why didn't you tell me? About the baby?" he said.

Annie sighed deeply. "I didn't want it to be so. I was hoping I wasn't."

"If God blessed us with another child, it would be a miracle, especially since we didn't think it was possible. How could you not want that?"

Annie said, "I think God realized that the timing wasn't right to give us another child in the middle of a war."

Max considered pursuing his questioning but accepted it was moot. "How is the pain?"

"It comes and goes. Molly said it could be several days before everything is out."

"Do you want me to bring a doctor?"

"No, I don't need a man interfering with what my body needs to do."

"Are you sure? A midwife, then?" said Max.

"If the pain gets too bad, I'll send Marie to get me something from the druggist."

Max kissed her forehead and stroked her arm. "I'm afraid to leave you, but I must go tonight." He lay on the bed next to her.

"I thought you were leaving tomorrow?" she said.

"I'll be sworn in tomorrow. Tonight, I'm going down to the river. General Wallace has asked Wesley Cameron to oversee building a pontoon bridge across the river to Kentucky. I'm going to help with that. We need a way for the troops to cross. Too bad Roebling's bridge isn't built yet; we could sure use it."

"It sounds like something right up your alley. You go. I'll see through this," she said.

"It doesn't feel right, leaving you here in this condition."

"We've never felt the need to have the other clinging by our side. Now is not the time to start. We both have much to do."

"Seeing you in so much pain—I wish I could help you… do something for you."

"Go. There's nothing that you can do." She forced a smile and closed her eyes.

He watched her for several minutes after she fell asleep. He kissed her forehead and slipped from the room.

#

Max met architect Wesley Cameron and several local builders on the levee. A crew of men carried lumber from carts on Front Street and piled it near the riverbank. Dozens more stood around talking, awaiting instructions.

Wesley ordered, "Saw those boards to a length of forty-five feet; the bridge needs to be wide enough to accommodate the width of two wagons. Stack the boards as close to the river as possible."

Max studied a row of coal barges moored on the river. "How do you plan to secure the barges?" he asked Wesley.

"We'll use the barges' anchors, but I don't know if that will be enough against the current."

"I can have some makeshift anchors forged if you need them." said Max.

"How soon?"

"I can get a couple of men working on them right away. We can have them by tomorrow."

"Do it," Wesley said. "We can add them after the bridge is built to ensure it doesn't drift."

"I have spools of heavy wire if you think that's needed to tie them together?" said Max.

"Bring them. We'll nail the planks to the hulls of the barges. That should be enough to keep them from drifting, but we'll use it if we start to see too much movement. We won't know for sure until troops and wagons start moving across it.

"How many nails did we find?" Wesley asked.

One of the builders replied, "We cleaned out every hardware merchant in town this afternoon. We should have plenty."

"We're still short a few barges. Does anyone know where we might find more?" said Wesley.

"The coal yard up the Licking River has several," said a man.

"Send some men across the river in a boat and get them," instructed Wesley.

"No one is there at this hour," objected one of the men.

Wesley ordered, "Take them. If you encounter any trouble, tell them General Wallace ordered they be used for the bridge."

Wesley spoke to the assembled men. "If we can get the barges in place and enough planks to allow workers to traverse the river, we can put three crews to work on nailing. Tim and Eddy, start positioning the barges and anchor them down. Max, Elliot, and Steven, can you supervise the nailing of the planks? Spacing between should be one to one and a half inches."

The sounds of construction filled the riverfront. Men maneuvered the barges into a line across the river, shouting instructions. A man fell into the river, and shouting and laughing echoed to shore. Max organized a line of men to carry the boards to piles at points across the skeletal structure, and the nailing began. Spectators stood on both riverbanks to watch the unprecedented project.

The men worked all night and into the next day. More spectators came to see the new bridge, built just east of the tall pillars of the unfinished suspension bridge. With the river now blocked, naval steamboat patrols intercepted river traffic and diverted it to the public landing.

After noon, Max bid farewell to the crews still nailing planks at his end of the new bridge. He stopped to talk with Wesley. "It's a fine piece of engineering. Last night, I wouldn't have believed we could do it so quickly."

"You doubted us?" said Wesley.

"Yesterday, there was nothing. Today, you've created a path for the defense of the Queen of the Union. You're a hero," said Max.

"I wouldn't go that far. I'm glad I could be of service. General Wallace came down this morning to inspect it and was impressed. He said it took weeks to build the pontoon bridge at Paducah, Kentucky."

"Look, they're already lining up to cross it," said Max, pointing to hundreds of men standing and sitting with their companies all along the riverfront. Walnut and Vine Streets were full of men as well.

"I'm off to my regiment. I'll salute you as we cross," said Max.

"Thank you," said Wesley. "You were a huge help." They shook hands. "God be with you."

#

Thursday

"How is she?" Max asked Marie as soon as he stepped through his front door. Lizzie ran to him, and he picked her up and kissed her. "How is my darling? What's this? You're covered in flour!"

"I'm helping Marie make biscuits for the soldiers," said Lizzie.

"You are a helpful patriot. Doing your part. Daddy helped build a bridge across the river so the soldiers can march into Kentucky. Maybe Marie can take you to see it this week."

Marie said to Lizzie, "Will you go in the kitchen and count the biscuits for me? Let's tell Papa how many we've baked."

Lizzie ran off to the kitchen.

"She's in the worst of it, I think. I slept by her bedside. She woke crying out in pain several times. I've changed her dressings. She's miscarrying for certain."

"Marie, I don't know what to do." He looked to his sister for solace, uncomfortable being in a position where he wasn't in control. "Is she going to live through this?"

"I don't know. I haven't been through anything like this before," said Marie. "I think so. Molly survived it."

"Jesus, please," prayed Max, eyes closed.

Marie hugged him. "She's strong. She'll survive."

Max went to Annie. He didn't wake her but washed up and changed his clothes. He sat on the bed. Her hair stuck to her face with sweat; her chest rose and fell with labored breath. He lay down next to her and fell asleep. He woke several hours later to her groaning. He wet a washcloth and placed it on her forehead. She opened her eyes briefly and then fell back to sleep. He kissed her goodbye and went downstairs.

"Thank you for taking care of her. You're a saint, Marie."

"We're all doing our part. I warmed you some soup to eat before you go."

He sat and told her of the bridge building and activity happening on the riverfront. "Thousands of men are already lining up to cross over it." When he finished the soup, he sat Lizzie on his lap. "Well, little lady, I need you to be brave and help Marie take care of Mama. Let her sleep; that's what she needs most right now."

"Are you going to fight the Rebs?" asked Lizzie.

Oskar came in from outside and stood in the kitchen doorway, listening to their exchange.

Max said, "I'm going to help build the forts to keep the Rebels away from Cincinnati so we will all be safe."

"Are you going to be a soldier like the ones in the streets?" said Lizzie.

"I'm not going to shoot a gun, but I will assist the soldiers."

"I'm going with you," said Oskar.

"Oskar, we've discussed this," said Max.

Oskar said, "The mayor and General Wallace have called for all able-bodied men to defend the city. Would you deny them and me my right to serve my country? The college is closed. I won't sit and do nothing. Let me come with you to work on the defenses, or I will join another ward's militia."

"You're ready for manual labor?"

"It's old men like you that should be worried about manual labor."

"Fine, go get the shovel from the basement."

Oskar hurried downstairs with a broad smile and a spring in his step.

Max gave Lizzie a hug and kiss, then hugged Marie. "Thank you. Please take care of her."

"She'll get through this," said Marie.

Marie hugged Oskar and handed him a bundle wrapped in cloth. "Some food for you two."

CHAPTER 28

Oskar stood on Vine Street in front of the firehouse, talking and joking with a group of volunteers. After several hours of waiting, a man came out of the building and announced, "Men, we are awaiting Captain Emery's arrival from headquarters. As soon as he returns, we'll march to Kentucky." He went back inside, and they continued talking. They moved to the side as another regiment of men walked past them in a haphazard formation.

Finally, several men, including Max, came outside. One stood on a wooden crate, and the men gathered around him.

"Men of the Fifth Ward, I am Captain George Emery and will serve as your commander of Company B. On behalf of General Wallace, I thank you for your service. You've taken an oath of allegiance to your country and your God. May he watch over us as we do his work to defend our community. Some of you choose to bear arms, and some the shovel. We need all of you to succeed in our mission—to prevent the Confederates from advancing from Kentucky into Ohio.

"We have requested muskets and ammunition from the armory, but none is currently available. We will march to our position with what you have and reinforce you with additional arms as they are delivered to us. Right now, our priority is to support the construction of the defenses of Cincinnati. The army has cannons on Mount Adams and Price Hill and armored steamships patrolling the river as a final line of defense." He held up a hand-drawn map of the

Ohio River and the areas south in Kentucky. "We are building a line of defense several miles south of the city to repel any Rebel troops that march toward the city. The army engineer has planned twenty-three batteries east and west of Fort Mitchel. Between those will be a series of rifle pits and trenches where men can take cover during an attack from the south. To man the fortifications, we now have over 20,000 volunteers to supplement the militias in the area. Our company's mission is to clear the land to construct a battery east of Fort Mitchel. We'll also dig trenches and rifle pits between it and the next battery in a line about a quarter-mile long."

Captain Emery continued shouting, "We're going to march down to the river, across the pontoon bridge, and up the Kentucky hills about six miles, just east of the fort. Right now, we need every man to help construct the fortifications. Now is the time for shovels and pickaxes. Soon enough, you'll need your arms. We've three men who will supervise crews of fifteen to twenty men each. Consider them your commanding officers for this mission." He introduced the men, who nodded. "Arthur Lang, William Martin, and Max Mueller.

"Fifth Ward, Company B, line up."

The men formed lines in the street.

Max pulled Oskar aside. "I need you to go to the stables where we keep the horses for the shop. Take a man with you, saddle up two horses, and meet us down on the riverfront."

Oskar said, "Mike, can you manage a horse?'"

"Yes."

"Let's go."

The leaders claimed the men who would make up their crews and attempted to put them in straight lines.

Captain Emery ordered, "Forward march."

The men walked south on Vine Street, carrying shovels, pickaxes, other tools, and rifles over their shoulders. Some cheered, excited to finally be in motion.

A crowd of women and children stood at one of the corners, "God bless you, men!"

"Hurrah for the Union!"

"Mr. Mueller," one of the ladies shouted. "We're so proud of you."

The man marching next to Max said, "Who is that?"

"I've no idea," said Max.

"She's a pretty lady. Maybe you should ask her for a sendoff kiss."

"My wife is waiting for me at home. Do you have a wife?" said Max.

"Me no, I'd take a sendoff kiss. Who knows if I'll ever be in the arms of a woman again?"

Another man said, "I'd be happy with a sendoff whiskey. I can't believe General Wallace shut down the saloons…deprive us of one last drink."

A man from behind tapped him on the shoulder and handed him a corked bottle. "Here you go."

"Why, thank you, kind sir. I won't die unsatisfied after all." He took the bottle, drank a swig and handed it back.

Along the street, a young boy and girl offered apples from a basket. Ladies waved flags and cheered the men. The crowd created a party-like atmosphere.

As they approached the Fifth Street market, Captain Emery shouted, "Halt." The men bumped into each other as their forward momentum was interrupted by a large crowd spreading out from the market. A line of men snaked back and forth into the street.

A woman wearing a sash that read "Sanitary Commission" approached the captain. "Sir, if your men would like a meal, please have them join the line here."

"Thank you, ma'am, but we're local volunteers. Most of my men have recently eaten at home. You've got thousands to feed. We'll let you feed the men who have traveled from other parts. Men, let's move on to the riverfront."

Another woman asked, "How about blankets then? Any of you men need a blanket—for sleeping?"

Several men who hadn't brought anything took one and put them over their shoulders or in their bags.

The company pushed past the market, reassembled into its sloppy formation, and started down the street to the riverfront. Crowds stood on both sides, cheering for them as they marched past. When they reached the bank, Max reunited with Oskar and assigned two experienced riders to mount the horses. The men stood pressed together, awaiting their turns to march across the river. A band played music. The tinclad steamships moved slowly up and down the river, with their cannons pointed at the shore.

"Move out," shouted Captain Emery.

The men marched behind a company of men dressed in farmer's clothes. Some wielded shotguns and other non-military weapons.

"Look at that, would you?" said Oskar. "He's wearing a cap made from an animal skin. I heard there were a bunch of squirrel hunters joining up."

"Squirrel hunters?" said a man marching ahead of him.

"That's what they're calling the volunteers from the farms. They've come in from Kentucky, Indiana, and upstate Ohio. They traveled by train from all over to help defend the line. I met a few of them yesterday. They were exploring the city, looking for an open saloon," said Oskar.

"It's probably just as well they ordered the saloons closed, with those boys running around town with their rifles."

"Those boys are going to help save us. I don't have anything against a squirrel hunter. They may not be used to our ways and talk a little funny, but they're on the same side of this fight," said Oskar.

As they moved onto the pontoon bridge, the sound of footsteps on the wooden planks rose above the conversation. The men quieted as they minded their feet on the bobbing bridge and felt the sense they were crossing from the familiarity of home into the unknown of the war. When they reached Covington, another crowd of cheering supporters lined the street on both sides. Ladies waved handkerchiefs and called to them from second-story windows. "God bless you, boys!"

They heard shouting on the curb ahead, "Negro lovers!"

"Union yellow bellies," another shouted.

Several squirrel hunters broke from their line and started attacking the shouting men, swinging fists and gun butts. The hecklers fought back. The long line of soldiers stopped behind the scuffle.

Two squirrel hunters held a man by the arms while a third punched him several times. "Let's marshal this one into service for the Union."

"Yeah, a prisoner of war, you traitor."

"Let him go," shouted the heckler's companion.

"What are you going to do about it?" said the squirrel hunter.

"You can't conscript him. Kentucky is neutral."

"The hell with that. Let's see how he likes being a slave to the Union army."

"Let me go. It's not right."

The squirrel hunter's captain stepped in, "Let him go."

Several from their company pulled the squirrel hunters back from the crowd.

The squirrel hunter captain shouted, "Save it for the Confederate army."

They shoved the man into the crowd and rejoined their formation. The line started moving again.

Captain Emery shouted, "Forward March. Steady men, they're not worth your trouble." They marched past the Rebel sympathizers, ignoring the continued taunts.

They marched up the muddy road. When they reached the summit, Max turned and looked back at the river and across to Cincinnati. The public landing was flooded with men, stretching from the bridge up into town. Max remembered seven years earlier when he and Annie spent the Fourth of July on the Covington hilltop and watched the city ablaze in fireworks. He prayed the city would be spared the fireworks of battle. He again thought of Annie, lying in pain at home, hoping her suffering would end soon without catastrophe. He hoped this would not be the last time he saw his hometown.

They headed east from the main road on a newly created dirt lane along tree-covered hills and valleys.

They passed another regiment of men clearing trees and digging a long trench. They had built up a tall mound of dirt and stacked tree branches and trunks in a pile behind it. The captain said, "Take a look. This is what we need to do. The rifle pits must be chest-deep to protect us when firing and wide enough to allow a second man behind the shooter."

They walked a little farther. "Halt. Men, this is us," said Captain Emery. "We first have to clear this area of trees, then construct the battery, rifle pits, and trenches to the east to Carlisle battery. We have a few hours of daylight left today, so let's use it. Bragg's army could be here within a day or two."

Max took command of his eighteen men, including Oskar. "We'll start here and work east. I'll leave the map here, under this rock. Those of you with shovels, start on the rifle pit. If you have an ax, start on the trees." He walked a few yards and pointed to a man with an ax. "Mark this one," he said, pointing to a large maple. "This one, this one." He continued down a line. The men began to work.

The sound of axes, shovels, and grunts replaced the parade's laughter and chatter.

Oskar moved several yards away from the other men and started digging. Max gave instructions, directing them where to dig and place the dirt.

One of the older men wielding a pickaxe took several dozen swings at the ground, barely loosening the dirt. He stood up, "Christ, this ground is hard. I can't do this."

Oskar walked over to him, "Would you be able to shovel the dirt if I loosen it?"

"Yes, I think I can do that."

Oskar nodded and held out his shovel, trading the man for his pickaxe.

"Thank you, son."

Oskar attacked the earth. After half an hour, he stood and removed his soaked shirt. His shoulder, arm, and chest muscles bulged as he worked like a machine.

One of the men said, "You're Max's brother?"

"Uh-huh," said Oskar as he continued to swing.

"You're not cut from the same mold, you two."

"He's just gone a bit soft. Spends too much time talking," said Oskar.

"You're about the same height but twice his size."

"I practice in the gymnasium."

"Practice what?"

"Gymnastics with the Turner Society—up over the Rhine. You know it?"

"No."

"It's a club for German men. We focus on physical fitness and fellowship. I compete in gymnast competitions in the rings, wrestling, and weightlifting events."

"Why aren't you with the 9th—the German regiment?"

"I was told I'm too young."

"How old are you?"

"Seventeen."

"You seem old enough to me, but I'm glad you're here. Hell, I don't even care that you're a Dutchman. In this fight, German, Irish, English—we're all Americans. We could use a few more like you. You're strong as an ox."

As the sun set, one by one the men set their tools down and sat on the ground, spent. Oskar continued to work alone, still pounding with his pickaxe.

"Brother, you should quit for tonight. Get some rest," said Max.

Oskar stopped and stood, letting his arms fall to rest. "We've got a long way to go. The Confederates could be here any day now."

"I know, but rest tonight. Tomorrow will be a long day."

"Fine then." He picked up his shirt and put it on.

"You've made quite an impression on the men. They said you're doing the work of two men. They like you," said Max.

"You surprised by that?"

"Well, I wouldn't have thought."

"Thought what? That your little brother can't do a man's work? Get along with men from all walks of life?"

"I guess I never thought of you that way," said Max.

"I'm not the ten-year-old boy you handed over to the Jesuits at school anymore."

"I see that."

"I can think and do for myself."

"I'm sorry. I underestimated you, but I still forbid you to enlist to fight. Papa isn't here, and I take responsibility for you until you're of age."

"That will be next year. Then I'm not your worry anymore."

"I'm proud of who you've become as a man. Finish your education. Don't let this war rob you of that or more," said Max.

"I'm proud to be here doing what I can. Next year, if this war is still on, I'm enlisting to fight."

"I'm glad to have you in the company. Let's go grab some food before we turn in."

They walked over to a campfire. The men ate salt pork, hardtack biscuits, with coffee to dunk and soften them in.

One of the men asked, "This all we have to eat?"

"For tonight," said Captain Emery. "Maybe we'll see some supplies and the guns we need tomorrow."

"That company down there," said a man. "They commandeered themselves a Negro to cook for them. I heard he made soup."

Max said, "What do you mean *commandeered?*"

The man laughed, "My buddy said his captain has a friend on the police force who delivered him to their company yesterday. The police rounded up a bunch of Black men and brought them over to support the troops. Told them they could either serve the army or be shot."

"These men freedmen?" asked Max.

"Well, yeah, they were all from Cincinnati."

"That's not right," said Max.

"I don't know. This is war and shit, the Blacks got more to gain from this war than any of us. They ought to be willing to support the war."

"Every man who's in the Union army so far has volunteered. There's no draft," said Max.

"Yet!" one of the men interjected.

"Yet!" agreed Max. "So it's not right that any man, Black or white, should be forced to work for the army against his will."

"I heard that some of the troops are making Confederate sympathizers work for them in the camps," said a man.

"I don't know anything about that," said Max. "But bringing a Black man against his will into Kentucky puts that man's freedom at risk. If they catch a Black man supporting the Union army here, God only knows what they'd do to him."

"I guess getting us our own Black cook is out the question?" said a man.

"Out of the question on my part," said Max. "Captain Emery, you support me on this?"

"Yes, we can take care of our own. There will be no slaves in my company. If you want soup, one of you needs to cook it."

Captain Emery said, "We'll assemble at sunrise tomorrow, men. Get some rest."

The men spread out to sleep. Some laid down near the fire. Oskar found a grassy spot with some of his new friends.

CHAPTER 29

As his men settled in for the night, Max walked in the moonlight along the path to the Fourteenth Ward company's camp. He approached their campfire. "Good evening, men."

A few grunted.

"Who are you? You a Confederate?" one of them said.

"No, I'm Max Mueller. I'm with Fifth Ward, Company B—we're working on the Hooper battery west of here."

"Hi, Max," said Michael Flynn, a stonecutter that Max knew from his business. He stood and shook hands with Max. "How is your company faring?"

"We just arrived today. Made good initial progress. How about you?" said Max.

"Been here a couple of days. We have a group of dedicated men. The laborers are the most valuable to us right now. They're used to the hard work."

"Might I have a word with you?" said Max, leading him away from the other men.

"What is it?"

"I heard you have a cook for your camp, a Black man?"

"Yes, Cookie, we call him," said Michael.

"You're eating better than we are, I suspect. We had biscuits and salt pork."

"Oh. You looking to use him?"

"No, I'm concerned that he's a freedman that was forced into servitude," said Max.

"Well, I couldn't say what his situation is, but he seemed amenable to doing the cooking, from what I saw."

"Could you take me to him?"

"You're not going to mess up a good thing we have going here, are you?" said Michael.

"I'd just like the opportunity to talk to the man. It doesn't sound right, forcing him into service."

"I don't think you should trouble yourself. It's not your concern."

"As a councilman, It's my duty to understand what circumstances led to his being here. If the city police were acting improperly, I want to know. Please, Michael."

"I think he's this way."

They walked to the top of a ridge where men lay on their blankets. "Cookie?" Michael called out in a lowered voice.

"Yes, sir?"

"Can you come over here?"

Max saw the silhouette of the man approaching. As the moonlight lit his face, Max recognized him. "John!"

"Max!"

They embraced.

"My God. How did you get here?" said Max.

Michael said, "You two know each other?"

Max said, "Yes. He's a friend. Can you leave us? I'll see him back. Thank you, Michael."

When they were alone, Max said, "John, are you all right?"

"I'm doing as best as can be expected. It's been a frightful couple of days."

"Tell me, please."

John relayed the story of his attempt to volunteer, seizure, and incarceration by the police, and then forced assignment to serve as cook and camp assistant. "I feel like my freedom is slipping away from me. I want to fight for the Union, but not like this."

"It's not right," said Max. "You and your friends were trying to do the right thing, and rogue policemen are making their own rules. I'm sorry. I'll make some inquiries tomorrow.

I don't believe the army command sanctions what they're doing to you."

"This world is full of nonsense. I don't know what to make of it. Where I fit?" said John.

"We're all feeling a little of that. I'm glad you're all right. How are they treating you?"

"These men are all right. They're glad to have a cook and someone to do the shit work. Some of them laugh with me. They call me Cookie."

"You're a good man," said Max. "You have a better attitude about all this than I would."

"I make the best of it, or I get shot. I think I'm in a better position than some of the others. Some of those men digging must feel like they've been pulled back onto the plantation. Their worst nightmare come true."

"I'm glad you're safe here. Be careful. If the Rebels get their hands on you, they'll be brutal."

"I know that," said John. "That's why I'm doing my part with these men."

Max put his hand on John's shoulder. "I never dreamed we'd end up in a war like this. We must prevail."

John nodded his head in agreement. "How are you doing? Where are you working?"

"I'm with the next company down. My brother Oskar is with me."

"He a soldier now, is he? Got his wish?" said John.

"No, he's a civilian volunteer. There's a difference."

"Miss Annie at home with Lizzie?"

"Yes. They're fine, I pray."

"Good, good. She's a strong, virtuous woman. She helping the wounded soldiers, sending the supplies. She's one of the most active ladies I've ever seen."

Max started to speak, then suppressed a sob by covering his mouth with his hand.

"What is it?" said John.

Max shook his head no.

"What's wrong?"

"Oh, God, John. Annie, she's sick. I had to leave her alone, in bed. She's bleeding, and I don't know if I'll see her again. I didn't want to, but I had to leave her."

John put his hands on Max's shoulders and then hugged him. Max pulled back, wiping his eyes.

"I'm sorry," said John. "I'll pray Miss Annie will be all right."

"Thank you. I should go. You take care of yourself."

"I've been doing that my whole life," said John.

Max returned to his camp and found an isolated spot over a hilltop. He spread his blanket on the ground, sat, removed his boots, and lay back, using his satchel for a pillow. He looked up at the bright moon and the star-filled sky, which seemed to hold even more stars this distance from the city smoke and lights. The only sounds were the chirping of insects and the occasional cough. Max closed his eyes and began his nightly examen, a Jesuit method of reflection and prayer that he had practiced since his days at Saint Xavier. He prayed for John and the other Negroes forced to serve. He prayed for Annie and wished that he were with her but knew that leading these men to prepare the fortifications for the city was where he needed to be tonight. He accepted his role in the war effort defending the city.

It was easy to lose sight of the war's purpose, but the original objectives didn't matter anymore. He was called to defend his home against an enemy that would be ruthless in its destruction and killing. He wondered how many soldiers fighting in the war were fighting for the cause versus just fighting to defeat the enemy before them and stay alive.

Now that the war had started, how would they stop it? Would one side come to see the other's point of view? Would one side admit the senselessness of it all and concede? Would one side defeat the other's army by killing hundreds of thousands of men until there were no more men to sacrifice?

What would he do next? When the pits were dug and the fortifications built, would he pick up a rifle? Could he shoot a man pointing a weapon at him? Could he stab a man as he ran over the top of the dirt hill and jumped into his hole? Could he defend himself? Could he kill? Would his killing of a man make a difference in the war? Would he need to kill two men? Three? How many? If he didn't fight and kill, would he be complicit in the slaughter of Cincinnati, his beloved home?

He lay on the blanket in the warm, humid night and tried to sleep. He was haunted by a vision of men running across a field toward him in his trench. He shot, and as soon as one soldier fell, another would appear on the horizon, running toward him. He had to keep firing. He knew if he stopped firing, stopped killing, he would be killed.

He lay awake, wondering when they would come and what he would do. Max didn't know how to shoot a gun. How many other men, who answered the call to defend the city, had never shot a gun? Would they be able to defeat the determined men of the Confederacy?

Sleep finally silenced his mind some time near dawn.

#

Friday

Max woke to a bugler playing reveille in the distance. He put his boots on and walked back to the fire, joining men in various stages of alertness. He wondered how many suffered from the same lack of sleep and similar dreams.

"Coffee and hardtack biscuits again? That's it?" complained a man.

"What were you expecting? Eggs and bacon? Griddlecakes?" said another.

"Something else."

"Quit your grumbling. It's the army."

"I'll send a message to the Sanitary Commission. See if they can provide something. For this morning, I'm afraid it's all we have," said Max. "Our goal is to complete our section of the defenses within three days. I ask you to work as hard as possible but take a break when necessary."

Max walked down the path and found Oskar, now using a shovel, already waist-deep in a trench section. "Good morning, brother. How did you sleep?"

"Good morning. I slept fine. You?"

"Not much."

"You're worried about Annie?" said Oskar.

"Yes, among other things."

"I'm sure it's difficult, not knowing how she is."

"You've made good progress already. Nice work."

Max greeted the rest of the men, then went to Captain Emery's tent and spoke with him. He sat at the captain's table and drafted two letters. He wrote a letter to Mr. Burnet, the president of the Sanitary Commission, explaining their situation and the company's needs. Then, he drafted a letter to Captain Wallace, the commander in charge of the Cincinnati defense, making him aware of the treatment of the Negro men the police had taken. He had Captain Emery sign that letter. He pulled one of the older men in the group aside. "Stevens, right?"

"Yes."

"Are you comfortable riding a horse to Cincinnati and back today?"

"Yes, of course."

"Deliver this letter to Captain Wallace. His headquarters have moved to Covington. Take this letter to Mr. Burnet in his office at the Mechanics Institute. Ask him if they have anything you can bring back with you right away. I've requested they send a wagonload of food to supply the companies along this ridge, but that might take a day or more."

Max and Stevens walked to the fortification site, where men were using one of the horses to pull a stump from the ground. "Where's the other horse?" Max asked. One of the men pointed down the path. Max convinced the crew to give up the horse for a few hours in the hope that the message would yield better food today.

Max picked up a shovel and began digging. He worked all day, taking breaks to walk up and down the line, encouraging the men and providing direction. One of his men collapsed from heat exhaustion in the heat and humidity. The men labored with few breaks, their hands unaccustomed to the work, plagued by blisters.

His courier returned with two saddlebags of food from the Sanitary Commission. The commission promised to bring a wagon of food by dinner. Max walked among the men sprawled under shade trees eating the improved lunch.

"Thank you for getting us the food, Max," said Martin, a bookseller in his late thirties.

"All I did was ask. You can thank the Sanitary Commission."

"You've got special connections with the Sanitary Commission, don't you? Your wife runs one of the Circles. Did she send us this?"

"No, I went straight to the top—president of the commission. The commission cares about the welfare of the men serving our country."

"Your wife. She's Annie, right? She's that women's movement lady," said one of the men.

"Yes, that's her," said Max.

"Well, I used to think those women were crackpots, but now they look like the smart ones. More women are working in factories. Many have to keep their houses and care for their families while their husbands are away at war. Some of them are lost. They don't know what to do without their husbands by their sides."

"Your wife's probably fine with you being gone, isn't she, Max?" said another.

"She's a capable woman, but I like to believe she misses me all the same. You married?"

"Fifteen years," said the man.

"How did your wife feel about you leaving?"

"She was pretty concerned reading the papers, knowing the Rebs were coming. She cried when I left, but gave me a going away roll in the hay so that just may have made it all worthwhile."

Another man piped in, "My wife didn't give me nothing. She took the children and skedaddled up to Medina county, where her family has a farm. How about you, Jonesy?"

"I'm not married. My girl didn't give me a roll either. She said if we fight off the Rebels and win this war, she'll marry me. Then we can have a roll. She's a good Catholic girl."

"You're dating a Catholic? Is her family taking their political direction from the pope?"

Jonesy said, "I don't know. I don't think it matters anymore. It used to be the Catholics, Irish, and Germans were the evil to be cast out. Now it's the Negroes, abolitionists, or Southerners. The way I see it—we're all just people. The politicians and the newspapers put labels on people to convince us to think like them so they can advance their position."

"You got that right, Jonesy. And this war is the biggest move ever to try to get half of us to succumb to the other half. All of us fighting this war are pawns in the politicians' game. Ol' Abe, he says we have to preserve the Union. Look at what the war has done to this country—all those dead soldiers in the battles at Bull Run, Pittsburg Landing, Mill Springs. Abe fooled us into this war, and now we're in it. No going back."

"You think this war is worth dying for?" one of the men said.

"Yes, I do," said Martin. "Those bastard Southerners have been milking this country with their slaves long enough. As soon as it looked like they wouldn't be able to keep their ways, they leave this country and attack us. We can't let men attack our people over something they don't like. If I have to die, so my children have the same America with the opportunities that I have, I'll do it. How about you, Max?"

"What's that?" said Max.

"You think this war is worth dying for?"

"I have to agree. I'll defend my family, even if I have to give my life for them. But we all must do that in a way our conscience allows."

"What do you mean?"

"I have to stand before God and be judged for my actions here on earth, and I intend to honor Him and do the best I can."

"We all have to do that," said Martin.

"That we do," said Max. "Men, let's get back to work. We still have a ways to go on our line, and the Rebels aren't waiting for us to finish."

#

After dark, Max went to check on John. He entered the Fourteenth Ward's camp and saw no sign of him. "Anyone seen Michael Flynn?"

"Who's asking?"

"Max Mueller, from Fifth Ward camp. I'm a friend of his."

"He's down by those trees, I think. Turned in already."

"Thank you."

Max stood at the edge of the line of trees. "Michael Flynn?"

"Here."

"It's Max Mueller. Sorry to disturb your sleep. Might we speak briefly?"

Michael came into the moonlight. "Max. How did you do today?"

"We made good progress. I'm a little sore in the back and shoulders, though."

"Me as well. I'm surprised how comfortable the ground feels. I heard you were the one that requested the food and supplies from the Sanitary Commission. We're all grateful."

"I just sent a message. The commission is a godsend, aren't they?" said Max.

"Hard to believe the army doesn't support our troops better."

"I don't think commissioned units are so bad off. This emergency call of men to action is an anomaly. General Wallace is doing a tremendous job, given the circumstances."

Michael shrugged. "I hope you're right, for the boys in blue's sake."

"I wanted to check in on your cook, John. Do you know where he is?"

"Cookie's gone."

"Gone where?" said Max.

"A General Dickson came into our camp today and ordered our captain to hand him over. He took Cookie and a bunch of Negroes back to Cincinnati. Dickson said that General Wallace ordered him to address the mistreatment of Negroes."

"General Dickson. Is that William Martin Dickson, the judge? He's been a vocal abolitionist for years."

"The same. Wallace made him a general and put him in charge of forming new regiments of Black volunteers."

"Black regiments? In the Union army?"

"That's what he said."

"Well, I'll be," said Max. "You lost your cook?"

"One of the men volunteered to take over the duty. He said it was better than digging holes."

"Thanks. Sorry to disturb you. Have a good night."

CHAPTER 30

By the time they crossed the pontoon bridge back into Cincinnati, almost five hundred Black men were gathered from the various regiments working on the defenses in northern Kentucky. White soldiers curiously watched the parade, led by General Dickson. The men taught each other songs to lift their spirits and keep them moving. A version of "John Brown's Body," a recent popular song, became one of the favorite cadence march songs. They sang to the tune of "Battle Hymn of the Republic:" "We're done with hoeing cotton, we're done with hoeing corn. We're Colored Yankee soldiers just as sure as you were born…."

They marched up to the makeshift Black Brigade headquarters at Sixth and Broadway. General Dickson addressed the men on the street.

"I am General Dickson. Under the orders of General Wallace, I will form and lead the Black Brigade of Cincinnati. Our mission will be to support the defense of this city, your city, in non-combat duties. Many of you were forced into service this week in a degrading and unjust manner, against your will. I apologize for the treatment you endured. The Black Brigade will be your opportunity to serve the Union in our fight for a unified, free United States. Should you choose to enlist, you will be assigned fatigue duty either here in the city, on one of the riverboats, or in the camps across the river."

The assembled men listened intently as Dickson shouted his address. "There is much work to be done, and your work is important to our cause. It has been a long day, with more long days to come. Go home tonight and say a proper goodbye to your families, returning here for assembly and assignment to duty at 5:00 in the morning. All Negroes are encouraged to report for duty, and my commitment to you is to treat you with the respect due a soldier in the army. You will be paid one dollar per day, the same as the white volunteers, for your service. May God be with you and your families, and may he bless the United States. You are dismissed."

John went home and spread the word about the Black Brigade to his neighbors.

He asked his friend, Charlie, to accompany him across town to visit Annie at home. Marie greeted them in the foyer.

"I'm sorry to bother you so late, Miss Marie. I wanted to see about Miss Annie's health. I saw Max working on the ridge yesterday. He told me she was feeling poorly. Tomorrow, I'm going back across the river and will try to take word to Max."

"Oh, John, thank you. How is Max?"

"He's doing right, like always. He's worried about Miss Annie, though. It's hurting his heart to be apart from her. Oh, I beg your pardon. This is my friend Charlie."

Charlie, hat in hand, was looking around at the elegant home. "Evening ma'am."

"Has there been any fighting with the Rebels?" asked Marie.

"No, the army is digging rifle pits and building batteries. It seems like all the men in Cincinnati are across the river building the defense. I think we'll be good and ready for them when they come."

"What about Oskar?"

"I didn't see him. I'm sure he's safe. There's no cause for worry yet. Miss Annie? Is she getting well?"

"She's still in a bad way, I'm afraid. Her body is still fighting her illness."

"She's going to get better, isn't she?" said John.

"She's drinking the soup I give her when she's awake. Hard to say with a thing like this."

"Anything you want me to tell Max?"

"Tell him not to worry about Annie. I'm taking care of her. Lizzie is safe too. We're proud of him."

#

Saturday

The following morning, seven hundred men stood outside the Black Brigade headquarters in the light of dawn. General Dickson climbed onto a box and addressed the men.

"Men of Cincinnati, I am heartened by your overwhelming response to the call of duty to your country and your city. We will form three regiments, each with five or six companies. Most of you are needed across the river to help finish the building of the fortifications and then to support the efforts of the men who will fight our enemy. Some of you can best serve by supporting the camps and hospitals here in the city. The fleet of steamships now patrolling the rivers also needs men. Before we assign you, I want to introduce Captain James Lupton, who will command the forces in the Negro camp. He has a presentation from the ladies of this city. Captain Lupton?"

The captain took the General's place atop the platform and made a speech thanking the volunteers and congratulating them on their valor and service in supporting the city's defense. The men cheered as they formed lines to sign up for duty.

John became part of Company C of the 3rd regiment of the Black Brigade. He and forty other men marched back across the pontoon bridge and the five miles up the Lexington Highway toward Fort Mitchel. They marched along the paths where men continued digging and building the defenses. Company C's assignment was to construct several rifle pits east of the Hatch battery.

As they marched past Company B of the Fifth Ward, John stepped out of line and approached Max, who was instructing a group of men. Max spotted John.

"John, you're now part of the Black Brigade? We heard about its formation. There are so many of you. Where did all of these men come from?"

"Most are freedmen from Ohio, but I've met a number who left their masters in Kentucky and came north to join the fight."

"Where are you headed?" asked Max.

"We've been assigned to build several miles of rifle pits and fortifications." John held up his shovel. "No weapons, but General Dickson and Captain Lupton have assured us they will allow us to work, like you other men, without harassment. Several companies are helping build a makeshift hospital behind the defenses."

"I'm glad you're here. We need the help. Scouts have seen Rebel troops as near as ten miles from the fort. There's no time to waste."

"I bring word of Annie. She's still resting," said John.

"You saw her?"

"No, but I was at your house. I spoke to your sister. She said not to worry, that Annie will be well. Lizzie is safe."

"You went to check on them for me?" said Max.

He nodded. "I pray her recovery will be soon."

"Thank you."

"I must go," said John. They shook hands.

John ran to catch up to his unit. Max watched the companies of Black men march by him, tools slung across their shoulders, heads held high. After they passed, two soldiers approached, leading two men behind them, their hands tied in rope.

Max greeted them, "Commander?"

"Sir?" the officer replied.

"Who are these men?" said Max.

"Traitors. These men were spying for the Confederacy."

"Under what circumstances?"

"They approached a company of men working on the barricade and offered them apples from their farm. Under the pretense of generosity and support for the Union, they were trying to obtain information about the defenses being built and our numbers of men. They had horses next to the highway, ready to take the information south to General Kirby Smith. Beware the locals around here. Many are secessionists, living amongst the good Kentucky people loyal to the Union."

"What's to happen to them?" asked Max.

"We're taking them to the barracks in Newport. After that, who knows? Likely the prison at Camp Chase in Columbus."

"Have you heard any word of Kirby Smith's troops?" said Max.

"No significant troops reported nearby, but our cavalry scouts encountered a few Rebels four miles south of here last night. After a few shots, they rode off. We're still trying to determine if the Rebs are heading our way, toward Louisville, or both. Kirby Smith had hoped the men in Kentucky would rush to join him in the Confederate army to grow his numbers, but we don't think that's happening. The Bluegrass men who don't support the Union are cowards like these two."

"Yankee pig," muttered one of the prisoners.

The officer hit him in the stomach with the butt of his rifle. "Shut up, you."

"Tell your men to be wary. Trust no one," the officer said to Max, then continued on his way.

#

The volunteers worked several long days finishing the battery and trenches. The cannons were put in place and tested. With construction complete, they settled into long, tedious days of sitting and waiting. They were issued guns. General Wallace and his staff rode along the defense line, inspecting the earthworks, rifle pits, trenches, and abatises made from fallen trees with pointed spikes facing the enemy's direction. There were now more than 70,000 men from Ohio, Kentucky, and Indiana in position across northern Kentucky and Cincinnati, awaiting the arrival of General Kirby Smith's and General Henry Heth's armies.

#

Tuesday

After lunch, the men sat along the road and in the pits. Some napped.

Oskar said to Max, "Have you heard any word of Annie?"

"No. I wish we knew when the Confederates might attack. I want to ride into town to see her," said Max.

"I know it has been difficult for you to be here, not knowing how she is."

"They've lifted martial law in town. Businesses are open, and schools have resumed. You should go back to school."

"I'm not doing that," said Oscar as he rubbed his fingers along the strap of the rifle hung over his shoulder.

"You've been a tremendous help to this company, but who knows how long this vigil of waiting for battle will go on? You're missing classes."

"I don't want to leave these men now. I've worked side-by-side with them for over a week. I can't walk out on them."

They stepped off the road to let a water cart and ammunition wagon pass.

"A battle is coming, and it's no place for a boy," said Max.

"I'm not a boy. I don't understand why you can't see that after seeing me here this week."

"Oskar, this is war. Men will die. You don't need to be here. You have your whole life ahead of you. We have plenty of men."

"You have a wife and a daughter. You're here. All these men with families are here. Why should I get to leave over them?"

"Because you're not of age," said Max.

"I want to be here."

"I know you do, and it's courageous and noble of you. I want you to take one of my horses and ride into the city. Check on Annie for me."

"No."

"Oskar."

"No, I'm not going. Why don't you ride into town?"

"I can't leave my men," said Max.

"Well, I can't either."

The sound of gunshots in the distance made them stop.

"Shots fired," a man yelled.

Men ran for the trenches, shouting.

Max and Oskar crouched down in a hole and searched the horizon with rifles pointed south. Max was breathing heavily, "Do you see anything?"

"No, nothing," said Oskar.

After a few minutes, Max sat back and closed his eyes, whispering prayers. Sweat ran down his face. He took deep breaths to calm himself.

"We're going to survive this," said Oskar.

Max looked at his brother. He wished he had Oskar's courage or his youthful ignorance of the severity of their situation.

"I'm going to go see what Captain Emery knows," said Oskar, climbing out and running down the road.

"Oskar, no. Stay down," called Max, but he was gone.

Max looked across the still field. He heard the crack of several rifles but saw no sign of troops. He stood scanning the horizon with his rifle resting on the dirt mound in front of his foxhole. He slid down into the hole.

"Casey, you see anything?" said Max.

"Nothing."

"Stay alert." Max gave him a reassuring pat on the shoulder as he moved down the trench, checking in with the men. He took up position again next to Miles.

"Do you think this is it?" said Max.

"I don't know. Those shots sounded pretty far off," said Miles.

"How far, do you think?"

"A mile, maybe?"

Jeff, the man beside Miles, said, "Hard to tell in these hills. I'd say more than a mile."

"Why do you say that?" asked Miles.

"The way it echoed. Of course, these military rifles sound different than the shotgun I use to hunt."

"You familiar with guns?" asked Max.

"Sure," said Jeff.

"Any advice for me? I've never shot a gun," said Max.

"You never shot a gun?"

"No."

"And you're out here leading us?"

Max shrugged his shoulders. "Doing what I can."

"Me neither," said Miles. "I own a bookstore."

"Shit," said Jeff. "Wait until you're close enough to see their eyes, then aim for the neck. If you're lucky, you'll hit them in the chest. If they reach this hole, stab them with your bayonet—in the stomach—too many bones in the chest."

They stood on alert. The sun set, and they continued to stand in the dark.

"What do you think?" said Max.

"Hmm."

"Are they coming?"

Jeff said, "I don't think they'll charge us after dark."

"You're probably right. We've got the advantage with these holes," said Max.

"In the morning, though. Might come then," said Jeff.

"You men try to get some sleep. I'll move back up the line, assign a couple of men to stand watch for an hour, then they can hand off duty to someone else," said Max.

"Gladly," said Jeff, turning and sliding down to a sitting position in the hole.

"I don't think I can sleep," said Miles.

"Try to," said Max.

Max worked his way down the military road and found Captain Emery in his tent behind the battery.

"Captain, any idea where the shots were fired from?" said Max.

"I'd say one to two miles away. It sounded like an exchange of ours versus the Rebs, but it could have been some Rebel scout encountering a local. I sent a man to the Buford battery where the vantage point is better, and I sent your brother and Roberts to scout it out on horseback."

"You sent Oskar?"

"I asked for volunteers, and they stepped up."

"He's a boy. He's not even eighteen."

"He doesn't look like a boy," said the captain. "He's here. He's got a rifle, and he's one of the strongest men in the regiment. I needed someone who could ride. The cavalry will scout things out on horseback in the morning."

"Jesus," muttered Max.

Able said to Max, "He can look after himself. They're under cover of darkness."

"How far did you tell them to go?" Max asked Captain Emery.

"I ordered them to travel south parallel with the Lexington Pike but stay hidden along the side. Two miles. They should be back in an hour or so."

"What are your orders for tonight?"

"Have men take turns standing guard about every hundred feet. The others can get some rest."

"Yes, sir," said Max. He returned to his men and gave instructions. He took a spot next to Casey.

Max closed his eyes and tried to sleep, but his thoughts wouldn't allow it. He thought of Annie, Lizzie, and his business which he hadn't checked on in over a week. He had agreed to let Oskar come with him to work on the fortification, then let Oskar convince him that he could stay and be part of the defense. Now Oskar wielded a gun and was off in the dark, searching for the enemy that would be looking to shoot any Union men they encountered. He was supposed to be leading this group of untrained men, and he, himself, couldn't master a weapon.

His feeling of inadequacy amplified his fear. He was frustrated by his inability to control anything anymore. The order of his life that comforted him and made him feel confident was gone, replaced by the war's uncertainty and disruption. He prayed to God to guide him, but the war seemed to be overpowering God. He had to stay strong for his men.

Max closed his eyes. His head swayed forward, jolting him awake. He closed his eyes again. In his dreams, a Confederate soldier ran across the open field toward him in the trench. Max fired his rifle, and the soldier fell. Another came in his place, and Max shot and killed again. Another came. Max fired, but the man kept running. The man jumped over the hill, and Max plunged his bayonet into his belly. Blood spurt from his abdomen as the man fell on top of Max. Max grunted, trying to push him off, his hands now dripping with blood. Max pushed the soldier off of him, and as he lay back on the ground, the man transformed into Annie in her nightshirt, the bayonet protruding from her abdomen stained with blood. Moaning, Max awoke suddenly, thrusting his rifle from his lap to the ground.

"Max, are you all right?" said Casey.

"Yes," said Max.

Casey handed him his rifle.

"I'm fine," said Max. "A dream."

Max closed his eyes and prayed, trying not to fall asleep but finally succumbing near dawn.

#

Oskar and Craig Roberts rode their horses slowly along the side of the road in the moonlight. Every few minutes, they stopped, listened, then moved on. About a mile south of Fort Mitchel, they saw campfire lights and movement through a stand of trees. They guided their horses down a hillside, tied them, then crawled back up the hill to survey the distant camp.

"How many men?" said Oskar.

"I can't tell. But there are a dozen fires spread across a quarter mile, at least," said Craig.

"We need to get into those trees to see."

"No!"

"Why not? We need to know how big their force is," said Oskar.

"Too risky. They'll have lookouts. If they see us, they'll shoot us," said Craig.

Oskar took in his statement for a moment. "Any place where we can get a better vantage point?"

"Those trees block our view. It looks like they took over the entire Whitfield farm."

"You know it?" said Oskar.

"My family has helped them harvest. Our farm is about three miles west of here."

"What do you think they did with the Whitfields?"

"They support the Union, so I don't think they welcomed the Confederates onto their property. My guess is they marched in and sent the family on their way. At least, I hope that's all they did. I pray they're unharmed."

"I say we go find out," said Oskar. "We need to see how many men and what kind of artillery they have and report back to Captain Emery."

"Son, that sounds mighty heroic of you, but we can't just go marching in there."

"Maybe we can," said Oskar. "Can you get us south of their camp without being seen?"

"We could ride along the western edge of the Nicholsons' farm, then take their road back to the Lexington Pike. What are you thinking?"

"We're in civilian clothes. What if we ride into their camp from the south, tell them we're looking for our runaway slaves and ask if they've seen them or if they took them? If you do the talking and we play like we're secessionists, they won't think a thing."

"I don't know. What if they catch on to us?" said Craig.

"They won't. You're from around here. You won't even need to pretend."

"You're a confident young man. All right, let's do it. We can rest at my farm tonight and approach them at first light."

CHAPTER 31

Wednesday

After another fitful night, Max woke to the bugler's reveille. He scanned his surroundings, then got up and walked to Captain Emery's tent.

Captain Emery and the other company leaders greeted Max as he entered. Max had a week's beard, and his blond hair stood out in some places and was matted to his head in others. He had bags under his eyes and smelled as rank as the other men in the camp.

"What did the scouts find down the Lexington Pike?" asked Max.

"They haven't returned," said Captain Emery.

"Captain, they were only supposed to be gone an hour. He's a boy, for God's sake."

"I've sent some cavalry south to look for them and scout for the enemy."

Max stepped outside and into the brush. He dry-heaved what little food was in his stomach. He pulled a handkerchief from his pocket and wiped his mouth and the sweat from his brow. He took a deep breath, then rejoined the officers.

Captain Emery said, "Your men need to be on high alert today. The enemy is close. The hillsides in the city are well armed with cannons, but we'll need every man's shots to count to prevent them from getting anywhere near the river.

We have reports that several other generals joined Kirby Smith's forces north of Frankfort and Lexington."

They heard several horses approach and men dismounting. Two men entered the tent and saluted Captain Emery. "What's your report?"

"We think it's General Heth's army. Many men— thousands," said the man.

"Where?"

"About a mile south."

"Christ. The storm is coming," said one of the other officers.

"Any heavy artillery?" asked the captain.

"We couldn't get that close; we didn't see any."

"Were they on the move?"

"No, sir, not yet."

"Did they look like they were preparing for an assault?"

"Again, sir, we couldn't get that close. They had scouts posted outside the perimeter of their camp."

Another man rushed into the tent. "Captain Emery, Lieutenant Hauser reporting, sir."

"What do you have to report, Hauser?"

"A large cavalry force attacked a standing guard along the Licking River, about two miles southeast of here. Several of ours were wounded."

"Where did the Confederates attack from?" said Captain Emery.

"They came from the south along the west side of the Licking."

"How many troops?" asked Captain Emery.

"Maybe sixty to eighty on horseback."

"Ground troops with them?"

"No reports of them, sir."

"Take your report to General Wallace, then ride back to the Licking. Send word of any troop movement."

"Yes, sir." As soon as the lieutenant saluted and left, another man stepped in.

"Captain Emery, headquarters sent this over the wire." The man handed the captain a note and left.

Captain Emery opened the paper and read it. "A messenger from Anderson's Ferry has intelligence that the enemy is about four miles from the Ohio River west of Cincinnati. A cavalry party was seen scouting there."

One of the civilian leaders said excitedly, "Damn, butternuts are crawling everywhere; they're like lice."

"Shut it, sir," said Captain Emery. "We need you all to be calm. If you panic, your men will panic. The order this morning is the same as yesterday. Stay alert. The men should remain in the fortifications unless they have a reason to leave them."

"Is taking a piss a reason?" asked one of the makeshift commanders.

The captain looked at him, trying to ascertain whether he was joking.

"I'm sorry, Captain, I don't know. I'm not a soldier; I'm a brewer."

"Of course. We don't need men pissing all over each other in the trenches. Unless we're being attacked, they should use the latrines we dug. We smell bad enough as it is."

The sound of horses preceded Oskar and Craig rushing into the tent.

"Oskar, thank God. You're safe." Max rushed over and hugged him.

Oskar pushed him away. "Don't," he whispered.

"What happened to you two? You were supposed to return last night with a report," said the captain.

Oskar said, "We couldn't get close enough to the Confederate position last night to learn anything of value. This morning, we approached the camp from the south, pretending to be local Confederate supporter farmers looking for our runaway slaves."

"You what?"

"We rode right into their camp headquarters and spoke to several officers. They questioned us, but Craig is from the area, and he duped them fantastically."

"What did you learn?" said Captain Emery.

"The camp is about a mile and a quarter south of here and is led by General Henry Heth. He has about 10,000 men."

"Jesus." Several of the civilian leaders voiced alarm and dread.

Oskar continued, "They camped there overnight. We saw hundreds of cavalry horses and some large munitions on wagons. They said that Kirby-Smith's army was nearby to the southwest."

"How far?"

"He didn't say."

"Were they advancing?"

"No."

"Preparing to move out?"

"Not that we could tell," said Oskar.

Captain Emery said, "What the devil are they doing? What are they waiting for?"

One of Emery's officers said, "Sir, could they be waiting for Kirby Smith's men to join them? That would more than double their numbers."

"It's possible. We know they've scouted our camps, and they know the size of our defense. Even though we're a ragtag bunch, we've over 50,000 guns pointed their way. Did you learn anything else?"

Craig said, "We know they ransacked some local farms for food. My family's included."

"Their supplies must be getting low. A starving army can't fight, so they've used that tactic all over the state. We heard reports that they took control of a mill about an hour's ride from here near Florence."

The captain turned to Craig and Oskar. "Good work. I'd like you two to accompany me to headquarters at Fort Mitchel to update General Wallace. Does anybody else have anything to report?"

No one spoke, so the captain ordered, "Spread the word along the line. Today is likely the day we've been preparing for. God be with you. Dismissed."

#

Max looked up at the American flag flying outside the captain's tent. He unbuttoned his coat in response to the already warm morning. He returned to his men, updated them, and then spent the morning speaking with men in the pits.

"What's that," said one of the men, pointing to a tree line across the valley. Smoke rose above the trees in several areas from the enemy's campfires. "There. I saw movement."

They all studied the band of trees.

"I don't see anything."

"There. A man."

"Shit, I wish I had a spyglass."

"I see him."

"Men, take your positions," shouted Max.

"I'm ready to kill these damn gray backs," said a man.

"They are not taking our city," said another.

"Yeah! It's time to kill them!" Shouts of encouragement rang out.

"Johnny Reb, welcome to your last day on this earth!" shouted one of the men.

Max moved down the line, meeting similar heightened spirits. After an hour and seeing no other movement across the field, the men stood down. Max sent them in small groups to eat lunch. He found a spot alone and pulled paper and pencil from his knapsack. Using his Bible for a writing surface, he wrote:

My Dearest Annie,

I sit amongst brave men who have taken up arms to defend our city, our families, and our way of life. We are awaiting the Confederates. All signs are that their attack is imminent. I have put aside my hesitancy to take up arms. I know God is on our side, and I will do my part in this battle in His name.

I have been blessed with so much. Most of all, your love and unwavering support. I pray that your weakened condition has passed, and you will again be the shining light in the lives of those around you. Lizzie is a reflection of your spirit and beauty, and a beacon for the next generation of citizens that I pray will allow each man and woman to seek their rightful place in our republic without government tyranny or unequal treatment from fellow citizens. My prosperity and place in the community are godsends that I have tried to use to help others, but I know, at times, that my vanity has caused me to fall short in doing so. I ask you and God to forgive me for my failures.

If I should perish in defense of our blessings, it will have been worth it, for you, for Lizzie, for all. Carry on your campaign, knowing I am always at your side.

I love you,
Max

Max folded the letter and put it in his coat pocket.

"Oskar!" Max stood and embraced his brother. "I'm so relieved you're safe."

"You worry too much," Oskar said.

"You're my brother."

"I'm unharmed," he said smiling, holding out his arms for inspection. "The Confederates had no suspicion. They're a stupid bunch. We're going to beat them."

"We will, won't we? We have to."

"Damn right," said Oskar.

Max said, "What you did…that was very clever and brave of you. I'm sorry I treated you as a child."

"I understand, brother. I'm grateful for everything you've done for me. You frustrate me with your parental inclinations, but I know I wouldn't be who I am without you."

"I'm proud of you."

Oskar nodded. "You look like shit. I've never seen you so disheveled, the proper Max Mueller."

"Enough from you. It's war."

"Are you going to be able to continue this pace, leading these men?"

"I am. Don't worry about me."

"I'm off to take up my position on the line, then. May God be with us and preserve the Union," said Oskar.

"Be careful."

"You, too."

Max watched Oskar approach a group of men, who heartily engaged with him as he joined them.

CHAPTER 32

Thursday

Max awoke with the first morning light on the quiet ridge. He felt exhausted as he contemplated another day of waiting—sitting, watching, wondering when they would come. He couldn't stop the thoughts of battle from invading his mind. Firing his rifle, fighting Rebel men at close range, fighting for his life. His heart raced, and he was suddenly hot, sweat forming on his forehead, neck, and back. Spots blurred his vision, and he labored to breathe. He pulled open his coat and ripped at the buttons on his shirt. He hated this. He wanted to be anywhere but here. He thought of Lizzie and Annie at home. He closed his eyes and took slow, controlled breaths. He prayed to God for strength, bravery, and safety in the battle that was to come. He breathed in and out, slowly regaining his composure. He had to do this—he had no choice. The distant coughing of a man pulled him out of his head. A soft breeze cooled his damp skin. He fanned his shirt and coat, allowing the air inside. After a few minutes, he buttoned his shirt, stood, and dusted himself off.

Max walked along the road toward Captain Emery's tent. Most men were still asleep, rifles at hand. As he walked, he scanned the southern ridge, looking for Rebel troop activity. He stopped when he realized there were no trails of smoke across the hills. He ran to the Captain's tent.

"There are no campfires this morning," Max blurted as he entered.

"Where?"

"To the south. The Confederate camps," said Max.

Several of the men rushed outside with him and surveyed the skyline.

"Are they advancing?" one of the men said.

"Not toward us. Maybe they're going to try to flank the city?"

"Our perimeter covers all direct attacks. To attempt it, they'd have to go several miles up or down river."

"Do we need to move troops? We need to find out where they are."

"Cool heads, men," said Captain Emery.

"Maybe it's a trick."

"We'll see them coming."

"We have to find out where they are. Captain, should we send scouts?"

"General Wallace already dispatched several. Give your men the same orders as yesterday. High alert. Eyes to the south."

Max walked back to his post, searching the hillsides and trees for activity. He relayed the morning's news to the men and commenced another day of watching and waiting. Word of several distant skirmishes and casualties from the day before spread through the camp, stressing already frazzled nerves.

Mid-morning, a messenger rode along the road. "Mueller?"

"Here," said Max approaching the man.

"Sir, word from Captain Emery. The enemy has retreated. They're gone."

"Where?" asked Max.

"Far to the southwest. They've abandoned an attack on Cincinnati."

"Are you sure?"

"Yes. Your men can leave their posts. The threat is over. They can go home."

Men overhearing the conversation started shouting in relief and celebration.

"Yellow Rebs turned and ran!" one yelled.

"Thank God," said Max, lips quivering as he suppressed tears of relief.

The messenger raised his voice to continue speaking over the men's celebrations, "Assemble your troops, gear, and weapons. We'll march back to Cincinnati at 1:00 PM today. Any men who were issued weapons will deposit them with the army in the city before being dismissed."

#

Max marched beside his men with the thousands from Fort Mitchel on the hilltop down to the river. People crammed the waterfronts and streets. Smoke from stacks billowed into the air, signaling that the city was alive again. Overwhelmed with the sight, Max took deep breaths, blinking away tears. As they marched, the men sang choruses of "John Brown's Body."

"John Brown's body lies a-moldering in the grave,
John Brown's body lies a-moldering in the grave,
John Brown's body lies a-moldering in the grave,
But his soul goes marching on.

The stars above in Heaven are looking kindly down,
The stars above in Heaven are looking kindly down,
The stars above in Heaven are looking kindly down,
On the grave of old John Brown.

Glory, Glory, Hallelujah
Glory, Glory, Hallelujah
Glory, Glory, Hallelujah
His soul goes marching on.

He captured Harper's Ferry with his nineteen men so true,
He frightened old Virginia till she trembled through and through,
They hung him for a traitor, they themselves the traitor crew,
But his soul goes marching on.

Glory, Glory, Hallelujah
Glory, Glory, Hallelujah
Glory, Glory, Hallelujah
His soul goes marching on."

Crowds cheered them as they marched through the streets of Covington. As they crossed the pontoon bridge into Cincinnati, steamships blew their whistles. The *Emma Duncan* fired her cannons in salute. A band and a mass of people on the banks of the Ohio greeted them.

The procession marched into town. The streets were crowded with people on every block, cheering, waving flags, and applauding. General Wallace stood on a platform at the corner of Twelfth and Elm Streets and reviewed the men as they passed. They, in turn, cheered him, the man who had organized and led the defense of their city. After they passed the review point, men laid their weapons in a pile in an empty lot and greeted their families and friends. The saloons were open again as the soldiers and citizens celebrated the passing of the threat of attack.

Max said goodbye to his men and then ran home. He opened the door and dropped his satchel on the floor. "Annie, I'm home! Marie? Lizzie?" He checked all the ground floor rooms, then ran up the stairs, "Annie?"

He found their bedroom empty, the bedclothes rumpled in heaps and stained with blood. A sour smell permeated the room. On the nightstand sat a half-empty glass of water, damp rags, and a bottle of laudanum, an opioid pain medication. Annie's blood-stained nightgown lay on the floor. He checked the other bedrooms, finding them all eerily quiet. In the kitchen, the table was covered with ingredients—tins of flour and sugar, salt, and apple peels. Dirty bowls and spoons sat unwashed in the sink.

Max ran next door and knocked. A middle-aged woman opened the door. "Mr. Mueller, you're back from Kentucky." She stepped forward and hugged him. "It's a glorious day for the Union."

"Mrs. Derr. Yes, it is. God has spared us from the ravages of war. I'm looking for Annie. Have you seen her?"

"No, I'm sorry. I know she was feeling poorly. Marie said she had quite a fever."

"I'm just home, and there's no one about."

"Have you seen Marie, Lizzie?"

"Not in a few days," said Mrs. Derr.

"Anyone been to the house lately?"

"A doctor was there. I haven't seen anyone since."

"I don't know where they could be." said Max.

"I'm sorry. Would you like to come in for something to eat? You look like you could use a warm meal."

"No, thank you. That's very kind of you. If you see them, tell them I'll return this evening."

"Yes, I will. God bless you."

Max encountered Oskar coming up the sidewalk. "No one is at home. I don't know where they are. I can't tell if they've just gone out or something has happened. There's blood!"

Oskar said, "Let's go inside and get some rest."

"No, I can't. I need to go to the shop. Jim has been managing things. I need to assess the state of the work," said Max.

"Can't it wait? The place isn't on fire. They've managed without you for a week. What are a few more hours?"

"No. Will you stay here? Come and get me when they return?"

"I will. I plan to use the bathtub and reacquaint myself with what a bed feels like."

"Good, good. You deserve it. You'll come get me then?"

"Yes, I promise," said Oskar.

"I'll run by the Eichen Garten on my way. Maybe they're there, or they have word."

Max entered the saloon, noisy and crowded with soldiers. Men greeted him, slapping him on the back or toasting as he walked through. He pushed his way out into the back garden, finding an equally large crowd, this one joined by families of the returning men. He scanned the courtyard. He spotted his sister, Helene, delivering beer mugs to a table and started for her. He pushed aside a man and then almost tripped over his daughter carrying two empty beer mugs. She tried to maneuver around his legs without looking up.

"Lizzie!"

The girl looked up at him, not recognizing him in his week's beard.

Max squat down on his haunches. "Oh, Lizzie, my girl." He took the mugs from her hands and set them on the ground.

"Papa!" she squealed as she recognized and hugged him tightly.

He picked her up and kissed her. "I'm so happy to see you. What are you doing?"

"I'm helping Oma serve the soldiers."

"You're doing a wonderful job."

"Your whiskers are scratchy, Papa!" She ran her fingers over his beard.

"Where is Mama?"

"She's at the hospital."

"When did she go there? Today?"

Lizzie shook her head no.

"Yesterday? Lizzie, how long has she been there?" Max said, raising his voice in panic.

Frightened by his agitation, she said nothing.

Max looked around the courtyard. "Where's Marie?"

"I don't know," said Lizzie.

Max scooped up the beer mugs with one hand and carried Lizzie through the crowd back into the bar. His mother and

Helene were now both behind the counter. They greeted him with smiles.

"Where's Annie? Marie? I went home. They were gone."

His mother responded in German, "She's gone to the hospital."

"What hospital? How is she?"

"Camp Dennison," she said.

"Why would you send a sick woman to a military hospital?" he shouted.

His mother touched his forearm gently. "Max. She's tending to the soldiers."

"What?" he asked, confused.

"She went last night for her shift. Marie dropped Lizzie off here this morning so she could bake for the soldiers returning home. Everything is all right now," said his mother.

"Annie's well?" said Max.

"Yes. It has passed. Annie felt well enough to go back to the soldiers."

"Thank God," said Max. "Do you know when she'll return?"

"No. How is my son? You look tired."

"I'm fine. Yes, I'm tired, but I'll sleep later. I'm just glad to be home."

"You fought the Confederates?"

"Thankfully, I didn't have to."

"I am proud of you."

"Thank you, Mother. I will leave Lizzie here with you. I must go to work now and check on the shop. They have been without me for too long."

"Lizzie, Papa has to go to work now. I'll see you at home tonight. I'll be there to tuck you into bed." He kissed the top of her head.

CHAPTER 33

When Max arrived home that evening, Marie was preparing dinner, talking with Oskar about their respective adventures of the last week.

"Brother, I hear you gallantly commanded a company of men," said Marie.

"I wouldn't go that far," said Max.

"Oskar tells me you led the men like a compassionate German commander."

"That is an unlikely combination," said Max.

"Maybe so, but I believe he speaks the truth. You have a way about you that brings the best of our heritage and combines it with the sense of the American way."

"Did Oskar tell you of his brave adventure as a spy amongst the enemy?"

"He did," said Marie.

"He also demonstrated an extraordinary combination of leadership and rapport with the men," said Max.

"I think our father would be proud of you both," said Marie.

"I wonder," said Max. "Do you think Annie is well enough to be nursing soldiers so soon after her illness?"

"She was in a bad way for several days," said Marie. "The doctor gave her some medicine for the pain. Her fever broke two days ago, and yesterday, she came downstairs dressed and said she was going back to Camp Dennison."

"Do you think that she is well enough?"

"You know Annie. It doesn't matter what you or I think. She makes up her mind and won't be dissuaded."

"Thank you for taking care of her and Lizzie. Once again, we would be lost without you."

"Mama!" Lizzie cried, running to greet Annie in the front hall.

Annie hugged Lizzie.

"Papa is home!"

Annie and Max stood in the hall, enveloped in each other's arms, crying tears of relief.

After dinner, they put Lizzie to bed.

"You need a bath," Annie said. "You smell like the soldiers at the hospital."

"What I experienced for a week is a fraction of the hardship and terror that the soldiers in battle endure," said Max.

"Even so, I won't sleep in the same bed as you, smelling like that."

Annie drew the bathwater for him, and he settled into it. She placed his dirty clothes in the backyard. When she returned, he said, "Will you wash my back?"

She leaned into the tub, washing him.

Max enjoyed the brief touch. Annie finished and dropped the cloth in the water. He touched her arm, but she pulled it away and stood.

"Stay. Talk with me. What's the matter?" he said.

"Nothing. I'm tired," said Annie.

"Marie said you had to call for the doctor?"

"The doctor was unnecessary. It was something I had to endure."

"You make it sound like a penance. You've been through a terrible ordeal."

She shook her head but wouldn't look at him.

"What is it? Tell me," said Max.

"I don't want any more children. After the doctor told us that I was unlikely to have more, I was relieved and put any thoughts of more children aside. When I realized I was pregnant, I was angry. I love Lizzie, but I don't want to start with a little one again. It's more years of being tied to the child and home. I don't want that. I was angry at myself for letting you, for succumbing to you in bed. The pain I endured last week was because I was weak. I love you, Max, but I won't be weak again." She left the bathroom.

"Annie, wait. Come back." Max buried his head in his hands, rubbed his forehead, then clasped his hands in front of his chin and took deep breaths. He closed his eyes in thought and prayer. After a few minutes, he dried himself and dressed for bed.

Annie was already under the covers when he slid under them and lay on his back. "Annie."

"What?"

"I'm sorry you had to go through it alone. I wish I could have been here for you."

"There was nothing you could have done," she said.

"I could have tried to comfort you. Held your hand."

"I managed on my own."

"Yes, you're a strong woman. When we made our vows of marriage, we promised to comfort each other in sickness and in health. Cherish, honor, and love each other until death. I want to help comfort you in your difficulties, and I need you to help me in mine. That's one of the gifts of marriage. We have each other, no matter what each of us faces. I want us to be here for each other, and if you're not ready to have relations right now, I can wait."

"No, not just now; I'm not sure I want to risk having another child."

"There are things we can do to avoid having children," said Max. "If that's what it takes. . ."

"I don't know. Another child? I can't contemplate it now. I'm tired," she said.

"All right. Let's not talk about that anymore tonight. We're both exhausted."

They lay silently for several minutes.

Max said, "I was so afraid of losing you. Lying in the fields at night, I worried that we'd never be together again. I'm relieved you're well, and I'm here, and we're together."

"I'm glad you're home safe, but I didn't let myself think about losing you," she said. "I knew you were somewhere at the front. We read that the Confederates were in central Kentucky, moving north. All we could do was wait and worry. I returned to work at the hospital as soon as I was well enough because I had to keep busy. If I stayed busy and focused on my work, I didn't have to think about the awful things happening in the war. When the papers reported troops just south of Fort Mitchel, some families left town. Mrs. Mills sent her silver with her son on a train to Cleveland. It was frightening not to know when the Confederate soldiers might come. I prayed you and the others would keep them from us, but I was afraid they might break through the defenses."

Max said, "For now, the threat of attack on Cincinnati has passed. We can go back to living our lives again."

"Our wartime lives," she said. "I wonder if we'll ever return to our pre-wartime lives? We can't go back, can we? I hope having the war at our doorstep will make more people realize we can't coexist as a country half free, half slave, and that we all need to actively support forcing a conclusion to the war. It was too easy for Cincinnatians when the war was elsewhere, down South."

"Do you think the threat of the siege was enough to convince people?" asked Max.

"I fear many more men will die before they are convinced."

CHAPTER 34

March 1863

Max stood with Aaron on the riverfront among a large crowd gathered for a demonstration of a new invention, the Gatling gun. Six metal barrels fused together allowed for rapid fire of bullets from the wheel-mounted gun at 200 rounds per minute. The inventor, Richard Jordan Gatling, contracted with Miles Greenwood of the Eagle Iron Works to build several prototypes. Greenwood scheduled the public demonstration to build support for the gun among the Union army leadership.

The crowd watched as two men loaded a cartridge atop the gun and began rotating the barrels, firing at a target set up in front of the river. The bullets assaulted the target, tearing it to shreds within seconds, as spent ammunition dropped to the ground below the weapon. The crowd burst into applause and cheers.

"Holy shit," said Aaron. "This could replace a dozen or more men with a single gun."

"Its destruction is shocking," said Max.

"How many do the Union army have?"

"None. The army is not convinced of its durability. Gatling is still working on perfecting the design," said Max.

"But Greenwood has built it. Look at it."

Max said, "I can't say what the army's leadership decision-making process is. Greenwood gave me a set of plans, and he and I met to consult on how to best manufacture it. That's as close as I've been to the process."

"Is it complicated to build?" said Aaron.

"No more complicated than other arms, but you must be precise in pouring the barrels and mounting them together."

"Could you build them at your factory?" Aaron asked.

"We could do it technically, yes, but Gatling has a patent on the technology."

"This could change the course of the war. What do they cost?" said Aaron.

"Only a few have been manufactured by Greenwood and several other manufacturers. No one has tried to scale building them, so the cost is prohibitive right now."

"There's a fortune to be made in this, don't you think?"

"Sure, but that's up to Gatling to negotiate with the army."

"What if we took this to a different market?"

"Like where?" said Max.

"The state militias, or other parties besides the federal armory."

"I told you, it's patented."

"That's a legal problem. I can resolve legal problems. My firm knows patent law. You make minor modifications to the plans and file a new patent. Then you manufacture it and sell it to the highest bidder. Could that be done?"

"Well, I suppose it could, but that wouldn't be ethical," said Max.

"Always the rule follower. As I said, I can get around the patent. Could you do a new set of drawings?" said Aaron.

"I'm not comfortable doing that. As soon as it was revealed what I had done, my reputation would be ruined."

"What if the gun buyer was outside your market, where you didn't have to worry about your reputation?"

"Like where?" said Max.

"Richmond, Virginia."

"The Confederate capital?"

"I think you'd find eager buyers there."

"Stop. Once again, you are willing to cross a line that I won't. How could you consider selling this to the enemy?" said Max.

"It's only a matter of time before the Confederates get a hold of this. Why shouldn't we make a profit before someone else does?"

"No."

"You don't have to manufacture them or make the design changes. Will you sell me a copy of the plans for the gun?"

"I will not. Greenwood entrusted me with the plans."

"There must be a price that you'd be willing to sell them. Name your price," said Aaron.

"Forget it."

"Think about it."

The soldiers fired off another round of shots at a Confederate soldier effigy. Cloth and cotton flew as the dummy fell to the ground.

#

Two weeks later, Max entered the unfamiliar saloon, which dockworkers and steamship crews frequented. Aaron stood at the rear and motioned him back.

"In here," Aaron said, directing him to a small room. A man sat at a table.

Aaron closed the door. "Do you have the plans?"

Max pulled a rolled-up set of drawings from his satchel. He spread them out on the table and explained them to the man, who asked several clarifying questions about the Gatling gun. The man nodded at Aaron, then rolled up the plans.

"My payment?" said Max.

"I have it. I'll deposit it into your account," said Aaron.

"I thought I would get it now."

"What, you don't trust me? Come on. We're family."

Max looked uncomfortably between the man and Aaron. "All right. Shall we drink on it?"

"Sure," said Aaron.

"I'll get it," said Max, stepping into the barroom. He returned with a bottle and three glasses. He poured a few fingers into each glass.

They picked up the glasses and toasted. "To American enterprise," said Aaron.

The door burst open, and three soldiers entered the room, pointing pistols at the men.

"What the hell?" shouted Aaron.

Max moved back against the wall.

The third man tried to run through them, plans in hand. One of the soldiers shot him in the chest, and he fell to the ground.

Max stood motionless, breathing heavily.

"Jesus," cried Aaron as another soldier shoved him against the wall, pointing his pistol at his neck.

"Move, and you'll be as dead as him."

Aaron muttered, "What the hell is going on?"

"You are under arrest," said the soldier.

"For what? We're respectable men of this community. I'm an attorney, and he's a city councilman. Un-hand me."

"You are under arrest for treason, conducting trade of arms with the enemy, and smuggling."

"This is ridiculous. He brought those plans here, not me," Aaron said, indicating Max.

The soldier said, "Indeed he did, just as he was asked to by General Wilson."

"What are you talking about? I came here for a drink," said Aaron.

"We followed you, saw you receive payment from this man earlier today. You're the orchestrator of this operation."

"You have no proof. No judge will let this flimsy evidence stand."

"Not sure you'll be seeing a judge any time soon. We're taking you to the city jail. From there, it's likely off to the prison at Camp Chase. That's where all the blockade runners and traitors are. You'll be in good company, you Rebel scum."

"I am not a Confederate. I am a loyal resident of the Union," declared Aaron.

"Rebel flows in the blood. It doesn't know geographic boundaries," said one of the soldiers.

"Max, tell them. I left Kentucky. I'm for the Union."

"Mr. Mueller isn't going to help you. He's on the good guys' side. He's working for us."

"Max, is this true?" said Aaron.

Max remained silent, uncomfortable with the confrontation.

"Max? We're brothers. I gave you half my inheritance."

"Aaron, you didn't give me anything. You relented and allowed half of our father's inheritance to go to me because it was the most expedient way to get your half. Everything you've ever done has been in the name of promoting yourself. You would do anything, at the expense of anyone, to further your interests."

"Christ, Mueller. Get off your high horse. You want to prosper in America? Well, this is what it takes. In addition to your rotten blood, you're too timid to win at business. You self-righteous, bleeding heart."

"I may be too soft sometimes, but this?" said Max. "You betray your country, the country that has provided you with a bounty of blessings well beyond what you deserve. That's not the American way."

"You gritless, dirty Dutch," said Aaron.

"Let's go," said the soldier, pushing Aaron into the bar room. The other soldier addressed the constable, now standing over the dead man.

Max sat down at the table, poured himself another whiskey, and downed it.

CHAPTER 35

Max stood in the front hall of his friend Patrick's house, whispering with Molly. "How is he?"

"He's not himself. He's been home a week, and all he does is sit in the parlor and read or look out the window. He's drinking quite a bit. I've had to go out to buy two more bottles of whiskey since he's been home. He has little interest in the children. He shouts at them to be quiet. It's made the younger ones afraid to go in there."

"He's been through a harrowing experience. It must be challenging for all of you," said Max.

"I'm so glad you've come to see him. Maybe your visit will cheer him up."

"I'll do what I can. How are you doing, Molly?"

"I'm happy to have him home. I am worried about his ability to work again. If he doesn't work, I'll need to do more than the sewing I've taken on."

"I understand. Until he does, I'll continue to help you with your bills," said Max.

"You've been so generous. I don't know how we'll repay you."

"No. He's like a brother to me. I'm happy I'm able to do it."

"Go on, then."

Max knocked on the door and entered the parlor.

Patrick smiled, stood, and embraced Max with his one good arm. His right sleeve dangled loosely due to the missing arm below the elbow. "Max."

"It's good to see you. I'm glad you're home safe," said Max. "You need a haircut and a shave."

"Bloody hell, man. You ever tried shaving left-handed? I'll cut my throat."

"Well, there's plenty of barbers. You only need to walk down the street."

"Hasn't been a priority since I've been home. I've nowhere to go, so there is no need to clean up. Besides, barbers cost money, and as you are well aware, I'm watching my pennies these days. How about a drink?" Patrick grabbed the bottle.

Max put his hand on top of Patrick's. "No, thank you."

"Come on now, have a drink with me. It's the least you can do for a United States infantryman injured in the course of duty."

"No disrespect, but no. You look like you've had plenty already today. Let's go for a walk."

"A walk? No. I did more walking during my year and a half of service. We marched halfway from here to Virginia and plenty of places in between. I'm not walking unless there's someplace I need to go."

"Let's go get you a shave and a haircut, then."

"I'm fine right here," said Patrick.

"Molly said you haven't left the house since you've been home. Let's get some air."

"I'm not interested in going out on the streets."

"Why not?"

Patrick raised his right arm. "People love to stare at a cripple."

"You can't spend the rest of your life here in this house."

"I'll go out when I'm ready," said Patrick.

"What are you waiting for?"

"You don't have any idea what it's like. I'm half a man. People either look at me like I'm deranged or treat me like a child who needs pity. It's degrading. I'll never be whole again."

"I don't know what it's like; you're right. And I'm sorry this happened to you. It's a catastrophe. Your life will be harder now than before, but you must try to move on. Your family needs you to do that," said Max.

"Where do you get off telling me what I need to do? You, who sat in your comfortable dining room, eating home-cooked meals, going to work, and embracing your wife, while I was marching in the mud, fighting Confederate scum and nearly killed by a cannonball. You haven't earned the right to tell me what to do." Patrick was yelling now. "You are safe and whole, and I'm screwed, screwed, screwed. It's not fair."

"I know it's not fair. Who knows why God does what he does," said Max.

"God? You think God did this to me?"

"No, of course not. It's just hard to make sense of it all. I hate seeing you like this. I'm so sorry. This damn war…"

Patrick softened. "I shouldn't be cross with you. You've been a true friend. Molly told me how you helped her with money…how you and Annie checked in on her. I appreciate that, but you need to back off. I'm not ready for help with this." He held up his arm again. "I'm still too angry."

"I want to help you get back on your feet. Just let me know. Whatever you need, I'm here."

"Right now, I need you to have a drink with me," said Patrick.

"One drink," said Max.

Patrick poured a drink of whiskey for each of them.

"This damn war," said Patrick. "What a sham. I signed up to defend the America that the Founding Fathers fought to create. The best damn country in the world that allowed me and thousands of other Irishmen to build a life. It was all going well until the aristocratic pricks down South were at risk of losing control of the government and their manor houses and plantations. So, they started a war to break up this country, and I signed up to fight them to keep them from doing that. I marched in the rain until my feet were bloody with blisters. I sat days and nights waiting to be told what to do next, eating rotten food and shitting in fields. I killed Rebs and watched them kill my friends right before my eyes. I fought Stonewall Jackson's army at a battle near Port Republic, Virginia, where I lost my arm for this war. They dragged me to a church, where a medic cut off my forearm. I woke up in a hospital in Washington, where I lay for four months, praying the infection wouldn't kill me.

"When I'm strong enough to sit up and sip watery soup with my left hand, I learn that President Lincoln has issued the Emancipation Proclamation, freeing all the Negroes in the Confederacy and changing the objective of the war from preserving our Union to freeing the slaves. That's not what I signed up for. If that had been the purpose of the war when I enlisted, I would have stayed home like you, and I'd have my right hand today.

"Can you believe that son of a bitch?" continued Patrick. "He's going back on his word. He said he wouldn't free the slaves. What a two-faced politician. He's as crooked as the rest of them."

Max said, "The country got caught up in the fervor of patriotism and jumped into war without a clear path to resolving our differences. And now we're in it, and thousands of men have died or been wounded like you. We're still no closer to settling our differences. Like you, I believe this country is the greatest on earth, and we must win the war to preserve it. Lincoln's proclamation is a tactic to help force an end to the war. It unites the people across the North against the South and will turn the Negroes in the South against their masters. It prevents the Confederates from using their slaves to support their armies. I don't see a path to ending the war if we remain a nation that's half free and half slave. I wish there were a way to resolve this peacefully, I do, but we're too far in it now. We have to finish the job."

"The man who has lived his life professing to turn the other cheek is now a warmonger?" said Patrick. "You now believe this war is justified?"

"I don't believe starting the war was justified, but I do believe we are justified in finishing it, in the name of protecting ourselves, our homes, our way of life, and yes, the lives of four million enslaved people in this country."

Patrick said, "Four million free Negroes. I fear for this nation. That's what you'll fight for? With the conscription act, there's a draft now. If you're selected, will you fight?"

Max rubbed his forehead. "You and so many other men have sacrificed so much, but I can't wantonly kill another man. I'm ashamed, but my soul won't let me. When I went to help build the fortifications for the city, and we prepared to defend ourselves, I decided I could kill in self-defense, but I can't kill otherwise. That's just who I am."

Patrick said, "Last year, when Lincoln called for volunteers, I thought you were soft for not enlisting. I sat around camp, talking with the other soldiers, and I'd think of you, back here at home. I was ashamed of you. But then I was shot and had months to think about the war. In Molly's letters, she told me what you did for her and my family. I thanked God that you were my friend and were here and not getting your ass shot off in some ridiculous battle. I realized that once again, you were the beacon that was going to get me through another difficult situation. As much shit as I've given you over the years for always doing the right thing or being rational, I'm sorry. You didn't go running off to war, excited to be shooting a musket. I realized I can't be ashamed to call you my friend. My God, you would do anything for me. I believe you would. You would give your life for me. But you're too astute to give your life to a pointless war."

"It's not pointless; it matters," said Max.

"Does it?" said Patrick.

"When we win this war, it will mean a better life for so many people," said Max.

"Will life be that much better? It's not going to be better for my family or me," Patrick said, raising his shortened arm. "Your faith won't allow you to kill another man, which saved you from a fate like mine or worse. I wish I had your faith. You've always been good. Those Jesuit priests would be proud of you."

"No, I'm not. Believe me; I'm not so good a Christian."

"Bullshit. If everyone had your moral conviction, just think how much better the world would be."

"It's never that simple, is it?" said Max.

"No, I guess not. What a messed-up world."

They sat for a minute in silence.

"I'm sorry, I have to go. I have to meet with a customer." Max downed the remainder in his glass.

"Somebody has to earn a wage," said Patrick.

"I'll come back later this week. We're going to the barber. I can hardly look at you. I'm sure Molly would like to see you cleaned up."

"She hasn't looked at me the same since I've been home. Things won't be the same with this," he said, holding up his arm again.

"I don't think it's your arm making her look at you differently," said Max. "You need to give each other time. You've been away a long while and have both been through quite a bit. Talk to her. Tell her some of what you told me. And listen to her; she's hurting inside too."

Max held out his arms, and they embraced. He patted Patrick on the back. "Things will look up for you; I know it."

CHAPTER 36

Annie sat beside a soldier's bed in the hospital barracks at Camp Dennison, writing a letter to his mother for him. The man spoke in heavy, labored breaths, requiring her to lean in to hear.

A young, handsome soldier in the next bed talked loudly, making it even more difficult for her to hear. "The Union will prevail over the rascal Confederates. We have more men, more commerce to supply our armies, and the Lord Almighty is on our side. We will emerge a stronger country with freedoms for the Negro and all men and women, making the United States the greatest nation ever to grace the earth. Men, I thank you for your courage and am proud to call you my brothers in arms."

Annie turned to the man, "Sir, I applaud your enthusiastic patriotism, but I ask that you orate more quietly so as not to disturb the other men's rest."

"Ma'am, I beg your forgiveness. I am happy to be a servant of the people of this nation. My enthusiasm sometimes gets the best of me."

"Apology accepted, and your restraint is appreciated by us all," said Annie.

A soldier across from them smirked at Annie's comment.

Annie finished writing the man's letter and promised to mail it. She moved to the vocal soldier's bedside. "You're new. I'm Annie."

"Well, pleased to meet you, Annie. I'm Will Mansfield, 21st Massachusetts Infantry."

"You're a long way from home. How did you end up here?" said Annie.

"The 21st, we fought at Bull Run, Antietam, Fredericksburg. Lost a good portion of our men when we ran up against Stonewall Jackson at the Battle of Chantilly in Virginia. After that, our orders sent us to fight with General Burnside and the Department of the Ohio. We were fighting the guerillas in Kentucky when I was hit by a sharpshooter while on patrol east of Lexington. Just arrived here last night."

"You've seen quite a bit of the war then. Thank you for your bravery. Is there anything I can do to make you more comfortable?" she asked.

"I…um, need to relieve myself. Can't walk yet." He pulled the sheet back, exposing a bandaged thigh.

Annie handed him a bedpan from under the bed. "Here you go. Use this." She left him alone and returned in a few minutes.

"How are you feeling?" said Annie.

"Leg hurts like a son of a bitch. Can you get me another opium pill?"

Annie came back with a pill and a glass of water.

"Thank you, Annie. What's your story?"

"My story? No story."

"How did you end up here?" he asked.

"I lead a women's circle for the Sanitary Commission. I was focused on sending supplies to soldiers, but then when the war started to result in so many casualties, and they opened this hospital, I started volunteering."

"Thank you for your service. The ladies of the Union have risen to the occasion with the same valor as our soldiers."

"I wouldn't go that far, but I've never been one to sit by when something needs to be done. Especially something as important as supporting the war," said Annie.

"I sense that. I've been observing you; you're different than these other ladies here. You remind me of some women I know in Boston. More confident, less timid. Like the Women's Rights Convention organizers in Boston in 1854."

"Were you there?" asked Annie.

"I was. Turned into quite a spectacle."

"I attended the Cincinnati Convention in 1855."

"I should have guessed. Did you get to hear Lucy Stone?" asked Will.

"Yes, she inspires me. What happened at the Boston convention—the spectacle?"

"Well, about a week before the convention, a slave named Anthony Burns, who had escaped from Virginia on a ship to Boston, was captured by slave catchers and put in the county jail. Abolitionists in town heard about this and organized a large protest outside Faneuil Hall. A group of them unsuccessfully tried to break into the jail and free Burns. On the day of the convention, officers led Burns from the jail to the waterfront to be put on a ship back to Virginia. A crowd of 50,000 people lined the streets to support Burns. Lucy Stone called a recess to the convention for us to go outside and show our support. We didn't stop them from shipping Burns back, but we made a hell of a statement. When the convention reconvened, it was agreed that the fight for women's rights should stand beside the rights of the Negro, the rights for all men and women."

"Fifty thousand people. That must have been exhilarating," said Annie.

"It sure was. There is strong support for both the abolition of slavery and for women's rights in New England. President Lincoln has our full support in pursuing this war."

Annie said, "Here in the west, people are more ambivalent about it. Even people I respect have beliefs but are hesitant to be open and forceful about them."

"It is almost a different world here. During my time in Kentucky, we knew that the farms in the surrounding area may have been friend or foe. It's hard to tell a man's heart by his appearance," said Will. "Did you hear about the National Convention on War and Women's Rights in New York in May?"

"No, I'm not familiar with it," said Annie.

"Elizabeth Cady Stanton led the convention. Lucy Stone and Susan B. Anthony spoke. They discussed the war and the importance of women fully supporting it to end the injustice of slavery. The women's rights movement is still here, but like everything in this country, the war overshadows and alters it."

"Your words reassure me. Sometimes, it is hard to face the injustices without supporters around me. Of late, I've been disappointed that the war has slowed the progress of the women's movement."

"Don't ever lose faith or stop fighting."

"I feel so alone."

"You're not, you're not. Oh, that pill you gave me has eased my pain. I'm feeling tired. Mind if I sleep now?"

"Oh, of course. I'm sorry. Yes, I should see to the other men."

"No need to be sorry. I enjoyed your company. Will I see you again?" said Will.

"Yes, I'll see you tomorrow."

#

Annie spent more time with Will Mansfield than with any other patient. She enjoyed his company and stimulating conversation. His life experiences in Boston were more similar to her upbringing in New York City than anyone she had met since moving to Cincinnati. She was impressed by his activism and passionate words about fighting for women's rights, words that had become lost in the war. She found herself looking forward to her shifts at the hospital and would extend her day to sit at Will's bedside.

"I brought you a treat today," said Annie, unwrapping and handing Will a piece of Marie's apple strudel.

Will took a bite. "Oh, it's heavenly. I haven't tasted anything this sweet since I left home. Did you make this?"

"No, my sister-in-law, Marie, made it. She bakes for the soldiers. It's one of her gifts. I can't cook anything."

"Well, you thank her for me. Tell her it made this soldier's day."

"I will."

"Your sister-in-law, you say? That implies there is a Mister Annie somewhere. Is he gone off to war?"

"No, he's at home."

"Hmm," he said.

"He's a councilman and owns a business. They do metalwork to supply the army. He feels he can better serve our troops in this manner than by wielding a weapon."

"Well, that makes sense. Fighting a war requires men and munitions. Someone has to supply the troops."

"Miller Industries is his company. I manage the accounts, schedule the work, and do the correspondence. I've helped him run the business for seven years now."

"I'm not surprised."

"He's a devout Catholic. He won't kill another man."

"Many Catholics follow their Church and have remained adamant about peace over war. Me—I believe that it became necessary to go to war to eliminate the injustice of slavery," said Will.

"What's this you're reading?" Annie said, picking up a book, embarrassed she had talked so much about Max.

"*Leaves of Grass. Poems by Walt Whitman.* Do you know his work?"

"I'm not familiar, no," said Annie.

"Would you read some of it for me?"

"Yes. Which poem?"

"'Poem of Walt Whitman, an American.' Start reading where the bookmark is," he said.

She opened the tattered book to a page marked with a photograph of Will and a young woman arm in arm. She studied the picture for a moment, then read:

"I am of old and young, of the foolish as much as
    the wise,
Regardless of others, ever regardful of others,
Maternal as well as paternal, a child as well as a
    man,
Stuffed with the stuff that is coarse, and stuffed
    with the stuff that is fine,

One of the great nation, the nation of many
    nations, the smallest the same, and the largest
    the same,
A southerner soon as a northerner, a planter non-
    chalant and hospitable,
A Yankee bound my own way, ready for trade,
    my joints the limberest joints on earth and
    the sternest joints on earth,
A Kentuckian walking the vale of the Elkhorn in
    my deer-skin leggings,
A boatman over lakes or bays, or along coasts--
    a Hoosier, Badger, Buckeye,
A Louisianian or Georgian, a Poke-easy from
    sand-hills and pines,
At home on Canadian snow-shoes, or up in the
    bush, or with fishermen off Newfoundland,
At home in the fleet of ice-boats, sailing with the
    rest, and tacking,
At home on the hills of Vermont, or in the woods
    of Maine, or the Texan ranch,
Comrade of Californians, comrade of free north-
    westerners, loving their big proportions,
Comrade of raftsmen and coalmen, comrade of all
    who shake hands and welcome to drink and
    meat,
A learner with the simplest, a teacher of the
    thoughtfulest,
A novice beginning, experient of myriads of sea-
    sons,

Of every hue, trade, rank, of every caste and re-
        ligion,
Not merely of the New World, but of Africa,
        Europe, Asia--a wandering savage,
A farmer, mechanic, artist, gentleman, sailor,
        lover, quaker,
A prisoner, fancy-man, rowdy, lawyer, physician,
        priest.

I resist anything better than my own diversity,
And breathe the air, and leave plenty after me,
And am not stuck up, and am in my place.
The moth and the fish-eggs are in their place,
The suns I see, and the suns I cannot see, are
        in their place,
The palpable is in its place, and the impalpable
        is in its place.

These are the thoughts of all men in all ages
        and lands, they are not original with me,
If they are not yours as much as mine, they are
        nothing, or next to nothing,
If they do not enclose everything, they are next
        to nothing,
If they are not the riddle and the untying of the
        riddle, they are nothing,
If they are not just as close as they are distant,
        they are nothing.

 This is the grass that grows wherever the land
        is and the water is,
This is the common air that bathes the globe."

"Enough for today?" Annie placed the picture back in the
book and closed it.
    "Yes, thank you," he said.

"It's an unusual style. The words don't flow like most poems. There's no rhyming," said Annie.

"In this part, he writes of the unique selves that collectively make up America. I fight for a country that thrives from the contributions of all of us—everyone."

"It's a beautiful vision. I wonder if we will ever achieve it." said Annie. "It's what we say we're about, but if you look closely, we're not."

"We must strive, even though we will never attain perfection. Don't you agree?"

"Yes, it's difficult sometimes," she said softly.

"Would you like to borrow the book? Take it home?" he said.

"What will you read?"

"Get me something from the shelves. I've carried that book since I left home, so I welcome a new one."

"Yes, thank you then. I will."

#

George Pendleton, a congressman in the House of Representatives from Ohio's first district, was a wealthy native Cincinnatian who had previously served as a senator in Washington. As the war proceeded and citizens' patience waned, Pendleton emerged as a champion of ending the war peacefully and negotiating a settlement with the South. As a Peace Democrat, he worked against Lincoln and the Republican party. The congressman was an old business acquaintance of Annie's stepfather, Stephen Neltner, an attorney. Pendleton asked Stephen to arrange a meeting with Max. They met in the meeting room of Simon Arnold's saloon on Eighth Street.

"Max, it's good to see you. It's been too long. How is Annie?" inquired Stephen.

"She is well, thank you. Annie has dedicated herself to the Sanitary Commission in support of the war. In addition to leading a circle of volunteers, she spends significant time aiding soldiers at Camp Dennison."

"Quite admirable. She is a remarkable woman. And Lizzie?"

"A reflection of her mother. She's seven years old now."

"Seven already? She'll be a debutante before you know it," said Stephen.

"She is focused on her schoolwork and assists with supporting the troops as well."

"Of course, a patriot like her parents. Max, I wanted George to meet you, as you are an influential member of our city, a councilman and a prominent figure in the German American community. George, Max's family has run a successful family-oriented establishment in Over-the-Rhine for more than twenty-five years."

Pendleton said, "The Over-the-Rhine neighborhood is one of the most populated in the city, and I recognize, as you do, the importance of listening to the voices of the people there. We, as elected officials, are obligated to represent those voices in our governing work. What would you say is the sentiment toward the war generally among your people?"

Max said, "By my people, are you referring to the citizens of the city's Fifth Ward, which I was elected to represent, or my family and friends in Over-the-Rhine?"

"I'm interested in both. You have a unique perspective I'd like to hear," said Pendleton.

"Congressman, it's difficult to generalize, as the opinions are as diverse here as they are across the country, and they are changing as the war drags on. I share this broadly: The most important thing to most men and women since before the war began is to preserve the Union. Natives and German-Americans alike appreciate the opportunities of this great nation and our representative form of government. They still believe in that. In addition, most believe in their hearts that slavery is an abhorrent stain on this nation which should be eliminated."

Pendleton asked, "We've been at war going on two years now. Do they still believe the war is worth fighting, or have they had enough?"

"Many are weary of war. Yes, they'd like it to end, but not at any cost."

"And what do they think of our president's proclamation of emancipation?"

"The general man is not in favor of it because there are politicians and those in the press that have instilled hysteria and fear that emancipation will result in a city overrun with Negroes, taking their jobs, assaulting their women, dirtying their communities, and needing food and shelter."

Pendleton said, "But this is what has already started to happen. I'm sure you've read the reports of the contraband moving across the river into the city and the North as they flee their masters in response to Lincoln's declaration."

Max said, "Granted, the freedmen seek safety and an opportunity to make a living, like any other men. The cities of the North are a natural destination for them, but they are hardly threatening the security of society as some newspapers, such as the *Enquirer*, would have their readers believe."

"Not yet, but if their numbers were to increase, don't you believe we would see a degradation of civility and society in general?" asked Pendleton.

"No, I don't believe that is a predestined outcome. Not if we as leaders establish policies and assistance to aid the assimilation of the Negro into society."

"Is that what your constituents want? To live side by side with the Negro?"

"They have been convinced they should be afraid. They need not be," said Max.

"Why are you so certain of this?"

"Congressman, are you acquainted with any Negroes?"

"Well, um, what do you mean?"

"Do you know any Negroes personally? Have you met with them? Spoken with them? Befriended any?" said Max.

"I have not had the opportunity or the need to do so, no. But neither have I befriended anyone of any race below my social class."

"By this lower status class, you mean most of your constituents?"

"Well, yes, I am a representative of all classes. That is how our government works. With my education and position in society, I am equipped to govern on behalf of them. Would you have common men leading government?"

"Some republic forms of government might suggest that, but putting that aside, as that is not how this nation's form has evolved, I would still suggest that you would better serve your constituents if you were more familiar with them. If they became people, rather than just an abstraction to you," said Max.

"You're quite a populist, aren't you? Negroes aren't citizens, so I don't need to know them. Are you friends with Negroes?" said Pendleton.

"I admit that I, like most men, find comfort when surrounded by people like me. And I don't pretend to know the life of the Negro, by any means, but I have become acquainted with several Negroes enough to empathize with their situation."

"Well, aren't you the enlightened man, then? Regardless of their situation, the immediate emancipation is unconstitutional, and an overstep of the president's powers. It's a dangerous precedent that exacerbates the divide between North and South and creates a growing divide among the Northerners that isn't helpful to the nation. The president has abused his powers as chief executive by declaring the Negro free, without constitutional authority. He has silenced voices of politicians and newspapers that disagree with his politics—an assault on the freedoms of our democracy."

"What do you advocate then as the best course of action for your constituents?" asked Max.

"We must cease this war, rescind the emancipation, and come together to negotiate a peaceful restoration of the nation."

"I no longer see a path to reconciliation without eliminating the institution of slavery," said Max.

"That's hardly reconciliation," said Pendleton. "That's a dogmatic, bull-headed position that will lead to thousands more casualties in Lincoln's war."

"Mr. Lincoln did not start this war, sir."

"No, but the black Republicans now own its continuation and consequences."

"You add to the hysteria by using terms like that—'black Republicans.' It degrades your reputation as a member of our federal legislature," said Max.

"I gather from your comments that you're now aligned with them," said Pendleton.

"I am, sir," stated Max.

"Well, that's disappointing to me and our common constituents. I had hoped we could collaborate to champion a peaceful end to the war and a bolstering of both of our reputations."

"I'm sorry to disappoint you, Congressman, but on this matter, I don't think we can agree."

"We're finished here then. Stephen, thank you for the introduction." Pendleton and Stephen rose.

Stephen said, "Please give my best to Annie and Lizzie."

"I will, thank you. Good day to both of you," said Max.

#

That evening after dinner, Annie sat in the parlor reading. Max came in and leaned down to kiss her. She turned her head to let him kiss her cheek. He sat in a chair and picked up a newspaper.

"How was your meeting with Stephen and Congressman Pendleton?" asked Annie.

"The congressman said he was disappointed in me."

"Oh, why?" said Annie.

"I think he and Stephen were both surprised that my position on the war has moved so far from where it was before the last election. Pendleton hoped I would be an ally in advocating for a peaceful settlement with the Confederates. He implied that if I did, it could help further my career. And he felt that I no longer represent most of my constituents on the matter."

Annie said, "Do you think that's the case? Do most citizens want us to negotiate a settlement with the Confederates?"

"I think that here in Cincinnati, with our proximity to the South, men fear an invasion of freed slaves. They know slavery is wrong but are afraid to embrace the unknown. No one can know how a reconstructed America will look after the war and the end of slavery. For this reason, they fear emancipation and are willing to accept a settlement."

Annie said, "A negotiation would include some form of continued legal slavery. I don't see how it couldn't. If the Confederates came to the table, they'd settle for nothing short of it. I'm saddened that so many people would be willing to let slavery continue. I hate to see us come this far in the battle against it, only to give up now. But I'm tired of the war."

"Me too," said Max.

"The killing, the lives ruined, the diverted supplies, the soldiers. It's everywhere, and the rest of our lives are stagnant. How much longer?"

"We must continue on, stay strong. With the new military draft enlisting men for one to three years, the president must believe we are far from the end."

Annie said, "The last report in the paper said that there are enough volunteers to meet the draft quotas for our district. Thank God for that. The bounty donations we make to pay the volunteers are at least keeping you from a potential draft into the army."

"For now, yes," said Max. "Most of the men are signing because of the bounty. They receive a couple of hundred dollars to enlist. That is a substantial sum for common men, especially those without adequate wages. It is becoming the poor man's army."

Max continued, "As I sat and talked with Stephen and Pendleton today, I became more convinced that we must persevere and win the war. It's the only way. Archbishop Purcell has advocated for the continued pursuit of the war in the name of abolishing slavery. He's broken with most of the Catholic Church, which advocates peace. I am comforted knowing I have one man of the cloth who supports my position; at least I'm not a heathen."

"You're no heathen," she said.

"It pains me to support killing, even to achieve a noble cause. I look at all the men lost and injured. Seeing Patrick last week…he's one of the hundreds of thousands of men who will return from the war scarred physically or in their souls. I hate to think that their sacrifices may be for nothing."

"Did Stephen share any news of my family?"

"No. He asked about you and Lizzie and sent his regards. We kept it business. It was awkward to be set up by him like that. You're sad that he sent no word from your mother?"

"I accepted our estrangement years ago. Deep inside, I still hope we might reconcile, but if having a granddaughter didn't overcome her disappointment in me, then I don't believe anything will."

"I'm sorry," said Max. "What's this?" he asked, picking up the tattered copy of *Leaves of Grass* from the side table.

"A book of poetry. One of the soldiers loaned it to me. He asked me to read to him from it. I was intrigued, so I wanted to read more."

"I've heard it's full of licentious garbage. You shouldn't have this in the house."

"Have you read it?" she asked in a sharp tone.

"No, but I read a review when it was first published. Hardly an appropriate book for a Christian woman."

"You can be so closed-minded. So set in your ways, like a sheep in the pope's flock. It's suffocating. Why don't you read it and form your own opinion before passing judgment?" She rose and retreated to her bedroom.

Max picked up the book and flipped through it. The photograph of the young smiling couple dropped onto his lap. He examined it, then put it back in the book and dropped it on the table. He poured himself a whiskey and returned to his newspaper.

CHAPTER 37

Annie set a bowl of water and a cloth on Will's bedside table.

"Good morning, Annie," said Will.

"Good morning. Here is your bath," she said.

"Aren't you going to help me?"

"You're healing quite nicely. You don't need my help anymore."

"It was the highlight of my day, having you tend to me."

"You need to look after yourself now. They tell me you'll be leaving soon," said Annie.

"Yes, I'm to rejoin my company in Kentucky. Having you care for me these past few weeks made me feel human again. After months in the field, it has been nice to have someone to connect with to help me remember what life can be like again after the war. I'll remember your kindness."

"What are you going to do after the war?" she asked.

"I'll go back to Boston. I'd like to help with the anti-slavery cause again. Traveling this country and serving with men from all over, I've learned that there are still too many people who are happy to let slavery continue in the South or worse, feel the Black man doesn't merit equal treatment with the white."

"Don't you think the war will resolve the question?" she said.

"Lincoln has declared that slaves in the Confederate states are free, but first, we must win the war to force the Southerners to accept it. Second, the Emancipation

Proclamation doesn't apply to border states like Maryland, Kentucky, and Missouri, where slavery still exists, but those states aren't in rebellion against the Union. They're an open question. Probably most important, once the war is won, and those issues are resolved, getting slave owners and even Northerners to accept a level of equality with Negroes will take time and effort. We can't rest even after the war."

"I understand all that, but I am frustrated and exhausted by the efforts to liberate the Negro, while the cause of women's position has been ignored these last few years. Women have demonstrated their ability to do men's work, lead organizations, and take care of house and home. Yet, we're no closer to being respected as individuals."

"That is another shift that will take time and continued effort," Will said. "I understand why the focus on slavery frustrates the women's movement. Please don't give up on it. You told me you were managing the accounts of your family's business. Doesn't that provide you a level of acceptance by the men in this community?"

"It's not that simple," said Annie. "Most men at the shop have come to respect me and accept my authority and abilities, but the men we do business with have not. Our customers and suppliers still look to my husband. The legal system still looks to my husband. My husband is still the final arbiter of all matters concerning the business. I am a vehicle to accomplish his objectives. He consults me and uses my talents when it is advantageous, but he doesn't truly see me as an equal partner in the business. He still expects me to be a mother to our daughter first and an assistant to the business second."

"Is there a practical alternative to that arrangement?" said Will.

"There must be," she said. "There is not today because men have prescribed the order of things. It has always been this way, and the schools, laws, and government reinforce it. I want the world to acknowledge that a woman's sex doesn't relegate her to a secondary position. I don't want my daughter to feel the weight of her sex smother her ambitions. I'm tired of it."

"I love your passion. Use it. Don't give up. You have to be patient until the war is over, but after that, fight for it all."

"I'm tired of being patient. It's always something else, some other priority. The war is endless; it will take years to resolve the issues that started the war. I don't have time to wait. My life is now. My daughter is growing up now. We are suffocating, and no one hears us." Annie began to cry.

Will reached and took her hand. "You are strong. Continue the fight."

"I'm just so tired."

"Things will get better. I'll continue to fight for the Negro, for women. You must continue too. Lead the fight here, knowing I'm fighting with you where I am. You are not alone," he said.

"I feel like I am, sometimes."

"You're not. There are plenty of us fighting for a better Union. You're a strong soldier in the fight too. Don't despair. Soldier on."

"I wish I could have you here near me. You're so strong, so brave, so encouraging," said Annie.

"Alas, our paths crossed in the midst of a national cataclysm. I must go soon and do my part to win the war. You must stay and do your part. We must fight from all fronts."

"Is everything all right here?" Sister Elyse stood at the foot of Will's bed, looking disapprovingly at Annie. Will withdrew his hand from hers.

"Yes, Sister," said Annie.

"There are other patients to attend to. Please see to them," said the nun.

Annie held Will's gaze for a moment, then stood and left.

#

When Annie arrived at Camp Dennison the following day, the in-charge nurse assigned her to attend to newly-arrived soldiers. She entered her assigned barracks and was assaulted by the persistent odors of soldiers and sickness. She began with one of the men who had his leg amputated at the thigh. She carried a pitcher, bowl of water, towel, and clean clothes to the man's bed. She washed and changed him and gave him his painkillers and something to eat. She made minimal small talk, working mechanically.

She spent the entire day in the barracks, nursing a dozen men without her usual level of engagement or enthusiasm. At the end of her shift, she went to Will's barracks. As she approached his bed, she realized another soldier was lying in his place.

He smiled at her as she stood at the foot of his bed. "Good evening."

"Sir. Will, the man who was here, in this bed…where is he?" said Annie.

"I don't know," said the new soldier.

"He's gone," said the man in the next bed.

"Gone where?" said Annie.

"Back with his company. They put him on a train this morning."

"Oh," said Annie.

"He said to tell you goodbye."

"Anything else?" she asked.

"No."

Annie reached into her bag and pulled out a piece of apple strudel. She handed it to the soldier.

"Thank you, Annie. He'll be fine. He was looking forward to getting back to his unit. He's a patriot."

"Thank you," she said and walked out of the barracks to the train platform. She sat on a bench until the train arrived, then took a seat in the back of a car, slumped down, closed her eyes, and slept the entire ride back to the city.

#

July 1863

In the east, the Confederates plotted to advance into the North and break the spirit of the Union population. They hoped to turn public sentiment against the war and apply political pressure to persuade the Union to negotiate a settlement. Fierce battles were fought at Gettysburg, where Grant's army repelled Lee's invasion and forced their retreat to Virginia. Still, the result was the largest number of casualties of any battle in the war. The North's casualties totaled more than 23,000 and the South's 25,000—more than a third of Lee's army. The dead were buried in makeshift graveyards, the wounded were sent to hospitals, and the captured were locked up in each side's prisons.

About the same time in the west, the Union forces took Vicksburg, Tennessee. The North now controlled the entire Mississippi River, splitting the South into two sections and cutting off supply and transportation routes for the Confederates. The North appeared to be gaining the upper hand in the war.

Later in July, Confederate General John Hunt Morgan began a raid with cavalrymen and artillery in central Kentucky. He raided farms and homes, taking food, valuables, and supplies as he moved northward. As reports of the fast-moving soldiers made it to Union leadership, they pursued the raiders but remained several days behind for more than a week.

Word reached Cincinnati that Morgan's raiders were approaching Ohio and the Queen City. Once again, the city sent more than 10,000 men to man the forts and rifle pits in northern Kentucky and the hills of Cincinnati. Martial law was declared as businesses were closed, and people stayed home, fearing their city would be ravaged and destroyed by the advancing raiders.

The Union troops chased Morgan across the river into Indiana, west of town. Morgan's men rode into Harrison, Ohio, then moved eighty-five miles from west to east in a line north of Cincinnati. Morgan considered an attack on Camp Dennison but was deterred by the number of forces there. The raiders struck farms and homes on a path east of the city, leaving Cincinnati untouched. The Union troops eventually caught up with and captured Morgan and his men. By July 26, the threat had passed, and relieved Cincinnatians again celebrated their avoidance of direct war violence.

#

November 19, 1863

Lincoln dedicated the national cemetery created at Gettysburg to honor the 3,500 fallen soldiers. Newspapers across the country published his concise speech, which crystalized the war's objective, recognized the men's sacrifices, and rallied the Northern citizens to remain steadfast in their support for the war.

Lincoln's Gettysburg Address

Four score and seven years ago our fathers brought forth on this continent, a new nation, conceived in Liberty and dedicated to the proposition that all men are created equal.

Now we are engaged in a great civil war, testing whether that nation, or any nation so conceived and so dedicated, can long endure. We are met on a great battlefield of that war. We have come to dedicate a portion of that field, as a final resting place for those who here gave their lives that that nation might live. It is altogether fitting and proper that we should do this.

But, in a larger sense, we can not dedicate—we can not consecrate—we can not hallow—this ground. The brave men, living and dead, who struggled here, have consecrated it, far above our poor power to add or detract. The world will little note, nor long remember what we say here, but it can never forget what they did here. It is for us the living, rather, to be dedicated here to the unfinished work which they who fought here have thus far so nobly advanced. It is rather for us to be here dedicated to the great task remaining before us—that from these honored dead we take increased devotion to that cause for which they gave the last full measure of devotion—that we here highly resolve that these dead shall not have died in vain—that this nation, under God, shall have a new birth of freedom—and that government of the people, by the people, for the people, shall not perish from the earth.

CHAPTER 38

May 1864 – Six Months Later

Lizzie opened her mother's bedroom door and approached the bed where Annie was still sleeping. She pulled the draperies back slightly, letting a small ray of sunlight into the room.

"Mama. Mama, wake up." She stood directly beside the bed.

"Hmm." Annie opened her eyes, startled to see Lizzie standing so close. She lifted her head suddenly. "What is it?"

"It's almost time to go," said Lizzie.

"Good morning," said Annie, beckoning Lizzie to join her in bed with her outstretched arm.

Lizzie climbed up into bed and hugged her mother. "Are you feeling melancholy again today?"

"I'm feeling better this morning. Thank you, darling."

"We mustn't linger too long. We'll miss the parade," said Lizzie.

"My little director. Just a few minutes. Let me wake up fully. Where is Papa?"

"He's gone to the shop. He said he'll meet us after the parade."

"And Marie?"

"She's already gone too. We went to the landing this morning. Then we made strudel for the soldiers."

"You've already been to the landing?" said Annie.

"Yes, a steamboat brought the soldiers home. It tooted its whistle and fired its cannons. We sang a song."

"What song did you sing?"

Lizzie sang, "When Johnny comes marching home again, hurrah, hurrah. When Johnny comes marching home again, hurrah, hurrah. The men will cheer and the boys will shout, the ladies they will all turn out and we'll all feel gay when Johnny comes marching home. Hurrah!"

"Very lovely. That's one of the nicest war songs, I think."

"We cheered the soldiers when they walked off the boat," said Lizzie. "We hugged Albert. Some of the ladies were crying. Marie said we'll feed the men this afternoon after the parade. They're coming home because their time is up in the army."

"These men have fought bravely in the war and deserve a hero's welcome," said Annie.

"Hugo's not coming home," said Lizzie.

"No, Hugo was killed in battle. It will be hard for Marie."

"She was happy this morning."

"She's happy on the outside but a little sad on the inside, missing Hugo. She's been a brave and strong woman, supporting the troops," said Annie.

"When I grow up, I want to support the troops like Marie. I already know how to make strudel, and I can feed the soldiers in the food lines."

"I think you can do much more than support the soldiers. You can run a business, like Papa and me, or become a lawyer or doctor."

"Or a nurse like Auntie Mary Berry," said Lizzie.

"Not a nurse; how about a doctor?"

"I'm a girl."

"Girls can become doctors too. If that's what you want to do."

"I think a nurse," said Lizzie.

"Nurses do wonderful work, but you can do even more good as a doctor."

"Maybe I'll work at the Eichen Garten, like Aunt Helene. She can carry six mugs of beer to the men without spilling any."

"Lizzie, we need to take a trip to New York City. Two sisters from Cincinnati became doctors and run a hospital there—Doctors Elizabeth and Emily Blackwell. Would you like to visit New York City?"

"Oh yes, when can we go?"

"We'll see. Maybe this summer."

"Yes, yes. Will Papa go too?"

"We'll ask him. He's never been to New York City either. I can show you both where I grew up."

Lizzie hopped out of bed and jumped up and down. "New York, New York, hurrah!"

"I guess I better get moving," said Annie. "Run downstairs and see what time it is. I'll get dressed."

#

Lizzie sat at the second-floor window above the Eichen Garten, looking out over Vine Street, watching for the parade. "It's coming. I see the flag. The band is playing. Oma, they're coming!"

"Here I am," said her grandmother, joining her at the window.

The Turner marching band led the procession up Vine Street. Crowds of Over-the-Rhine residents lined the streets to welcome home the *Die Neuner*, one of four German regiments that had been among the first in the city to volunteer for the war effort. The men had completed their three-year commitment and were returning to their families. They would receive their back pay and a $100 bonus for serving the entire three years. They had fought fiercely and lost men in battles at Rich Mountain, Carnifex Ferry, Mill Spring, Perryville, and Chickamauga, including Marie's beau, Hugo.

The uniformed men marched with their bayonets, looking weathered, with sunburned faces, faded uniforms, and worn boots. Several who had lost limbs were pulled in carts. Occasionally spectators from the crowd would descend on one of the men with cheers and pats, hindering the parade's progress. Some stopped to hug friends along the way and then ran to join their place. The neighborhood collectively welcomed their sons and husbands home, full of pride.

"Where are they going?" asked Lizzie.

"Up the street to the Turner Hall for a party."

"Can we go?"

"You and I will join your parents there later."

#

Max pushed through the crowd inside the main room of Turner Hall, decorated with a large "Welcome Home Soldiers" banner, American flags, and streamers. Friends stopped to greet him at nearly every step as he worked through the packed room. Spirits were lighter than they had been in a long time. Max took a beer from a server's tray. He hugged and congratulated returning soldiers he knew from his boyhood. He joined a circle of men in conversation, several standing arm in arm.

Max asked, "How many from the 9th are re-enlisting?"

"Not many. Your brother Albert is one of the few. He's a brave soldier," said one of the men.

"To Albert," one of the soldiers toasted.

"To Albert!"

"May God continue to watch over him."

The men chatted, the war the predominant topic. "With so many men's three-year commitments up, we need to replenish the ranks to finish off the Rebels. The president ordered a draft of 500,000 men."

"In the First Ward, they had a blindfolded seventeen-year-old boy draw the names out of a drum. Elliot Hunt

Pendleton, the congressman's brother, was drafted while away on his honeymoon."

"Won't that be a rude surprise for his new bride when they return?"

"The draft in the Third Ward selected two city councilmen—can you believe it?"

"Max, you weren't one of the councilmen drafted, were you?"

"No, not me," said Max.

"I understand your shop is now working on gunboats?"

"We are. We launched an iron-clad battery steamboat, the *Catawba*, in April. We're working on a couple more. We're so busy that I've applied for an exemption from the draft for my employees. If any of you returning soldiers are looking for work, I could use you, especially if you've experience in iron work."

"I saw the gunboats that captured Morgan's raiders moored opposite your factory last week, Max. It was a bizarre scene. People were taking rowboats out on the river to glimpse the prisoners on the boats. People are fascinated by all aspects of this war."

"I guess Morgan's men are celebrities of sorts."

"The army put the cannons captured from Morgan on display near the river at Front and Broadway. There's been a steady crowd of people curious to see them."

"The drafts are heating up. Men who can afford to are paying the $300 commutation fee or paying substitutes, so additional drafts are required. We're in a race to replenish the army to outman the Confederates. Thousands are reporting to Camp Dennison each week to be mustered out. They had to move all the patients to other hospitals in the city to make room for the returning soldiers there."

"I've heard numbers of seventy-five Negroes signing up to fight every day. They're flooding into Covington and Cincinnati from the South. Many are walking off their plantations now that Lincoln will let them in the army."

Max said, "My friend, John, was one of the first to sign up for the 5th U.S. Colored Infantry. No problem getting enlistments in the Colored regiments now. They're making a significant impact in our numbers and our ability to out-fight the Confederates."

"Here's a man who volunteered—Oskar!"

Oskar greeted his friends.

"When are you reporting, Oskar?"

"I'm off to Camp Dennison next week," said Oskar.

"The peace Democrats are openly campaigning against the draft."

"Damned Copperheads—they really are snakes! It's hard enough to fill our numbers without those traitors working against the president."

"I heard the governor put the National Guard into active service to assist General Grant in a hundred-day push against the South."

"Jesus, we're pulling out all the stops."

"We can't let up now. The Confederates don't have the numbers of soldiers to compete with the North. We have to finish them off with a show of force they cannot deny."

"It's making it difficult to maintain a sense of normalcy here at home. The school board even met to decide how to address the loss of teachers from the draft."

Marie broke into the group of men with a tray of beers.

"Marie!" The crowd reached for the beers and set their empties on her tray. Several kissed her cheeks and touched her arm.

As she looked at the soldiers, Marie's eyes moistened. "Welcome home."

"It's great to see you."

She lingered for a few minutes, then retreated to the kitchen.

After several hours, the ladies served a banquet. Judge Stallo made a speech and thanked them for their service. The regiment commander, Colonel Kaemmerling, thanked the citizens for their generosity and welcomed them home. They cleared the banquet tables and pushed them to the end of the room. A German band played while the partiers danced and sang.

Annie arrived and stood next to Max.

One of the drunk soldiers said, "The city seems to have more Negroes than when I left. Max, can't the city council do something about it?"

"What do you mean?" said Max.

"They're going to drive wages down. Soon, we'll compete with them for the jobs, and our position will fall even further."

Annie spoke, "What would you have city council do? It's a free labor market."

"Well, maybe you should pass an ordinance preventing them from entering the city, or at least keep them south of the canal."

"That's undemocratic, wouldn't you say?" said Annie.

The drunken man said, "Look here, no one asked you your opinion. Why don't you go fetch us some more beer?"

"I am not your servant," Annie said sharply.

"Annie," said Max.

Annie continued, "I've as much a right to state my opinion as any of you."

"Yeah, yeah, you're Max's high society wife. You're both too good for us. Supposed to represent the citizens, and like the rest of the politicians, you do what fattens your pockets."

Another soldier added, "You say you're working for us. You, who abandoned the neighborhood, married her. Too good to fight in the war, like a decent self-respecting man."

"I hear he's too yellow to fight," chimed in another.

"Why are you even here? You're not a soldier. Do you even support the war?"

"I support the war," said Max. "I am as committed as you are to defend the Union."

"Defend with what? Your money? You are an aristocratic coward."

Oskar stepped in the man's face. "My brother is not a man of arms, but he's a staunch servant of God that has done as much as any man in this city to defend the Union. His factory has built ironclad ships, converted passenger steamboats into tinclads to defend our waters, and built cannons to supply our armies. He has donated thousands of dollars for causes, including supporting families whose husbands are at war. He's a patriot. For God's sake, we need to stop fighting each other and put our passion toward defeating our enemy."

"Fine," said the man, "but I don't like the look of him." The man left the group.

"Annie, I think you should go home," said Max. "These men are drunk. This is no place for a woman."

"Count yourself among the drunk. Men," she scoffed as she pushed her way toward the door.

CHAPTER 39

October 1864

"Where are we going?" asked Lizzie, struggling to keep up with her father's brisk pace.

"We need to visit a relief camp on our way to the rally," said Max.

"What's a relief camp?" asked Lizzie.

They arrived at the makeshift camp in a building between Fourth and Hammond Streets. "It's a place for men and women to stay until they find a home and can support themselves." About thirty people stood on the sidewalk in front of the building, huddled together. Max held Lizzie's hand as he navigated through the crowd and went inside.

Two men greeted them.

"Good morning; I'm Max Mueller from city council."

"Mr. Mueller, good morning. What can we do for you?" said one of them.

"I wanted to stop by to see your operation. I heard you've taken in a group of freed men and women."

"Yes, we learned of a group of emancipated people arriving by steamship from Arkansas. They had nowhere to go and spent their first night sleeping on the public landing. We brought them here, fed them, and provided beds, but it's crowded."

"How many have you?" asked Max.

"Nearly 150, including a number of children."

"What do you need?" said Max.

"Nothing immediately. We have donations of food and clothing and can keep them here for a week or two."

"What about after that?"

"Not sure," said the man. "We're talking to several communities in the northern part of the state that offered to help freedmen establish homesteads. That may be an option. Most of these people are farmers from plantations in Arkansas. They're good candidates to farm upstate. But the government needs to get a plan together quickly for aid. Our city can't handle the influx of people if we don't have assistance, and there needs to be better coordination across the country. They can't all come to Cincinnati."

Max said, "Congress is still debating the particulars of the proposed National Freedmen's Bureau to support the emancipated. They're arguing over whether it should fall under the Department of War or Treasury."

"Meanwhile, the flood of freedmen pours into the city."

"I'll bring it up at council," said Max. "See if we can't get some local governance and funding to assist until the bureau is established."

"Thank you, Mr. Mueller. Anything you can do is appreciated. Also, sir, if there's anything you can do to influence the national program, we're going to need it to do more than feed and house people."

"What do you suggest?"

"Feeding and housing is a start and a temporary solution. There needs to be a coordinated effort to provide schooling and employment. Without that, they'll remain vagrants and wards of the government."

"It's a large problem. I understand," said Max.

"Anything you can do to help."

"Thank you both and all your volunteers for all you're doing. God bless you."

Max shook hands and made his way back outside. Lizzie held his hand tightly and pressed against him as they walked.

"What's the matter?" Max asked Lizzie

"I'm frightened."

Max asked, "What are you afraid of?"

"The Negroes."

"Why?"

"They're ugly and dirty."

"Lizzie, why do you say that?"

"Their skin is dirty, and they're not nice. They talk funny. Jennifer said that we have to keep them down South, or they'll come and hurt us."

Max stopped and squatted down to eye level with her. "Lizzie, you don't need to be afraid of Negroes, honey. Jennifer is wrong. They won't hurt us. You know Mr. John, the Negro who comes to our house?"

She nodded.

"You like John. He's a nice man. He wouldn't hurt you. Negroes have dark skin, but they're not dirty. The Negroes have been mistreated by the slave masters in the South. They made them work without paying them, and they wouldn't let them go to school, so the Negroes need our help. God wants us to help them and be nice to them, the same as anyone. Do you understand?"

She nodded again. Max was unconvinced but stood and walked on. Cannons boomed a few blocks away.

"What was that?" asked Lizzie, grabbing him around the waist.

"Cannons. It's all right. It's part of the rally." They reached the crowd of more than 100,000 who gathered for the Union rally. There were bonfires on several street corners. Men shot rockets and Roman candles. Two bands played music amongst the crowd. They met Annie on the agreed-to corner.

"Let's try to move closer to the stage so we can hear," said Max as Salmon Chase took the stage.

"Can you hear anything?" asked Annie.

"No, he's likely pledging support for Lincoln for reelection," said Max. "Even though he resigned from Lincoln's cabinet as Secretary of State, the press says he still supports him for reelection. The word is that Lincoln made a deal to appoint him to Chief Justice to appease the radical Republicans who want Chase to run against Lincoln for the Republican party nomination."

"Lincoln has to win," said Annie.

Max said, "I never thought I'd be advocating for a war candidate, but it's our only hope to put an end to slavery and the war. Congressman Pendleton tried again to get me to speak on behalf of the Democratic ticket of General McClellan for president and Pendleton himself for vice president at the Democratic convention last month. He made me publicly rebuke him, so it's on the record that I support the Republican candidate now. I don't know what that will do to my bid for re-election next year, but I couldn't let that sway my position."

"Ever since Sherman's army burned and captured Atlanta and began his march to the coast, public sentiment seems to be going our way. Most people in this city now believe that the war will be won if Lincoln is reelected," said Annie. "This is frustrating, standing here and not being able to hear. Let's go home."

Max took Annie's hand as they walked.

"For the first time in a long time, I'm hopeful," said Annie.

"I am too. I'm glad you're not feeling so blue anymore. It's good to see you out and about," said Max.

Annie said, "We need to talk about Lizzie's schooling. When the war ends, I think we should send her to a boarding school in the east."

"At this age?" he said.

"Yes, it would do her good. She needs to be challenged intellectually in a more open environment."

"You think she needs an education like yours, a young women's school?"

"I think she needs to go to a progressive school, where they accept girls as equal classmates with the boys."

"She's too young to go away to school," said Max.

"You went to boarding school when you were about her age."

"A boarding school less than a mile from my family."

"It doesn't matter. You gained independence by living on your own," said Annie.

"But."

"Don't say it," she said.

"What?"

"Don't say she's a girl."

"She is," he said.

"We were having such a nice walk, and now you go and make me angry."

"Would you feel comfortable with Lizzie halfway across the country?" asked Max.

"I would," said Annie.

"I want the best for her too," said Max. "She needs a good Catholic education in an environment where the students and the faculty are committed to living a Christian life. She needs that foundation to develop fully and become a good citizen."

"I don't agree that a popist perspective is the best way to a full life for her. She needs a more open-minded set of perspectives and a broader set of experiences."

"She is nine years old. How full can her life be?" said Max. "There's time for that."

"I know your faith and Jesuit education mean so much to you. It provided you what you needed to develop into who you are today. But if we leave her as a girl in Saint Mary's School, she will be treated as a second-class student. That is the hard truth. Same if she were to go to the common schools here in Cincinnati. I know. Remember, I taught in the schools. I want her to have a better chance."

"A better chance at what—becoming a lightning rod of attention to be ridiculed and ostracized? Why put her through that?"

"Is that how you see the cause for women's rights?" said Annie.

"Can you honestly say that it's not! Championing the cause for women's rights has led to negative reactions everywhere you go."

"I'm surprised at you. You didn't shy away from a fight for your rights or what you wanted as the son of immigrants. Why don't you expect your daughter to do the same thing?" said Annie.

"Because I also know the pain of it. It hurts not to be accepted, to be on the outside trying to get in. I don't want her to go through that," he said.

"You can't protect her from that. As a woman, she'll face that every day of her life, no matter what we do for her. We need to give her a fighting chance, with a progressive education, so that her choices are broader than mine and she can make an impact on the world around her."

"She needs the foundation of Christian teaching to inspire her to do good and face adversity with grace. Our young people need that, or we don't stand a chance as a country."

"That's not enough for her. You were a man, so finding a way to fit in with the world as it is, worked for you. Don't you see that if she settles for the accepted path, she will miss the opportunity to live up to her potential? She'll be pushed down until her dreams are smothered by the weight of men."

"That is a pretty dim view of her future. Is that how you feel? Is that your life?" he said.

"Yes. Can't you see that? We have to help her change society. It's not enough for her to just focus on herself—that's only the start."

"That's a lot to put on a nine-year-old."

"Yes, it's daunting," said Annie. "It's not fair, but the world's not fair, so we all must work to change it. We're talking about the country where Lizzie will live. We're not asking her to do it alone. We need to be there for her every step of the way. She needs your active help too."

"Is it truly so terrible for women?" he said.

"Yes. You can't see it; you're a man. Every breath we take is heavier than yours. Men's dominance permeates every inch of the world we live in."

"I'm sorry. I can't understand what it's like."

"It's impossible for you to feel what we feel. I understand that. I only ask that you try to empathize with me, Lizzie, all of us. Do what you can to understand and work with us for change."

"I need to think about this," he said.

"I know."

"You're making my head ache," he said, running his fingers through his hair.

"Good," she said.

"You know that I love you."

"I know. I love you too."

CHAPTER 40

As the Union army won more battles, public support for finishing the war led to Lincoln's landslide reelection in November 1864. The Confederate capital of Richmond was captured, and General Robert E. Lee surrendered to General Grant at Appomattox Courthouse in April 1865, ending the war. Cities across the North held euphoric celebrations in streets, churches, and halls. The South and its peculiar institution were defeated.

Six days after the surrender, President Lincoln was assassinated, and the country mourned the loss of the champion of democracy, the Union, and equal rights for all men. Lincoln's vice president, Andrew Johnson, was sworn in to lead the efforts to reconstruct the United States without slavery.

#

May 1865

John and Max knocked on the door of Aaron's house. Mary greeted them and escorted them to the back garden.

"Aaron, Max and John are here," Mary said.

"Mueller." They shook. "John, how are you?" he said, nodding at John.

"I'm happy to be alive, thank you," said John.

Aaron said, "I understand you served in the 5th Colored Infantry?"

"Yes, I did. Served and fought in Virginia and was there when the war ended. It's good to be home."

"Very honorable of you," said Aaron.

"Thank you. And how are you since release from your incarceration?" asked John.

"Happy to be home as well. I'm thankful that President Lincoln offered amnesty to so many in the name of reuniting the country," said Aaron.

"How did that work?" asked Max.

"I signed an oath of allegiance to the United States Constitution and the Union and agreed to abide by any acts passed by Congress related to slaves. I signed it, and they let me walk out of prison."

"It's a tragedy what they did to him. He was an amazing man with a true Christian heart. Our country will miss his leadership," said Max.

"He proved himself an able politician. I, like many, underestimated him and what he was capable of," said Aaron.

"Aaron, I must ask—why did you do it?" said Max.

"Why did I sell the Gatling gun plans to the South?"

"Yes, among other things that betrayed the Union."

"I lived my whole life in-between my mother and father's beliefs," said Aaron. "I saw the good and bad of both sides, and neither was clearly in the right to me. So I didn't hold allegiance to either. I was willing to play one against the other to win. It was business for me."

"You're an opportunist then?"

"If that's what you want to call me. The way I see it, I'm no different than you or most of the men in this country. I use my abilities to advance myself within the commercial and political systems in place."

Max scoffed. "That's a twisted view of our society."

"Is it?" said Aaron. "How is my behavior different from the powerful congressman in Washington who introduces and passes laws that bring economic advantage to himself?

Or you, Max, who used your relationships to secure contracts to supply the armies and fill your coffers with government money? Even you, John, with your newfound status among the proper Colored of Cincinnati, using your earnings to begin to acquire things that your former brothers on the plantation can't imagine. Aren't we all using our abilities to better ourselves and, in doing so, gaining advantage over others?"

"The difference is you broke the law and betrayed your country," said Max.

"Who made the laws? The government of the Union made up of men, who destroyed the society built by another group of men—both groups living according to their own defined rules."

"But your behavior was immoral," said Max.

"Ahh—the morals as defined by the Holy Catholic Church. The Church made up of men who took the teaching of Christ and created a set of laws its flock is supposed to follow. I never bought into it, Mueller, but I know you did."

"I see. So you believe anything goes? Anything is fair game if you can get away with it?"

"No, I understand there must be limits; otherwise, we have anarchy. I spent a lot of time in prison thinking about it. But in our society, there are going to be winners and losers. I'd rather be a winner."

"You feel no obligation to be fair, then?" said Max.

"Fair? There's no fair. That would mean we're all the same, and we're all committed to the common good. We're not all born the same and we don't all work toward a common good. Do you believe men are capable of that?

"I do," said Max. "Some of us are born with greater abilities. It's our obligation to assist others to help them better their position."

Aaron shrugged. "We like to profess that in this country that if we apply our abilities, we can succeed, but that's not really what allows some to succeed more than others. Chance and circumstance matter more. My parents owned Given

House and its riches due to my mother's family bloodline. You grew up in the slums Over-the-Rhine, and John was born a slave in a cabin. We're all born into our circumstances, and there's very little we can do about it. Unless everyone decides to give up what they have and share equally. That's not going to happen—it's the way of the world. It's human nature."

"You're so cynical. Man doesn't have to be driven by self-promotion," said Max.

"Self-promotion, self-preservation…, it's human nature. I don't see you sharing your acquired wealth with John here. Where's your sense of equality? Oh—you donate to your charities, help out your friend Patrick—just enough to make you feel like you're not like me; like you're not looking out for yourself."

Max looked at Aaron, not sure how to respond. John looked between the two men.

Aaron said, "Don't worry, Mueller. As I said, it's human nature. I understand. But don't judge me for being like you."

"I'm not like you," said Max. "I don't go out of my way to take advantage of others. I try to help others where I can."

"I know you do. Good for you. I'm sure it makes you feel better. We're the same, Mueller. It's just degrees."

"You resent me because I turned you in, don't you?"

"No, I don't resent you. I understand you. There's no mystery with you. I should have known better than to ask you for your assistance; you're a man of unwavering values," Aaron said sarcastically. "I had to earn a living. I miscalculated, and I lost. I don't harbor ill-will toward you for it."

Max shook his head. "You and I couldn't be more different."

"You believe that if it makes you feel better," said Aaron.

John, uncomfortable with the conversation, changed the subject. "How are things at Given House? Do you know what happened to the rest of the Coloreds?"

"I don't know where they are," said Aaron. "They're gone. I heard through a neighbor that several joined the Union army as soon as they took Negroes in their ranks. The rest left after the war was over. Probably came North, I suppose."

"What's the condition of Given House? Is Lyle going to continue to farm it?" asked Max.

"You want to know if you'll ever receive your full payment?" said Aaron.

"I'm curious as to how the estate fared. I know troops from both armies moved through central Kentucky during the war. Houses were ravaged and burned."

"You're never going to see the rest of your money, Max. The farm is bankrupt. Lyle had to sell most of the furniture. The bank has foreclosed on the property."

"I'm sorry to hear it," said Max.

"Me too," said Aaron. "My childhood home is gone. Central Kentucky will never be the same. Why are you two here? I doubt you came for a social visit."

John said, "We came to see you, Aaron, because I'd like to ask for your help."

"With what?"

"Finding Jenny, my mammy. Can you tell me where she is?"

"Hmm." Aaron said, "I'll tell you what I know, but she could be anywhere by now."

"Do you know where they sent her?"

"I don't know for certain. I remember she was sent to Mississippi. Lyle and my mother's father, William Reed, owned a large cotton plantation on the Mississippi River south of Greenville called Western Magnolias. She could have gone there. The other family plantation where she might have ended up was Matthew Henry's plantation near there. Matthew Henry is a cousin of Lyle and my mother's. I heard Lyle talk of selling other slaves to Matthew in later years. I never visited Mississippi, so I can't tell you much more about the plantations."

"Can you think of anything? Anything at all that might help me find her?" said John.

"Lyle did tell me that when the Union troops were advancing toward Vicksburg, they occupied and burned plantations near Western Magnolias. I don't know if it was spared. The Union troops liberated the slaves after Mississippi was occupied. The slaves could have stayed on the plantation and worked as sharecroppers—many of them did—or they could have left and gone anywhere."

"Do you think Lyle would tell you where she went?" asked John.

"I don't think so. He's one angry, defeated Confederate and not a friend of the Black man. Besides, he's written me off since the war."

"I guess I'm going to have to go there then," said John.

Max said, "John, I don't think it's safe for you to travel there. I've heard stories about vigilantes in the South attacking freedmen. Maybe we can hire a man to go there for you. There are plenty of returning soldiers looking to earn a fee. Maybe we can find one who fought in Mississippi and knows the territory."

John said, "I want to go myself. I can't trust someone else to go."

Max said, "Would you even recognize her? It's been twenty years."

"I think I would."

Max said, "Let's start by placing ads in the newspapers in Mississippi. I've seen ads placed by freedmen looking for lost family members."

"That doesn't sound hopeful," said John. "It's like shooting a gun into the night sky, hoping to hit a star. Now that she's free, I have to find her. I want to take her to my sister and brother; put our family back together. I'll do whatever I need to."

Max said, "Aaron, is there anything you could do? Write your family a letter? Anything? It's the least you could do for

John and his family, after what they did for your family... all those years."

"Maybe I could write a letter. I'll consider it," said Aaron. "Anything else?"

"No. Anything you can do to help, I'd appreciate it. I've got to find her," said John.

Then men stood and shook hands.

Max said to Aaron, "He's not asking for much. We're appealing to your sense of human decency."

"I said I'll think about it."

Max & John met each other's eyes, signaling skepticism, hope, and solidarity. Then said their goodbyes to Aaron.

#

Max drove the carriage with Lizzie seated in between Annie and him. The horse labored as they moved up the steep hill from the city into the growing suburb of Mount Auburn. Annie and Max had purchased a lot with a city view before the war and had an architect draw up plans for a house. When labor and supplies were diverted to the war, they suspended construction. Max drove the carriage onto the overgrown lot amidst several completed homes on the street. He helped Lizzie and Annie climb down.

They looked down toward the city. Streets stretched the mile from the bottom of the hill south to the river. They could see the partially completed stone support structures rising out of the Ohio river, awaiting construction of the bridge that would someday connect Cincinnati with Covington. The tree-covered hills of Kentucky formed a lush backdrop above the river basin.

"I forgot what a beautiful view there is from up here," said Annie.

Max said, "It's so peaceful. Do you remember our first carriage ride after you arrived in Cincinnati from New York?"

"Our first outing together. It was very romantic. You brought a picnic, and we sat right over there," she said, pointing to the grape vineyards on Mount Adams. "We stood there and looked down on the city. It was the first time Cincinnati started to feel welcoming to me."

"Where?" said Lizzie.

Annie pointed again. "And your Papa and I agreed to marry over there, across the river on the Covington hilltop. Max, remember? We watched the fireworks on the Fourth of July and discussed what an equitable marriage would mean to us."

Max said, "If I had only known then what I know now. I should have swum all the way back across the river."

"Be nice. You wouldn't have it any other way."

"I wouldn't. There's the shop—that big building by the river," Max said, pointing. "There's the canal. The Eichen Garten is right there, just this side of all those trees."

"Where's our house?" asked Lizzie.

"Let's see, right in between that street and that street. There's Saint Mary's. See the steeple?" said Max.

"Are we going to build a house and live up here?" asked Lizzie.

"I don't know," said Max. "That was our dream before the war. Mama, what do you think?"

"We were excited about building a home up here, away from the bustle of the city, but the war changed us, Lizzie. Papa and I don't look at the world the same as we once did."

"How did it change you?" said Lizzie.

Annie said, "It made us both think about what's important and what our duty is. I realized that I need to become more active in fighting for the rights of people. We won the war, but there's still much that needs to change to give women and the Negroes equal rights and opportunities."

"How did the war change you, Papa?"

"I learned that there are plenty of men in this country willing to cast aside people to further their own interests. I can't take anything for granted and need to fight for those less fortunate than myself."

"I don't understand."

"Mama and I want the same thing for you, and we each will do our part to build a country that is more just for everyone."

"I still don't understand," said Lizzie.

Max placed his hand on Lizzie's shoulder. "We love you and will do everything we can to make America a better place for you. Does that sound all right?"

"By building us a better house?" she asked, looking up at her father.

"I suppose that's a simple way to put it," said Max. "We need to build a better house."

AUTHOR'S NOTE

As I wrote Book One, *Queen of the West* and created Max and Annie, they became living characters to me. I didn't know where their lives would take them, but I was excited to find out. In order to write their next chapter in this book, I first had to understand America and Cincinnati during the Civil War.

I knew the general history but lacked the understanding of the people's motivations. I also had minimal knowledge of the role that Cincinnati, just across the Ohio River from the border state of Kentucky, played and how its people viewed the events of that time.

I became a student of Civil War history, sourcing materials primarily from the Cincinnati History Library, the Cincinnati Public Library and the Library of Congress. I visited Ward Hall, a Greek Revival antebellum plantation in Georgetown, Kentucky, to put myself in the space of a plantation home, like the one where Aaron and John grew up.

As I researched, I began to appreciate the era's complexities and politics. Because communication was print media, scant wires and face-to-face conversations, the politics and positions were much more fragmented and localized than today's national politics. I tried to understand and reflect the day's sentiments in the characters and put them in a Cincinnatian's perspective. There was as wide a range of opinions about slavery, secession and the war as any contemporary issue. I imagine many Cincinnatians didn't want to be bothered by it all and hoped these critical issues would be quickly resolved so they could return to their lives. It would have been easy for them to think about the war happening somewhere else. The siege of Cincinnati brought it to their doorstep and caused fear, but they were spared the devastation that so many others endured.

Queen of the Union could have been an epic in itself. My intent wasn't to tell the full story of the Civil War, but my hope is that readers will gain enough understanding of the events and attitudes to appreciate how they contributed to where we are today.

In telling the story, I injected actual events and, in some cases, took from published information about them. I want to acknowledge the following elements I took from the historical record and placed into my fiction.

General Wallace's orders to Cincinnatians when he declared martial law and instructed volunteers to report to defend the city was described in the article "The Siege of Cincinnati" by Joseph S. Stern, Jr. in the *Bulletin of the Historical and Philosophical Society of Ohio*.

I placed John into the actual events and created the dialogue, but the rounding up of Black men and placement in a pen by Cincinnati Police, as well as General Dickson's address to the Black Brigade, was told in *The Black Brigade of Cincinnati* by Peter H. Clark, written in 1864.

The Walt Whitman poem in the story was excerpted from an 1855 version of "Poem of Walt Whitman, an American," accessed from *The Walt Whitman Archive*.

I included the text of "Lincoln's Gettysburg Address" in full, as it was widely read across the country and provided a concise summary of the state of War and sentiment of the North at the time.

It is hard to find joy during war, but at the conclusion of *Queen of the Union*, the characters have reason to be optimistic. I hope you'll read the forthcoming Book Three of the *Queen of the West* series, which continues their journey during the American Reconstruction era.

ACKNOWLEDGEMENTS

I am grateful to the following for their help in completing this book. Jill Beitz at the Cincinnati History Library for her assistance with my research. Ericka McIntyre for her thoughtful editing and enthusiasm. Those who read early drafts and provided feedback and encouragement, including Alison Jones-Pomatto, Mary Ann Russo, Calista Hargrove, Beth Tschop, Kathleen Logan, Jill Beitz, and my OTR book club readers: Jeff, Kim, Jerry, Marci, Roseann, Kevin, Marilyn, Sarah. And my wife, Peggy, for her continued encouragement and support.

ABOUT THE AUTHOR

JR Zink enjoyed a successful career as a consultant and corporate leader before stepping away from the business world to develop his right-brain talents as an author. In addition to writing, he coaches high school swimming and enjoys running, backpacking, bicycling and travel. JR and his wife raised a family and now live in the historic Over-the-Rhine neighborhood in Cincinnati.